My
Lord
Foxe

My Lord Foxe

Constance Gluyas

DAVID McKAY COMPANY, INC.
New York

Gluyas, Constance, 1920-
    My lord Foxe.

    I.   Title.
PZ4.G5673Mf3 [PR6057.L87] 823'.9'14 75-44063
ISBN 0-679-50568-7

For my husband, Don,
with all my love

Chapter One

Henrietta Maria was very young and very pretty, and at this moment she was filled with misery and foreboding. She did not wish to be where she was now, in this strange and chill England. She did not wish to be England's Queen, and certainly she did not wish to be the wife of Charles the First of England. She had known that childhood could not be expected to go on forever, but she had never expected to be cut off from those gay and carefree years at the tender age of fifteen.

She blinked tears from her eyes. As a Princess of France, her life had been an unusually happy one. It was perhaps for that reason that the shock, when it came, was the greater. "There is a time to marry," she had cried out to her mother. "But, Madam, that time is not now!"

But Marie de Medici had been unmoved by her daughter's passionate plea. At the end of the hysterical sobbed-out words, she had fixed the girl with her cold eyes and bade her remember that it was the lot of Princesses to marry advantageously. "It is hoped that this marriage will bring about a lasting and firm

1

alliance with England," she went on. "For England has ever been the enemy of France. Therefore, I expect you to remember that you are a daughter of France. You will do your duty, and you will not whimper."

Henrietta Maria cried out in rebellion. "But I do not love him! And well do you know that the King of England is not of our faith."

"Then it is for you to bring him back to the True Faith, is it not?" Marie de Medici had answered her calmly.

"I have said that I do not love him."

"Love! Must you babble on so foolishly? What has love to do with a royal marriage?"

"What of yourself, Madam? Did you not love my father when you wed him?"

Marie de Medici flushed. Yes, she had loved Henri of Navarre. Indeed her love had bordered on idolatory. But his interest in her had been, at the most, tepid. "We are not talking of your father or of myself," she answered sharply. She saw the trembling lips and relented slightly. "It may be, child, if you are lucky, that love will grow up between you. If it does not, then you must comfort yourself in the knowledge that a great destiny lies before you. I ask you to remember that your brother married without love. Yet, or so I believe, they are happy enough together."

Henrietta Maria's brother, Louis XIII of France, had married Anne of Austria. With a wisdom unusual for her, Henrietta Maria refrained from pointing out that her brother could scarcely be happy or contented of mind when Anne's passionate love affair with the English Duke of Buckingham had, at one time, been the scandal of the Court. The affair was over now, and Anne was very subdued. As for the Duke of Buckingham, he had been forbidden, under pain of death, ever to set foot in France again. Nevertheless, that affair would be long remembered.

Frowning, Henrietta Maria dismissed thoughts of her mother.

Of what use to think of her when Henrietta Maria's pleas had all been in vain? She was in England, she was married, and she awaited the husband she had seen but once.

Henrietta Maria glanced about her. For the first time in many long and weary hours, she was entirely alone. Seated at the oval breakfast table, she made no attempt to eat. She realized that she was shivering convulsively, and she drew her wrap closer about her. It was cold in the big gloomy room with its high walls and its carved and gilded ceiling. She was conscious of an icy chill that seemed to penetrate to her very bones. Looking down at the numbed hands clasped on her lap, she wished that she had not insisted upon solitude. The laughter and chatter of her ladies might have served to distract her thoughts from her misery. Henrietta Maria rose to her feet and walked over to the window, wondering if she would ever be warm again.

Outside, the benign June sunlight bathed the land in a gentle warmth. Sunlight crowded the narrow-paned windows seeking, but not finding, entrance into the room. Its golden light touched the childishly rounded planes of Henrietta Maria's face; it lit the large, brown, dark-lashed eyes, the pretty petulant mouth; and brought out unexpected red glints in her intricately piled black hair. She frowned at the sunlight that brought her only an illusion of warmth. At her back was the frigid air. She wondered if sunlight, however fierce its rays, could penetrate the thick stone walls of Dover Castle?

Turning away again, she walked over to the oval table and sat down. And suddenly, despite her bitter disappointment with the match, she felt a touch of excitement and wonder. She, Henrietta Maria, was Queen of this land. At fifteen years of age, she had become Queen of England. She thought back to the one and only time she had seen her husband, Charles Stuart. When Charles, the Prince of Wales, as he was then, had visited the French Court, on his way to Spain, he had seemed to Henrietta Maria quite handsome but far removed from her by his great age. But his ten years' seniority had not mattered then, for he did not seek a French bride; his heart had been set on a match with the Infanta of

3

Spain. Nothing had been asked of Henrietta Maria then, and so she had admired him from afar. She had been pleasantly thrilled with the fluttering of her pulses when he had addressed her. But now that she was his wife, she found herself remembering that he had not always smiled. Sometimes she had noted quite a stern set to his mouth. Doubtless, from the lofty pinnacle of those ten years, he would think her to be naught but a frivolous child.

Henrietta Maria's heart began to beat very fast. Child she might have been, but when the Prince had arrived at the French Court, she had been immediately captivated by his dark and smiling eyes. She had been no different from the rest of the ladies at Court in that she had fallen easy victim to his warm and effortless charm. She remembered now being piqued because he had treated her like the child she was and not as the mature young lady she fondly imagined herself to be. Long after the Prince had departed for Spain, Henrietta Maria found herself the prey of a strange inner turmoil that she did not understand. Lying in her bed at night, she stared into the darkness and hoped quite fervently that the Infanta of Spain would prove to be fat, ugly, and bad tempered.

Whether the Infanta had been any of these things, Henrietta Maria was never able to find out. She only knew that Charles's hopes of a Spanish match had met with disappointment.

But Charles, it seemed, had not been entirely indifferent to the little French Princess. As the year 1623 was nearing its close, Lord Kensington, who had apparently come in the guise of Charles's unofficial ambassador, arrived at the Court of France. Soon after that Henrietta Maria's brother Louis, supported by Marie de Medici, began to speak of the English Prince with great favor. They pointed out to her his charm, his handsome appearance, the desirability of such a match, until Henrietta Maria, fearful of losing her pleasant life and of being parted from her beloved France, found that her budding infatuation for the Stuart Prince had been quite slain under the barrage of words that poured over her. If anything, she actively disliked the thought of him. It was no consolation to her when she learned that her religion would not be interfered with in any way, and that she and her attendants would be allowed to practice it freely. Naturally she was happy in that knowledge, for her religion meant a great deal to her, but even this did not console her. Neither did the further knowledge that the children of her body would remain under her religious guidance until they were thirteen years old. She could not imagine herself with children, she who had but recently put away her dolls. The marriage would bring yet another benefit, her brother told her. Because of the union of England and France, the lot of the practicing Roman Catholics of England would be eased. They would at least be tolerated and the persecution of old would cease.

Henrietta Maria moved restlessly. How very far away France seemed now. And how foolish was the romantic dream she had once cherished for Charles Stuart. She was his wife, that was the reality, and she was terribly afraid. Would Charles be kind to her? Would he be angry because she was not the Infanta of Spain? And what of his promise? Would he keep it, or would he try to turn her from her religion?

At this terrible thought, Henrietta Maria's hands clenched and her eyes flashed with anticipated anger. He was a Protestant Prince. Might it not be that he would attempt to force her to embrace his religion?

"Nay!" she spoke aloud. "I will not allow it!" She had been brought up in the Catholic faith and it was to her the one true religion. In that faith would she live and die. Would Charles keep faith with her brother? Would he, as he had promised, lighten the severity of the penalties now meted out to the Catholics of England?

Henrietta Maria glanced over at the door. Although she dreaded the impending arrival of Charles, yet she wished that he would come soon. Good Lord, she prayed silently, make me pleasing in his eyes!

She closed her eyes, remembering the proxy marriage, and the Duc de Chevreuse who had represented Charles in the ceremony, standing tall and straight at her side. The marriage had been celebrated on a raised platform outside the great cathedral of Notre Dame. The platform, which led from the palace to the cathedral, had been covered with a deep-purple velvet lavishly embroidered with the golden lilies of France. She herself was radiant in a gown of cream satin frothing with golden lace and sewn all over with tiny pearls. She had found, despite her unwilling complicity, that she was enjoying every moment of the ceremony. She did not mind being a bride, it was simply that she did not wish to be a wife.

She looked at the door again. When Charles came the marriage ceremony would be performed again. Publicly this time. It would not be the Duc de Chevreuse standing at her side, but her bridegroom, Charles of England. The marriage must be made legally binding in the eyes of the people of England. The ceremony would allow them to view at their leisure the French Princess whom their King had married.

Would the people resent her? Henrietta Maria shrugged and made a wry face. It was delightful and comforting to be loved, and so she would prefer them to love her. But if they did not, if they resented her, she did not think it would trouble her unduly. Like it or not, she was their Queen. She was young, she was beautiful, or so she had been repeatedly told. Henrietta Maria smiled. Without undue vanity, she was pleasing to look upon with her cloud of silky dark hair, her large dark eyes, and her creamy skin. Henrietta Maria's smile faded, and she hastily crossed herself and asked God's pardon for the sin of vanity. She added to her prayer that if she must bear children for England, as of course it was her duty to do, that they be many and healthy.

Henrietta Maria's thoughts drifted. Perhaps, after all, she would not be homesick for France. She had, in a way, brought France with her in the persons of the hundred and fifty French noblemen and the ladies who made up her entourage. She had no intention of learning the barbarous tongue-twisting English language. It would be absurd to try when it made her head ache so abominably. Every member of her entourage was necessary to her comfort and well-being. So were her twenty-nine priests. Her

Grand Almoner, the Bishop of Mende, and her favorite confessor, Père Berulle. It might be with her personal and religious friends all about her that she would not miss France at all. There was of course Mama, she thought, her self-satisfaction fading slightly. But Mama would have many opportunities to visit England. And, after all, her mother was not a particularly maternal woman. If one did not love her, as was one's duty, it might be truthfully said that she was a cold woman. And one moreover who was inclined to be irritable if her children made too many demands upon her time. Sometimes when they had clamored for affection she did not seem to have any to give.

Shrugging, Henrietta Maria rose to her feet. Forgetful now of the cold, she flung her wrap to one side and began to twirl about the room. Her green silk skirts flew out in a bell with her movements. "It is nice to be loved," she sang out in her high sweet voice, "so nice to be loved. My husband will love me, my children will love me. Everybody will love Henrietta Maria of France."

"Henrietta Maria of England, Madam," a quiet voice said from the doorway. "And you, Madam, will you love them in return?"

The glow fading from her face, Henrietta Maria swung round to face the tall, slender woman standing there. "Saint-Georges," she said petulantly, "must you creep about? You startled me. As for your question, naturally I will love them in return."

Madame Saint-Georges advanced into the room with a rustle of red skirts. "I am very happy to hear it, Madam," she said dryly. "I know well that you are good at receiving love, but sometimes I think you find it difficult to give."

Henrietta Maria was annoyed at this reminder of her mother, Marie de Medici. Nay, she was not like her mother. She was young and ardent and willing to love if opportunity presented itself. She stared at her maid of honor with hard eyes. Then, remembering that she could rarely intimidate the woman, she remarked in a light voice, "You are quite absurd, Saint-Georges. I love my mother, my brother, my country, and my religion. You

7

may believe me when I tell you that I am also prepared to love my husband."

"Nay, Madam, you are by no means prepared to love your husband. I fear that your resentment will be apparent to him."

Henrietta Maria lost her temper. Stamping her foot, she shouted, "You forget yourself, Saint-Georges! It is not for you to tell me of my innermost feelings. If I say I will love my husband, then I will love him. I will also love my children, should God see fit to bless me with them."

Madame Saint-Georges smiled. "For your sake, Madam, I pray that you will remember that children are born with various needs. Yours will be no exception. You must not let your love of your religion blind you to those needs. It is with your happiness in mind that I say this, little Majesty."

"My happiness? You are stupid and impertinent! I will not listen to you, for I have no notion of your meaning."

Madame Saint-Georges remained unruffled. She loved the girl, and she had learned to deal with her in her many moods. "You are well aware of my meaning, Madam. It may be that some of your children, perhaps all of them, will incline to their father's faith rather than to yours."

Henrietta Maria's face flushed a deep red, and in that moment her eyes looked fiery and dangerous. "My children will be good Catholics, Saint-Georges, or I will know the reason why!"

Sighing, Madame Saint-Georges looked away from those revealing eyes. It had always been difficult to reason with Henrietta Maria. She seemingly could see no other point of view than her own. On the question of her religion, Henrietta Maria, unless she was greatly mistaken, was already showing signs of the developing fanatic. She was young, but the signs were nevertheless there. As the years passed fanaticism would take firmer hold of her, Madame Saint-Georges thought, deeply troubled. God help her children should they attempt to follow a different religion!

Henrietta Maria's flash of anger had already passed. She was devoted to Madame Saint-Georges and she hated to indulge in heated words with her. Nevertheless there were times when the woman could be quite stupid and very trying. Henrietta Maria smiled her forgiveness and regarded her with amused impatience. "What is it you want, Saint-Georges? I told you that I desired to remain undisturbed."

"You did, Your Majesty. I came to tell you that the King has arrived."

"What!" Henrietta Maria stared at her in dismay. Her hands flew to her hair. "Why did you not inform me at once, imbecile? How dare you stand here wasting my time with your idle chatter!"

"I had meant to tell you immediately, Madam, but I was diverted."

"Arrange my hair," Henrietta Maria cried. "Move quickly, quickly! Get out my blue gown. Oh, you are so infuriating. o not stand there gaping at me with your mouth opened like a fish!"

Madame Saint-Georges started across the room. " 'Tis a pity to change your appearance, but I will get the blue gown. As for your hair, it is a little loose, but it looks very pretty."

Henrietta Maria hesitated. "I would not wish to change my gown, Saint-Georges, if 'tis not necessary. I wish to present a pleasing appearance. If you can assure me that I will do so, then I will greet the King as I am."

"I do assure you, Madam," Madame Saint-Georges answered. She smiled. "France need not be ashamed of her representative."

Henrietta Maria, well pleased, cast dignity aside and flew over to the door. "Saint-Georges," she cried, flinging the door wide, "what do you suppose the King will think of me?"

"I will be very surprised, Madam, if he does not love you at first sight."

"You are prejudiced," Henrietta Maria said, laughing. "Now come, Saint-Georges, follow me quickly. And tell the other ladies to attend me at once."

"Yes, Your Majesty."

Henrietta Maria did not hear her. She was already running

along the corridor, her small silver-slippered feet soundless on the thick red carpet. Reaching the head of the staircase, she stopped to catch her breath. She looked down into the great hall below.

The King, clad in dark-blue velvet trimmed with lace, a plumed hat tucked beneath his arm, stood before the fireplace with his slender ringed hands held out to catch the warmth of the blazing logs. Henrietta Maria could see the ruddy glow of the flames through the fine ruffles that spilled from his wide cuffs. Behind him stood a group of gentlemen, their attention on the antics of three dogs. On the King's left was the Duke of Buckingham, a man whom Henrietta Maria detested both for his smiling affability which, she felt sure, masked insolence, and for the hurt he had dealt her beloved brother by his blatant love affair with Anne of Austria. On the King's right was another gentleman. She could not see his face. He was very tall and broad shouldered, with long dark curling hair that fell to the shoulders of his red-velvet jacket. As Henrietta Maria watched, he turned his head and addressed a remark to the King in a low voice. He had a finely carved, almost arrogant profile. There was something about him that caught her interest at once.

"Brett, you damned young cub," the King said in a laughing voice, "what the devil do you mean by that remark?"

Henrietta Maria had not taken in the sense of the remark, for she understood little English. It was by his tone that she knew Charles was amused rather than angry. Henrietta Maria's heart warmed to the tall young man. Whatever the remark had been, it quite evidently did not please Buckingham. The Duke was looking quite sour.

Henrietta Maria hesitated a moment longer, then she began to descend the stairs slowly, one hand holding her skirts aside from contact with the stairs.

She was almost at the bottom before the rustle of silk betrayed her presence. Charles Stuart turned his head sharply. His dark eyes widened. He saw a tiny childlike figure. A pretty and slightly flushed face framed by a gleaming mass of soft dark curls, downcast eyes with lashes so long that they cast tiny shadows on her cheeks, and full provocative lips that were faintly smiling.

Charles felt an instant response to her fragile femininity, but at the same time he was conscious of a pang of dismay. He had forgotten how very young she was. Indeed she looked far younger than her fifteen years. How would they get on together, he wondered. Buckingham had told him that though the French Princess understood some English, she obstinately refused to converse in that language. Buckingham, who thought only of his King's interests, had also told him that the Princess Henrietta Maria was hostile to all things English. She had been greatly opposed to this union between the two countries.

Smiling, Charles went toward her, his hands outstretched. "Welcome to England. Welcome to your new country, Madam."

Henrietta Maria's smile vanished. She frowned, trying to puzzle out the King's words. Buckingham said in a low voice. "You see, Sire, did I not warn you? Your words have not pleased her."

The King, obviously enchanted with his child bride, answered Buckingham in a curtly impatient voice. "I doubt the lady understood me, my lord. You are too hasty in your judgment."

The gentlemen gathered in the hall looked at one another in astonishment. The King had administered something that sounded very like a snub to the Duke, his prime favorite.

Buckingham flushed darkly. If Charles chose to use that tone to him, why must it be in front of these sniggering fools? His anger deepened as he saw the covert glances cast his way. Price-Walker, that dolt, was openly smiling at his discomfiture! His hands clenched. It would seem that Henrietta Maria would bear watching. He had no intention of allowing her to gain too great a hold on the King, lest it weaken his own influence. He glanced quickly at Brett Foxefield. There was another who needed to be watched. The King found too much enjoyment in his company. No wonder he is called my lord Foxe, Buckingham thought, for he knew well that Charles did not give his loyalty and affection easily. Thus far the loyalty and affection had all been for himself, and be damned if he would share it with Foxefield. Allowing nothing of his thoughts to show, Buckingham turned a blandly smiling face to the Queen.

Charles was carefully repeating his greeting in French. His efforts were rewarded by Henrietta Maria's radiant smile.

"You know my language, Sire," Henrietta Maria said. "It rejoices my heart."

Charles looked at her with mock reproach. "Can it be that you have forgotten our first meeting?"

"But no, Sire. How can you think so?"

"At our first meeting, I spoke to you only in French."

Henrietta Maria looked dismayed for a moment, then she said quickly, "It is because I am so happy to be here, Sire, that I am confused." Remembering her mother's careful coaching, she added in a prim little voice, "I know that I am very young to be the Queen of your great country, but I will learn. I wish to please Your Majesty, and your people."

Touched, Charles said gently, "They are your people now, Madam. As for pleasing me, you will find it an easy task. In all truth, I am already well pleased."

She made to kneel before him, but Charles caught her hands tightly in his. "Nay, Madam, you must not kneel to me." He hesitated, then, putting his arms about her, he gave her a soft kiss on the cheek. "There. That is the way a husband should greet his wife, is it not?"

Henrietta Maria saw his shy smile, and her heart softened toward him. Obeying a sudden impulse, she raised herself on her toes. Putting her arms about his neck, she kissed his mouth. "Your Majesty will agree that this is a better way?" she said breathlessly.

"I—I—I do indeed." Charles's slight nervous stammer caught him unawares.

Henrietta Maria smiled at Charles's suddenly puzzled expression. His eyes traveled downward, lingering on her shoes.

12

Instantly she understood. "I am taller than you expected, is it not so?" she inquired.

Charles returned her smile. "Aye, you have grown since our last meeting. You are not tall, but nonetheless taller than I had been led to believe." He glanced at her shoes again.

Laughing, Henrietta Maria drew her skirts to one side and revealed her silver slippers. "Your Majesty can plainly see that I do not stand upon built-up shoes." She dropped her skirts, her eyes meeting his. "Sire," she said in a demure voice, "I stand upon my own two feet, and I have no help from art. Thus high am I, neither higher nor lower."

"So I see, Madam," Charles said huskily. He saw the warm look in her dark-brown eyes, and he had a mad impulse to crush her in his arms, to touch her caressingly. He thought longingly of the moment when they would be alone. To divert his thoughts from that pleasing but, at the moment, impossible path, he looked at the Duke of Buckingham. "You have already m—m— met my lord B—Buckingham, Madam," he said, flushing as the stammer caught him again. Turning to Brett Foxefield, he motioned him forward. "Madam, may I present the Earl of Foxefield." He smiled at her. "I call him my lord Foxe, because he is such a wily fellow."

"Your Majesty." Brett Foxefield bowed over Henrietta Maria's small white hand. He added in French, "Your Majesty is a most beautiful addition to our country."

He suffered a slight sense of shock as, smiling, she looked at him fully. There was something in her eyes that set his heart beating uncomfortably fast. He felt a great sense of excitement, and he could not but marvel at himself. She was a child, Brett told himself quickly. Aye, a child. Yet somehow he knew that beneath Henrietta Maria's childlike exterior there was a lush sensuality. Instinctively he knew, too, that no matter how arrogant and demanding she might conceivably be, she had that magic quality that could well enslave a man and bring him to his knees. Here indeed, he thought, in the person of Henrietta Maria was a budding *femme fatale*.

Henrietta Maria was fascinated by my lord Foxefield's dark-blue eyes that were heavily fringed with thick black lashes. By his tanned and rugged face, and the deep cleft in his chin. Her hand tingled in his. It seemed to her that he was the most fascinating man she had ever met. He was handsome, but in such a strongly masculine way that she felt suddenly weak and helpless. It shocked her a little to find that she was thoroughly enjoying the sensation. "My lord Fooxe," she said, trying out the name and finding it pleasant to her tongue.

"Foxe, Madam," Brett corrected her in his deep pleasant voice. "But let me assure you that my nature does not harbor the least foxlike tendency."

"He speaks truth," Charles said, "though his is a cursed, complex nature. He is direct and honest, qualities which I like well."

Brett dropped the Queen's hand, knowing even as he did so that he had a great desire to go on holding it. "I fear I do not deserve such flattery, Sire," he said, smiling at the King.

"Mark the moment well, then, my lord. I am not often given to honeyed words."

There was an affectionate gleam in Brett's eyes as he answered. "I will mark the moment, Sire."

Once more Buckingham found himself fuming at the easy comradeship that existed between the two. He was about to say something that he hoped might amuse Charles and divert his thoughts from Foxefield, when he was caught by the Queen's expression. She moved through the ensuing introductions like one in a dream. And he noticed that her eyes seemed to be continually seeking out and lingering on Brett Foxefield's face.

She is a fool, Buckingham thought. If she feels an attraction for Foxefield, why must she show it so plainly? Charles could be very jealous and possessive over what belonged to him. He would not like it. Buckingham's eyes narrowed in sudden thought. No, Charles most certainly would not like it. He would not feel kindly disposed toward Foxefield, and certainly not inclined to listen to any counsel the Queen might have to offer him. Well pleased, Buckingham smiled. A word here, a word there, and it might be that he could fan smouldering embers into a flame. It was a pity the King seemed so unaware of Henrietta Maria's obvious attraction to my lord Foxefield. But that could be remedied at the earliest opportunity.

"Mr. Brewster," Henrietta Maria was saying to the red-headed young man now bowing over her hand, "I thank you for your good wishes." As the young man moved away, her eyes sought Brett's face. He was not looking at her. How handsome he is, she thought. How white his teeth are against the deep brown of his face. His eyes glow like blue lamps. She looked at the short black cape swinging from his shoulders. And how elegant of figure he is. She knew that she was behaving like a love-sick chit, but it did no good to tell herself that. She felt a deep longing welling up inside her. If only my lord Foxe had been the King! She looked at Charles blankly. She had no memory in that moment of the instant attraction he had had for her when first he came to the French Court. His eyes were as deep and as dark and as warm, but she had looked into dark-blue eyes. She was stirred by violent and painful emotions. She wanted to shout to him, "Look at me, my lord Foxe. You are such a man as I had thought came only in dreams!"

Charles beckoned her to his side, and Henrietta Maria went to him dutifully. "My lord Foxe has a favor to ask of you, Madam," Charles said.

"Indeed." Henrietta Maria's smile unconsciously caressed. "Ask your favor, my lord."

Brett Foxefield was looking faintly embarrassed. " 'Tis too soon, Your Majesty," he murmured. "I had not meant to speak of it until much later."

Charles laughed. "From what you have told me of little Miss Vixen, it cannot be too soon."

Henrietta Maria tried to retain her smile, but she could feel her face hardening. "Who is she, this Miss Vixen?"

15

Brett reddened beneath the amusement in Charles's eyes. "His Majesty is pleased to jest," he said. "Though I will agree that the lady well deserves to be dubbed vixen."

"But a sweet and pious vixen, you will admit?" Charles put in.

"Aye. And in her sweetness and piety so damned exasperating that I could wring her neck. How the devil piety can bring about such an uproar in one household is something I have never been able to fathom." He caught the Queen's eyes and said hastily, "Your pardon, Madam. My language is perhaps overstrong."

Henrietta Maria shook her head. "The lady's name, my lord. And the favor, if you please."

"She is but a chit of seventeen, Madam," Brett said. Suddenly recollecting Henrietta Maria's age, he added hastily, "Once more I must ask your pardon."

Henrietta Maria moved restlessly. "You are forgiven, my lord. What is her name?"

"Her name is Meredith Hartford."

"She is perhaps your sweetheart?"

Brett shuddered. "God forbid, Madam. She is my mother's ward. The daughter of some friends of hers."

"Her mother and father are dead?"

"Aye, Madam." Brett hesitated. "I wished to ask if Your Majesty might have a place for her in your household?"

"It may be." Henrietta Maria's smile came easily now. "You dislike her so much, this girl?"

"No, Madam," Brett said, frowning thoughtfully, "I do not dislike her. Though often she arouses me to intense anger. She believes herself to be very devout. She is a Puritan, you see, and she insists upon forcing her damned religion on us. But beneath her meekness and her long-suffering smile, I suspect that there is the very devil of a temper."

"And now he wishes to inflict this termagant on the Court," Charles said. "What say you to that, Madam?"

Henrietta Maria seemed to be considering. "She is pretty, this Mademoiselle Meredith?"

"Pretty? I have never thought about it, Madam. I suppose she might be considered so." He smiled. "But in all truth she angers me so much that I am blind to any attraction she might have. There is another reason why I wish she might be found a place at Court. She has recently come under the influence of a neighbor of ours. The fellow has served to make her the more infuriatingly determined to reform us."

Henrietta Maria looked at him with soft eyes. "And this neighbor, he is also a Puritan?" She knew that she was going to assent to my lord Foxe's request, but she wished to prolong the conversation.

Brett's lips hardened. "He is, Madam. I believe him to be a scoundrel and a mealy-mouthed hypocrite."

"Mademoiselle is in love with him?"

"No, indeed, Madam, I think not," Brett answered curtly. "But she is considerably under his influence."

"And the name of this man?"

Charles gave her a puzzled look. "You know, Madam," he said gently, "the name of this man can scarcely be of interest to you."

Henrietta Maria's head rose imperiously. "I am interested in all things, Sire. I wish to know his name."

Brett inclined his head. "His name, Madam, if you insist, is Oliver Cromwell."

"Oliver Cromwell," Henrietta Maria repeated. "I do not think I like this name. It has a hard sound."

"He is a hard man, Madam, and surly to boot."

"But if mademoiselle is not in love with him, might it not be that this Cromwell is in love with her?" Henrietta Maria did not know why she persisted.

Charles caught the flash of anger in Brett's eyes and the tightening of his lips. Not for the first time, he wondered if my lord Foxe might be more interested in Mistress Hartford than he himself realized. "My dear," Charles said to Henrietta Maria in soft rebuke, "the feelings of Mr. Cromwell can be of no possible interest to us."

Henrietta Maria smiled vaguely at the King. She too had noticed my lord Foxe's anger. Bitter jealousy curdled inside her. If he had no interest in the difficult Mademoiselle Meredith, why should the thought of this man loving her anger him. "Well, my lord," she persisted. "Is he in love with her?"

Brett looked at her with carefully blank eyes. "I would not imagine so, Your Majesty," he said in a cool voice. "I believe that Mr. Cromwell is happily married." He frowned, then said arrogantly, "However, whatever his feelings might be for my mother's ward, he would not dare to so presume."

Buckingham, who had been listening intently to the conversation, saw the look on the Queen's face, and the King's sudden startled awareness. He is beginning to take notice, Buckingham thought with satisfaction.

"Madam," Charles's voice was so cold that even Buckingham was momentarily startled, "be so kind as to give my lord Foxe an answer. Will you or will you not take Mistress Hartford into your household?"

Henrietta Maria's eyelashes fluttered nervously. But she was far more devious than Buckingham had given her credit for. She turned to Charles, and her smile was sweet and enchanting. It would, she thought, be better to have this girl under her eyes. She said in her demure voice, "Does my lord King desire it so?"

"I do, Madam," Charles answered her shortly.

Henrietta Maria placed her hand lightly on the King's arm. "Then so it shall be. It is my desire to please Your Majesty in all things." She looked at Brett, including him in her smile. "But, of course, my lord Foxe. I will be most happy to receive Mademoiselle Hartford. I trust she is able to converse in French?"

"She speaks the language tolerably well, Madam," Brett answered.

"Splendid. The members of my household are all French."

"But we must mingle some Englishmen and Englishwomen in that household, must we not, Madam?" Charles said. "And it would be as well were you to take immediate instruction in the English language.''

Buckingham saw the rebellion in Henrietta Maria's eyes. The smiling mouth now looked faintly sullen. He waited for the outburst he felt sure would come. Again she disappointed him. "May we not talk of that later, Sire?'' she said in a soft voice. Her fingers caressed his sleeve.

"But of course.'' Charles's easy pleasant smile had returned. "Well, my l—lord Foxe. It would seem that your r—r—request is granted.''

Buckingham heard the King's stammer with some dismay. Charles was only so afflicted when he was angry or emotionally stirred, and his anger had passed.

Buckingham stepped forward and bowed before the King. "Charles—'' He broke off, biting at his lip. Henrietta Maria, watching him, had the feeling that his slip had been deliberate. "I beg your pardon, Your Majesty,'' Buckingham resumed. "It is my feeling that we should soon be on our way. The weather is pleasant enough at the moment, but the clouds are gathering. It might well rain.''

"On our way?'' Henrietta Maria said, puzzled. "What means my lord of Buckingham?''

"We are to journey to Canterbury,'' Charles answered. "The sooner the better, for my people are impatient to see their Queen. If we make good progress, we should reach Barham Downs before nightfall.''

Henrietta Maria looked at him coldly. Drawing herself to her full height, she said haughtily, "But that is quite impossible. I am very tired. I do not wish to travel today.''

Charles might have understood this, but he was stung to anger by her tone. "I am sorry you are tired, Madam. But the carriage is well provided for your comfort. We will journey t—today.''

"We will not!'' Henrietta Maria gave him an outraged look. "I refuse, Sire!''

Charles took her arm gently. "And I insist, M—Madam.''

19

"You may insist all you please, Sire. I will not stir." She was about to say more, but at that moment she met Brett Foxefield's eyes. Their expression was one of icy disapproval. Without thinking, she capitulated. "Oh, very well, Sire, if you do indeed insist."

Charles's hand shook slightly as he took her arm again and led her toward the stairs. He looked at her ladies, who stood grouped nearby. "It would seem, Madam," he said in a carefully lowered voice, "that your desire to please my lord Foxe is greater than your desire to please your husband."

Henrietta Maria looked at him scornfully. "Nonsense!" she said in a loud voice. "How dare you say such a thing to me!"

Charles's fingers tightened painfully on her arm. "Never again address me so in front of others. Perhaps you have forgotten, Madam. You do not s—speak to a lackey, but to the King of England."

She stared at him with hard eyes. "And perhaps you have forgotten, Sire," she said in the same loud voice, "that I am the daughter and the sister of kings. I ask you to remember that I am your wife, not your slave. I will address you in any manner I choose!"

Despite her arrogant words, Henrietta Maria was frightened by the look in the King's eyes. "By my faith, Madam, how dare you!" his soft voice was infinitely more intimidating than a raised one. "Were we alone, I would teach you what it means to defy me!"

Henrietta Maria wrenched her arm away. "By your faith, Sire? What faith? You are naught but a heretic!"

"Be silent!"

"I will not be silent. I am Henrietta Maria of France. I am neither slave nor dog, Sire."

Brett Foxefield thought that she looked quite insane with her heavily flushed face and her blazing eyes. Embarrassed for Charles, he turned his eyes away.

Whatever Charles might have replied, Henrietta Maria gave him no chance to do so. With an imperious gesture to her frightened ladies to follow, she swept up the stairs, her skirts clutched in both taut hands and her head held high.

When Charles turned to face them, the gentlemen were appalled by his expression of fury. The King, normally so good-natured and even of temper, had obviously been driven to the limits of his endurance. He had married a virago, was the general opinion as they studiously avoided his eyes. Hurried spasmodic conversation broke out.

Only Brett Foxefield and Buckingham kept their eyes on the King. Brett found himself unable to endure the fury that, he could see, was fast turning to acute embarrassment. A muscle at the side of the King's mouth twitched. He must be extricated.

"Your Majesty," Brett said, strolling forward, "I ask your pardon, but I have a most damnable ache in my head. Perhaps you will do me the honor of accompanying me for a turn about the grounds?"

The lazy almost indifferent voice had a steadying effect upon Charles. "Gladly, my lord Foxe," he said after a moment. "It is stuffy in this hall."

Buckingham's eyes were triumphant as he watched them go.

They walked in silence for a few moments, then Charles stopped and said awkwardly, "My lord Foxe, I would prefer you to forget the scene you have just witnessed." He gave a difficult laugh. "I would also prefer you to forget the crumbling of your king's dignity."

Brett stooped over a rosebush. "I cannot recall a scene, Sire," he said, his finger carefully ruffling the petals of a red rose.

"Brett, I—"

"No, Charles"—Brett turned to him swiftly—"do not go on, I pray you." His steady eyes held the King's. "As for your dignity, Sire, in my eyes there is nothing, no situation, that could crumble it."

"Thank you, my lord Foxe."

Brett smiled. "Your Gracious Majesty is most welcome."

He was relieved when Charles returned the smile. "You are a rogue, my lord Foxe," Charles said in a normal voice.

21

"But of course, Sire. Have you not often said that I was born to be hung?"

Charles laughed. "Aye, I have. And damn me if I don't believe it to be the truth."

"I thank Your Majesty for those kind words."

Buckingham watched them through the window. Hearing their laughter, he turned away scowling and stared into the fire. He was unaware of the other men. But they, seeing his black look, were delighted. If my lord Foxe could break Buckingham's malign influence over the King, then they were heartily in favor of the black-haired giant who had sprung so recently into renewed prominence.

The friendship between the King and Foxefield was, of course, an old story. Foxefield and the King, or the Prince as he had been then, had played together as lads. In those days Prince Charles had been weak and sickly, his legs so unsteady that he had found great difficulty in walking. It was Foxefield, so the story went, who had protected the weaker boy from harm. And, greatly daring, had even endeavored to shield him from the anger of his father, King James. The King had expected too much from his son. It was Foxefield too who had stood between the young Prince and the harsher realities of life. He who had first introduced, and then produced in the Prince, that passionate love of sports which had, eventually, built his weak and underdeveloped body into new strength and grace. As Charles grew older, and the pressures brought about by the death of his older brother began to weigh heavily upon him, the two boys had inevitably gone their own ways, though not without regret on both sides. It was only lately that the King, suddenly encountering the Earl of Foxefield in the course of a hunting expedition, had resumed the old friendship with enthusiasm and pleasure.

As he accompanied the King to his waiting carriage, Brett was thinking of the Duke of Buckingham. He did not dislike Buckingham. The truth was that he had no particular feeling for him at all. But he felt that the Duke was perhaps too ambitious for his

22

own good, or for the good of the King, who stood so loyally and solidly behind him. Buckingham's all-consuming ambition might well bring disaster to his sovereign. The people murmured against Buckingham, and because of the King's close friendship and association with him, against the King also.

"Why the frown, my lord Foxe?" the King said lightly, stopping before his own carriage. "Your thoughts appear to be mighty unpleasant. Are you thinking of Mistress Hartford by any chance?"

Brett shook his head. "Your Majesty must know that I seldom think of Mistress Hartford if it can possibly be avoided."

Charles gave him a laughing sidelong look. "So you would have me think. But it seems to me that your conversation of late has been quite extravagantly sprinkled with many and varied references to Mistress Hartford."

"I trust that Your Majesty is jesting," Brett said stiffly, looking at him with cold eyes. "To the best of my knowledge, the only references I have made to Mistress Hartford have been unfavorable in nature."

"God's sacred bones!" Charles cried. "Must you look at me like some infernal threatening thunder cloud? I do not recall saying that your remarks had been favorable."

"I beg Your Majesty's pardon."

"So I should think." Charles suppressed a smile. "But you will not deny that the wench, pesky though she is, has been blessed with quite extraordinary looks?"

"It would depend on one's taste," Brett said thoughtfully. "I have no doubt that she could be deemed passable. But to my mind, she has an overbold look."

"Overbold?" Charles coughed to hide a laugh. "Nay. Surely you wrong the demure lass."

"I do not, Sire. She is not what she seems, and I would wager a fortune on it." He paused, then went on feelingly. "As for her blasted tongue, 'tis akin to the stinging of a thousand wasps."

"That is because you refuse to obey her, my lord," Charles

said, not troubling to hide his amusement now. "Were you to give her her way in all things, and refrain from argument, I doubt not that she would out-coo the turtle dove."

"Her own way?" Brett exclaimed, his frown formidable. "I assure you, Sire, that the only thing I shall give her is the soundest thrashing of her life. I'll not be dictated to by an ignorant, prating chit!" Brett's mouth tightened. "When I return to Foxefield Hall I intend, despite my mother's protests, to establish new rules. I will no longer overlook Mistress Hartford's defiance. I intend to be obeyed."

Charles put his hand on the carriage door. "Do you so? Blister me if I don't think you mean it."

"I do mean it, Sire."

"You are not the only one to suffer, my lord. On my last visit to Foxefield Hall, the wench attempted to reform me."

"You, Sire?" Brett stared at him. "This time she has gone too far!"

"But I enjoyed it. It was a new experience."

Seated inside the carriage, Henrietta Maria stared at the King's hand on the door. She sat upright, her piquant face framed by a feathered bonnet, and her hands clenched on the fur-trimmed lap robe across her knees.

Seated across from her, Madame Saint-Georges regarded her young mistress uneasily. Henrietta Maria's lips were pressed tightly together, and she had a strained, listening look. The King would shortly be entering the carriage. Surely, she thought, the youthful Queen did not intend to repeat the earlier distressing scene she had witnessed in the hall? How could she have spoken to the King so! Madame Saint-Georges eyes softened. She thought the King, with his slender and elegant figure, his warm dark eyes, and his little pointed beard that was so black against his brown face, a figure of romance. Her mistress was lucky to have made such a match. She sighed. Were she Henrietta Maria, she would be down on her knees thanking God for such a marriage.

Hearing the woman's sigh, Henrietta Maria glared at her

impatiently. "What is it, Saint-Georges?" she snapped. "Why are you snorting?"

Madame Saint-Georges raised her fair brows in polite protest. "I beg your pardon, Madam," she said mildly. "However, I was not aware of snorting."

"Well, you were. I find it most irritating."

"Please, Madam! The King will hear you."

"Indeed. I care naught!"

Madame Saint-Georges leaned forward and placed her red-gloved hand on the girl's knee. "Madam," she whispered urgently, "I beseech you to have a care. It would not be wise to anger the King again."

Henrietta Maria's look was icy. "You forget yourself. You speak to the Queen!"

"And you, Madam, if you recall, were speaking to the King." She shook her elaborately curled blond head when the Queen would have interrupted. "Hear me out, Madam. I do not need to tell you that I love you. Nonetheless, I also owe a duty to your mother. She will not care to hear of your behavior. As for myself, I cannot in good conscience stand by and see you destroy yourself."

At this mention of her mother, the Queen's face clouded. Shivering, she said quickly, "You also owe a duty to me." The cold look left her eyes as she added appealingly, "Saint-Georges, 'tis not necessary to report everything to my mother, is it?"

The woman smiled at her reassuringly. "No, little Majesty, and I will not. But again I must beg you to have a care."

Henrietta Maria hesitated, biting at her lower lip, then she said unwillingly, "I—I will do my best."

Madame Saint-Georges was about to reply, when the carriage door was jerked open and the King put his head inside. "Madam," he began, smiling pleasantly at Henrietta Maria, "the day is fair. We will have pleasant journeying. I—" He broke off, seeing the maid of honor. "Madame Saint-Georges," he said, regarding her with some surprise, "we are about to

25

depart. Would it not be as well to take your place in your own carriage?''

"My own carriage, Sire?" Flushing, Madame Saint-Georges looked at him inquiringly. "I do not understand. It is customary for me to accompany my mistress.''

Charles entered the carriage and seated himself beside the Queen. "In France, perhaps," he answered, "but it is not the custom in England.''

"Forgive me, Sire. I did not understand.''

"But of course, madame." Charles held out his hand. "Allow me to assist you.''

"Wait!" Henrietta Maria looked from the King to the woman. "You will please stay in your seat, Saint-Georges. You will travel with me.''

There was silence in the carriage. In an agony of embarrassment Madame Saint-Georges lifted her fur muff to hide her face.

"Madame Saint-Georges," the King said at last, "pray leave the carriage.''

"Do nothing of the sort," Henrietta Maria snapped. She looked at the King. "Sire, I am accustomed to Madame Saint-Georges traveling with me. It is a French custom. I wish it to continue.''

"I have said, Madam, that the lady will leave this carriage.''

"She will not!''

The King's nostrils were pinched, his face taut with rage. Madame Saint-Georges looked at Henrietta Maria, and she saw her stubborn determination to have her own way. Feeling a little sick, Madame Saint-Georges whispered urgently, "Oh, please, Madam, please! The King must be obeyed.''

"So the King must be obeyed, eh?" Henrietta Maria shouted. Her face scarlet, she jumped to her feet so hastily that she banged her head on the roof of the carriage and knocked the little feathered bonnet to one side. For a moment she appeared dazed, then she found her voice. "I would have you remember that I am Henrietta Maria of France. I am the sister of Louis the Thirteenth, and I will not bow down before this—this English King.

Remember, Saint-Georges, I am the Queen. I too have a voice. I say that you stay! Do you hear me, woman?''

Madame Saint-Georges dared not look at the King. Fixing her eyes on a point just beyond him, she faltered. "I—I will remove myself at once, Your—Your Majesty."

"What did you say!" Henrietta Maria's voice rose to a scream. "Do you dare to defy me, you miserable woman? You will obey me, you will, you will!" She laid violent hands on Madame Saint-Georges shoulders, shaking her to punctuate her words.

"By God, but this is too much!" Unpleasantly aware of the staring faces outside, the King tore Henrietta Maria away from the woman. Pushing her down on the seat, he held her there by force. "I can only think, Madam," he said in a terrible voice, "that you have taken leave of your senses!"

Gasping with rage, Henrietta Maria opened her mouth and began to scream wildly.

"Be silent!" Perspiration glinted on the King's forehead as he continued to hold the struggling girl to the seat with one hand. With the other, he beckoned to the Queen's chaplain to approach the carriage.

The man came forward with obvious reluctance, his narrow brown eyes apprehensive. "Yes, Your Majesty?"

"You will speak to the Queen," Charles commanded. "There are so many priests in the Queen's entourage that I think it safe to assume that you will have some influence over her."

"And is that wrong too, you Englishman?" Henrietta Maria shouted.

The chaplain wrung his hands together in agitation. He did not like the look on the King's face. He felt that it boded no good for the Queen and her French household. "My daughter," he began, forcing himself to speak sternly, "I beseech you to calm yourself. There are many listening. You would not wish to lower your royal dignity?"

"Be quiet, you fool!" No sooner were the words out of her mouth than a surprising change came over Henrietta Maria. She looked frightened, almost cowed. "I pray you to extend me your forgiveness," she said in a chastened voice. "I did not mean to speak to you so."

The chaplain brightened visibly. "You do well to ask forgiveness, my daughter. But you must also ask it of the King, your husband."

For a moment it looked as though Henrietta Maria would rebel, then she said in a barely audible voice, "Must I?"

"You must." The chaplain glanced quickly at the King. "It may be," he went on, "if you have a contrite heart, that His Majesty will allow Madame Saint-Georges to travel with you."

Henrietta Maria looked at Charles. "Forgive me, Sire." A faint smile appeared. "If you will be kind enough to indulge me, I would like Madame Saint-Georges to attend me on the journey."

Realizing that he had been neatly trapped, the King could do no less than agree to the sweetly worded request. At the same time he was unpleasantly aware of the mockery in her eyes that told him she was savoring her victory. "Very well," he said curtly. "Since you seem to wish it so urgently, madame may travel with us."

"Thank you, Sire." Charles could not control an angry flush at the mockery in her voice. "You are so good to me," she went on softly, flashing him a brilliant smile.

Charles inclined his head stiffly. Seating himself comfortably, he folded his arms across his chest. He would long remember the embarrassment of these moments, he thought grimly. Turning his head, he stared unseeingly out of the opposite window. Something primitive and alien to his nature began to boil inside him. He dared not look into Henrietta Maria's smirking face lest he be tempted to hurl her across his knees and administer the beating that she deserved. Like it or not, she was his wife. In the future, he intended to see that she behaved as became a wife and a Queen of England. In wedding this shrew, this screaming, hysterical, spoiled child, what had he done to himself? More impor-

28

tant, what had he done to his people? What manner of Queen would she make, what manner of helpmate? To add to her many faults, she was staunchly Catholic. He had heard that she was almost fanatically so. With a sinking heart, he thought of the majority of his people who were against Catholicism in any form. Well, against sage advice he had entered into this marriage, and now he must make the best of it.

Charles turned his head again and looked at the chaplain, who was beaming indulgently upon the Queen. Priests! Charles fought a flash of savage anger. He would not have the black-garbed soft-spoken hypocrites cluttering his Court! He himself was a devoutly religious man, but his Protestant soul could not abide these representatives of the Catholic faith. For the moment he was forced to put up with them, but that would change. Sooner or later he would ship them back to France. Aye, he would, he promised himself, and with them would go most of the other perfumed, mincing, chattering French parrots who made up the Queen's entourage. He was not a vindictive man, but, nursing his bruised dignity, he took pleasure in the thought. And, Henrietta Maria must learn to speak the English language. She must learn to behave and to think as befitted a Queen of England. A pox on the French. He had never liked them! Becoming aware that he was being less than charitable to the French men and women, most of whom he had not yet met, he gave a rueful smile.

Brett Foxefield, with Buckingham beside him, approached the carriage. Charles heard Henrietta Maria's soft, delighted murmur as Brett leaned into the carriage and bowed over her extended hand. "My lord Foxe," Henrietta Maria said.

By God! Charles thought, his anger returning in full force. How gentle she sounded now. How her childish voice lingered over and caressed the nickname he had given to Brett Foxefield.

Brett moved round to the window where Charles sat so stiffly. "Your Majesty?" he said, the two words an inquiry.

Charles could not restrain a smile. "My lord Foxe."

Brett bowed. "Charles," he said in a soft whisper, "do not

show anger. Be calm, be easy of manner. There are doubtless many skirmishes ahead. 'Tis but a little battle you have lost.'' Brett's dark-blue eyes smiled into his.

It was the same voice that had so often reassured him in his lonely and delicate boyhood, and Charles responded as he had always done. He relaxed against the seat, feeling much of the angry tension leaving him. One would not think that Brett was one year younger than himself. ''I hear you, my lord Foxe,'' he said in a quiet voice. ''I will remember.''

''I pray so, Sire.''

Charles cleared his throat. '' 'Tis a pity you do not accompany us, my lord,'' he said with his accustomed calm. He felt rather than saw Henrietta Maria's start, and he smiled grimly.

''A great pity, Sire,'' Brett answered. ''But Your Majesty, being gracious enough to take note of my small problems, is aware that it is imperative that I return immediately to Foxefield Hall.''

Charles laughed. ''Do not play the smooth courtier with me, my lord, it does not suit you. Remember that you are commanded to rejoin me with all possible speed.''

''I will remember, Sire.''

Henrietta Maria watched them, her mouth sullen. It might be that, for the sake of courtesy, the King and my lord Foxe spoke in French. But she had a shrewd idea that Charles, having guessed at her attraction to my lord Foxe, wished to make quite certain that she understood that he would not be accompanying them.

Charles was nodding to Buckingham, who was bending over his hand. ''We will miss the knave, will we not, George?''

''Indeed, Sire.''

Buckingham's words came so reluctantly that Brett laughed aloud in genuine amusement. ''I am sure you did not intend to make it sound so, my lord Duke,'' he said, patting Buckingham's shoulder, ''but your tone was hardly complimentary.''

''Was it not?'' There was such malice in Buckingham's pale-blue eyes that Brett felt shock. He had not known that the man hated him so. ''My lord Foxe mistakes me,'' Buckingham said smoothly. "I pray you to believe that I will rejoice with His Majesty in your return."

Brett grinned. "So that you can keep an eye on me, I suppose?" he could not resist saying.

Buckingham did not answer, but Brett knew from his startled expression that he had hit the mark. "You must try not to grieve too much, my lord Duke," Brett drawled. "In a very short space of time I will be back to brighten your world."

Charles glanced from one to the other. "That will be enough, gentlemen!"

Henrietta Maria listened dully to the rest of the conversation. She felt cold and tired and bitterly disappointed. She glanced through the window at the sky. "The sun has disappeared behind the clouds," she said sharply, breaking rudely across the conversation. "Why may we not proceed?"

Charles shrugged. "Calm yourself, Madam," he said coldly. "In a few moments we will be on our way."

She tossed her head petulantly. "I hope so, Sire. In my country ladies are given every courtesy and consideration."

Again Charles fought the urge to turn her over his knee. He smiled at her politely. "One must act like a lady if she wishes to be treated as such."

"What mean you, Sire?" Henrietta Maria said, her voice rising indignantly.

"At a more convenient time, Madam, I will explain my meaning fully. In the meantime, I request that you lower your voice."

She glared at him. "And if I will not?"

"I think you will be very sorry, Madam."

She opened her mouth to challenge his statement, then closed it hastily. The expression in his eyes had frightened her. Sulkily, she flopped back against the cushions. "As you wish, Sire," she muttered.

When it was time for the carriages to proceed, Brett stood to one side, choking a little on the dust raised by the turning wheels. He stared thoughtfully after the swaying vehicles. The lady is a virago, he thought, but she has that magic quality when she chooses to use it. Should she use it on you, my poor Charles, you may well be lost. I doubt if you will be able to manage her, or even wish to do so.

Troubled, he turned away and walked back to the stables. His face tightened as he thought of Henrietta Maria. "Were she mine," he muttered, "I'd gentle her in a very short space of time. If she did not come to heel, she would feel more than the length of my tongue. She would feel my hand smarting on her backside!"

Mounted once more and on the road to Huntingdon, Brett thought of the note delivered to him two days ago. It had been brought to him by a groom from Foxefield Hall. The note had been from his foolish and pretty mother. Lady Sarah Foxefield had expressed great anxiety over that thorn in the flesh, Mistress Meredith Hartford. Brett did not doubt that it was another storm in a teacup. His mother was given to these sudden alarms. And certainly Mistress Meredith was not calculated to soothe a troubled soul. Damn the chit! There had been nothing but trouble of various natures since first she had come to live at Foxefield Hall. Brett's brows drew together in an ominous black line. If he found that the tone of his mother's note was justified, Mistress Meredith would find out what it meant to defy him!

Chapter Two

Lady Sarah Foxefield sat stiffly upright on the rose- and silver-brocaded couch. With a trembling hand she fluttered a delicate ivory and lace fan before her heated face. She wore a hunted look, and, as she darted several furtive glances toward the door, her large, soft, still youthful brown eyes were apprehensive. It was almost as though she expected the door to burst open at any moment and reveal some frightful vision. When it did open, however, it was to admit a tall, slender, serene-faced girl. She was carefully holding a round silver tray in both hands, on which stood a glass tankard filled with a steaming raspberry-hued liquid.

The effect on Lady Sarah was precisely the same as if she had, in actuality, been confronted with the frightful vision of her imagining. Uttering a shriek, she fell back against the piled up cushions. "Oh, Meredith!" she moaned. "I begged you not to wear those clothes. How could you? You'll be the death of me yet!"

"Aunt Sarah," Meredith Hartford said calmly, "why will you indulge in these absurd dramatics?"

The lady opened suffering eyes. "I have told you to call me Sarah, not Aunt Sarah." She plied the fan again. "I do not care to be addressed as aunt. It makes one feel so ancient."

"I'm sorry, Sarah." Meredith approached the couch. "I have brought your cordial," she said in a soft voice, depositing the tray on a side table.

"And that is another thing, Meredith. Why must you do work best left to the servants?"

"I like to keep busy," Meredith answered, smiling down at the agitated little lady. "Here, allow me to arrange your cushions, so that you may be comfortable while you drink."

Lady Sarah suffered her ministrations in sulky silence. She took the glass tankard from Meredith's hand, then exclaimed bitterly, "Comfortable! Is that what you expect me to be? I doubt, my love, that I will ever be comfortable again in this world, or, with the ill luck that so constantly dogs my footsteps, in the next world either." She plucked with thin jewel-laden fingers at the collar of her filmy pale-blue negligee. "As for this cordial, you know very well, you wretched girl, that if I drink it in my present state of mind, I will be seized with severe palpitations." Absently, she took a sip from the tankard, then, meeting Meredith's eyes, she clutched at her heart and gave vent to a low, quivering moan. "I am quite sure you have driven me out of my mind, for I scarce know what I am doing. Have you no compassion, my love? Must you indeed wear those abominable black garments and that—that apron. It makes you look like a serving wench."

"And what of that? 'Tis an honorable occupation."

Lady Sarah dismissed what she considered to be a frivolous remark with a wave of her hand. "I see that you are intent on hurrying me into my grave, you wicked, ungrateful girl!" She caught at Meredith's hand. "Change into something pretty, my love," she pleaded. " 'Tis the least you can do for me."

"But why must I change?"

"Because I desire it. Oh, Meredith, you must know that I am not long for this world."

Meredith laughed. "I know nothing of the sort, Sarah. You are excessively healthy."

"Cruel!" Lady Sarah moaned. "Hard! I am only just beginning to realize how hard and unyielding is your nature. What your poor mother would have said, could she but listen to you now, I shudder to think!"

Meredith's wide hazel eyes, which were fringed with absurdly long and curling black lashes, twinkled, and the sensitively beautiful face, framed by a severe, stiffly starched white bonnet, expressed amusement. "Mama would doubtless have agreed with you," she answered. "She ever despaired of me." Thinking of her parents, both dead these many months, the lovely eyes were shadowed momentarily. "I miss them both very much," she went on firmly. "But in character, or so I have been told, I am more like my father."

"Yes, yes." Eager to concede the point, Lady Sarah said quickly. "You are very like dear Jack. I have often remarked upon it, have I not?"

"No, indeed you haven't."

"Must you bark at me so abruptly, my love. I have a severe migraine, and a loud voice only aggravates the pain." With a show of spirit, she added, "Anyway, if I have not mentioned it, I have always thought you to be like your dear father. Meredith, will you at least take off that hideous bonnet? It hides your hair. Hair, you must know, has ever been considered a woman's crowning glory."

"Vanity is a sin," the girl said severely.

"I daresay you are right," Lady Sarah said despondently. "Though I remember there was a time, my love, when you gloried in luxury and rich fabrics."

"That was before I saw the light."

"I daresay," Lady Sarah repeated on a note of petulance. Sighing, she tried again. "For my sake, Meredith, pray take off those garments."

Meredith's dimpled chin set firmly. "For your sake, Sarah," she said after a thoughtful moment of silence, "I might do so. But I am well aware that you do not ask it for your sake, but for the sake of your son, my lord Foxe."

"Hush!" Instinctively Lady Sarah's eyes darted over to the door. Do not let him hear you call him that, I pray you. I am quite sure he must dislike to be called so. But in one thing you are quite correct. He will be very displeased with your appearance."

Let him be, Meredith thought. Mayhap he will notice then that I am a woman and not a child. So let him be angry, let him be anything he pleases, just so that he notices me. She took a deep, steadying breath. It would not do to let Lady Sarah guess at the emotion that the mention of Brett's name always aroused in her. "I know he will be displeased," she said in a loud clear voice, "and I care not a snap of my fingers. Had I cared, I would have fared very badly, would I not?"

"What do you mean, my love?"

"You know well that he is always displeased with me." Meredith sat down on a small chair beside the couch. "As for the name of my lord Foxe," she said, folding her long white hands in her lap, "I am quite sure that he is very proud of it, since 'tis the King himself who bestowed the name upon him."

"If you think that, Meredith, then you sadly misjudge him. Faults he has, but vanity is not one of them."

I know it, Meredith wanted to shout. No, you are not vain, my dearest lord Foxe. Again she was forced to struggle for composure. It was Lady Sarah's fondest dream to see them wed. But even if Brett gave in to his mother's matrimonial plans, which she doubted, she herself was not willing to take a reluctant bridegroom. "Perhaps you are right," she answered calmly. "He is very independent and quite disagreeably arrogant."

"Meredith! Do not say such things, I beg you." Lady Sarah's round pretty face crumpled, giving her the look of a grieving child. Facile tears welled into her eyes, fell down her delicately tinted cheeks, and splashed upon her negligee. "But I cannot altogether blame you, I suppose. Brett can be so very difficult," she wailed. "Sometimes, my love, I vow that I am quite afraid of him." She mopped at her eyes with a wisp of silk and lace. "And now you, determined to shatter my poor nerves, have resolved to be difficult too."

"Oh, come now," Meredith said quickly. "It is true that in my eyes my lord Foxe has very few virtues, but I do know you have no need to fear him. He is extremely fond of you. His manner when conversing with you is invariably kind, one might almost say tender." She stopped short as if struck by a sudden and surprising thought. Tender? What would she not give to hear tenderness in my lord Foxe's voice when he addressed herself. "You know, Lady Sarah, if I had not seen and heard for myself, I would never have believed him to be capable of such a soft emotion."

Elated by the note in her voice, Lady Sarah said with a bewildering change of direction, "He has always been a good boy." She sighed mournfully. "But Brett is just such another as his father. I loved my poor Hugh very much, and I love Brett too, but neither father nor son can ever have been said to appreciate and to understand the extreme delicacy of my constitution. Sometimes, when Brett looks at me, his eyes appear to me to be quite hard."

"He does but seek to draw you from your self-indulgence," Meredith answered her briskly.

"Self-indulgence! I?" Lady Sarah looked outraged. "How can you, Meredith! I am a sick woman. I—I have been so since the d—day my H—Hugh died."

Meredith felt a touch of pitying impatience. Lady Sarah's pampered and perfumed body, she was sure, had rarely known the touch of pain. As for her heart, she'd stake her life that there was nothing wrong with that organ. Nonetheless, this very healthy little lady truly imagined herself to be a fragile invalid. In appearance, of course, she was frail, but very far from the brink of the grave. Meredith's dark-bronze brows drew together thoughtfully. Lady Sarah must, at one time, have been very different, else she would not have appealed to the autocratic

Hugh Foxefield. Meredith had seen him many times when, as a small child, her parents had taken her on visits to Foxefield Hall. She had been secretly afraid of the brusque, good-looking man, she remembered, though drawn by his smile, and the dark-blue eyes so like Brett's. Her memory, hazy where Lady Sarah was concerned, gave her only a fleeting picture of a pretty, vivacious, and extremely spirited young woman. Brett Foxefield she had never met until three years ago, when, after the death of her parents, she had come to Foxefield Hall as Lady Sarah's ward. On those earlier visits, Brett had been away at school. So it must be her husband's unexpected death that had plunged Lady Sarah into this mournful state.

Lady Sarah fidgeted on the couch. "What is it?" she said at last. "What are you thinking of?"

Meredith started out of her abstraction. "I was thinking that I must apologize to you for my words. I am sure you must know the state of your health better than I. I am very sorry, Sarah. I am sure that everything must be very difficult for you."

Lady Sarah, believing she scented sarcasm, gave the girl a sharply suspicious look. Apparently reassured, she said pleadingly, "My dear, you must not let Brett see you in those clothes. He will know at once that it is all due to that hateful man, Mr. Cromwell."

Meredith's sympathy faded. "How can you say that Mr. Cromwell is a hateful man? He is upright and honorable, he is all things fine and decent. As for my clothes, though I know you detest them for their somber hue, the choice was my own. It is true that Mr. Cromwell said that the color of my hair is flaunting, and that it gives me an undeserved wanton look. It is also true that he suggested I cover it with a bonnet, but he did not insist. So once again the choice was my own."

Thinking of that shining mass of bright bronze hair hidden from sight under that atrocious Puritan cap caused Lady Sarah to wince. "Brett will be very angry," she warned once more. "You know well that he detests Mr. Cromwell."

"I am not afraid of my lord Foxe."

Lady Sarah looked faintly surprised. "Are you not, my love?"

"I am not. Doubtless, with his many faults, my lord Foxe is ashamed to be in Mr. Cromwell's presence."

"But, Meredith, I cannot bear Brett to become angry. He has such a very violent temper. Indeed, my love, you would do well not to aggravate him."

Now Meredith felt the first flash of a genuine anger. She might yearn for the arms and the caresses of my lord Foxe, but she'd not become humble before him. She had thoughts and opinions of her own. "I shall not coddle him," she said coldly, "if that is what you mean. And I shall not cringe or beg for his smile."

The thought of Meredith cringing before anybody, even Brett, brought a smile to Lady Sarah's lips. The girl was a spitfire, and fully as arrogant as Brett. But the discomfort she would inevitably be subjected to, should Brett become angered, caused Lady Sarah's smile to disappear. "You know you provoke him, Meredith," she cried, wringing her small hands together in agitation. "Oh, yes you do, so there is no need to be giving me such a fierce look! You do it deliberately. How can you my love! Why can you not be gentle? Why will you not obey him?"

"Why should I? Though even were I of a mind to do so, Sarah, I could never bring myself to obey an unreasonable tyrant."

"He is not a tyrant."

"He is. But," she went on, telling the truth despite herself, "I admit that I do deliberately provoke him. I like to shake him out of that icy, contemptuous calm of his. His eyes are so cold when first he looks at me, but very soon they are blazing with fury."

Lady Sarah shuddered. "And that pleases you, Meredith?"

"It does."

"But why?"

"I—I—How should I know why?" She looked down at her folded hands. "Oh, I suppose it is because then he must look at me. Because then he can no longer pretend that I do not exist. So, you see, it is no use asking me to become gentle and obedient."

Lady Sarah sighed. "I suppose I do ask the impossible. I doubt very much that you will be brought to obey any man. I know not why you must always be so stubborn and headstrong, so intent upon forcing your extraordinary religion on others. I fear, my love, that you will come to a bad end.''

''Not I. My religion is the true one. It is only because I love you that I struggle to make you see reason.''

''Puritanism?'' Lady Sarah said faintly. ''My dear, I fear that it will never become a fashionable religion.''

''Fashionable? What a thing to say!''

''You know what I mean. The Puritans lead such a terribly grim life. They do not seem to care for pleasure in any form. Such terribly uncomfortable people! Mr. Cromwell is a typical example. He is so stern, so sober. I cannot bear those piercing pale-blue eyes of his. And, my love, I feel quite sure that he heartily disapproves of me. Did I tell you that, on the last occasion he called upon me, my palpitations afterwards were truly terrible? I believed that my time had come. My heart did not resume a normal beat for quite an hour.''

Meredith suppressed a smile. ''But we were talking of your son, were we not?''

''Were we? Oh, yes. Yes, so we were. Meredith, I expect Brett at any moment. He sent word to me by a groom that he would come. Oblige me for once, if 'tis possible, by not angering him.''

''What!'' Meredith exclaimed, staring at her. Bright color tinged her creamy skin. ''He is expected today? Oh, Sarah, why did you not tell me?''

''Did I not?'' Lady Sarah asked, looking at her vaguely. ''I had meant to do so. Do you promise not to provoke him, my love?''

''No, I do not.'' Her heart beating uncomfortably fast at the thought of his imminent arrival, Meredith rose to her feet and began to pace the room with long, agitated strides. ''I tell you to your face, ma'am, that I care nothing for his opinion. I tell you also that your son is a brute! Aye, a brute and an abominable boor!''

''He is nothing of the sort,'' Lady Sarah said hotly, betrayed into a flash of maternal indignation. "You shall not say so!" Meredith's hands clenched. "He is," she insisted. "And further to that, he is a great hulking bully!"

Wondering a little at the girl's agitation, Lady Sarah put a hand to her head. "My love," she said plaintively, "must you whirl about the room? And, tell me, what has Brett ever done to you that you should dislike him so?"

Meredith could have said, and, in fact, was almost tempted to do so—It is because he will not see me, because he looks straight through me, because he does not care for me! That is why I must pretend to a hatred that I do not feel. For if Brett ever guessed my true feelings, if he should ever laugh at me, I would want to die!

"Meredith, I asked you a question. What has Brett ever done to you?"

"What has he not done, Sarah, is more the question. When the great m'lord Foxe condescends to look at me, which is seldom, it is always with a scowl. He lectures me continually in that cold, precise voice of his. He criticizes my friends, my manner, and my dress. Oh, yes, Sarah, I assure you. No matter what I wear, I cannot seem to please him. And there is another thing. He has taken a strong objection to my religion."

"Well," Lady Sarah ventured mildly, " 'tis scarcely to be wondered at, is it, my love?"

"Nevertheless, there is no need for him to speak slightingly of Mr. Cromwell. He calls him a dull dog with treasonable ideas. And one who would be far better off to be married to another dull dog like himself, rather than to the nice little Mistress Cromwell."

"Treasonable ideas?" Lady Sarah said in dismay. "What mean you? Does Mr. Cromwell indeed speak treason?"

Meredith came back to the chair. "It would depend how you construe treason," she said, sitting down again. "He does not approve of the King. He believes him to be a heedless and inconsiderate rogue, with little thought for the people. And now that he has married that Frenchwoman, Mr. Cromwell is even more concerned for the people and the country."

"Very good of Mr. Cromwell to concern himself, my love," Lady Sarah said dryly. "But with or without his religious and moral guidance, I feel sure that we will all manage to stumble along."

Surprised at her unusual tone, Meredith went on slowly. "He believes too that Buckingham is an evil influence over the King, just as he was over King James. He says that the King and Buckingham are frittering away the country's substance. 'Tis no use to look so outraged, Sarah. You should not lightly disregard Mr. Cromwell, I tell you. I believe that he will rise to become a great man. It is men like Mr. Cromwell who should be governing this country, and not a weak excuse for a king."

"Meredith! Oh, my love, you cannot mean it."

"Well, perhaps not," Meredith answered laughing.

"Listen to me, Meredith," Lady Sarah cried, sitting upright. "You are never to see that man again!" Panting audibly, she put a hand to her heart. "The audacity of the creature, to dare to speak so of the King! To be sure, I do not like the Duke of Buckingham, but the King is gracious and charming. He is a good man. This Cromwell person should be punished for his wicked lies!"

"But are they lies, Sarah?" Meredith stood up slowly. "But whether they are not, do you mean that we should not feel, that we should not think for ourselves? Do you mean that we should follow blindly after the King, no matter how wrong he may prove to be?" She swept a mocking curtsey. "Yes, Your Majesty. No, Your Majesty. Pray to pardon me, Your Majesty!"

"What has happened to you?" Lady Sarah cried. "I do believe that man has bewitched you! Meredith, the King has several times been a guest in this house. I know that you have spoken together many times. You liked him, or so I did believe. What has changed you?"

"I have not changed, Sarah. I both admire and like the King. In truth I found him to be quite charming."

"Well then?"

Meredith laughed. "But if he should prove to be wrong for

42

England," she cried, making a chopping gesture with her hand, "then I say off with his head."

Lady Sarah gave vent to a small scream. "Meredith!"

"Oh, Sarah, you take everything so seriously. 'Twas only a joke, you know."

"I do not like such jokes."

"Nor I, Mistress Hartford," a cold voice said from across the room.

Lady Sarah started violently. "Brett! How you startled me." She stared at the tall figure of her son, blinking nervously at him. "I d—did not hear the door open. But, my dear, I believe Meredith spoke truth. 'Twas really only a joke, I believe."

"I trust so." Brett inclined his head to Meredith. Crossing the room, he took Lady Sarah's hand in his. "Well, Mother, how do you fare?"

"I—I—" Gently, Lady Sarah drew her hand from his. Her fingers touched a lock of her soft brown hair, twisting it. "I am in a very unstrung condition. My—my nerves, you know."

"I see." His eyes smiled into hers. "Then your condition is unchanged?" he said, touching her cheek with caressing fingers.

"Quite unchanged." She looked up at him wistfully. "I am sure that I must be a very great bother."

"What nonsense. I would not change you for the world."

Meredith watched them, her heart pounding as she looked with loving eyes at his tall stooping form. So lost was she in her usual dream, so carried away, that she was disagreeably surprised when Brett came toward her, a forbidding look on his face. "I know not the meaning of this mummery, Mistress Hartford," he said, his eyes appraising her costume, "nor do I care to know. However, it will not do. I wish to speak with you on a matter of some importance. But first you will go to your room. You will remove that garb and dress yourself in normal apparel. I will see you downstairs in the Red Room, in precisely ten minutes." His curt nod dismissed her. "It is understood?"

Burning color flooded her face. "No, it is not understood," she cried, glaring at him. "I will wear what I please. Nothing you

43

may say or do will persuade me to discard these clothes. And you cannot force me to do so.''

"Can I not?'' He looked at her with that faint amusement that she had learned to detest. It was the same look that he might give to a bad-tempered obstinate child. An amused look, but quelling. "I believe, Mistress Hartford,'' he went on, "that you know better than that. However, since my form of persuasion might be construed as rough, it might be as well, while you reside in this house, to do exactly as you are told.''

"Then I will not reside in this house. I will leave!''

"By all means do so, if such be your wish. But I fear you would not care to be dragged back in humiliation. Until you are of age, you are under our care. I would advise you to remember that.''

"Oh, you—you beast!''

He took a threatening step toward her. "It seems, then, that I must treat you like a child.''

"What do you mean?''

"I mean exactly this. If you have not left this room within the space of one minute, I will personally carry you to your room and undress you myself.''

She backed away from him. "You would not dare.''

His dark brows rose. "You know that I would, Mistress Hartford. If you do not, then I must warn you that you now have less than a minute in which to find out.'' He turned away from her. "By the way,'' he added casually, "you will not see Mr. Cromwell again. I forbid it.''

"You forbid it! I will see him whenever I like. I will do exactly as I please, and I will see whomever I pl—''

"Meredith!'' came a faint moan from the couch. "Oh, Meredith, please!''

Meredith cast Lady Sarah a fuming look. "Oh, very well.'' She glanced quickly at Brett. He was looking at her with cynical amusement. She lifted her head high, turned her back on him, and left the room with a dignified step.

Lady Sarah eyed Brett. The thought came to her that he looked very handsome, despite the splashes of mud on his clothes, his wind-tangled hair, and his general air of weariness. He was very like his dead father. Hugh had had the same dark curling hair, the dark-blue eyes, and the deeply clefted chin. Then her maternal pride in him was swallowed up in a surge of anxiety for Meredith. Despite many trying moments, she sincerely loved the girl, and did not wish her to be exposed to the blast of Brett's fury. Again like his father, he could be so very formidable, so intimidating. Even now, as he loomed over her, he looked dark and forbidding, she thought. As if sensing her thoughts, he smiled, and his whole expression softened.

"Mother," he said, "why do you look at me like that? Do I indeed terrorize you?"

"S—sometimes."

"But I do not mean to do so, you know."

Oddly touched by something she saw in his eyes and heard in his voice, Lady Sarah impulsively took his hand and cradled it against her face. "Forgive me, my dear boy. I am really very silly, I know. You must blame it on my precarious health."

His hand still held in hers, he sat down on the side of the couch. For a moment he regarded her steadily, then, smiling, he said, "But, Mother, you know that you are not really ill. You do know that, don't you?"

Tears came into her eyes, and she looked at him defensively. "You say that I am not ill. Then tell me why I always feel so weak and nauseated? Tell me why I have such terrible palpitations."

"You have been examined many times, and all of the medical men have given it as their opinion that there is nothing wrong with you. Did they not impress upon you the need to take more exercise, and to perhaps try to live a little outside of yourself?"

"Yes." She turned her head away. "Then I suppose that what you are really saying is that I am a selfish woman? And not only a selfish woman, but one who only imagines herself to be ill."

"If it sounded like that, I am sorry." He wiped her trickling tears away with the tips of his fingers. "I admit that I have believed your illnesses to be largely imaginary. But even if they

45

are only imaginary, if you believe your symptoms to be genuine, then it is one and the same thing, I suppose.''

Her lips quivered. ''I rarely speak of your father, Brett. I—I find that it is much too p—painful. But I do miss him so very much. It was as though my whole world crumbled, when he died. And though I seek to restore the pieces and make my world whole and steady again, I cannot find them.''

''I know, Mother, I know.'' He put his arms about her and drew her into his embrace. ''And that is really the trouble, isn't it? But the damned leeches find very few cures for the afflictions of the body, so we can hardly expect them to find a cure for a broken heart, can we?''

''No, I suppose we cannot.'' She was silent for a moment, then she said timidly, ''Are you very angry with me, my dear?''

''Nay, how could I be?'' He laughed softly. ''Do you really believe that I could have the temerity to be angry with my own mother?''

''I don't see why not. And anyway, you know well that you have often been angry with me.''

''Nay, surely not!'' He took his arms away and pressed her back against the cushions. ''You must try to forgive me, must you not?'' He touched her chin with a teasing finger. ''You should have beaten me more when I was a lad.''

She laughed with him. ''Aye, perhaps I should. But you were such a dear little boy, and even then promising to become the very image of your father.''

''' 'A dear little boy,' '' he repeated wryly. ''Was I really?''

''You were indeed. Everybody thought so.''

''But it would seem that I have not grown into a dear little man,'' he said, grinning at her. ''As Mistress Hartford and a great many others would very quickly inform you.''

''I'll not hear a word against you.''

''Will you not? I rejoice to hear you say so.'' He hesitated, then went on quickly, ''Mother, will you, for my sake, try to take more exercise?''

''I will, darling,'' she promised eagerly. ''I will indeed.''

"I have your word?"

Her eyes wavered. "I will—will try."

"I believe you." His smile faded. "You know, Mother, there is a tide of unrest in this country. England will need strong men and women if she is to overcome it."

Lady Sarah bridled. "I am not a child, Brett, so you do not need to hold out a bribe."

" 'Twas not meant as a bribe, I assure you."

Her face changed. "Then what can you mean? What unrest do you speak of?"

"I should not have spoken of it at all." He shrugged. "Come now, there is no cause for alarm. There is nothing definite as yet. At the moment it is more something I sense, I suppose."

Lady Sarah looked at him indignantly. "You frightened me."

"I'm sorry." He leaned forward and kissed her cheek. "I must leave you for a while. I have an appointment with the chit."

"Brett! Do not call her that. You must try not to be too hard on her. She does mean so well, you know. You know, dear boy, you do have such an unfortunately savage temper."

"Evidently she is a wench who must embrace some cause or other. But I will try not to be hard on her," he promised gravely. "And I will do my utmost to control my savage temper."

Taking his leave of Lady Sarah, Brett walked along the hall. Reaching the stairs, he descended slowly. As his mother had said, he did have a hot temper, a temper that sometimes impelled him into violent action. Thinking of Meredith, he could not help but wonder why it was that she so easily aroused his rage. Just now, when he had walked into his mother's room, the mere sight of Meredith dressed in those hideous clothes had instantly antagonized him. But for all that, he had not meant to speak to her quite so harshly, or, if it came to that, to threaten her. He could only assume, unreasonable and unfair as it was, that everything about her not only annoyed him, but seemed to bring out the worst side of his nature. Everything, that is, except her courage, which was a quality in her that he could not help but admire. If only she would endeavor to be less irritating, less prone to follow slavishly the ideas of a man like Oliver Cromwell. He shrugged. But if it were not Cromwell, it would doubtless be some other crack-brained ranter. Damn Meredith, anyway! It seemed that whenever he thought of her, his thoughts always became angrily chaotic.

Reaching the wide hall, which gleamed like a mirror and smelled vaguely of lemon polish, he stood there for a moment in deep thought. Just before he had entered the gates of Foxefield Hall, he had encountered his neighbor, Oliver Cromwell. The man had greeted him politely enough, but he himself had returned the greeting rather curtly. The very thought of Meredith being so constantly in the man's company, perhaps imbibing his treasonable ideas, had made him long to smash his fist against the man's thinly smiling mouth. Brett frowned. But perhaps he was being less than fair to accuse the man of treason, even if his accusation was unuttered. If Cromwell truly believed the things he was quoted as saying, then he should be at liberty to say them. The time had not yet come when Englishmen must tremble like terrified slaves before the wrath of the monarchy. Perhaps it had been so in the time of Henry VIII, but it would not be so in the time of Charles I.

Thrusting thoughts of Oliver Cromwell from his mind, Brett walked across the hall and entered the Red Room.

Meredith looked up as he entered. "As you can see," she said unsmilingly, "I am admirably punctual."

Brett moved slowly toward her. "So I note," he said, standing over her. "However, there appears to be a little matter you have forgotten. You have neglected to change your clothes. But perhaps I did not make myself clear before?"

"You made yourself perfectly clear, my lord Foxe. I have not forgotten to change. It is simply that I had no intention of doing so."

"I see. That is indeed unfortunate for you."

"Unfortunate? What do you mean?"

"I will answer your question with another question. Do you prefer to be undressed here, rather than in your bedchamber?"

"What!" Meredith shook her head. "Nay, m'lord, not even you would dare."

Her eyes were the color of amber, he thought. Amber speckled with green and blue. Had she been any other wench than this one, he might well have been tempted to draw her into his arms and kiss the full, soft mouth. He said drawlingly, "Would not dare? So you remarked before, Mistress Hartford. Do you know, I find it very curious, since we have encountered each other frequently in the last three years, that you have not yet made a more accurate assessment of my character."

She could not look away from him. "I think you are wrong, my lord Foxe," she countered. "I have made a very accurate assessment. I know you for a bully and a beast."

His mouth tightened very slightly. "You might add to that, Mistress Hartford, that when I say a thing, I mean it. However, if you truly believe that I am a bully and a beast, would it not be wiser to mount the stairs to your bedchamber and remove the clothes yourself?"

"I am to be given a choice, then?"

He put out his hand. Taking hers, he pulled her to her feet. "Yes, you are to be given a choice. I have, unfortunately for myself, a very tender heart. Go now, and I pray you to hurry."

"You are not accustomed to being kept waiting. Is that it, my lord?"

"It is indeed." He smiled faintly. "When I am kept waiting, it arouses all that is evil in my nature."

"Bah!" she turned from him abruptly and walked over to the door. "Do not speak to me of your tender heart. I would find more compassion in a stone!"

"Mistress Hartford," Brett said softly as she flung the door wide, "I wish to tell you that I have a key to your room."

"I have the key."

"So you have. But there are two keys to every room. You might remember that, should you have conceived the foolish notion of locking yourself in your room."

"I hate you!"

49

" 'Tis not necessary to refine upon the point. I had arrived at that conclusion for myself."

Meredith hesitated. She dallied with the tempting idea of resuming her seat and so arousing in him that anger which both frightened and fascinated her. She wondered, as she had wondered often before, what he would do if she pushed him beyond a certain point. She bit her lip. But no. This time it might prove to be really dangerous. She was suddenly sure that he was quite capable of carrying out his threat.

"There is something you wish to say, Mistress Hartford?" came Brett's voice.

She opened her mouth to reply. Instead of the words she had meant to utter, words she had sworn never to say, came out. "Why do you not call me Meredith?" she said sullenly. "Or Merry, as you were used to do?" Her face flushing, she waited for his answer.

"I believe, unless memory deceives me, that 'twas yourself who first established formality between us." He smiled lazily, mocking her with her own words. "Why do you not call me Brett, as you were used to do?"

She stared at him, longing to run into his arms, but at the same time longing to strike him hard. Confused and shaken, she burst out rudely, "Because I loathe you, that's why!" Without waiting for his answer, she rushed from the room, banging the door loudly behind her.

She brushed past a manservant who was making his way through the hall. His stately progress interrupted, the man turned his head and looked after her as she fled up the stairs. What's up with our little Puritan, he wondered. For all her sweet words, 'tis plain to me that she's got a nasty temper when roused. He chuckled. But master's back, I'd forgot that. Master's a rare one for making little miss lose her temper. More like a demon than an angel when he's around, that she is.

Some ten minutes later a transformed Meredith entered the Red Room. Nodding approvingly, Brett rose to his feet. "Much better," he commented.

She was wearing a low-necked gown of apple green, and she had tied back her hair with a ribbon of the same color.

"Green becomes you," Brett said, motioning to her to be seated.

She sat down. "Since I care nothing for your compliments, my lord, perhaps we might proceed to this matter you wish to discuss."

"Oh, did you think I had paid you a compliment? It was merely a statement of fact."

"Was it so? Then, m'lord, I concede the difference."

"Will you take a glass of wine?"

"No, thank you. You know well that I do not approve of strong drink."

"Do I, my little pious one? On the occasion of my last visit, I seem to remember that you indulged in several glasses of the sinful liquid. So I could hardly be expected to remember, could I?"

"I have changed since then. And that is another thing. I do not wish you to laugh at me. You are laughing, are you not?"

"A little," he admitted. "You will admit, Mistress Hartford, that you are as variable as the wind?"

"I admit nothing of the sort."

"Be that as it may, and at the risk of lowering your already low opinion of me, I believe that I will take some wine."

Fuming at his casual attitude, the mocking smile with which he regarded her as he slowly filled his glass from the crystal decanter on the table, she waited until he had resumed his seat.

"Well?" she said.

He sipped the wine slowly. "Very good," he said, holding his glass up to the light.

"I am glad you are enjoying it, m'lord. Will you now condescend to speak?"

"Why, yes, I believe so. May I first ask you a question, Mistress Hartford?"

She hesitated. Eying him with deep distrust, she said, "I suppose so. What is it?"

Brett placed the glass on the table beside him. Leaning forward, he subjected her to a long cool stare. "I would be most interested to know what new guise this is that you are now adopting?"

"New guise?" Her fingers twisted nervously in her lap. "I fail to understand you?"

"I will elucidate. When last I was at Foxefield Hall, you were all sweet murmurings and blushes. It is true that I could still read your dislike in your eyes. It is also true that your sweet murmurings were ofttimes edged in acid, but on the whole you were satisfactorily meek, one might almost say pliable. What has happened to change this happy state of affairs? Why, when I return, do I now find you bold and brazen?" He shook his head at her. "These changes, I believe you will admit, are apt to be bewildering. More especially since you were wearing the costume of a Puritan lady. Tell me, what caused you to drop your mask of simpering hypocrisy?"

At his first words she had flushed scarlet, and her face still felt uncomfortably warm. But it was more relief than anger she felt. So he could read her dislike in her eyes, could he? How little he knew. "How dare you?" she said without much conviction. "I have not changed."

"But of course you have," he said, smiling. "It causes me to wonder if, when next I see you, you will be wearing the habit of a nun."

"I refuse to discuss the matter with you."

"A pity. I find it all so fascinating. You are never twice the same."

"My lord," Meredith said in a muffled voice. "The matter of importance, if you please."

He lifted the glass, drank from it, savoring the wine, then he replaced it on the table. "I have joyous news for you, Mistress Hartford." He laced his fingers together. "I feel sure you will thank me for my thought on your behalf."

Joyous news? What new trick was this? she wondered. One of

his ruffles was torn, she noticed. "The lace at your cuff is torn," she said.

"Is it? Are you telling me that you wish to repair it, Mistress Hartford?"

"Indeed not." She looked at him haughtily. "That is work for the seamstress. I will inform her, when next I see her."

"Thank you."

"But perhaps," she said, giving him a malicious look, "you would prefer to inform Bessie yourself. I have several times noticed that you are not unappreciative of her ample charms."

"And that troubles you, Mistress Hartford?"

"Certainly not!" she snapped. "Your movements are of no interest to me. Why should they be?"

"I have no idea. I thought perhaps you had decided to record my sin in your impeccable mind."

Meredith was close to tears. He cared nothing for her, it was plain to see. But then she had always known that, hadn't she? Only today it seemed to hurt much more than usual. Forcing herself to control, she said, "What is this joyous news?"

"I have captured your interest?"

She felt bewildered. If, as he had said, she had changed, what of himself? She had offered him provocation, and he should by now be losing his hold on that precarious temper of his. He had not, and she was conscious of a keen sense of disappointment. If she must be nothing to him, then she would prefer his violence, the whiplash of his tongue. Anything, to the cool indifference he was now displaying.

"Well?" he persisted. "Have I captured your interest?"

In her despair, she shouted at him. "Nay, you have not! And you never will, my lord Foxe. So there, and be damned to you!"

"Such shocking language from a Puritan lady!"

"Oh, be quiet! Be quiet! Tell me the news."

"Very well. The Queen has granted you an appointment to her household."

"The—the Queen? That Frenchwoman?"

53

"That Frenchwoman," he agreed. "Though it would be more accurate to say that French child."

"You mean I am to live in London? At the Court?"

"You are. Or wherever the Court may happen to be at the time."

He was looking at her with that faintly quizzical expression. Was he jesting? "I refuse," she said finally. "I will not go."

Brett sighed. "Enough! The game is over, child, and I find myself wearied of argument. I have said you will go, and go you will. That is the end of the matter."

"Is it? And another thing, m'lord. I would have you know that I am seventeen years of age. Scarcely a child. Do you not agree?"

"Seventeen? 'Tis worse than I thought. You are but a babe in arms."

"I do not care to live at Court, m'lord. I wish to stay here."

Brett forced down a surge of anger. "Under the guidance of Oliver Cromwell, I suppose?"

"Yes, if you will have it so. Yes."

Brett rose to his feet. Meredith eyed him warily as he stretched both arms above his head and yawned. "I had a cursed hard ride," he said sleepily, strolling over to the door. Opening it, he turned his head to look at her. "You will be packed and ready, if you please. We will leave in two days' time."

"I have already told you that I will not go. Do my wishes count for nothing?"

"In this case, Mistress Hartford, nothing at all."

"Lady Sarah will miss my companionship."

"Then you will be pleased to know that after the plague has abated, I will be—"

"Plague?"

"Aye, there is plague in London. It is not uncommon at this time of the year."

"I see. So you do not mind subjecting me to it?"

He gave her an impatient look. "Were you to be in any danger from such a move, I might conceivably give the peril to yourself

54

some thought. However, you will find that the King and his Court have already decided to seek healthier air.''

He waited for her comment. The sun from the window at her back shone directly on her hair, and he felt a fleeting admiration for its color and texture. She had lovely hair. Why had he never noticed it before? "As I was saying,'' he went on, "as soon as the plague has abated, I will close Foxefield Hall for a time. I intend to take a small house in London for my mother. So you see, once the Court returns to London, you will be quite near to her, and you will be able to visit her frequently.''

"Lady Sarah does not like London.''

"On the contrary. She will be quite enchanted with the idea. She has long wished to reside in London.'' He nodded to her amiably. "All your problems have been swept away, have they not? So,'' he repeated, "you will be packed and ready.''

"No!''

"You really have no choice, you know.'' Nodding to her again, he left the room.

Left alone, Meredith burst into a storm of angry tears. She would not mind going so much if she could be sure of seeing Brett frequently. But she knew him too well to suppose that her forcible entry into Court life would have such a happy conclusion. Brett detested her, and he would make certain to keep away. She would be robbed of even his infrequent visits to Foxefield Hall. Her unhappy thoughts drifted to Oliver Cromwell. Always highly suggestible, she was much impressed by that stern man. She was remembering now how seriously he had spoken to her of the decadent life lived at Court. His face grimly set, he had told her that while he himself could not make claim to a personal knowledge, he had been made familiar with many of the licentious details. It had been bad enough, Cromwell said, indeed a thorough disgrace in the reign of King James I. But King Charles did not seem to be in any hurry to cleanse the Court of the results of his father's sinful living, or to reestablish a decent and moral life.

Meredith twisted her damp kerchief between her fingers. She

would not think of Brett, she would think instead of Oliver Cromwell. Desperately concentrating her thoughts upon him, she forgot the numerous times when Oliver Cromwell had inspired in her a feeling that was close to guilty dislike. Guilty, because she herself loved luxury and entertainment and all the things he frowned upon, and dislike because he made her ashamed, and she did not like to feel ashamed. She remembered instead how good the man was. Never once had he deviated from his austere life, in fact he seemed to enjoy its bleakness and self-sacrifice. The least she could do, Meredith thought, was to strive hard to follow his good example and to suppress her own frivolous longings. As proof of the firm hold her talks with Oliver Cromwell had taken on her vivid imagination, she even forgot Brett. She firmly believed that, should she be forced to take part in the life at Court, her soul would be in grave peril.

Meredith jumped to her feet and ran over to the door. She must find Mr. Cromwell, she must tell him of the terrible prospect before her. It might be, since he had once studied law, that he would be able to put a stop to my lord Foxe's plans for her damnation.

As she ran swiftly across the wide lawn and down to the gates, Meredith, who was normally possessed of a keen sense of humor, felt it striving to take over and to show her how ridiculous was the dramatic turn her thoughts had taken. What was she doing? Why was she running for protection to the formidable Mr. Cromwell? Meredith closed her mind firmly against that inner laughter that struggled to be free. She must know Mr. Cromwell's mind on the matter. He was a wise and a good man, and she felt sure he would advise her with his usual wisdom. What if he did believe in hell and damnation, in a stern and terrible and avenging God, what if she did shudder away from the picture he painted? She was silly and frivolous, and if he believed it, then she would do her best to believe it too.

Meredith stopped short in sudden dismay. What would Mr. Cromwell say when he saw her hair flowing free, giving her once again that distressingly wanton look? What would he think of the vivid color of her gown, and the neckline that was indecently low and revealed the cleavage between her breasts. Had Brett noticed? Had he seen, by the clear evidence of those thrusting breasts, that she could no longer be looked upon as a child? Well, she did not care if my lord Foxe had noticed or not. Yet it did sting to remember the blank indifference in his eyes.

Meredith began to run again. She must risk Mr. Cromwell's displeasure, there was no time to change her dress. Doubtless he would tell her that she should have taken a few minutes to resume her decent black. She thought of the black garment with its wide stiff white collar, and she grimaced. Wearing the gown, she felt very saintly, when not wearing it, she could only think of it with distaste. No, Mr. Cromwell would not like her present appearance. He would lecture her severely, she was sure. He would speak of wantonness and of willing abandonment to the devil. Well, let him. She must find him, and at once.

Chapter Three

Elizabeth Cromwell watched her husband walk heavily along the rutted lane. He did not pause at the end of the lane to wave to her before disappearing from view, as once he would have done.

Elizabeth shook her head, and her brown eyes clouded with worry. Poor Oliver, so serious, so dedicated to God. She too was dedicated to God, but sometimes she had the feeling that she and Oliver spoke of different Gods. Her God was a loving God, who wished His children to revel in the sunshine and the flowers, in the song of the birds, in the beauty of face and form, and in all good things that He had created. But it would seem that Oliver's God demanded that the eyes be blind to beauty, especially the exotically beautiful, for it was apparently a sin to notice such things. Oliver's God demanded that he be grimly serious and fanatically dedicated to His cause. Elizabeth had often wondered if her God would not believe fanaticism to be a sin? She felt that He would wish His servant Oliver to take a little time for innocent pleasure, rather than taking upon his shoulders, as he did, his neighbors' burdens as well as his own.

Elizabeth frowned. She had recently asked the local doctor to call in and examine Oliver. The doctor had been with her husband a long time. Then, when he had finally sought her out, he had given it as his opinion that Oliver was suffering from a severe depression.

Thinking of the doctor's words, Elizabeth shivered. It might be that Oliver would, in time, get over it. But would he? There seemed to be so many things on his mind. Only last night Oliver had raved for well over an hour about their new king, Charles I, and about Henrietta Maria, the Catholic Princess the King had taken for a wife. The sins of the King's favorite, the Duke of Buckingham, had not been left out, or the money the pair of them were squandering on, as Oliver put it, their vicious pleasures. Adding to the list of those people who came under Oliver's grave displeasure was the handsome Earl of Foxefield, another favorite of the King's.

Closing the door, Elizabeth reflected that she loved Oliver, and she had not the slightest doubt that she would always love him. She was not sorry that she had married him. But somehow, when she had been plain Elizabeth Bourchier, living with Sir James, her father, in their London home, life had been so much more light-hearted. Aye, it had been a joyous thing to wake up in the morning and begin to plan her day. She had indulged in pleasures, but they had been innocent pleasures and surely not offensive in the eyes of God? As Elizabeth Bourchier, she had been a considerable heiress, and she could have married a man whose fortune matched her own. Instead, she had chosen Oliver. He had changed a great deal since their marriage at St. Giles's Church, in Cripplegate, London. He had seemed warmer, more human and approachable then.

Feeling a tug at her skirts, Elizabeth smiled down at the little boy clinging there. She bade him play with his brother, and he ran off obediently.

Walking across the room, Elizabeth sat down at the clean, well-scrubbed kitchen table. Her body was heavy with pregnancy and there was a nagging ache in her back. God forgive her, she thought, putting her hands on her swollen stomach, but she had not wanted this child. What sex would it be? she wondered. Would it be born with an intuitive knowledge of its mother's reluctance to bear it?

Elizabeth felt suddenly and overpoweringly weary in both body and spirit. Hastily she dismissed thoughts of her unborn child and instead, allowed her thoughts to revert to the Earl of Foxefield. My lord Foxe, as the King was reputed to call him. Although they lived near enough to be called neighbors, Oliver had little to do with my lord Foxe, but he seemed to nourish for him a hatred that was fully as virulent as that he nursed for the Duke of Buckingham. A scoundrel and a wastrel, Oliver called the Earl. But Oliver's vehemence did not make sense, Elizabeth thought, frowning. On her chance encounters with the Earl, she had found him to be both courteous and charming. He had showed little trace of the dissolute rake Oliver had described. But perhaps she was unable to see her husband's point of view because she had allowed herself to become dazzled by the Earl's outstanding looks. Was that it? Still, it was nice to have one's hand kissed. It was pleasant and flattering to see that warmly intimate look in the Earl's blue eyes when he stopped to exchange conversation.

"My lord Foxe," Elizabeth said softly. She put her hands to her cheeks, still warm and flushed from the morning's baking. It was wrong of her to allow her thoughts to stray so often to the dark-haired Earl. She kept thinking of his intensely dark-blue eyes, and she chided herself for behaving like a green girl. Nay, she must not indulge in daydreams. She must not allow herself to be so swayed by a handsome face that she entirely forgot the arguments Oliver put forth against him. She did not think it possible that the romantic Earl could be all that Oliver said he was. But then again, he might be. This last thought displeased her so much that her frown deepened.

A chuckle from behind her caused her to look round. The little boy was making a staggering run toward her. She made to lift

60

him into her arms but, still chuckling, he ran away from her.

Straightening up, Elizabeth tucked a straying strand of dark-brown hair under her starched white cap. How she wished that Oliver would take more moderate views. On the subject of clothing, for instance. Was it such a terrible sin if one wished to wear a color now and again? She did not think that God would consider such a small vanity to be a major transgression. When she had told Oliver so, he had scowled at her blackly. Instead of answering her, he had begun to talk of his imminent death, for he was sure that his demise was rapidly approaching. She had heard it so many times before that she was no longer fearful for him. Now she endured in silence. When first he had begun to speak of his early death, she had tried to soothe and comfort him. But he always pushed her away, saying impatiently that she did not understand. So she no longer tried to reason him out of his fear. But just lately he had begun to speak on a new obsession. Visions of Divine wrath, he told her, had been frequently vouchsafed to him. This frightened her. Oliver seemed to be convinced that God was calling upon him to save England from some dreadful peril.

Oliver? Elizabeth shrugged and smiled indulgently. She could not take Oliver seriously, even though his ravings terrified her. She could not believe that God had chosen Oliver to save England. Her husband, in common with many others, was a man who worked his lands and provided a good living for his wife and children. Oliver was a good man, a devout and loving man, but she could not picture him as the savior of England. Let the dukes and the earls vie for power. Let them, through the King, rule England. Such a task was not for Oliver Cromwell.

A squabble breaking out among the children distracted her attention. She rose to her feet. Aye, she must certainly ask the doctor to call in again, she thought, as she went toward the children. Mayhap he would have some new physic that would enable Oliver to get a restful night's sleep. Certainly he could not go on as he had been doing. He was so morose, so irritable, that she had the terrible fear that his brain was about to snap under the strain of his real and imagined problems.

Oliver Cromwell walked beside the river. His hands were clasped behind his back and his head downbent. Why were so many people troubled? he was thinking. Why was he so troubled? Dear sweet Jesus, there was trouble everywhere! So much of it seemed to come his way that sometimes he would feel his brain reel in horror at the load. But nevertheless he must try to shoulder all trouble that came, and to be of good cheer. Someone must think for England. Someone must make plans to save her from disaster. His thoughts turned to the corrupt King James the First, the present King's father. King James, who had put such a monstrous drain on England's coffers. Then there was the evil Duke of Buckingham, a vile and sinful man! The Duke, not content with having been the favorite of King James, had now fastened like a leech upon King Charles. James, Cromwell considered, had looted the country to finance the sinful pleasures of himself and Buckingham. James had brought to dishonor all that the great Elizabeth the First had built up. And now Charles seemed to be set on the same course. But Charles had two favorites, Buckingham and my lord Foxe. Would my lord Foxe prove to be another leech, another looter of the country's revenues? It seemed more than likely, Cromwell thought bitterly.

His mind raced. There had always been trouble and doubtless there always would be. Unless—unless a strong man grasped the helm and brought England into safe harbor. The Stuarts should be swept away into oblivion! Had they not always brought disaster in their train? One had only to think of the flaunting and shameless Queen of Scots. Her conduct with David Rizzio, reputed to be her lover! Rizzio, murdered before Mary's very eyes by her outraged husband Lord Darnley, and his faithful followers. And later, Mary had continued her shameless conduct with the Earl of Bothwell. Cromwell's lips tightened as he thought of the many

62

who went to great pains to defend the red-headed harlot Queen. Those people said that the poor lady had been much maligned. But it was only he, Oliver Cromwell, who knew the truth. Aye, he knew it in his heart, in his soul. God had opened his blind eyes and had revealed to him the sordid truth that was hidden from the ordinary man. He knew that he was the chosen of God. He knew!

Cromwell felt the now familiar drumming in his ears. The sunlit landscape seemed to dip and waver. The Queen of Scots had passed on the evil seeds of lechery and decadence to her son, James, and he, in turn, to his son, Charles.

Cromwell wiped his sweating forehead. He had been just four years old when, upon the death of Queen Elizabeth, James had ascended the throne of England, in 1603. And he had been six years old when Guy Fawkes and his companions had attempted to rid England of James. That plot, unfortunately, had been discovered in time. Guy Fawkes and his fellow plotters had been captured. They had died a miserable and tortured death.

Frowning, Cromwell's thoughts dwelt on Guy Fawkes. He considered that the man had been a martyr to a great cause. He should be reverenced rather than condemned. He himself, though he had been very young, far too young to understand the dark shadow that was slowly but surely enveloping his beloved England, had listened to all these tales with enthralled interest. Now he was no longer too young to understand. He was, in fact, one year older than Charles, King of England. Now he could easily follow the trend of affairs, and he knew that something must be done to avert calamity. Something would be done! When, or how, he did not know. He would trust in God to reveal to him the time to strike. He felt a sudden ecstasy as his mind went to his recurring dream. In that dream Charles Stuart mounted a scaffold. He knelt before the people, his lips moving in prayer to the God he had offended so often. Then the executioner would lift his arm, the axe would come swooping down, and then—!

Clenching his hands tightly together, Cromwell forced himself to calm. He must remember that it was only a dream. Certainly he did not desire the King's life. Nay, he was not a vindictive man.

He only wished for justice for the people of England. And yet, was it really only a dream? Or was God endeavoring to point out the path that he must take? He, Oliver Cromwell, was destined to participate in momentous events, and perhaps God was trying to tell him that. His walk slowed. "I am not a vindictive man," he said aloud. "Is there not another way, Blessed Lord? Show me, I pray, another way!"

He stopped, listening for an answer to his plea. The only sounds that came to him were the rustling of the birds and the gentle lapping sounds of the river. To divert himself, he thought of the time when King James had negotiated for a match between his son, Charles, and the Infanta of Spain. Terror had swept England then. The people could only think of the burnings at Smithfield, in the reign of Queen Mary. Bloody Mary, she had been called. The people feared that the same thing would happen if, through this marriage, Catholicism were brought back to England. The union, however, had come to nothing, and once more the people relaxed.

Cromwell stood on the grassy bank and stared moodily into the murky depths of the River Ouse. But after all, what had the country really gained? Nothing. Nothing at all! For was Charles's marriage to the Frenchwoman, the Catholic Henrietta Maria, any better than that dreaded Spanish alliance?

He began to pace slowly. He could not help wondering why, since he was the chosen of God, he should constantly torture himself with thoughts of his approaching death. God's chosen could not die until he had completed the task allotted to him. For the first time he felt doubt. Had God really touched him, or did he only dream a glorious and impossible dream? He thought hard, then smiled as a quiet conviction came to him once more. He had been singled out for glory. The calm and quiet life of a husbandman was not for God's chosen. Now he knew he could put thoughts of death from him.

Cromwell lifted his chin arrogantly. He knew well, though he had no proof, that his wife laughed at his grandiose ideas, but he would climb to the heights. He would be the savior of his country. Oliver Cromwell had not been meant to live and die in obscurity. A husbandman, he? Well, mayhap for a time, but only until the call came.

His brow wrinkled as he thought once more of his wife. Why could he not make Elizabeth see him as he really was? She looked at him with love, sometimes with pity, and she had no knowledge of that other man who lurked in his body. That man, could she but glimpse him, would terrify her. Aye, she would go down on her knees before him, before the terrible power of that man, no longer hidden. He had strength, he could be ruthless, but his ruthlessness would be in God's cause. In God's cause, and the cause of his country. Cromwell felt a warm glow. That hidden man waited so impatiently to be set free, and one day, perhaps soon, God would release him. "England needs me," he prayed aloud. "Thou knowest it. Release me soon, blessed God, soon! Soon!"

Cromwell stopped pacing. He felt suddenly exhausted and drained of strength. Sitting down on the bank, he rested his back against the gnarled trunk of an oak tree. He should not complain of Elizabeth. She was a good wife and, in many ways, she understood him completely. Then why was it so hard for her to envision him in a position of power? He felt a twinge of resentment. He was not a no-account. He came of a good family. His dead father, Robert Cromwell, though he could not be said to be outstanding, had been a good husband and father. As had been his grandfather, Sir Henry Cromwell. And was he not descended from Thomas Cromwell, the Earl of Essex? Then there was his mother. His mother's maiden name had been Elizabeth Steward. She was reputed to be connected with the royal Stuart line. It could not be proved, of course, though he had tried. There were always obstacles put in the way of one who tried to lay claim to royal blood. He often thought of the possibility of this connection, and his heart would race with pride. Pride was a sin, he knew, especially too great a pride in lineage. But although he detested all Stuarts, still that pride would not be denied. He had spent countless hours on his knees, asking God to forgive him for the sin of pride.

Cromwell sighed. Elizabeth, his much-loved wife, had lately added to his burden. Aye, she had begun to trouble him increasingly. When she had stopped to converse with the Earl of Foxefield, he had noticed something in her attitude, something coy, almost flirtatious. It had caused him severe displeasure. But when he had remonstrated with her, Elizabeth had merely stared at him. Then she had looked down at her body which was swollen with child, and she had laughed. He had not liked the sound of that laughter, or her scornful words which sought to brush the matter aside. When first she had become pregnant with her third child, she had not seen it as the will of God. She had railed at him angrily, crying out, "Another child to bear, Oliver! Oh, dear God! Why did you not have more thought for me? It is too soon after the last birth!"

When he had coldly rebuked her, she had become yet more hysterical. It was not God's will. It was not a joyous gift from Heaven. It was a calamity and a nuisance. He had forgiven her outburst, of course. She was his wife, and he loved her. But since that time, there had been many things to trouble him. Pregnancy, he had heard, sometimes did strange things to a woman, but could that really explain her many frivolous ideas? She wished to wear lace at her neck and her wrists, she had told him. She wished to discard her black gown occasionally and wear silken and colored materials. Shameless! Sinful folly!

Remembering, a vein began to throb in his temple. He massaged the throb with his fingers, trying to soothe it away. He had so many things on his mind. It was so hard for him to relax. He brought his will to bear upon the problem, and little by little he felt the tension draining away. The sun was warm on his upturned face, and he took off his hat to enjoy it the more. He found himself wondering how Mistress Hartford fared, now that the Earl had returned to Foxefield Hall? When first he had met Mistress Hartford, he had thought her to be naught but a silly child with giddy ideas and a far too light-hearted outlook. At first she had been disposed to laugh at the things he considered to be holy and serious, but he had shown her the way. He had wrestled with her in prayer. He had had the satisfaction of knowing that her demons were driven out. She was meek now. She looked at him with admiration. There were times when he fancied he saw a gleam in her eyes, a curl to her lip that might indicate repressed laughter, but he told himself it was only fancy.

Cromwell clasped his hands together. That was the trouble with the world today. There was too much laughter. Too many people feverisly intent upon enjoying themselves, no matter what the cost to their immortal souls. There was not enough time taken for prayer, for humble thanks to God for His bountiful blessings. Why, there were people who would rather go to a bear baiting, to a cockfight, a puppet show, or even a theater, rather than spend a few precious moments with their Creator. How ungrateful was man! His breath caught in his throat and tears rose to his eyes.

Meredith Hartford stopped short as she saw Oliver Cromwell seated on the bank. The sun shone on his fine, light-brown hair and flushed his pale freckled skin with color. For once, his short, rather stocky body looked entirely relaxed. He was wearing his usual severe black, but he had loosened his plain white stock. He looked, Meredith thought, less severe than usual. Looking at his slightly tip-tilted nose, she thought once again of how incongruous it looked on that stern and unsmiling face.

Intensely conscious of her gown, Meredith approached him somewhat hesitantly. "Mr. Cromwell," she addressed him in an uncertain voice. "Might I speak with you, please?"

He had been deep in thought, and he started violently at the sound of her voice. He did not look at her at once. Flushing guiltily, he hastily restored his stock to order. Picking up his hat, he rose to his feet. His pale-blue eyes surveyed her, narrowing as they took in her gown and her bright uncovered head. He felt a spurt of anger that she should dare to appear before him so. His anger was the more severe because she had caught him in a rare moment of relaxation.

With something of an effort, he mastered his anger and forced a gentle note into his voice. "You have been crying, my child. What is your trouble?"

Meredith did not answer him at once. She looked at his tightly compressed lips, the ascetic face with its incongruous nose, and the thought came to her that, mingled with respect for him, there was also a small touch of fear.

Waiting for her to answer, Cromwell touched his little tuft of beard with nervous fingers. The finger moved to his full, shaggy mustache. It was a mannerism of his when annoyed or uncertain how to proceed. How the child did stare! To a lustful man, those golden eyes of hers which were speckled with blue and green and gray, might prove to be far too alluring and inviting. He must remind her, whenever possible, that it would be best to keep her eyes lowered. He smoothed his mustache again. "Well," he said, a touch of irritation manifesting itself in his voice, "why do you stare at me? What ails thee, maiden?"

"First I must apologize for appearing before you like this," Meredith said. She saw his small smile and was suddenly angry with herself. Why should she apologize to him? He was but a man, after all. Certainly he was not the god he pretended to be. Now shame replaced anger. Nay, she was wrong. He did not pretend to be a god, but he was God's representative. The next moment, she found herself appalled by a sudden surge of dislike. She glanced at him fearfully. Those eyes of his had always seemed to her to be able to see right through her. Could he read her mind now? she wondered.

Evidently he could not, for he said on a note of satisfaction, "You must not apologize to me, maiden, but to your Creator." His eyes dropped to her bosom, lingering on the cleavage between her white breasts. His mouth went dry, and he turned from her abruptly. "What is it you wish to say to me?"

Meredith moved to face him. "My lord Foxe is taking me away, Mr. Cromwell. I am to go to London. I am to live at Court and attend upon the Queen."

His eyes averted, Cromwell fumbled in his capacious pocket.

Drawing out a large square of clean white linen, he thrust it at her. "Cover yourself," he said harshly. "Your appearance is unseemly in the eyes of the Lord. Your breasts are as wantonly exposed as your brazen and flaunting hair."

Bright angry color stained Meredith's cheeks as she took the kerchief from him. Her impulse was to throw it in his face, but, conquering it, she attempted to obey. Her nervous fingers would not obey, and the kerchief fluttered to the ground.

Cromwell looked at her for a long moment, and she shifted uncomfortably before the look in his eyes. Bending abruptly, he picked it up. "I will help you," he said in a strangled voice.

His shaking fingers touched her flesh, lingering against the swelling curves as he worked. His heart began a hard rapid beating as the mad impulse came to him to pull those soft breasts from her bodice. Horrified and sick with shame, he admitted to himself that he wanted to gaze upon them, to touch them with the fingers and the mouth of a lover. Perspiration broke out on his forehead as he imagined how her nipples would harden and thrust beneath the touch of his caressing fingers. Would Mistress Hartford's breasts be as soft and as round and as delicious, as rosily nippled as the bare and jerking breasts of the London harlots? Their nipples were painted of course in a further effort to attract, and some of them were not merely rosy but a bright scarlet. He remembered a time, before he had come to God it had been, when, for a few coppers, he had played sensuously with the breasts of a harlot. His senses, normally fastidious, had been dulled to the rank odor of unwashed flesh. His mouth had suckled first one nipple and then the other, and in his ignorance he had truly believed he had discovered Paradise. When he entered deeply into the harlot's body and felt the clutch of her legs about his neck, heard her moans mingling with his own, he had been sure of it. But that episode had been some time ago. He had come to God, he was washed clean of carnal desire. Why should he feel this way now? Was Satan endeavoring to lead him from his broad and sunlit path to God into the dark and steaming chasms of sin? His heart was thundering in his ears and he felt a great sickness.

This young girl with her bright hair, her wanton mouth, her harlot's eyes, was Satan's instrument, he felt sure of it. Anger mingled with his shame. He wanted to strike her, to shout "Begone! Get out of my sight!" Instead, he stepped quickly away from her.

Wondering at his extreme pallor, Meredith thanked him in a subdued voice. There was something about him, a something that made her want to pick up her skirts and run. How strange to feel this crawling fear in the presence of such a saintly man. To make up for her thoughts, she gave him a sudden and brilliant smile.

Cromwell flinched as though she had lifted her hand and struck him. "You were saying something a moment ago, Mistress Hartford," he jerked out the words with some difficulty. "I—I fear that I did not hear you. What were you saying?"

She looked blank. "Oh. Oh yes, I was saying that my lord Foxe is forcing me to go to London. I am to attend upon the Queen."

Cromwell was momentarily diverted. "The Queen!" he gave a short bark of laughter. "That Frenchwoman!"

Meredith felt the welling of impatience. "Frenchwoman or no," she said tartly, "she is nonetheless the Queen." Seeing his tightly compressed lips, she feared that she had angered him. "I do not wish to go," she added softly. "Is there aught you can do to help me, Mr. Cromwell?"

Help her? He would as soon help a snake! She was Satan's instrument! Let her but go to London and his temptation would be removed. After a long pause, he said with a note of finality, "Nay, there is nothing I can do to aid you, maiden." He paused, licking his dry lips, but the habit of truthfulness was too deeply ingrained. Fighting his reluctance, he said slowly, "You could of course appeal to Lady Sarah Foxefield. She, after all, is your legal guardian. Her—her decision would naturally come before that of my lord Foxefield."

Meredith shook her head. "I know that. But you see, Mr. Cromwell, Lady Sarah is entirely under the thumb of her son. She will agree to anything my lord Foxe may suggest or command."

Hoping to hide his relief, he gave her an austere look. "Then there is nothing further that I can suggest. It would seem, maiden, since you are to go to London, that I have labored with thee in vain."

Meredith looked at him with mournful eyes and gave vent to a dutiful sigh. Inwardly, she was aware of a pounding excitement. Why had she come to Cromwell in the first place? She was a hypocrite, she had known all along that he could not help her. But to satisfy something within herself, she had had to make the gesture. Well, she had made it, and she was to go to London, she thought in sudden wild elation. Brett! words sang in her head. "Oh, Brett, Brett, I love you, and one day I will make you love me!" She knew now that she cared not whether she were in Huntingdon or London, as long as she could manage on occasion to be in my lord Foxe's company. She looked into Cromwell's eyes remembering the disquieting dislike she had felt for him now and again, and she was ashamed. She touched his hand gently with her fingertips. "I would not say that you have labored in vain, sir. I will strive to remember your wise and gentle teachings and your goodly thoughts."

Why did she call him sir? He was of much the same age as my lord Foxefield. Did she think of him as old, because he was not steeped in sin like Foxefield? He could still feel the touch of her fingers, it burned into his skin like a brand. Her touch! It had brought about a return of the sensuous sickness. His imagination showed her lying naked upon the sun-bleached grass. He could see himself touching her, mounting her, entering deeply into her body. Oh, dear God! Save this miserable sinner! He turned his hot face to her and looked at her with eyes that he strove to make expressionless. He saw that she was looking at him with a faint frown, wondering why he did not answer. "I trust you will remember, maiden," he said harshly.

Anxious now to be gone, she nodded eagerly. "I will remember. And if there is aught else I can do to further your teachings, you may be sure I will do it."

Cromwell's pale eyes blazed in sudden excitement. He drew

himself to his full height and said in a deep, throbbing voice, "To those who trust and believe in God, He will make His face to shine upon them. He will instill into His chosen servants the wisdom to know and understand His divine plan. Thus it may be that He has chosen you to report upon the corruption at Court."

"Chosen me? I do not understand."

Trembling, he burst out, " 'Tis simple, maiden. You must watch the French drab closely for any indication that she is trying to spread the evil teachings of Rome. You must watch the King, my lord Foxefield, my lord Buckingham, and all who are close to the King. Where you see evil, you must do your duty and report it to me. 'Twill be easy enough to find a messenger you may trust. The Court is the vineyard in which you must labor. Do you understand?"

Meredith drew back. "You mean that you wish me to spy for you, Mr. Cromwell?" she said in a hard voice.

"Call it not by so hard a name as spying," he said rebukingly. "You will be doing God's work."

"Call it what you will, but I fear that I cannot spy for you."

"You do not understand. It is not for me. You will be working in God's Cause."

She shook her head. "Good-bye, Mr. Cromwell," she said, holding out her hand.

Unthinkingly, he took it in his. The smallness and softness of her hand fired him with uncontrollable excitement. Heat flushed his body, and he could feel a quickening, a throbbing all through him. Tears filled his eyes, and he began to shake like a man in the grip of a fever.

"What is it?" Meredith's voice seemed to come from far away. "Are you ill, Mr. Cromwell?"

He made a moaning sound as he snatched her into his arms. "You were formed by Satan, sent by Satan to test me! Oh, dear Christ, I have lost the battle!" His hot lips touched her face, traveled lower to her breasts.

It was when his hands began to fumble at her bodice that Meredith recovered from the paralysis of surprise. "What are you doing!" She struck at him, wrenching herself away. "How dare you touch me, you—you—"

He stood there, hands hanging at his sides. He saw the horror in her face, the expression in her eyes that told him he was unclean, and it was like a thunderclap in his brain. "Mistress Hartford," he took a step forward, "Meredith!"

Instantly she retreated. "Do not come near me, you vile man!" With another withering glance, she turned and walked away.

All Meredith's instincts bade her run, but her pride would not allow it. Her ears alert, she walked on, a little faster now. She could hear no sound of pursuit. She had had her moments when she disliked Cromwell, she thought, but she had believed him to be a saint. She was seventeen years old, but not too young or too innocent to misunderstand what she had seen. No saint he. In his sweating, trembling eagerness to possess her, he had revolted her. Nay, he was not what she had thought him. Now that pride need no longer be considered, she began to run. The bitter disappointment and disillusion she was experiencing gave way to a delicious excitement as she thought of facing my lord Foxe again. As she neared the house there was no thought in her mind of Oliver Cromwell. With the easy contempt of the very young, she had determined to erase him as though he had never been.

Cromwell watched her out of sight. Unclean! She had looked at him as though he were unclean! Was he? Gradually, as he sought excuses for his behavior, his trembling ceased. It was true that he was God's chosen, but he was a healthy man for all that, a man with normal sexual appetites, though only for the procreation of children, of course. He was not to be blamed for his lapse. It had been so long since he and Elizabeth had lain together. His thoughts broke and scattered and he felt a surge of new confidence. It was as if a light was shining inside him, so certain was he of God's understanding love and His approval of His servant.

He turned and began to make his way along the bank. Secure in

God's understanding, what need had he to feel guilty? Luxuriously, slowly, he let his thoughts revert to the soft cushiony breasts of the harlot. His mouth worked, as, in imagination, he suckled her once more. Almost he could feel her hard-muscled experienced body responding to his own.

He was almost running when he turned into the lane and came within sight of his home. Elizabeth understood him. She knew that his sexual frenzies were few and far between, but that when they did come they must be instantly appeased. She was in her sixth month of pregnancy, and her body was so swollen that it was thought by the doctor that she might well bear twins. Nevertheless, he knew that she would accommodate herself to his needs. She must! Besides, had she not recently complained that he was neglecting her? She was right. He also had a duty to his wife.

Elizabeth looked up as he came through the door. She saw the blaze in his eyes, his working mouth. Not now, she thought. She was so big, so uncomfortable. Oh, please, not now!

There was determination in the very way he moved toward her. He put his hand on her shoulder. She could feel the heat of his flesh through the thin material of her gown. "Send the children out to play," he commanded hoarsely. He thought that he saw rejection in her eyes, and he could not bear it. "Send them to play with the neighbor's children," his voice was unsteady, overloud.

Elizabeth Cromwell knew then that he would not be denied. Sighing, she bowed her white-capped head meekly. "Yes, Oliver."

Chapter Four

Henrietta Maria started up from the bed where she had been sitting as the door opened abruptly to admit the King. She cast a quick look at the two ladies, her guardian angels, as she had come lately to think of them, who had been preparing her for bed. They were not looking at her. She knew that they, fearing her imperious demands and her anger, dared not. Their eyes meekly lowered, the two ladies curtsied before the King.

Unwillingly making her own obeisance, Henrietta Maria said with a hard note in her clear young voice, "Perhaps I am mistaken, Sire, but I did not hear you knock."

Her tone suggested that he was in grave error. His smiling mouth tightened ominously. "Possibly because I did not knock, Madam."

"Your visit is inconvenient, Sire. I am being prepared for bed."

"It would seem to me that you are prepared," he said shortly. His cool gaze warmed as it rested upon her. She was wearing a fine white linen shift embroidered all over with tiny rosebuds. Her hair had been brushed, and it lay on her shoulders like a gleaming black cape. There was candlelight behind her, and he could see the shadow of her limbs through the thin material. She was very lovely, this bad-tempered, obstinate, and hysterical child he had married. So lovely, in fact, that he could almost forgive her the constant scenes she made. Perhaps, too, if tonight she would come to him willingly, he might forgive her for her openly expressed hatred of himself, her ceaseless complaints, her contempt for everything English, except, of course, my lord Foxe. He might even forgive her the insult she had offered him night after night with her firmly barred bedchamber door. Christ's wounds! he thought with a spasm of anger. Her attitude suggested that he sought to rape an innocent and unprepared child. She was his wife. And, by Christ, before they entered London on the morrow, she would be his wife in truth! He had been very patient with her, but his patience was now at an end.

He looked suspiciously at the two ladies, searching their faces for a trace of a knowing smile. They stood very still, their heads still downbent. "Have you finished with the Queen, Madame Saint-Georges?" Charles inquired.

Madame Saint-Georges raised her head to look at the King, and the smile she gave him was warm and sweet. "We have both finished, Sire." She indicated the other lady. "Madame Duval and I were about to depart."

"Good. Then I bid you a pleasant good-night, ladies."

Ignoring Henrietta Maria's gasp of protest, Madame Saint-Georges cast her willful charge a warning look, then, taking the other woman's arm between firm fingers, she hustled her from the room.

The door closed behind them. Henrietta Maria's lips tightened to a thin line, and the eyes she turned upon the King blazed hatred and defiance. "It was for me to dismiss my attendants, Sire."

"Then why did you not do so?"

"I did not wish to."

Charles shrugged. "No more childishness, Madam, I beg of you."

"Do not beg me for anything," she retorted, "for it will avail you nothing." She reached out a hand to pick up the white lace wrap spread out upon the bed.

Charles' hand grasped her wrist. "You will not need the wrap, Madam."

She snatched her hand free and backed away from him. Her back to the wall, she said commandingly, "Leave me!" Warned by something in his eyes, she added, "I am tired, Sire, pray have the chivalry to leave me in peace."

He laughed. "Not this time, Madam. Besides, have I not often heard you say that an Englishman knows not the meaning of chivalry?" He put his hands on his hips and regarded her smilingly. "We have been several days on the road. Each night when I came to you, you were either too tired, or you had a headache, or some other of the numerous excuses you women make. Tomorrow we reach London. You may call it a whim of mine if it pleases you to do so, Madam, but I will not enter my city with the knowledge that you are not yet a wife."

"I did not wish to marry you, Sire."

"What Princess, unless she be very lucky in her parent's choice, ever wishes to marry the chosen one?"

Henrietta Maria ignored this. "I dislike you exceedingly, Sire."

Charles shook his head. "Nay. Despite your viperish tongue, your hostility and your insults, which, by the way, I must tell you I will endure no longer, I have seen that in your eyes which gives me hope."

She gave a shrill laugh. "Hope? I fear, Sire, that you are quite mad."

"We shall see."

Henrietta Maria's eyes slid over to the door as he began to walk toward it. "What are you going to do now?" she demanded. Then, on a note of hope, "Are you leaving?"

77

"Why, Madam. How could you think that I would disappoint you? I merely wish to lock the door."

"Don't!" she cried out in genuine terror. "I have told you to leave me, Sire. How—how dare you l—lock the door!"

Charles shot the bolt into place. "There is nothing to fear, you know," he said gently. "I will not hurt you, Henrietta."

With a strangled cry, she rushed toward him. Before he had divined her intention, she hurled herself against the door and began to batter at it with her fists. "Help!" she screamed. "Help! Somebody help me!"

Charles stared at her. That even she would go this far! It was unbelievable. Had she no sense at all of the dignity of his position and her own? An anger so intense seized him that he trembled with the force of it. "Madam, you will cease this unseemly screaming at once!"

"I won't!" Red-faced, her eyes screwed up in terror, she continued to batter at the door. "Help me! Help me!"

Charles seized her so hard that her black hair fell over her face, "But this is too much, Madam!"

She went limp beneath his hands. Charles's anger was beginning to fade, and he found himself touched by the terror in her face. "Come, Madam, be reasonable," he said. He slid his arms about her. "A kiss first, then we will talk this out in a reasonable manner."

She spat in his face. "I will die before I let you touch me!"

"Then die, Madam." Charles took a strand of her hair and wound it tightly about her throat. "It can easily be arranged!"

"Kill me then!" Without warning tears began to fall from her eyes. "I had rather you killed me."

He looked into her swimming eyes. "You are the first wench to tell me that. Usually they enjoy my embraces."

"How dare you call me a wench! I would remind you that I am Hen—"

"I know," he finished for her wearily, "you are Henrietta Maria of France. But you are also Queen of England, and my wife, so forget it not, Madam. Aye, I called you wench, but 'twas not meant insultingly.''

" 'Tis a name you would call a tavern slut.''

Charles shrugged. "True. But one may also call the Queen a wench, if she behaves like a tavern slut.''

"Then it was meant insultingly?''

"Not originally.''

"I have asked you to leave, Sire,'' Henrietta Maria snapped. "Will you now take heed?''

He unwound the strand of hair. "I have no intention of leaving, Henrietta.''

"That is your final answer?''

Smiling, he shook his head. "But no, Madam, this is my final answer.'' He hooked his fingers into the ruffled neckline of her shift. With a mighty wrench he tore the thin garment from her body. "That, may it please you, is my answer.''

She screamed, a thin wailing sound of despair. "Mother of God!'' she panted. She shook her long hair forward, trying to cover her breasts. "How could you do this to me!''

He watched her frantic efforts to shield herself from his gaze, and he smiled almost tenderly. She was beautiful, like a delicately and lovingly carved figurine. "Henrietta,'' he said, touching her arm, "why this terror, this outraged modesty? Hast forgotten that I am your husband?''

She hung her head. "You have shamed me,'' she whispered. "Think you that I can ever forget this moment? I will never forgive you!''

"You will not only forgive me, Henrietta, but you will remember this moment with amusement and pleasure. For it will be the moment when you first fell in love with your husband.''

"Love you?'' She looked up at him. "You delude yourself, Sire, if you think that. I tell you that I will never love you. Oh, I know well that I must eventually come to my duty. But if you touch me now, against my will, there will not even be liking between us. You will have to force me every time.''

"I think not." He moved closer to her and put his arms about her rigid figure. Swinging her up from the floor, he marveled at her smallness, her softness, the subtle fragrance emanating from her body. "That which you call your duty, Henrietta, you will find to be a very pleasant duty."

She made no answer. He carried her across to the bed. He was about to lower her, when she came to sudden frantic life. Writhing in his arms, sobbing, she lifted her arm and clawed at his face with her long, pointed fingernails. "Leave me alone! Go away!"

Swearing beneath his breath, he flung her down on the bed. She rolled to the far side. "Go away! Go away!"

He hesitated. Should he give in to her pleas? She was naught but a sobbing, terrified child, and he had never before forced himself upon a female, there was something particularly distasteful in the thought. She moaned, and his moment of hesitation passed. Nay, she was his wife. It was true that she was but fifteen years of age, but in the position in life in which she found herself, the child must grow quickly into the woman. Tonight he would teach her how to be a woman, a queen. "Henrietta," he said softly.

"Oh, please! I have told you to go away!"

He lay down beside her. Pulling her toward him, he tried soothing her. Holding her tightly against him, he stroked her hair with a gentle hand. "It will be all right, Henrietta, I promise you."

"Please!" she began to struggle again. "Please, Charles!"

The touch of her fired him. Raising himself up, he turned her over on her back. Straddling her, he pinioned her flailing arms on either side. His breath caught in his throat as he looked at her. Her hair was a dark shadow against her white skin; her stomach was as flat as a boy's, and her small firm breasts were tipped with pale pink. Those breasts rose and fell rapidly with her agitation as he began to caress her. It was like gentling a terrified horse. Gradually her trembling ceased, and except for an occasional nervous shudder, she lay quiet beneath his stroking hands. When his lips touched her breasts, she gave a convulsive leap, and then was quiescent. She did not seem to notice when he drew back for a moment. He untied his robe and threw it to one side. He continued to caress her, and, when he finally entered her, she made only a token struggle. Even caught in the grip of his own spiraling excitement, he was aware of her response. Small at first, then growing stronger, until she was clutching at him with hot frenzied fingers, and her voice was moaning his name, her body arching upward and urging him on and on.

Later, lying quietly at his side, his head heavy on her breast as he slept, Henrietta was aware of a sharp, sweet pleasure. She had not known it could be like this. She would never fight him again, never! He would find his wife willing, nay, eager for his caresses. She thought of my lord Foxe, and her full lips curved into a sensuous smile. If Charles could give her such ecstasy, what would it be like with him? A flush rose in her cheeks. It was wrong to have such thoughts, but she could not help it. She could love Charles, she knew that now, but if she had never glimpsed my lord Foxe, had never looked into his eyes and found herself filled with breathless excitement beneath his dark-blue gaze, it might be that she could love Charles the more wholeheartedly.

Henrietta closed her eyes and composed herself for sleep. No matter how old she might grow, she would remember this day, the 15th of June, 1625, when first she became a woman. Her contentment grew. Perhaps tomorrow, just before they entered London, my lord Foxe would be with them again. Had he not told the King that he would rejoin him with all possible speed. Snuggling close to Charles, she sighed happily. His body, that vastly exciting body, was warm and relaxed. Perhaps if she woke him, he would wish to—Even as she formed the thought, sleep claimed her.

Chapter Five

Henrietta Maria looked at the waiting barge with contempt, not caring that that contempt showed plainly in her expressive face. Tapping her small silver-shod foot with imperious impatience, she coldly acknowledged the greetings of the bowing officials. The officials had brought with them alarming reports of the plague which was at present ravaging London, and they expressed great concern for the safety of the royal couple. In her own mind, Henrietta Maria had no doubt but that the reports were grossly exaggerated and expressly designed to humiliate and insult her. She did not ask herself why the English people should wish to insult her. It was not her way to reason, but only to feel.

Henrietta Maria turned her head away and looked down into the gray waters of the Thames. It was not thus, in a barge, that she had thought to enter her husband's capital. Tears of anger filled her eyes. She knew that she was looking her best in her soft, silk-lined gown of supple light-green velvet. The wide hem of the gown and the square low-cut neckline were edged with bands of diamonds and pearls; her bodice was laced with silver ribbons, and a jeweled Medici collar provided a charming background for her lovely face. Long glossy black curls escaped from beneath a wired silver cap which had been intricately cut and shaped to frame her face with the ruffled petals of flowers. In the heart of each silver flower there nestled a single large diamond which, glittering in the sunlight, sent out rainbows of color. She had looked forward to riding through decorated streets with the ovation of the crowds ringing in her ears. But this almost furtive entry, by barge, along the River Thames to Somerset House, was something that she should not be asked to tolerate.

Her discontent was reflected in the faces of her French attendants. Except for the priests, they too were dressed in their best, and, like Henrietta Maria, it did not please them that their finery was only to be seen by the loyal crowds along the river bank. They stood in small sullen groups, ribbons and flowers and plumes fluttering in a wind that had abruptly grown chill. That they were gorgeously arrayed and colorful objects of wonder to the people on the bank, did not make up for their overwhelming disappointment. Henrietta Maria was Queen of England, why then could she not enter London as a queen? The plague! Bah! What of that? Did they not have plagues in France? The English might cower, but they were not afraid of a little infection.

Charles was aware of Henrietta Maria's disappointment, and he was annoyed by her ungracious attitude toward the anxious officials. Unlike the Queen, he was not concerned with display or with the loss of a larger celebration. His people suffered, and he was seriously concerned with their welfare. Almost two hundred were dead of the plague, and there appeared to be no relief in sight.

The sun disappeared behind a cloud; the heavens darkened, and large fat drops of rain began to fall, rapidly increasing to a soaking downpour. The people on the bank huddled closer together, their eyes on the tall, white-clad figure of their king. They responded with a rousing cheer as the King took off his white hat with its jaunty curling green plumes, and waved it at

83

them. "God save the King!" they roared. "God save the Queen!"

Henrietta Maria ignored the enthusiasm from the bank. Haughtily, she turned to the King. "I will not enter London in this way. You must request that fresh arrangements be made." She frowned as the wind blew a gust of rain into her face. "Pray do so quickly, Sire. I am becoming most uncomfortably damp."

At this arrogant speech, the embarrassed officials avoided the King's eyes. But the Duke of Buckingham, standing behind the King, smiled maliciously. The lack of harmony suited him well. The Queen's influence over the King would be considerably weakened by such conduct, and his own influence strengthened.

Charles's face had reddened. Always aware of his dignity and the respect owed to him, he felt anger grow and swell. How dare she! How dare the French chit speak so to him within the hearing of others! He had a sudden almost overpoweringly primitive urge to sweep her off her dainty feet and throw her into the water. His mind played with this satisfying picture for a moment, then, exerting control, he mastered his anger. "Madam," he said coldly, "I must request you to enter the barge."

Henrietta Maria hesitated. She was of a mind to defy him and to demand her own way. But there was a look in his eyes that was suddenly intimidating, and then, too, she was conscious of the damage being done by the rain to her elaborate gown. Her head held high, she sullenly allowed herself to be assisted aboard.

Seating herself on the long, padded seat, Henrietta Maria's eyes searched the faces of the cheering crowd. Where was my lord Foxe? Somehow she had fully expected to see him. But it was all one with this disappointing entry into London. She looked down at the gray turbulent waters of the Thames lapping against the sides of the flower-decorated barge. Doubtless, in this cold and alien land, she would have to grow used to disappointments.

Charles, followed by the Duke of Buckingham and several of the officials, stepped onto the swaying barge. Ignoring Henrietta Maria's trembling anger, Charles seated himself beside her. Rain drummed fiercely on the scarlet and gold-embroidered canopy

84

above their heads. Thunder, followed by blue-white streaks of lightning, growled in accompaniment to the guns of the Royal Navy as they made booming welcome to the new queen.

The shrieks and cries of the people on the bank, competing with the thunder and the guns, rose in volume. Charles raised his hand in response, but Henrietta Maria merely sat there, her gloved hands folded tightly in her lap, her face set.

"Please to respond, Madam," Charles commanded her, a hard note in his voice. "Your people are greeting you."

"My people!" Henrietta Maria flashed him a quick look. "I do not feel that they are my people."

"Nevertheless, Madam, they are. They are gathered here in greeting, at some considerable discomfort to themselves. They have a right to a response from their queen." He put his hand on her knee, his fingers gripping tightly. "You will respond, and at once!"

Henrietta Maria jerked her knee away. "How dare you handle me so!" she hissed at him. "Your fingers have made marks on the fabric of my gown."

Charles was not by nature a vulgar man, but the provocation was great, and he succumbed to temptation. "Behave yourself, Madam, or you will find that my hand will make considerable marks on your behind."

Charles had spoken in a whisper. But it was though he had shouted, for bright scarlet dyed her cheeks. "You will regret your impudence, Sire."

He stared at her. "My impudence! Madam, you are becoming ridiculous. Respond to your people, please."

Reluctantly, her face mutinous, she raised her hand and waved. Almost instantly she found herself consoled by their cries of admiration, and her angry resentment drained away.

The guns ceased their salute, and the raucous cry of the gulls could be heard again. One woman, teetering dangerously near to the edge of the bank, and apparently overcome with admiration, screamed out, "Jus' look at her! Ain't she pretty? Ain't she the prettiest little sweetheart you ever did see!"

Henrietta Maria leaned forward in her seat. Looking directly into the excited face of the woman, she smiled. The woman rose to fresh heights of enthusiasm. "Smiled at me, she did," she shrieked. "God bless her darlin' little face! God's blessings on Your Majesties!"

The people took up the cry. "God bless you both! Long may you reign. Long life and good health to Your Majesties!"

Buckingham, at a smile of encouragement from Charles, strolled to the side of the barge and waved a lazy hand in greeting. The cries of the people faded and an ominous silence fell. Somebody booed. A man shouted, "Down with Buckingham! Down with the bleedin' scoundrel!"

Buckingham stepped back, shrugging indifferent shoulders. But Charles frowned angrily. Watching him, Henrietta Maria could not help but wonder at his blind affection for a man who was little better than a rogue, and had, by his influence, led his King into many difficult situations, had advised him badly, and had, by so doing, lowered his popularity with the people. Henrietta Maria had heard this from her brother. And, in a rare moment of confidence, from that taciturn man Lord Kensington, Charles's unofficial ambassador, who had arrived at the Court of France to further his King's wooing of herself. Since arriving in England, she had noted the strength of Buckingham's influence, and had resented it.

With one of her bewildering change of moods, Henrietta Maria put her hand on Charles's arm and smiled at him tenderly. She saw his face change, and his instant response, the smile in his dark eyes caused her heart to flutter wildly. She found herself remembering last night. The touch of him, his lips against her breast, the sweet and tumultuous excitement of their joining; her own response, the throbbing of her pulses, and afterwards, the lovely lassitude of her body. Her fingers tightened on his arm. He seemed to know what she was thinking, for he leaned close to her and whispered in her ear, "Tonight, Henrietta Maria?"

"Tonight," she answered. "May it come quickly."

"Did I not tell you that you would enjoy your duty?"

She was all generosity now, her petulance and her anger forgotten as she relived her sensuous memory. "You were right, my lord King." Unthinkingly, she rested her head on his shoulder. And the people, seeing this loving and wifely gesture, forgot Buckingham and roared their loyalty anew.

By the time the barge reached Somerset House, Henrietta Maria's imagination had caused her body to become a throbbing urgent ache of desire. Even my lord Foxe was temporarily forgotten. Tonight! she thought. Tonight! Tonight!

Madame Saint-Georges watched Henrietta Maria. Her mistress was happy. It would seem, from the look on her face, that she had enjoyed last night's initiation into the mysteries of sexual love play. But remembering the note in Henrietta Maria's voice when she had spoken of my lord Foxe, Madame Saint-Georges felt a return of her original worry. Henrietta Maria was fanatical in all things she loved and enjoyed. Should she decide to pursue my lord Foxe, she would be fanatical in that too. Royal dignity, discretion, all these things would be forgotten. She knew this trait in her mistress's character only too well.

Entering Somerset House, Henrietta Maria's eyes found the Earl of Foxefield. Clad in dark-blue velvet, the tunic embroidered in gold, a black velvet cloak fastened to either shoulder by large gold clasps, he stood at the end of the lane of bowing men and curtseying women. As the King and Queen approached him, he swept off his wide-brimmed plume-laden hat and bowed low.

"Welcome to London, Your Majesty," the Earl said, smiling at the Queen.

Henrietta Maria paid scant attention to the curtseying girl who was standing beside the Earl. One part of her mind told her that the girl was beautiful, but then instantly dismissed her. She listened to Charles, who was greeting the Earl with unfeigned delight, but now her thoughts were in confusion, her contentment and her desire fled before the onrush of a new and stronger desire. She frowned. My lord Foxe was obviously very dangerous to her peace of mind. She wanted Charles's body, but she wanted my lord Foxe too. How could she be a good wife if the mere sight of my lord Foxe brought this surge of unseemly desire? Was she a common strumpet that she should feel this way? Nay, she was the queen. She must not allow the slightest breath of scandal to touch her. And yet, if she encouraged my lord Foxe, and if he proved to be willing, would she be able to resist?

Henrietta Maria's eyes grew thoughtful as they rested upon the Duke of Buckingham. It might be that she could satisfy her desire for the Earl of Foxefield without the affair being discovered. After all, it was only a very unlucky accident that had brought to light the Duke's love affair with Anne of Austria, her brother's wife. What if she were careful? What if she made certain there would be no accidental discovery? Might it not be that she could enjoy the embraces of my lord Foxe? It was typical of Henrietta Maria that she gave no thought to the possible reactions of the Earl of Foxefield, should she encourage him to make advances. Her only thought then, as she met the Duke of Buckingham's coldly smiling eyes, was one of shock. He looked sly and knowing. It would not surprise her to discover that the man could read her mind. She turned her head away, but she could still feel Buckingham's eyes upon her.

The line of presentation seemed endless to Henrietta Maria. She felt an overwhelming weariness as she murmured agreeably, nodded, smiled, until the smile seemed to be frozen to her lips. But finally it was over.

Seated at last, Henrietta Maria allowed herself to relax for the first time in many weary hours. Of the few people remaining in the large white and gold reception room, the girl standing beside the Earl of Foxefield arrested the Queen's attention. She was a tall, beautiful girl, with creamy skin and bronze hair. She was dressed in a gown of white satin with a draped overskirt of the palest green. Long white lace gloves with flaring cuffs of white satin covered her arms to the elbow. A small white bonnet lined with green, and tied beneath her dimpled chin with wide green satin ribbons, was perched on her vivid hair.

Smiling, Charles turned to the Queen. Taking the girl by the hand, he led her forward. "Madam, may I present the ward of Lady Sarah Foxefield, Mistress Meredith Hartford."

The difficult Mistress Hartford. Henrietta Maria felt an instant antagonism as she looked into the girl's brilliant hazel eyes. She was too beautiful, too closely linked with the Earl of Foxefield, upon whom her own desire was set. "Mistress Hartford," she murmured. "We are delighted to welcome you to our Court." Her smile, though she tried to force warmth into it, was chilly as she gave her hand to the girl to kiss.

Meredith rose from her curtsey. This then is the French-woman? she thought. This dressed up little girl with the hostile eyes and the bad-tempered curve to her soft pretty mouth. Meredith felt like laughing. Oliver Cromwell's detested and feared Frenchwoman, who was no ogre, but only a petulant child. Her inner laugh faded as she met those eyes again. But no, Henrietta Maria's eyes were not those of a child, but of a woman. A sensuous woman, she added, as she saw the Queen return the Earl's bold glance.

Meredith felt a flare of resentment and jealousy. How dare he look at the Queen so? What was wrong with him? Did he not know that the King's eyes had missed nothing? Her hands clenched at her sides. She had a great desire to kick my lord Foxe in the shins, and an even greater desire to smack the smile from the Queen's lips.

"Mistress Hartford," the King's voice said, "I pray you to be seated. You must be very tired."

Meredith took the chair he was indicating. "I thank you for your thought, Sire," she said. Her eyes returned to the Queen. "My legs are tired, but other than that I have never been more wide awake."

"I see." Charles gave a soft laugh. "Aye, Mistress Hartford, I do see, and I quite understand."

Chapter Six

Brett looked at the King curiously. The King's eyes had a far away expression. It was as though he had forgotten that he was on his way to attend his first Parliament. The Duke of Buckingham, seated on Charles's left in the barge, wondered if the King's stormy marriage with Henrietta Maria had blinded him to the solemn business ahead of him. Avoiding the eyes of my lord Foxe, for whom his hatred and jealousy daily grew more acute, the Duke stared straight ahead of him.

The King was aware of neither of his friends. His thoughts strayed from one subject to another. To Henrietta Maria, his troublesome wife, now installed with her French retinue at Hampton Court. The disturbed atmosphere, which he believed to be caused by the misleading advice of certain of the French men and women, and, in some cases, by the priests who hovered constantly about her. Charles's mouth tightened. There would never be peace, he was sure, until he had rid the Court of the French. He distrusted their influence over the Queen, and he was certain that they were the cause of many of the quarrels between them. As was her too obvious infatuation for my lord Foxe.

The King glanced quickly at Brett, but there was no censure in his eyes. The Earl, though respectful to the Queen, was indifferent to her as a woman, if one could call her such. Nay, Brett was far more interested in Mistress Hartford, with whom he constantly quarreled. He would deny that such an interest existed, of course, but it was there.

From Henrietta Maria, the King's thoughts drifted to the time when Henry, his dead brother, had been Prince of Wales, and heir to the throne. There was no triumph in Charles. He had loved Henry dearly. He had been very young at the time, but he could remember with great clarity Henry's investiture as Prince of Wales. He could hear the solemn chanting, see the look on the face of the Archbishop of Canterbury, a look that was at once loving and anxious, for everybody had loved Henry. The Knights of the Bath had escorted Henry to his place. He saw again the shimmer of their purple satin robes and hoods, and the stark contrast of the white silk lining framing their grave faces. Henry had worn a cloak of deep-blue velvet over a blue robe; the robe had been slashed and edged with gold brocade. How proud his father had been at that moment. Charles could remember the smile on his face as he had replaced Henry's blue cloak with the purple mantle of state. His hands had trembled with the excess of his emotion as he placed upon Henry's head the cap and coronet. And when he had girded the sword about Henry's lean young waist and had invested him with the rod and the ring, there had been actual tears glistening on his ruddy cheeks. Aye, he had been very proud of Henry, and he had loved him so dearly. Had his father been disappointed and resentful when, in the year of 1616, he had had to perform a similar ceremony for his younger son? Had he been haunted and ravaged by thoughts of the dead Henry as he had placed the cap and coronet on the dark head that was so unlike Henry's sun-bleached bright blond head?

Charles came to himself with a start. He was too prone to live in the past. It was the present that counted, the solemn present that now seemed to weigh unbearably on his shoulders. He was the king, though he had not yet been crowned. His people were still sickening and dying of the plague. There were unpaid debts left by his father, and the pressure of the growing war with Spain. War with Spain? Why must his reign be burdened with some-thing that was not of his making? But nevertheless, since there was a war, he was in honor bound to carry it through in his father's name. But from where was the money to come? Would the Commons, already disapproving of the staggering debts under which the Crown labored, be amenable to granting further money to prosecute the war? Charles's chin lifted arrogantly. They must grant the money, he would demand it. It was not for them to dictate to their King. The next moment he felt inclined to laugh. Why create imaginary obstacles? Why make ogres of the gentlemen of the Commons? It might well be that they would see things his way.

The King's sober mood passed. He was light-hearted, full of hope, and feeling friendly to all as he walked into Westminster. Taking his place, with the Earl of Foxefield seated to his right, the Duke of Buckingham, the Duc de Chevreuse, and several of the Duc's compatriots seated to his left, the King scanned the faces of those present in the House of Commons. He looked at thin-faced John Hampden, who was smiling nervously, his fingers playing with a piece of parchment on the desk before him.

John Hampden, noticing the King's eyes upon him, looked quickly away. Almost immediately he forgot the King and the business at hand. He was thinking of that strange, moody man, his cousin, Oliver Cromwell. Oliver, though often vociferously disapproving of the King, and his wealthy and powerful friend, the Duke of Buckingham, would have enjoyed being present at this, the first Parliament of King Charles's reign. He had heard that Oliver was being considered as a candidate for Westminster. He hoped that it might come to pass. Oliver, with his sobriety, his single-mindedness, his dedication to any cause he embraced, would be a considerable addition to the gathering. John drew his fingernail across the parchment. Did he like Oliver? He was not sure, he had never been sure. There was something about the man, something that was almost frightening.

From John Hampden, Charles's eyes went to Sir Edward Coke, who, he had heard and had seen for himself, was a great lawyer, though a smooth rascal, and a man who was reputed to make a merciless enemy. Seated near to Sir Edward were Sir Thomas Wentworth and Edward Hyde. Charles's eyes went from one face to another. Their expressions, he noted, except for the nervous John Hampden, were all similar—polite but carefully blank.

A stir in the House indicated that it was time for the session to begin. The King had worn his crown to this momentous opening. He now removed it, veiling it with a thin silk scarf in deference to his uncrowned state. The gesture caused the gentlemen to stare, but faces brightened at the King's unexpected courtesy.

Charles rose to his feet. "Gentlemen," he said, "may the doors be closed." He smiled. "Bishop Laud is waiting to officiate. I know that you would wish to unite with me in prayer before opening this session."

There was a stunned silence. It was not so that Parliament had been wont to open. Sir Edward Coke smiled sardonically. Then, at a wave of the hand from the Speaker of the House, there was an immediate bustle. Velvet-clad attendants, the purple plumes on their flat white caps fluttering with the speed at which they sprang to obey the command, slammed the great doors shut. And once again silence fell as Bishop Laud came forward to begin the prayer.

Listening to Laud's rich sonorous voice rising and falling, Charles was filled with a new hope for the future. He clasped his fingers tightly together. He would be a good King, he vowed silently. He would be as a devoted father to his people. He would enrich the lives of the poor with culture that had hitherto been denied them. He would relieve their burden of poverty, and he would see that education was available to all. "This do I vow," he muttered beneath his breath. "So help me God."

The Earl of Foxefield listened to the King's speech, which,

coming so soon after the prayers, seemed to have taken on an added and touching simplicity. Charles spoke of the war with Spain. "A war which I deplore, gentlemen. But since it must be, I have a great need of money with which to vanquish our enemies and bring this war to a successful and honorable conclusion."

Faces stared back at him, some wooden, some inimical, and others as though startled by his request. Charles waited for a moment, then he went on, "I trust that you do remember, gentlemen, that you requested me to advise my father to break off the treaties with Spain. It may be that I was rash to do so. I now tell you that I come into this sorry business unwillingly, but freely. Yet I do beg you to remember that my intervention with my father proved to be very much to your own interests. Since it was all begun on your advice, would it not dishonor both you and me if the war should fail for lack of that assistance which you are well able to give me?"

Brett Foxefield moved uneasily. It was evident to him that the King had not reached them. Hating, malicious eyes were turned on the Duke of Buckingham, who was lounging nonchalantly in his chair. Brett could see a fine dew of perspiration on the King's forehead, and Charles's ringed hands, which rested on the rail before him, trembled. He felt their hostility, for they had never made a secret of their undying animosity toward the Duke. Brett knew that Charles was fiercely loyal to his friends, and the more the Duke was reviled, the more tenaciously would he cleave to him. Both Lords and Commons, so Brett understood, blamed the Duke's counsels for much of the evils afflicting the kingdom.

Robert Spaulding stood up. He bowed his gray head in a token gesture of respect. Fixing the King with his small, glittering brown eyes, he said in an unctuous voice, "Your pardon, Sire, but may I ask if you now intend to put into force the existing laws against the Roman recusants, and those who would be inclined to follow after them in this evil?"

Charles's face flushed. Spaulding's words seemed to him to be a direct attack against his Roman Catholic wife. It was no secret that he was honor-bound by the treaty he had signed, in which he had promised to treat those of his wife's faith with at least a measure of indulgence. But he could not help a feeling of dull anger when he remembered the French noblemen and noblewomen, the overabundance of priests now infesting the palace. But he'd be rid of them, he resolved, and at the earliest opportunity. He answered Spaulding with admirable calm. "That is a matter we may take up on another occasion. At the present moment there are far more urgent matters to engage our attention."

Spaulding, whose hatred of Catholicism was virulent, was somewhat taken aback. "As Your Majesty wishes." He sat down. Folding his hands before him, he fixed the King with malicious eyes.

Brett was not interested in politics, and he listened sleepily. His presence at this session was at the request of the King. Voices flowed on. He heard the works of Doctor Richard Montague on the study of the existence and the laws of God condemned. A fierce argument broke out in which the King took little part. Montague, it seemed, had appealed to the late King James for protection against his enemies, and James's answer was to make the man his chaplain. This action was voted then and now to be a contempt of the House.

Brett made no attempt to understand the various accusations. It was becoming increasingly hot and he had some difficulty in keeping his eyes open. It was only when the House began to deliver a stinging rebuke on the sorry state of the King's finances that he took notice. A further insult to the King was added when they agreed that they would only supply the King with the amount of one hundred and forty thousand pounds "for supply."

"Th—that is ridiculous, g—gentlemen." Charles's stutter showed the depths of his angry bewilderment. "You must know well that s—such an amount would be of little m—moment."

"We regret, Majesty," John Pym said, standing up, "but it is all that we can in good conscience allow.'' He looked down at the paper in his hand. ''Furthermore, on the question of tonnage and poundage, we further regret that it must be limited to Your Majesty for the period of one year only.''

Charles stared at him. ''Is it your intention to insult me, gentlemen?'' he said at last. ''You know that the subsidies from tonnage and poundage have always been a lifetime grant to each sovereign.''

The House was in an uproar. Charles's quiet voice reproached them for their boorishness, their lack of trust in himself, who was as yet untried. He reminded them of the war, of public needs. He spoke of the vow he had made to relieve the burden of the poor, and to provide adequate education. It was all to no avail. Either the House could not see, or refused to see, the necessity of further subsidies. They were not impressed with the King's obvious sincerity, his willingness to submit any or all documents for the inspection of the House. They were, it seemed, singularly unimpressed with their new, young King.

Traveling back to Whitehall Palace, the King was very quiet. The Duke of Buckingham, with rare tact, was silent. Brett, meeting the King's eyes, contented himself with a reassuring smile.

Charles had need of reassurance in the days that followed. The House remained obstinate and unwilling to see the King's point of view. The death toll of plague victims mounted so rapidly that the King, in sympathy for those forced to stay in London, suggested that Parliament should adjourn until August 1st, when they would meet again, in Oxford.

On the way to Hampton Court, Charles put his worries aside. There was a look in his eyes that touched Brett. It was the look of an eager bridegroom. Henrietta Maria, Brett thought, was not worthy of such a look. She was a bad-tempered shrew. She was arrogant, headstrong, fanatical in her religious beliefs. She was equally fanatical in her attempts, within the scope of her limited power, to bring back the heretics to what she called the ''True Faith.'' She treated the King with light insolence, sometimes not troubling to lower her voice as she berated him in the presence of others. Why did Charles, who was very proud, very conscious of his dignity, stand for such treatment? Because, Brett guessed, Charles was caught fast in that enchantment Henrietta could exude even at her worst. One could boil with resentment and anger, but she had only to lift those slumberous eyes, to smile that smile that hinted at so much, and a stronger man than Charles might well be lost. Sometimes Brett wondered if she herself realized the extent of her sexual powers?

Almost as though Charles had guessed at his thoughts, he looked at Brett and smiled. "Being, I trust, a gentlemen," Charles said lightly, "I will name no names, my lord Foxe. Yet, because I know you have been worried on my behalf, I will tell you that, upon my honor, there is a certain lady whom I shortly intend to master."

Startled that he should speak on such a personal matter, Brett returned the smile. "The lady is undoubtedly a shrew, Sire," he answered casually. "May I advise severe and repeated thrashings?"

"Good advice, my lord. You do not, of course, refer to the Queen, I trust?"

"Nay. I refer only to a certain lady, as did Your Majesty."

Charles laughed. "So, in your opinion, the lady is a shrew?"

"She is, Sire. And again I advise the thrashings."

"You are a rogue, my lord. But it may be that I will follow your advice. But what if this certain lady should be in love with another?"

"The lady in question, Sire, is very young and impressionable. If she imagines herself to be in love with a gentleman other than yourself, I assure you it is all in her imagination."

"Why so, my lord?"

"I have seen the look in the lady's eyes. She loves you, though I believe that she does not yet know it." Brett gave Charles a swift sidelong look. "As for that other gentleman, he is honored by her interest and fully conscious of her beauty, but unfortunately he is quite uninterested."

Charles said slowly, "And is this gentleman studying to be a monk, or could he perhaps be in love with another?"

"Neither, Sire. He is uninterested in the lady because he happens to love and revere his King."

Charles's hand covered his briefly. "The King is fortunate, and greatly honored to know this."

As they approached Hampton Court, Brett wondered if Charles would indeed adopt a sterner attitude toward the lovely but hideously spoiled Henrietta Maria.

Henrietta Maria, seated with a group of her ladies, lifted her head sharply as she heard the cry from the corridor. "The King comes this way! Make way, make way, the King comes!"

Henrietta Maria noticed how Mistress Hartford's eyes flew to the door. If the King came, so did my lord Foxe. She had realized from the first that the girl was in love with the Earl of Foxefield. She smiled to herself. She did not like Mistress Hartford, and she was determined to frustrate her. Henrietta Maria moved uneasily in her chair. Was her own feeling for my lord Foxe merely a lust of the flesh? What was this strange new feeling she had for her husband? Why did she cry into her pillow at nights, when he was especially angry with her? Could it be that she had fallen in love with him? She was suddenly angry. She did not like this new emotion. It made her unsure of herself. Just as she had determined to frustrate Mistress Hartford, so she now determined to frustrate her own emotion. The feeling was too tender, too new. She did not trust it or herself. Was she in love with Charles? Oh, surely not! Had she not driven and bedeviled him, almost alienated him?

As Henrietta Maria rose to her feet her ladies rose with her, all save Mistress Hartford, whose eyes were still fixed on the door. The Queen's lip curled and she made a remark in French to her ladies. They tittered and glanced with sly eyes at the unheeding Meredith.

"Mistress Hartford," the Queen addressed Meredith sharply. "We do not require your presence. You may leave us."

Meredith rose. "Leave, Madam? I do not understand."

"Do not argue with us, Mistress Hartford."

Meredith had a sudden desire to strike the Queen's lovely, haughty face. Today, Meredith thought unwillingly, the Queen was looking particularly lovely. Her big dark eyes were bright, her thick black hair was piled on top of her small head and held in place by a jeweled band. The color in her cheeks matched the rosy color of her daringly low-cut gauzy gown. The jeweled butterflies decorating the wide skirts glittered brightly with her every movement. Meredith, in her own simply cut green gown trimmed at the neckline and the cuffs with a discreet edging of small pearls, felt dowdy and plain in comparison with the radiant Queen.

Meredith's opinion, however, was not shared by Henrietta Maria. She considered that the blaze of the girl's hair against the green of the gown, her soft white skin, and the golden glow of her eyes, made her look far too beautiful. "Mistress Hartford," she snapped, "unless you have an affliction in your hearing, pray have the courtesy to answer us!"

"Your pardon, Madam. I heard. You require me to leave your presence." Her eyes lowered to hide her anger, she curtsied, then quietly left the room.

The Queen turned to her ladies. "I am going to walk about the grounds for a while. You may tell His Majesty, should he inquire for me, that I wish to be alone."

Madame Saint-Georges's eyes took on that faint look of worry ever present in them these days. What was the foolish, headstrong child plotting now? She thought she knew. Suspicion grew into certainty as she approached the Queen. "Madam," she said in a low voice, "I beg you to be discreet. Allow me to accompany you."

"You will stay with the other ladies, Saint-Georges."

Feeling driven, Madame Saint-Georges put a pleading hand on the Queen's arm. "Madame, please! What you contemplate is folly."

"How dare you! You do not know what I contemplate."

"I know you, Madam."

"Be silent!" The Queen thrust her hand away impatiently. "Do as you are told, Saint-Georges."

"But, dear Madam. The King knows that you detest walking. He knows too that you hate to be alone."

"You will tell him what I have said."

"Nay, Madam, not I. Forgive me, but I would prefer that you dismiss me."

"But you are not dismissed!" Shaking with rage, Henrietta Maria lifted her hand and struck the woman sharply in the face. "You will never question my actions again. You will do as you are told!"

Henrietta Maria whirled about and stared into the shocked faces of the other ladies. "Well? Do you all understand?"

With the marks of the Queen's fingers flaring red against her pale cheek, Madame Saint-Georges turned away. She felt no anger, but she felt a great sorrow for her beloved charge, who was and had always been her own worst enemy. The silly child was in love with her husband, any fool could see that. So why would she not admit it to herself? Why must she continue her pursuit of my lord Foxe? It was a pity that she did not stop to search her heart before plunging into new folly.

Giving the ladies a hard, warning look Henrietta Maria made for the door. Outside, she took a deep breath, then she began to run swiftly along the marbled corridor. Startled glances were turned her way, but she did not notice them. Temporarily she had forgotten the dignity she owed to her position. Her object was to meet with my lord Foxe before she was forced into the ceremony of greeting the King. Surely my lord must desire her, she thought, as she desired him? She was beautiful, and it was not everybody who could boast of bedding the Queen of England. But my lord should have that honor. Thinking of that certain look in his eyes whenever she was near, she dismissed lingering doubt.

Outside the white and gilt-trimmed door that led into the Earl of Foxefield's apartments, Henrietta Maria hesitated. A thought of Charles came to her, and she was conscious of pain. Charles!

When he held her in his arms it was as if only they two existed. She did not think of my lord Foxe then, but only of him, her Charles! Henrietta Maria clenched her hands tightly together. The love she refused to acknowledge was striving to push its way to the surface of her mind. She frowned in fierce resistance. In all her short life, she had thought only of herself. It disturbed her acutely that she must now think of another. I do not love Charles, I do not! I desire my lord Foxe, so how can I love Charles? She heard that inner voice again telling her that it was Charles she loved, Charles alone whom she desired. No! Frightened and defiant, she silenced the voice.

Henrietta Maria looked about her. It was as though this moment had been specially prepared for her. The short corridor before the Earl's apartments which was usually crowded with strolling figures, was empty. Doubtless they were all preparing to greet the King. If one of her own countrymen should see her, it would not matter. A Frenchman would never think of betraying her. Not unless, that is, a betrayal would prove advantageous to a soaring ambition. Even so, many Frenchmen had been known to regard a love affair as being fully as important as ambition. They were more romantic, more civilized and understanding of the hungers of the body than ever an Englishman could be.

Smiling, Henrietta Maria entered the apartment. As she had anticipated, the Earl of Foxefield and his personal attendant, Bruce Seton, had not yet arrived. She looked about her. The furnishing were all in shades of delphinium blue and silver. The heavy drapes drawn across the two long windows were of blue velvet lined with silver tissue. Over the rooms there hovered that subtle fragrance she had come to associate with the Earl's immaculate person. No doubt, she thought, it was something he used after shaving.

She walked slowly into the bedchamber. Her eyes dwelt on the huge bed with its blue velvet hangings. A shiver of anticipation went through her as she thought of lying in that bed, locked in the Earl's arms.

Her heartbeat quickened. He and his attendant would be arriving shortly. The Queen frowned. She did not like Seton, he had sly eyes. It might be that the man, for a suitable reward, would be only too ready to betray her. But she felt sure that she could rely on my lord Foxe to silence the man and to protect her from scandal.

She looked at the tall, blue-painted cupboard with its elaborate silver scrolling. The cupboard stood between the two large windows. The door was standing half open, and this gave her an idea. She would hide herself in the cupboard. Entering, she had some difficulty in concealing herself behind the garments that crowded the space, but she managed it.

Now that she was safely hidden from view, Henrietta Maria found herself beset by doubt. Beginning to regret her impulsive behavior, the thought came to her that she must be quite insane. Her behavior was such as would be condemned in the meanest scullery maid. The thought of confessing this episode to her priest brought a vivid flush to her cheeks, but, eager to placate the stern voice of her conscience, she thought, I will confess, no matter what it costs me in shame.

Why had she come here? It was so hot in this cupboard, and she was beginning to feel very foolish. Her gauzy bodice felt as though it were plastered against her breasts, and there was a prickling of perspiration along her hairline. Then, despite the heat, she began to shiver. What if Seton should arrive before his master? What if, in the absence of the Earl, he should be accompanied by another servant? Oh, God, how would it look if she should be discovered cowering in the cupboard like a common slut! Tears crowded her eyes, and she felt like sobbing aloud. Saint-Georges should have braved her anger, she should have prevented her. Why else had she accompanied her to England, if not to protect her from folly? Charles, dear Charles! He would be anxious to see her. He might even now be searching for her. In the stuffy darkness of the cupboard, she at last admitted the truth to herself. She loved Charles! She thought of the tender look in his dark eyes, his shy smile, his slight stammer when he was moved or angry, and she was consumed with an aching tenderness. "Oh, Charles, my darling," she whispered, "how foolish I have been. I have mistaken desire for love. But it is you I love, only you!"

She must leave these apartments at once. She pushed the cupboard door wide. If God be with her, no one need ever know.

God was not with her. She could hear footsteps in the outer room and the sound of voices. What was she to do?

"Seton," the Earl of Foxefield's deep voice said, "why the devil did you allow my shirts to become so badly crumpled? Do something about it, please."

"Aye, my lord, at once."

Footsteps were coming toward the bedchamber. Whose footsteps?

Unthinkingly, she stepped back to press herself more firmly against the wall of the cupboard. Her clumsy and hurried movement set the cupboard swaying, bringing several pairs of shoes falling from the shelf above her head.

"Who is there?" came the Earl's sharp voice.

Henrietta Maria cringed. She closed her eyes tightly as the door was jerked open.

"My God!" the Earl exclaimed. "What in plague are you doing here, Madam?"

She wished that she might die of the shame consuming her. Opening her eyes, she looked into his astounded face. "Please, my lord!" she whispered. "Do me the courtesy of lowering your voice."

Fury blazed from his eyes. He muttered something beneath his breath. Then, with an abrupt movement, he closed the door in her face.

She could hear his voice telling Seton that he would not require his services for an hour.

Seton was saying in a puzzled voice, "But, my lord, your garments are in need of care. I have much work to do."

"Forget the work. You have my permission to go. Doubtless you will wish to refresh yourself after our journey."

"Very well, my lord." Seton did not understand this about-face, and his voice sounded stiff with offense.

Henrietta Maria heard the Earl's easy laugh. "Oh, lord," he said, "do not poker up, lad. If you must have explanation, I want you out of the way because I have just remembered that I will shortly be receiving a visit from a lady."

"What alrcady, my lord?" The offense had left Seton's voice. He gave a throaty chuckle. "The ladies do not waste any time when you are around, do they, my lord?"

"Watch your tongue, Seton," the Earl answered good-naturedly. "If you wish to avoid a clout round the head for your insolence, you will go at once."

Another throaty chuckle. "I'm going, my lord."

When the door had closed behind the man, Brett walked back to the cupboard and opened the door. Silently he extended his hand. "Now, Madam," he said, when she was standing before him, "have the goodness to explain your presence."

He was looking at her with open contempt, and a welcome stir of anger mingled with her fear. "You speak to the Queen," she reminded him in a sharp voice.

His lips were a tight grim line as he regarded her. "So I do," he said at last. "You do well to remind me. I had not thought to find the Queen hiding in a cupboard in my bedchamber. I will ask you once more, Madam. What are you doing here?"

She looked at him wide-eyed. Even in his creased and travel-stained red velvet jacket and breeches, faint lines of fatigue beneath his eyes, his dark hair disordered, he was very hand-some. She loved Charles, but was it not possible to indulge in a small affair with this exciting man? No one need ever know. She would die before she brought hurt to Charles, but if he did not know, what harm would it do? She said slowly, "Is it necessary to explain, my lord? You must know why I am here."

"Very necessary, Madam. I have not the slightest idea why you are here."

He was lying, of course he was lying. She could see the desire in his eyes. He knew. He wanted her, he could not hide it. She said in a low, halting voice, "I am here because I want you, my lord." The bald words sounded stark and terrible. Heat flushed her face, and she could scarcely bear to look at him.

His heart began such a rapid beating that he felt slightly sick. A pulse began throbbing in his temple. So she wanted him, did she? Well, he wanted her, by Christ he did! It would be so easy to take her here and now. He would be quite undisturbed, Seton would see to that. Charles would not seek him out. Why should he? They had parted but a short while ago. Charles need never know. He took a quick step toward her, another, and then he halted. Charles might not know, but *he* would, damn it! He could not have such a thing on his conscience. Impossible to betray the trust that he knew Charles had in him. He wanted this royal slut, he would not attempt to deny it. Wanted her so badly that his body ached. He thought of the long years of loyalty and friendship between himself and Charles, and he winced. Was that friendship to be broken by this tempting child-woman? For if he took her, he would have to go away. He could never face Charles again. Her fascination was such for him that fine beads of perspiration broke out on his forehead. He lifted his hand to wipe them away, and quite suddenly the struggle was over. How could he have thought for one moment of bedding the Queen? Charles was his King as well as his friend. He loved him like a brother. With an effort he forced a smile. "I fear you must brand me ungallant, Madam," he drawled, shrugging his broad shoulders, "but I do not want you. You are my Queen, though you make that fact damnably difficult to remember. As my Queen, it is my duty to honor and revere you. As a woman, you do not interest me in the slightest."

Henrietta Maria almost choked on her angry disbelief. "You lie! I know that you want me. Do you think I have been blind to the way you look at me?"

He was in a fever to be rid of her. "Don't be foolish," he said in a curt voice. "I look at every pretty woman in that way."

In that moment she even forgot the sweet new discovery of her love for Charles. She thrust discretion aside and allowed the hot tide of her outraged pride and anger to carry her out of her depth.

She would teach the handsome, insolent cur! She would show him the folly of treating Henrietta Maria with contempt. "Can you tell me in all truth that you do not desire me, my lord Foxe?"

"In all truth, Madam, I do not. You are charming and delightful to look upon, but I do not want you." He turned away from her and moved over to the door. "I will make sure that it is safe for you to leave."

Her breasts rose and fell with her rapid, angry breathing. He would reject her, would he? He would turn the Queen from his door as though she were a woman of small account. "Do not trouble yourself, my lord," she said loudly. "I have no intention of leaving."

Brett turned and came back to her. Looking at her, he felt that mad temptation again. He crushed it down. "Then would you care for a glass of wine first, Madam," he said, his eyes mocking, "or would you prefer me to tear the gown from your body on this instant? Shall I throw you down on the bed and mount you as I would a riverside doxie? Will such an action ease the burning in your body, Madam Slut?"

Madam Slut! He dared! Tears of rage and humiliation filled her eyes. "Curse you, you insolent swine!" she screamed. She raised her hands, her fingernails ready to claw at his face. "I will kill you for that!"

"Be silent!" He caught her hands in his and held them tightly. "You are a slut, or so you would have me believe. But for the sake of the King, I would protect you from the consequences of your foolish actions."

"Let me go!"

His grip tightened. "Gladly, Madam, if you will stop struggling. Come now," his voice roughened, "do not goad me too far!"

The hard, determined glitter of his eyes frightened her. There was no trace in them now of desire. Unwillingly, she stopped struggling. "Do you have the insolence to threaten me, my lord?"

"Aye," he answered. "If you do not leave at once, I will slap your pretty backside hard. Do I make myself understood?"

She could not believe it. No one, not even her brother, had ever spoken to her in such a fashion. "You would not dare!" she panted. "I—I am the Q—Queen!"

He smiled grimly. "Do not remind me of that lamentable fact."

Fresh tears crowded her eyes and fell down her cheeks. "You are cruel, my lord."

His heart softened, but he kept his voice hard. "Cruelty comes easily to me, Madam. Ask Mistress Hartford. She will tell you that it is all too true."

"Do not speak to me of that creature," she snapped. "She is naught but a great clumsy fool! She is in love with you. Did you know that?"

Meredith Hartford! In love with him? Ridiculous! "Nay," he said. "And we are not discussing Mistress Hartford or her emotions, Madam."

"You spoke of her first. If I wish to discuss her, my lord, then I will."

The child in her was showing. Brett's patience snapped. "You will leave this room at once. I hope to God that it will be a long time before I set eyes on your face again!"

She was past anger now. But she wanted to win from him that admiration to which she was accustomed. She wound her arms about his neck and laid her wet face against his chest. "My lord," she said in a small voice, "do not be angry with me. You know well that you will be forced to see me. If—if I can have nothing else, may I not have your friendship?"

He was full of suspicion. Yet her slim young arms clung to him in appeal, and there was a quiver in her voice that touched him. He was a fool, he told himself, as he felt his hard-sustained anger draining away. She was naught but a spoiled and willful child. She had behaved like a trollop, it was true, but he did not believe it was truly her nature to be so. With the years, he felt sure, she would gain in dignity and restraint. One tended to forget it, but she was only fifteen years old. He must not forget that this sobbing little girl who clung to him now was the Queen of England. For a moment he wondered how she would have responded had he given in to her desire? He put the thought quickly from him. She was not entirely to blame, he knew how it was in the forcing-house of royalty. Had he not seen Charles struggling in vain to retain his childhood? If you were royal, you must grow up quickly. Henrietta Maria would come to realize that very soon. Perhaps she was entitled, as any other girl of her tender years, to her brief and fragile infatuations. But Charles must not know of this visit. He must not be hurt. Incredible, the strength of his love for this pretty little fool who was his wife.

"Henrietta Maria," Brett stroked her hair gently. "This will not do, you know. You do not really want me."

"Perhaps I do not, my lord," she said in the same small voice. "But I—but I thought I did."

"I am glad you have realized it for yourself."

"I do realize it now. But will you make me a promise, my lord?"

"What is it?"

"Promise me that you will never fall in love with Mistress Hartford?"

He sighed. There spoke the jealous and possessive child. If I cannot have you, then neither can Mistress Hartford. "If I can avoid it, Madam, I have no intention of falling in love with any woman."

"With another woman, perhaps," she answered. "I would not mind that. But not with Mistress Hartford. I do not like her."

"Why?"

"She thinks of me as a little girl. She does! I can see it in her eyes."

"That is easily remedied, Madam. Do not behave like a little girl."

Henrietta Maria was no longer listening. My lord Foxe was exciting and fascinating, but she was forced to admit to herself that she wanted to be with Charles. Her Charles! How she loved him! She was filled with wonder and pleasure. She had given her mother a dutiful affection, and in a mild way she had loved her brother. Other small loves she had had. But all that had gone before was a poor pale thing when compared with this feeling she had for her husband. She loosened her arms and looked up into Brett's face. "My lord," she said in a humble voice, "please forgive me for my actions and for my words."

Brett smiled at her. "I forgive you freely, Madam. Might I suggest that you give your desire as well as your love to your husband?"

She began to laugh, and it was a joyous sound. "I am a fool, my lord, I am everything you called me. For only today did I find out that I am very much in love with my husband."

He stared at her startled, but something in her face told him that she was telling the truth. "Why, then, did you come to me, Madam?"

She shook her head helplessly. "I suspected that I loved him. But it was only when I was hidden in your cupboard that I finally admitted it to myself."

His bewilderment grew. "Then why did you say such things to me?"

"I thought I desired you, even though I loved the King. I—I was playing a part, I suppose. I d—did not want to be in love. It frightened me. Perhaps, when I said that I desired you, I was still trying to fight it."

"Don't you know?"

She shook her head again. "I know only one thing. I love Charles."

"You are sure of that, Madam?"

"Oh, yes!" Her smile was radiant. "Yes, my lord Foxe, I am very, very sure!"

"Then all is well."

"All is well. Never again, my lord, will I forget my dignity or the King's, I promise you." She put a coaxing hand to his cheek. "We will be friends, my lord Foxe?"

"Friends," he assured her.

"Then will you give me a kiss in token of our new understanding and friendship?"

In this mood she was irresistible. Nevertheless, he was uneasy. "A kiss, Madam? Do you think it necessary?"

She saw the alarm in his eyes, and she laughed aloud. "Nay, my lord, you need not fear. 'Twill be only a kiss upon the cheek."

"I see. In that case, Madam, it will pleasure me." Even as he bent his head and kissed her cheek, he was surprised to find that his desire for her was gone as if it had never been.

Henrietta Maria clung to him for a moment. "I love you too, my lord Foxe, in a way. But I could never love you as I love my Charles."

Holding her lightly, Brett knew that she spoke truth. She did indeed love Charles. For these few moments he found her very sweet, but he did not believe that she would change too drastically. Her love for Charles would not cure her vanity, her ill-temper, or the highly dramatic scenes she so often threw. She was a highly emotional and dramatic person. Aye, there would always be the scenes. But if there was love between them, mayhap Charles would learn to tolerate her faults as well as her virtues. He smiled to himself. She did undoubtedly have virtues. It was a pity she so constantly hid them beneath her displays of temper and hysteria.

Henrietta Maria raised herself on her toes. "One more kiss, my lord, as a further token, and then I will go." Smiling, she pressed her soft lips on his cheek.

Neither of them had heard the opening of the outer door, or the footsteps, muffled by the thick blue carpeting.

The King stood at the open door of the bedchamber, with Mistress Hartford beside him, staring at the spectacle of the Queen kissing the Earl of Foxefield. The Queen was whispering something to the Earl, but he could not make out the words. Charles felt physically sick with the force of the pain that attacked him now. His Henrietta Maria! In the past he had had many light affairs with women, but never before had he been in love. But Henrietta Maria, with her pettishness, her often vile temper, her arrogance, and her unbridled tongue, had, despite all this, managed to find her way into his heart.

"Remember, my lord Foxe," Charles heard Henrietta Maria say, "please remember that I love you."

"I will remember, Madam," Brett said gently.

Charles felt a rush of bitterness. The traitor, the false friend! Why did he call her Madam, when it was so obvious that they were familiar together? Charles's bitterness increased as he realized that he was unalterably in love with Henrietta Maria. No matter what she had done or might do, he would always love her. Ironic indeed to know that he was in love with the wife he had taken in unwilling exchange for the Infanta of Spain. He had returned to Henrietta Maria so eagerly, fool that he was! He had anticipated not only the delights of her supple young body, but this time he had hoped to woo her, to win her love. Even more than this, he had hoped to bring her to a complete understanding not only of himself, but of her adopted country. He had wanted to inspire in her a love of the people such as he had himself. He knew that he was often moody, often given over to melancholia, but, with her love to sustain him, he had felt that he could become a different and more vital person.

Meredith shivered and wondered why the King did not speak. Why did he stand there so motionless? She looked at him quickly, and was appalled by the naked pain she saw in his face. If only he would say something. Anything! Damn Brett, the lecherous fool!

Charles had forgotten Meredith. He was aware of nothing except his own pain. He drew a deep silent breath. If only he could roll time back. If only he had never set eyes on Henrietta Maria. He had obviously been deluding himself. She had nothing to give to him or to his country. His hand clenched tightly on his silver-headed cane. He had meant to laugh with her about the cane, his latest affection. Now there was no laughter left in him. Nothing but the wish to kill them both. To drive them from his life and never have to look upon their faces again. The hand clenched on the cane felt damp. He must not give in to his feelings. He must not behave like a savage. He would control himself. If these two, one whom he loved, the other who he had trusted, were lost to all dignity, he was not. He was the King. More was expected of him than of an ordinary man. In a moment he would speak, but he needed that moment to gain control. He prayed that they would not become aware of his presence before he had managed this difficult feat. Startled, he became conscious that his eyes were wet. He lifted his hand slowly and brushed the betraying dampness away. If Henrietta Maria saw his emotion, she would believe him to be a weak fool. And what would my lord Foxefield, his erstwhile friend, think?

Meredith saw the gesture. Tears came into her own eyes. She swallowed against the constriction in her throat as fear for the Earl of Foxefield fought with her rage and her jealousy.

The iron control Charles had early been taught to employ came to his aid now. The pain left his face and his expression went blank. "S—So here you are, Madam," he said quietly, painfully aware that he could not control his slight stammer. "I m—must confess to a certain surprise at f—finding you here. I had thought you to be s—strolling in the grounds."

Henrietta Maria was rigid with horror. Merciful God, that Charles should find her in such a compromising position! He would never understand. Her mind reeled as she sought for some explanation that might excuse her conduct. Or, at least, how her conduct must appear to him.

"My lord King!" She wrenched herself free from Brett's light hold. She looked at the King, her face scarlet, her eyelashes fluttering nervously. It was an effort, but she managed to force her shaking limbs into a curtsey. "I am greatly rejoiced to see you, Sire," she said in a high, breathless voice.

Charles, looking at her with unconcealed contempt, inclined his head stiffly. In the silence that followed her words, Henrietta Maria glanced pleadingly at Brett. She saw a muscle twitch beside his mouth, and she was not reassured by his grim expres-

112

sion. She said desperately, "I encountered my lord Foxe in the gardens, Sire. There was something I wished to discuss with him in private."

Sickness swept over Charles again. The wanton! The lying jade! He would like to raise his cane and strike her. He would like to beat her until she crawled at his feet and begged for mercy! Instead, he said in a colorless voice, "Why, Madam, I have observed for myself that you found that privacy."

Oh, what had she done? Tears came into Henrietta Maria's eyes. Charles stood before her, yet somehow it was as if he had removed himself to a great distance. His eyes were remote, and there was a nonchalance about the way he stood, but she could sense his pain. He was looking directly at her, but she had the odd, chill feeling that he did not really see her.

Henrietta Maria looked at Meredith. The girl's eyes were very revealing, and the scorn in them brought another rush of blood to the Queen's cheeks. "Mistress Hartford! What are you doing here?"

.The King gave Meredith no chance to reply. "Mistress Hartford is in no way to blame for her presence here, Madam," He said in a smooth, cold voice. "Meeting her in the corridor, I asked her to accompany me. I assumed that she would wish to give greeting to the Earl of Foxefield."

Brett stiffened. So it was to be the Earl of Foxefield now? Was he, from now on, to be barred from Charles's friendship? He was aware of a dull ache at the back of his eyes, a great feeling of loss. A plague on it! A plague on the stupid, heedless chit who had brought this situation about! His eyes were drawn to Meredith. The freezing contempt in her face brought a rush of savage anger. By God, was he to be condemned out of hand? What right had the blasted wench to look at him like that? One would think him to be guilty of an act of murder! He looked at Charles again, and he was shaken out of his anger. Perhaps murder had been committed in this room, the murder of a man's heart. The King's eyes looked dead. Did Henrietta Maria, of the vanity and the pretensions, know how much she was loved?

113

He must speak, Brett thought. He must say something to Charles. He could not allow him to believe that he had betrayed him. The thought had been there, he remembered with deep shame. But in the end his great affection for this man had conquered. Perhaps he could explain it in such a way that Henrietta Maria would be absolved from blame. His intentions were good, but his first words were tactless. "Your Majesty," he said, "I know what you must be thinking. But things are not always as they appear to be."

"Not always as they appear to be?" Charles repeated. His dark brows rose haughtily. "I fail to understand you, my lord."

"If Your Majesty would allow me to explain."

Charles's smile was bleak. "There is no need of explanations, my lord. I believe that we now understand each other perfectly."

"Nay, Charles. I have said that it is not as it seems. You must listen to me!"

"Must I?" Charles traced a pattern on the carpet with the tip of his cane. "No, my lord, I think not."

The coldness of his voice chilled Brett. For the moment, he thought, he must accept temporary defeat. But later he would find a way to make him listen. Charles must believe that he had walked in on a passionate love scene between his wife and his friend. But not for one moment would he allow himself the emotion of anger, or any other emotion for that matter. He would be reminding himself that he was the King. He was deeply hurt, furiously angry inside, and at the moment he would neither listen to nor accept an explanation. Certainly he would never admit to the need of one.

Meredith clenched her hands so tightly together that her nails bit into her palms. She was afraid that Brett intended to explain further. Do not say any more, you fool! she thought, trying to will him to silence. Cannot you see how deeply you have hurt him? Anger leaped in her, and she had a longing to hurl herself across the room and batter at his face with her fists. A pox on him for a lecherous swine! How dare he make love to that dark-haired, doll-faced French trollop! Oh, God, she was not worthy to be the

Queen! Henrietta Maria, she had heard it said, wished to name her first-born son Charles. God preserve England if the boy, rather than taking after his father, should instead take after his mother! If the morals of Charles the Second be like to those of his mother, how would England fare under such a licentious King? Meredith, in her young and sweeping scorn, believed what her eyes had seen. There could be no excuse. They were both guilty. But scorn would not erase her love for Brett, she knew. Later, when her first anger had passed, she would possibly find herself seeking to excuse him. But the Queen, never!

Meredith glanced at the King's half-averted face. She felt a surge of affection for him. Why did he have to love the false jade? Better by far had he been indifferent.

The King suddenly turned his head and looked at her questioningly. "Was there something you wished to say, Mistress Hartford?"

Meredith curtsied. "I wished to ask Your Majesty's permission to retire. I fear, Sire, that I have neglected my duties for long enough."

Charles's eyes softened. Long ago he had guessed that she loved the Earl of Foxefield. He felt a bond with her, for she must be suffering now. Mistress Hartford was very lovely and appealing, but she was not noted for her tact. But somehow he knew instinctively that, in this particular instance, he could rely upon her discretion. "I feel sure that the Queen will excuse you from your duties, mistress," he said gently. He looked at Henrietta Maria, who nodded. "That being so," Charles continued, "I feel it only civil that you stay and give the Earl your greeting."

"If Your Majesty pleases," Meredith burst out, "I have no wish to stay."

"But I am quite sure you do not mean that, Mistress Hartford," Charles said. He turned to the Queen. "Come, Madam, we will leave them together." He inclined his head to Brett. "My lord." Walking to Henrietta Maria, he took her arm.

Henrietta Maria shivered as she felt the cold firm clasp of his fingers. She had a sudden wild feeling that she was a prisoner, and he her implacable goaler. There seemed to be nothing that she could say to him. Nothing that he would wish to listen to. Gone now was her arrogance, her customary haughty bearing. Her head was drooping, and, as the King led her from the room, she looked like a guilty child.

As soon as the door had closed behind them, Brett's simmering anger turned on Meredith. He looked with hard eyes at her hostile face. "What the devil are you looking at me like that for?" he exploded. "Do you actually have the impertinence to sit in judgment upon me?"

Meredith came to stand before him. "It is not necessary to shout, my lord."

"Guard your tongue, wench!"

She smiled at him tauntingly. "Oh, I will, my lord, if I have your promise that you, in your turn, will guard the morals and the reputations of yourself and the Queen."

"Take care!" he said, anger blazing in his eyes. "If you, Mistress Hartford, are under the impression that you may address me in any manner you please, then let me tell you that you do not know me."

"My lord, after what I have seen here this day, I have no wish to know you."

"Blast your insolence!" His hands shot out and clamped down hard on her shoulders. "I warn you," he said, shaking her, "that I have had quite enough for one day!"

"So I would imagine!" she shot at him. "And so has the King. He believed you to be his friend. And yet the moment you could contrive it, you went behind his back and took his wife!"

His hands dropped away. "By Christ, you little fool! Are you insane? Do you realize what you are saying?"

His face was frightening. Hiding her fear, she tossed back her tumbled hair and glared at him defiantly. "Aye, I know what I am saying. You should be ashamed! As for the Queen, I can't imagine for one moment what she finds in you to attract her from her husband's bed."

He stared at her for a long moment, and the line of his mouth looked cruel. "Can you not, Mistress Hartford?" He thrust his face close to hers. "Mayhap I will show you what she finds."

She stood very still, her face flushing as Brett's eyes traveled from her face to her partially exposed bosom. When his eyes rested on her lips, she found her voice. "Do not show me, my lord. I believe, if you were to kiss me, that I would vomit!"

"Would you?" His hands grasped her hair. "I would see this interesting spectacle."

His hands were twined cruelly in her hair, but she would not show that he was hurting her. "Your touch makes me want to vomit, my lord. I fear that your kiss would be even worse."

"Then vomit, and be damned to you!" He ground his lips savagely against hers.

She could hardly breathe beneath his bruising, punishing lips. She had dreamed of the magic moment when he would kiss her. But this kiss, given in contempt and anger and from a desire to humiliate her, roused her to an almost insane fury. Her fingers tore at his hair, trying to hurt him as he was hurting her. He released her suddenly, with an abruptness that threw her off balance. Stumbling backward, her foot twisted and she fell heavily to the floor.

"Be damned to you!" he said again, coming to stand over her. He looked down at her. Her hair was in wild confusion, her cheeks were scarlet, and her mouth looked bruised. In that wild struggle, her breasts had sprung free from her bodice. He laughed as she tried to cover herself.

Beside herself, she watched him stride over to the door. "Do you think you are God?" she shouted. "Do you think you can stride about this earth and take whatever pleases you?"

He turned to look at her. "May I suggest that you cover yourself decently, Mistress Hartford? 'Tis surely a sin for a Puritan lady to so wantonly expose her breasts." The sneer in his voice stung as he added, "As for the other. If you are under the illusion that you please me, you are sadly mistaken. If you will make an effort to cover yourself, I would be happy if you would get out of here."

"Oh!" She grasped the pearled edge of the bodice and drew it up with a violent jerk. "There, damn you!"

He nodded. "They are the better for being covered. I have no doubt that there are some who would find them admirably shaped, but for myself they hold no temptation."

He was laughing at her! How dare he. "You pig!" She leaned forward and tore off her green velvet slipper. "I hope—I hope you die!" she shouted, hurling it at him.

The slipper struck the door. "I am happy to know that you wish me well, Mistress Hartford. If I assist you to your feet, will you depart?"

She shrank back. "Do not dare to touch me! Will you let me go out of that door, my lord, without offering me some kind of explanation for your conduct with the Queen?"

He stared at her in amazement. "You know, wench, there are times when your audacity is beyond belief." He walked over to her. Reaching down, he jerked her to her feet. "My conduct with the Queen, or with any other woman for that matter, is none of your infernal business."

"Lady Sarah would not approve of such conduct, as you well know."

"Then might I suggest that you refrain from telling her." Grasping her arm, he pulled her ruthlessly to the outer door. "Out with you, before I forget that you are supposed to be a lady."

"I am a lady, but you are not a gentleman. You are" her words broke off with a gasp as he jerked open the door and pushed her out into the corridor.

Seton, about to enter the room, received the full impact of her body. He staggered. Then, grunting, he fell to the floor with Meredith sprawled on top of him in a tangle of petticoats.

For a moment she lay there stunned. Then, hearing the Earl's laughter, she got shakily to her feet. With a muttered apology to the prone Seton, she gathered her skirts in both hands and fled down the corridor as if pursued by demons.

The Earl looked down at Seton, who was staring at him with

118

pained eyes. "Get up, man," he said. "You look damned silly lying there." He nodded his head to a group of ladies and gentlemen who had paused to watch. "You are attracting attention, Seton," he went on, his eyes glinting in amusement. "Have I not told you repeatedly that too much wine taken at this time of the day is bad for you?"

Laughing, he turned away. The indignant Seton followed him into the room.

"My Lord," Seton said in a grieved voice, rubbing at his elbow, "I am in some considerable pain." He sniffed. "I would remind you, my lord, that I do not drink." Wincing, he drew himself to his full height. "You have taken my reputation from me. It will now be rumored that I am a drunkard, and unfit for your lordship's service. You know well that I am not a man of full or bibulous habits, and 'tis scarcely fair to me to spread this rumor."

Brett grinned. "Well, you are unfit to be in my service. Had you been back within the hour, none of this would have happened."

Seton limped to the chair and picked up his lordship's cloak. "I returned in two minutes under the hour. However, since your lordship chose to eject the lady so brutally, I am glad that my body was there to break her fall. I will not speak of my own pain, for I assure you, my lord, that I have grown accustomed to suffering in silence."

"Silence, Seton? Bah! You have been blathering since first you picked yourself up from your drunken stupor."

"My lord!"

Brett turned away, his smile fading. What the devil was he to do about the unholy mess in which he found himself? He could not let Charles go on believing that he had betrayed him. He could believe anything else he chose, but not that.

Limping painfully about the room, Seton was surprised at his master's black scowl. What had he to scowl about? Was my lord Foxefield the injured party, or was it he?

119

Chapter Seven

With a flourish of his lace kerchief, the Duke of Buckingham bowed low as the King and Queen approached him. The pleasant smile he had quickly assumed vanished, as the King, who would normally have paused to speak to him, passed his elegant satin-clad figure by without apparent recognition.

The Duke's offense at this slight passed, and a thoughtful gleam lit his light-blue eyes. There was something wrong, he was almost sure of it. It seemed to him that Charles was looking unusually grim for a man who had made no secret of the fact that he was eagerly anticipating a reunion with his wife. Aye, and now he came to think of it, the Queen looked different too. Her appearance was slightly dishevelled, and she had looked almost afraid.

Absent-mindedly, the Duke acknowledged the bows and curtsies of the passing people. If something had happened, then he should know about it. It behooved him to have a knowledge of all that went on, for one never knew when such knowledge might prove useful. Making up his mind, he began to stroll slowly in the same direction.

A little distance from the Queen's apartments, the Duke stepped behind a great gilded statue of the late King. The King had paused by the door and he was saying something to the Queen. Henrietta Maria, in reply, put out her hand. There was something wild and appealing about her attitude. It was as though she begged a boon. Whatever it might be it was instantly refused, for Charles's only response was to bow stiffly and turn away.

The Duke, as he waited for Charles to pass him, thought he heard the sound of sobbing as Henrietta Maria entered her apartment and slammed the door behind her.

The Duke stepped from behind the statue as the King came abreast of him. "Sire," he said, "might I speak with you?"

The King stopped and turned to look at him. "Aye, my lord," he answered, "if 'tis important." He began to walk on. The Duke fell into step beside him. The slight stoop of the King's shoulders, the weariness in his face and voice, was not lost on him.

" 'Tis important to me, Sire," he said in a low voice. "You seem troubled. I would know of that trouble, in order that I might bear part or all of your burden."

The King seemed not to hear him, for he made no answer. After a moment Buckingham went on. "Charles, forgive me, but is all well between yourself and the Queen?"

The King stopped walking. "My lord Buckingham," he said in a freezing voice, "you forget to whom you are talking. The affairs of the Queen and myself are not your concern."

The Duke was dismayed, but he did not allow that dismay to show in his eyes. That Charles, who had always treated him as dearest friend and confidant, should rebuke him as one would a stranger!

He bowed his dark-blond head before the King, as if accepting the rebuke. It was not easy for a man of his arrogant pride to assume a humble air, but, when it was expedient, he could do so. He looked at the King with mournful eyes. "Forgive me, Sire.

You know well that I would die rather than offend you. The question was impertinent, I freely admit it. I only ask you to remember that it was prompted out of my loving concern for you."

The King had always believed in Buckingham's sincerity. No amount of scandal, and there had been plenty, could shake that belief. No proof of the man's perfidy, and it had been offered to him, could convince him that Buckingham was other than he seemed. There were many sides to the Duke's character. Charles had no notion of it, but in all the years that had passed he had been allowed to glimpse only one, the side that Buckingham wished him to see. He had created an image of himself in Charles's mind, the image of a loving and concerned brother, or, perhaps, by a stretch of the imagination, a father. Looking at him now, Charles felt the pull of old loyalties, of the confidences between them, the laughter they had enjoyed, the plans they had made, the adventures they had shared. One adventure in particular, that never-to-be-forgotten and light-hearted journey to Spain. It had been made in order that Charles might catch a forbidden glimpse of the Infanta, who was, at that time, his promised bride. Nay, he should not have spoken so to Buckingham, who, unlike my lord Foxe, was his true friend. Buckingham, he was certain, would die rather than betray him, and he deserved better from him. He had no intention of confiding the real truth, his pride would not allow it, and not even to Buckingham could he be persuaded to show his wounds. But he could say something that might be accepted by this old friend.

The Duke, watching him narrowly, was not surprised to see Charles's lips soften into a smile. He had always been able to play on the emotions of this impressionable young man. "I fear that I spoke too sharply, George," the King said. "I ask you to forgive me for that."

Buckingham's answering smile was radiant. " 'Tis not for such as I to forgive the King. Come, Charles, you know well that the King can do no wrong."

"I would that that were truly so," Charles answered with a

wry smile. "But you wished to know what troubled me. I will tell you."

"Only if it is your desire to confide in me," Buckingham put in hastily.

"It is my desire," the King assured him. "It is the Queen's household that troubles me, George. While she is surrounded by Frenchmen and Frenchwomen, to say nothing of her cursed priests, she makes no attempt to learn the English language." He clasped his hands tightly together as he felt the flaring of the old resentment and anger. "In truth, concerning that situation, there are many things that trouble me."

It was a genuine grievance, he had spoken of it many times before, and always he had displayed that same tight, angry control. Buckingham was suddenly convinced that this was indeed the cause of the trouble between the King and Queen. "Might I suggest, Sire," he said soothingly, "since Mistress Hartford is the first English lady to enter the Queen's household, that others might mingle admirably."

"Perhaps." Charles looked at him thoughtfully. "Have you anyone in mind?"

Buckingham hesitated, his eyes watching Charles warily. "Well, Sire, my wife would be greatly honored were she to be offered the position of Lady of the Queen's Bedchamber. There are also my niece and my sister, who would be equally honored."

Charles nodded. "A good choice. I will speak to the Queen and suggest that she bear these ladies in mind. However, I must tell you that my real intention is to rid the Queen's household of all her French followers."

"All of them, Sire?" Buckingham said, looking somewhat taken aback. "But would not such an action on Your Majesty's part be construed as a breach of the marriage contract? Richelieu, you know, who greatly favors the Queen, has considerable influence with her brother."

"I know that," Charles said impatiently. "But there must surely be a way to circumvent both the marriage contract and Richelieu's interference. It is not that I wish to break promises or avoid my obligations, but this is an English Court and I will not have it turned into an imitation of Louis's Court. And especially will I not have those long-faced, dismal priests creeping about. Wherever one turns, one encounters them.''

"I understand, Sire.''

"I should not have signed such a marriage contract, I know that now. I did not peruse it carefully enough, and so I did not realize how unreasonable were the articles provided for, nor how exasperating. My patience, even after this short time, is at an end. I tell you now that somehow or other I will be rid of these French!''

"Of course, Sire, of course. We will find a way. There is always a way.''

"I trust so.''

The King, with a last smile, turned and abruptly left him. Buckingham bowed, but other than that he did not move. For a full ten minutes he continued to stand there. He had few friends at Court, and the eyes that observed him were mostly those of his enemies, who wondered what his absorbed air might portend. Buckingham did not see them, or hear their light, malicious voices. He was thinking that he saw in the King's confidences a chance not only to oust the Earl of Foxefield from favor but to bring to fruition a personal ambition. If his wife might be installed in the Queen's household, to say nothing of his sister and his niece, they would have the indiscreet and impulsive Queen under their eyes. Aye, they would be his eyes and his ears, and the Queen would be unable to make a move without his knowledge.

He moved at last. He would go to the Queen now. For the sake of the King, it was his duty to do so. He would speak to her of the King's dissatisfaction with things as they were. He might even, in a subtle way, of course, threaten her with the possible consequences of her continued defiance of her royal husband. Aye, my lord Foxe might amuse the King and help to lighten the gloomy moods that sometimes attacked him, but in the end Charles would be brought to see that in matters pertaining to his comfort, his happiness and his general welfare, it was only his old friend Buckingham upon whom he could safely rely.

Armed with this thought, and fired with ambition for himself and the women of his household, he hastened toward the Queen's apartments.

When Henrietta Maria was informed by the timid Antoinette Dubois that my lord Buckingham was without and craved an immediate audience, she instantly refused. "I will not see him!" she cried out. "I never wish to see him. I hate the man!"

"Wait, Antoinette," Madame Saint-Georges said quietly.

Henrietta Maria stared at her. "What do you mean? Do you actually dare to countermand my order!"

Madame Saint-Georges, in whom the weeping Henrietta Maria had confided that fatal encounter in the Earl of Foxefield's bedchamber, calmly continued to minister to her mistress. "It is not a case of countermanding your order, Madame," she said, mopping at the Queen's tear-blotched face, "it is merely that I suggest we think for a moment."

"What is there to think about?"

"Madame, my darling," the woman answered, "would it not be wiser to see the Duke?"

Henrietta Maria broke down again. "You are cruel and unfeeling!" she sobbed. "Am I not unhappy enough to suit you, Saint-Georges? Must I now add to my unbearable sorrow the detestable company of that hateful man?"

Madame Saint-Georges put the kerchief aside. Picking up a brush, she began to smooth the Queen's tangled hair. "Why must you always be so dramatic, my little one?" she said tenderly. Henrietta Maria stiffened, and she added hastily. "Ah, no, Madame, I do not seek to make light of your unhappiness. I think that I knew, even before you realized it yourself, that you loved the King."

"You knew? Then why did you not tell me, imbecile?"

"Would you have listened, Madame?"

"I might have done," Henrietta Maria said sullenly. "But what is all this to do with that—that creature out there?"

"Shortly after the King left you, Duval saw him in conversation with the Duke of Buckingham. Might it not be that he has come with a message from the King?"

A gleam lit Henrietta Maria's dulled eyes. "Oh, Saint-Georges," she said eagerly, "do you really think so?"

Madame Saint-Georges did not think so, but she nodded dutifully. She was anxious that Henrietta Maria grant my lord Buckingham an audience, because, through Buckingham's not inconsiderable influence, a way might be found for her darling to approach the King and come to an understanding.

Sighing, Madame Saint-Georges stroked the girl's black hair. She loved Henrietta Maria, her happiness meant everything to her. Always with the thought of that happiness in mind, she willingly endured Henrietta Maria's frequent insults and abuse. She had always felt that the girl, despite evidence to the contrary, loved her in return. "Well, Madame," she coaxed, "will you see him?"

"But of course. How like you to ask such a stupid question, Saint-Georges!" Henrietta Maria looked across at the girl, who waited with respectfully lowered eyes. "Do not stand there, Dubois," she cried. "Go to my lord Buckingham. Inform him that I will see him shortly."

"Yes, Madame." Antoinette Dubois curtsied, then turned and ran from the room.

The smile Henrietta Maria turned on Madame Saint-Georges was radiant with relief and happiness. "You are right for once, Saint-Georges. Of course the King has sent him to me. You will see. He has regretted his cold leave-taking, and he has chosen this way to convey his regrets. Oh, I am so happy! So happy!"

"Madame, do not hope for too much."

"Cease your croakings, you stupid woman." Henrietta Maria frowned suddenly. "You do not want me to be happy," she accused.

"Oh, Madame, I do. But it did occur to me that my lord Buckingham might be here on a different matter."

"It did not seem to occur to you before."

Madame Saint-Georges shrugged helplessly. "Will you promise to be gracious, Madame," she pleaded, "no matter what he might wish to discuss?"

Henrietta Maria jumped up from the chair. She was all animation now, all joy and hope. "Of course I will be gracious. Am I not always so?"

"No, Madame."

"What!—Oh, never mind, I refuse to let you depress me, you dismal creature. Do hurry, Saint-Georges, you move like a snail. Come, come, we must not keep my lord Buckingham waiting. I will wear my red gown. And you must do something about my face and my hair. Oh, why am I forced to endure you, you infuriating woman? Hurry!"

When Henrietta Maria entered her sitting room some fifteen minutes later, Buckingham got quickly to his feet and bowed low. "Your Majesty," he murmured, kissing her small hand, "you are looking quite radiantly beautiful."

Henrietta Maria, who had an uneasy suspicion that the red of her gown did disastrous things to her tear-swollen complexion and her puffy eyes, eyed him sharply. "Do you think so, my lord?"

"I do indeed, Madam," Buckingham lied smoothly. He had never been a great admirer of Henrietta Maria's particular style of beauty, though he pretended to be. At this moment, he thought, she resembled nothing more or less than a sick monkey.

Henrietta Maria's suspicion was allayed. She could never really like the man, but that was forgotten now. In her present state of mind he seemed to her to resemble a shining angel. He was here to relieve her misery and to lead her back to happiness with the King. Of course he meant what he said. Saint-Georges, who had no doubt hoped that she would appear ugly in his eyes, would be vastly disappointed.

"Pray be seated, my lord," she said, smiling at him. "I would hear what you have to say without further delay."

Seating himself, Buckingham was confused by the brilliance of the Queen's smile. Why was she looking at him like that, like someone who was anticipating a treat? Hitherto he had been accustomed to receiving scowls from her. Her voice, when forced to speak to him, had always been high pitched and arrogant; but now it was soft and low. There was a light in her eyes, and her smile caressed him.

Henrietta Maria had seated herself opposite to him. "Well, my lord?" she said eagerly. "Pray, tell me why you have requested this audience." She held up her hand as he was about to answer, her nose wrinkling like a mischievous child's. "No, wait, I think I know. His Majesty has sent you to me, is it not so?"

"Why no, Madam, though I do admit that I come upon the King's business."

"The King's business?" Disappointed, Henrietta Maria's smile quickly disappeared. "I do not understand."

Buckingham was completely at his ease now. He crossed one satin-clad leg over the other, and regarded her with eyes grown stern. He was a consummate actor and he addressed her in a bell-like voice that held a fine blending of sorrow and reproach. "I do not have to tell you, Madam, that my King's happiness has ever been first with me. To achieve this, I would do and say anything. I wish to make quite sure you understand me, Madam."

Apathy crept over Henrietta Maria. She did not care now what he might have to say. She only knew that he had not come to lead her back to happiness. Her fingers plucked restlessly at the red brocade of her chair. "Say what you have to say, my lord," she said, shrugging.

Buckingham pressed his fingertips together. Now what was the matter with the stupid wench? he thought impatiently. She had been all light and sparkle a moment ago, but now she looked dull and cold and older than her fifteen years. He was not sure that she was listening to him either. He said slowly, "I regret that I must say this, Madam, and I beg you to forgive me, but you are causing the King great unhappiness."

Henrietta Maria's head lifted, her eyes flashing with indignation. "I do not care for your words, my lord!" Color flared into her face. "Is it for such as you to tell me of my faults?"

Buckingham nodded. "Aye, Madam, when my King's happiness is at stake."

She stared at him in genuine amazement. "How dare you speak to me so! The King shall hear of this impertinence!"

The Duke shrugged his shoulders. He knew women and their eternal curiosity. "If you will not hear me, Madam, then may I beg your leave to retire?"

As he had anticipated, she cried out, "Nay, I do not give you leave to retire. You are either drunk or insane, yet it behooves me to hear all of your ramblings." Her narrowed eyes conveyed a threat.

Buckingham was unmoved. Let her tell the King, it mattered not to him. It was for the sake of the King that he was here. Charles, once he fully understood his purpose, would understand and forgive.

"Well, my lord, I am waiting."

"Your French household does not please the King, Madam. He has endured enough. They must return to France immediately. As for—"

"You dare!" The color had left Henrietta Maria's face. It was white with rage.

"Yes, Madam, for my King I would dare anything. Neither does your own indifferent attitude please him."

"Be silent!"

"I regret, Madam, I cannot. I must say it all." He leaned forward in his seat, his eyes holding hers. "If you do not show him the love and respect to which he is entitled, you will find that you will become the most wretchedly unhappy woman in this world."

Henrietta Maria laughed, a high, hysterical sound. "Are you threatening me, my lord?"

"I would not so presume, Madam. Say rather that I am warning you."

Her hands clenched on the arms of the chair. "Warning me of what, my lord?"

Buckingham smiled. "There are some unhappy Queens, Madam," he said, not caring that his tone was openly menacing, "who have paid with their heads for far less offense than you have given to His Majesty."

Henrietta Maria rose slowly to her feet. "You will leave my presence at once, my lord." There was dignity about her small figure now, yet still she could not resist her small touch of drama. Her head held high, her eyes flashing, she pointed a trembling finger at the door. "Go! Go! And remember this, my lord, I am not unprotected. And more noblemen have paid with their heads than have Queens in this wretched and barbaric country."

Buckingham rose and bowed before her, and there was mockery in his deep obeisance. "This wretched and barbaric country, as you choose to call it, is also your country. I advise you to remember it."

"Say no more. You will regret this, I warn you!"

"No, Madam, I will not. I am a loyal servant of His Majesty. I felt that I had to speak."

"Go!"

Buckingham bowed again. As he walked to the door, he was satisfied with the impression he had made. He did not fear Henrietta Maria. He could manage Charles, and that was all that mattered. He worked in the King's interests, and his own, too, of course.

For a long time after he had left, Henrietta Maria stood in the center of the room, her hands before her face. She did not believe that Buckingham had come of his own accord. He would not dare! Charles had sent him. The threats he had uttered were really Charles's threats. He had done this to her, the husband whom she loved with all her heart? He had dared to send Buckingham to her, that vile man! He had dared to submit her to this indignity! All thoughts of explaining her behavior and begging humbly for his forgiveness fled. She would never explain, never, never! Not until he got rid of his creature!

She began to moan, but she was not aware of it until Madame Saint-Georges' quiet voice spoke. "Madame, my dearest. Come, let me bathe your head. It will soothe you."

Henrietta Maria's hands dropped. She stared wildly at Madame Saint-Georges, who was standing by the door of the bedchamber, a group of ladies behind her. She did not see their frightened faces, she saw only Saint-Georges, her rock, her comfort!

"Saint-Georges!" she cried. Her face working, she stumbled forward. "Saint-Georges, the King sent that man to threaten me!"

Madame Saint-George's arms closed firmly about her. "I heard it all, Madame," she said in a low, crooning voice.

Henrietta Maria burrowed her hot face against the woman's shoulder. "Save me! Someone must save me! The King will take my head if I do not instantly obey him!"

Madame Saint-Georges gestured to the women to depart. They fled into the next room, casting fearful glances over their shoulders at the distraught Queen.

"Come, Madame, you will feel much better if you lie upon the bed." Madame Saint-Georges led her, unresisting, into the bedchamber.

"I am threatened, don't you understand?" Henrietta Maria cried out as she flopped down on the bed.

"No more drama, Madame. This is no time for it." With brisk capable hands, Madame Saint-Georges settled the Queen on the large canopied bed and drew the scarlet and gold coverlet over her shaking form. "You are not threatened. The King is a kind man, and he loves you."

"Loves me!" Henrietta Maria laughed bitterly. "Ah, how he loves me! You imbecile! Did I not tell you that he sent that man to threaten me?"

"I do not believe it. I will not believe it. I'll warrant that the King knows nothing of this."

Henrietta Maria was not listening. Her head rolled wildly from side to side on the satin pillow. "I will never explain to him now.

I will never tell him I love him, not until he rids himself of Buckingham.''

"You must tell him, Madame. You know well that you are entirely to blame for that episode with my lord Foxefield. You owe it to the King, and to my lord Foxefield, whom, you have assured me, is guiltless.''

"Only I am to blame, I suppose?''

"Only you, Madame. You have admitted it.''

"How can you speak to me so? I—I thought you loved me!''

"I do, Madame. I desire your happiness.''

Henrietta Maria's face contorted. "Liar! Hypocrite! You have given your loyalty to the King!''

A peculiar expression crossed Madame Saint-Georges' face. She clasped her hands together as though fighting an urge to slap the hysterical girl. "My loyalty is to both you and the King,'' she answered with an effort. "But still I say, Madame, that you must explain to him.''

"I will not! Why should I?''

"Madame, you must. 'Tis for your own sake.''

Henrietta Maria burst into loud angry sobs. "You hate me! I have always known it.'' She sat up on the bed and pushed her hair away from her face. "Do you dare to deny it?''

"Aye, I do dare.'' Madame Saint-Georges sat down on the side of the bed and drew the girl into her arms. "Hush!'' she said softly, rocking her like a baby. "Be calm, my little one, my Queen. Saint-Georges is here, and nothing shall happen to you.''

"But he will send you away,'' Henrietta Maria mourned. "He wishes to send all my friends away!''

"Do not think of it now.''

Madame Saint-Georges turned her head as a shadow fell across the bed. She smiled faintly as she saw the slight figure standing in the doorway. "Oh, it is you, Mistress Hartford.'' She tightened her arms as Henrietta Maria made a convulsive movement. She shook her head warningly at Meredith. "The Queen does not require your presence at this moment.''

Meredith was taken aback as she caught sight of the Queen's red and swollen face. She stepped back hastily before the intimidating glare of those dark eyes. "Very well, if you are sure there is nothing I can do."

"I wish nothing from you!" the Queen shouted. "Get out! Get out, you abominable Englishwoman! I hate you, do you hear? I hate England and everything English. I want to go home!" Her voice broke into sobs. "Tell her to go, Saint-Georges."

"Mistress Hartford has already gone, Madame."

"Oh, what am I to do? Saint-Georges, Saint-Georges! What am I to do?"

"You will sleep now. Later on, when you are calmer, we will talk."

A tap sounded on the door. "How do you expect me to sleep," Henrietta Maria shouted, "when fools are forever intruding? Am I deaf that you expect me to sleep with the thunder of rapping in my ears?"

Cecile de Villiers looked at the Queen apologetically. "I regret to disturb you, Madame," she said, coming farther into the room. "I would not have done so if—"

"What do you want?" Henrietta Maria interrupted impatiently. "Am I never to have peace?"

"Madame," Cecile whispered urgently, "the King is here."

Henrietta Maria gave a stifled scream. "Oh, God! He has come to threaten me again!"

"Please, Madame, he will hear you." Madame Saint-Georges looked at Cecile. "Tell the King that the Queen will be with him in a few moments."

"I will tell him." Cecile hesitated. "He wishes to speak with the Queen in complete privacy," she said, directing her words at the older woman. "We are all dismissed."

"Very well," Madame Saint-Georges answered quietly. "Go now, Cecile."

Henrietta Maria moaned. "You must not leave me, Saint-Georges. Please! You will destroy me if you do!"

"You know that I must go, Madame, since the King has commanded it. 'Twill be only for a while. We will be nearby, for I will direct the ladies to stand in the courtyard just below your windows. Come, get up. Allow me to bathe your face and make you look pretty."

"No! You must not leave me. I am—I am afraid of him!"

Madame Saint-Georges took a deep breath of exasperation. She knew that the words she was about to speak would be remembered against her when Henrietta Maria had recovered from her fear, but she had no patience with such dramatics, and it was for the girl's own good. She must be calm when she faced her husband. "Nonsense, Madame!" she said cuttingly. "I would remind you that you are not a play actress. You are the Queen of England, little though I can believe it at this moment. I would have you act as a Queen. You must compose yourself. You must call upon your courage and dignity. The white silk gown will look beautiful upon you, Madame. If you hurry, we need not keep His Majesty waiting for too long."

"I care naught if he waits for the rest of the day." For all her words, Henrietta Maria rose from the bed. She delivered herself into Madame Saint-Georges hands and allowed her to do with her as she pleased. She was conscious of a misery and despair so devastating that she did not even complain when the brush caught in her hair and jerked her head back painfully.

While he waited for the Queen, Charles prowled restlessly about the room. Frowning, he halted before the bust of a long-gone King, standing on a tall pedestal beside the window. He stared unseeingly at the blind eyes and the sternly carved lines of the face. He loved Henrietta Maria. No matter what she had done, he would always love her. But despite this, he knew it was the desire to punish her that had brought him here. He did not believe that he was normally a vindictive man, nonetheless he would punish her for the wound she had dealt him. It might be that in time he would forgive her, but only when his pain eased, if indeed it ever did.

He heard a rustling of silk, and he turned quickly. Henrietta

Maria stood there, her hand holding Madame Saint-Georges' hand in a tight grip.

Charles scarcely noticed when Madame Saint-Georges, after pulling her hand free, curtsied to him and hurriedly left the room. His attention was all on the Queen. She was very pale, he noticed, and he wondered if it was the unrelieved white of her gown that had the effect of draining the color from her face. She seemed smaller, too. He found himself remembering her laughing words on that first meeting in Dover Castle. Believing him to be critical of her height, she had drawn her skirts to one side to show him her dainty silver slippers. "Thus high am I," she had remarked, "neither higher nor lower."

Conquering a traitorous rush of tenderness, he bade her harshly to be seated.

Henrietta Maria shook her head. "If Your Majesty has no objection, I would rather stand."

She wanted to rush into his arms, to feel them close about her in love, instead she said sneeringly, "I am surprised to see Your Majesty here, since you told me it would be a long time before you would wish to look upon my face again. My strumpet's face, I believe you said."

"I did, Madam, and I make no apology for my words."

Her resolution weakened, words rushed out passionately. "If you would only listen, I would tell you the whole story. I admit that I was foolish, and in that moment of foolishness I went to the apartments of my lord Foxe. He was—"

"Indeed?"

Henrietta Maria ignored the interruption. "My lord Foxe did not take advantage of my foolishness, though he could not be blamed had he done so. He told me to leave. He was rude and blunt in the telling. I knew then that I loved you, and only you. It was a kiss of gratitude you saw, nothing more."

Charles wanted to believe. Rude and blunt. Aye, it sounded like my lord Foxe. Was it so? Should he give my lord Foxe the chance to explain? After all, they were old friends. An explanation from Foxefield would not be as humiliating as it might be from another. He stared at Henrietta Maria. He could almost swear it was truth he saw in her eyes. But even if it be so, did she not still deserve her punishment?

"Madam," he said coldly, "I shall be most interested to hear your story at another time. But I am here because I have something I must say to you."

Her shoulders sagged in defeat. "I believe I know what you have come to say. I suppose you were disappointed with the failure of your creature's mission?"

His eyebrows drew together. "My creature? What the devil are you talking about, Madam?"

She put her hand to her throat to stem her hysterical laughter. "Do you expect me to tell you what you already know, Sire?"

What did she mean? Whatever was behind her words, he had no intention of finding out now. He would say what he had come to say, and to the devil with her! "We will unravel that puzzle later, Madam. I have come here to tell you that, at the earliest possible opportunity, I am determined to send your French retinue back to their own country."

A strangled cry escaped her lips. She stared at him, her eyes looking enormous in her white face. It was even as Buckingham had threatened. First the King would rid himself of her ladies and gentlemen, perhaps her priests too. Then he would proceed to deal with her. He believed her to be an unfaithful wife, and so he would give orders that her head be severed from her body. She put a hand to her shaking mouth. She was not a Queen in that moment, she was only a frightened child, and, like a child, incapable of reasoning.

"No!" she panted. "No, you cannot do this! I will not allow it! My—my brother w—will come to my aid."

Her punishment had begun to lose much of its zest for him, but her words brought his rage rushing back. Fiends seize her brother! She would not allow it? She! "You have nothing to say in the matter, Madam," he answered her violently. "They will all go back, all of your cursed French! I'll not endure them mincing about my Court a moment longer than I can help. I'll no longer endure their barely hidden sneers, their patronizing manners and their damnable carping criticisms!''

This was a man she had never seen before. His face was heavily flushed, his dark eyes blazing, and he was running his thin fingers through his hair in agitated sweeps.

''My priests?'' Henrietta Maria whispered. ''Am I not to be allowed the comfort of my priests?''

''Damn your priests! It might be that I will allow you one, perhaps two, but the rest of them go!''

''No!''

''I have said it, Madam. If necessary, I will drive them from me like wild beasts!''

It was too much! With a frantic scream, she went rushing past him to the window. With a strength born of desperation, she picked up the heavy bust from its stand and hurled it at the window. Glass splintered and exploded outward, much of it spraying back into the room. Careless of jagged edges, Henrietta Maria climbed out onto the wide windowledge. Startled faces were turned upward, and all activity in the courtyard ceased at the amazing spectacle of the Queen intent, it seemed, upon hurling herself to her death.

''Help!'' Henrietta Maria screamed at the paralyzed onlookers. ''In the name of God, help me!'' She struggled madly when she felt Charles's tight grip on her waist. ''I am to die! I am to be bereft of my friends. I am not even to be allowed the comfort of a priest!''

Her loud voice was like something out of a nightmare! Beads of perspiration started out on Charles's forehead as he fought to drag her back into the room. He was strong, but the terror-crazed Queen was almost a match for that strength. Sweet Christ! He dug his fingers into her waist, and felt her resistance lessen slightly. What was the meaning of her wild words, her piercing screams? Did she actually believe what she was saying?

His breath was coming in sobbing gasps when he finally managed to pull her back. They both collapsed on the carpet, heedless of the glass splinters. Henrietta Maria's head lolled weakly, but her cries did not cease. Blood was smeared over her face, blood that came from her lacerated hands, and there was blood on her bodice and her skirts.

My God! Charles stared at her in horror. "What are you doing to yourself, Madam? What are you trying to do to me?"

Sobbing, she held out her bloodied hands in appeal. "I—I did not m—mean to displease you, S—Sire. There—there was no betrayal. M—My lord Foxe will tell you. Do not order my death! Do not deprive me of my friends! Please, my lord King, if you will but have mercy on me, I will endeavor to—to be all that a wife should be. I—I will obey you in all th—things."

"Henrietta! Do you really think I would order your death?"

His dignity, his wounded pride and his pain, all were forgotten as he drew her into his arms and held her close. "Oh, Henrietta, a man does not knowingly kill the thing he loves. And I do love you. So much more than I could possibly tell you!"

"D—Do you, Charles?"

"Yes, my darling, so very much!" His lips touched her soft hair. "I will never hurt you, Henrietta. I ask you to believe that."

There was a short silence, then she whispered timidly, her eyes closing tightly as she said the words, "Then you do not believe that I betrayed you with my lord Foxe?"

She felt him start. He said in something like the cold stiff voice he had used before, "I know not what to believe. But, if it pleases you, I will speak with my lord Foxefield."

Her eyes opened wide with relief. "Oh, yes, dear Charles, pray do that. He will tell you all that occurred. I ask you beforehand to forgive me for my folly, but not for my unfaithfulness, for there was none." She did not add that the intent had been there. Perhaps he need never know.

Charles did not believe for one moment that Brett would tell him all. Despite his somewhat brusque and almost brutal way with women, he was nonetheless a gentleman. He would not betray the extent of the Queen's folly, but perhaps he would tell him enough to convince. Charles felt a faint sense of surprise as he realized that he was already halfway to believing in the innocence of the episode. "Then I promise you, my dear, that I will speak with him."

"Charles, thank you. Oh, Charles, I do love you so very much!"

He could not speak, he could only hold her. He was a prey to so many emotions. She bewildered him, exasperated him. Her violent temperament, the rapid changing of her moods, the heated shrewishness of her tongue could rouse his anger and cause his more retiring nature to shrink with distaste, and yet still he could not help this love he felt for her. She was so small in his arms, so soft and desirable. He could hear her breathing catching on an occasional sob, and he was filled with tenderness and a desire to please.

Henrietta Maria closed her eyes again. She was happy when she had thought never to be happy again. She loved him, she knew it to be truth. With Charles by her side, his love to support her, her life could not fail to be gloriously happy. A thought struck her, and she frowned. But if he loved her, he must give her her way. He would not send her little French Court from her, not if he knew it would make her unhappy. Nevertheless, she would not speak of it now. She was content with the happy moment. Later, she would approach him about it. She had a list she intended to present to him. There were various favored people whom she wished to administer her dower lands. These, naturally, were her own countrymen. Should he prove adamant about the administration, should he indeed insist upon sending them all back to France, then, dearly as she loved him, he would have to be punished. She would not eat or drink, she would not sleep until he promised to allow her to keep her servants. But he loved her. Of course he would give way. She sighed happily.

Charles wondered what she was thinking about. Her terror might never have been from the way she snuggled against him now. How quickly he had grown to love her! Nonetheless, she could not be allowed to have her will in everything. The French must go. Only then, left to themselves, without spying or interference, could they be truly happy. Her head moved, and he felt her lips touch his neck. Dear, sweet, lovely Henrietta! His wife, his Queen, his darling! It was not necessary to be unduly harsh with her. Perhaps he might allow her to keep a very few of her servants, and one priest. There was Father Pierre, for instance, or Father Philippe, who seemed to him to be the more bearable of the priests who moaned and droned in Henrietta's wake. At least these two seemed human. Sometimes they smiled, and when they spoke it was not always to discuss mortal sin. But the rest must go, he thought, his mouth tightening with resolution. He would give them presents as a token of appreciation for their services to the Queen, and he would return to them any monies they might have spent while in that service, but that was all they might reasonably expect of him. Although he did not know when or how this expulsion might be effected, he had faith in Buckingham, who would surely find a way. Louis, his brother-in-law, would be angered at the expulsion of Henrietta's French household, but the anger of Louis XIII held no terrors for him.

Henrietta Maria stirred in his arms. "Sire," she said in a sleepy voice, "it might be as well to reassure my ladies that no harm has come to me."

Charles released her reluctantly. "Aye, it is your duty to show yourself, Madam, lest they think that I have murdered you."

So he could even joke about the insane assault she had made on his royal dignity, he thought with a wry inner smile. What had he come to, he who was normally so proud? What would he come to in the future with such a wife? Of what like would be the children of her body? What a thing to think of at this moment! Henrietta was young, she would learn to bear herself with dignity and restraint. He himself would teach her to be more gracious to those who served her, and, above all, to bridle that damnable tongue of hers.

Wincing as a small splinter of glass pierced the edge of his hand, Charles got to this feet. He carefully brushed glass from his breeches, and assisted Henrietta Maria to pick the glass from her skirts. For a long time he had been dimly aware of a babble of voices outside the door, and now he must open the door and face the owners of those voices. He felt a rush of humiliation and anger, but Henrietta Maria was looking at him with such trusting and shining eyes, that he forced it down. Picking up her hand, he kissed it lingeringly. "Go to your bedchamber, Henrietta. I will send your ladies to you."

But Henrietta Maria was full of love and remorse. "We will go to the door together, Charles, my darling. They will see then that there is nothing wrong."

Charles looked at the blood on her face, her hands, her skirts, and he had some difficulty in restraining his laughter. How like her to forget her appearance so completely. "I fear, Madam," he remarked gravely, "that, were they to see you now, they would believe me to be the most complete villain. Nay, Henrietta, you have done enough damage for one day."

"Oh!" she began to laugh. Delightful little girl laughter, giggling, mischievous. She ran her stained hands through her curls, ruffling them widely, "Move aside, Sire. I will now go to the door."

"You dare!" He caught her about the waist and swung her. "I would put nothing past you, minx."

"Charles! Charles! Put me down. You are making me giddy."

He set her on her feet. Looking up at him, Henrietta Maria's smile slowly faded. "Charles," she said pleadingly, "say that you believe me."

Still he could not entirely commit himself. "We will see."

Henrietta Maria sighed. "When you have spoken to my lord Foxe, you will come to me, please?" She hesitated. She was of a mind to tell him of the Duke of Buckingham's visit, but he had softened to such an extent that she felt it might not be wise. She was not unaware, unfortunately, of his attachment to Buckingham. Later, perhaps, when this trouble between them had been cleared, she would tell him. For she had no intention of allowing the Duke to go unpunished. She said again, "You will come to me, Charles?"

"I will come, Madam," he said, looking deeply into her eyes, "if my lord Foxefield's explanation prove satisfying. If it is any consolation to you, I want to believe. You are very dear to me, and so too is the friendship of my lord Foxefield.''

He turned to the door. ''If you will hide yourself, Madam, I will allow your ladies to enter.''

She fled to the door of her bedchamber. She was laughing again, and Charles, watching her, thought, how little impression it seems to have made upon her. Can she be entirely without conscience, or has she told me the simple truth? But would a person without conscience spend so much time with the priests? She must be telling the truth. Charles, who had a very simple code of ethics by which he lived and which he rigorously observed, felt his heart lifting with hope as he strode toward the door.

Outside, shocked faces stared at him. Madame Saint-Georges, the only one with the courage to speak, said boldly, ''The Queen has need of us, Sire. May we go to her now?''

Charles smiled absently, for he saw the Earl of Foxefield coming toward him. ''By all means, ladies.'' Taking pity on Madame Saint-Georges' obvious anguish, he added gently, ''You will find the Queen in good spirits, Madame.'' His eyes twinkled. ''I have never seen her looking better.''

He stood aside as the ladies curtsied to him, and then filed into the room. Mistress Hartford, the last to enter, smiled at him, and he patted her arm as she passed him.

The Earl of Foxefield paused before the King. His face impassive, he bowed. ''Your Majesty,'' he said.

Charles stopped him as he was about to pass on. ''My lord,'' he said in a low voice, ''you will accompany me, please.'' For the benefit of those passing, he added. ''Walk with me in the grounds, I have something I wish to say to you.''

Brett looked into his unsmiling face. He thought that he knew Charles's every mood, yet he could not fathom the expression in the dark, somber eyes. ''Certainly, Sire.''

They walked for some time along the winding paths, in silence. Now and again Charles paused to examine a flower, but he might have been alone for all the awareness he gave of his companion. Brett seethed. If Charles had something to say, why in the plague didn't he say it? He was guiltless, and he felt he could convince Charles of this, but he was helpless against such stony silence. He could not even speak of the matter, unless Charles gave him permission to do so.

Charles paused before a bench set beneath an arbor of roses. "Pray be seated, my lord."

Brett's anger showed plainly in his eyes as he complied. Seating himself beside him, Charles said quietly, "You are angry, my lord Foxefield?"

"Your Majesty is mistaken," Brett mumbled the conventional reply. "Oh, to the devil with it!" he said in a louder voice. "Aye, Charles, I am angry. Angry because you are suffering need-lessly." He saw the King's cold smile. "Plague take it!" he rushed on. "Can we not forget for the moment that you are the King? Punish me, do with me what you will, but for Christ's sake allow me to speak!"

"It would seem that I cannot stop you, my lord," Charles said mildly.

"Nay, that you cannot. We have had a long friendship, you and I, Charles. I would regret more than I could possibly tell you to see it end. But, curse it, even at that risk, I must speak! And with all respect, I'll not be stopped!"

"Will you not?" Intently Charles studied the labors of a trail of ants on the path. "I have said, my lord, that I cannot stop you."

Brett's eyes narrowed slightly. Did he mean that he was willing to listen, or was he employing sarcasm? "You will hear me, Sire?"

"You have given me no choice, my lord."

Brett was easier now. He had caught an inflection in the King's voice. Not friendly, but not hostile either. In a low voice, he began his story. Charles still studied the ants, and Brett could not tell if he was listening or not.

When his voice faded into silence, Charles said quietly, "Have you ever studied ants, my lord?"

"Ants? What the devil have ants to do with—" he broke off. "I beg Your Majesty's pardon. No, I have never studied ants."

"You should." Charles turned his head and looked at him. "You really should, my lord Foxe. The creatures are endlessly fascinating."

My lord Foxe! Brett smiled broadly. "Damn, Charles! I'll study the pesky things, if it pleases you. Though I have always felt the world would be a better place if rid of them."

Charles rose. "As to that, my lord Foxe, I cannot agree with you. Everything has its place. Well, get up, you lazy oaf, would you sit in the presence of your King?"

"By no means, Sire," Brett said, rising with alacrity. He grinned. "Knowing Your Majesty's aversion to snakes, would you say that they too have a place?"

Charles considered this. "If they do," he said at last, "it is not around me."

Not one word of blame for the Queen, Charles thought as they made their leisurely way back to the Palace. I like you for that gallant lie, you damned rogue! As to the rest, I believe it. Since you are ofttimes too outspoken for your own good, my lord Foxe, you will doubtless curse yourself later for painting Henrietta as an angel, but I like that too. 'Twas a noble effort, my friend. Nay, no angel is my pretty willful bitch, but she'll learn. Aye, she'll learn, or I'll know the reason why!

"Your Majesty is still thinking of ants?" Brett asked, halting before the entrance.

"Of two ants, my lord Foxe, and of one particular spider. You may leave me now, you scoundrel. But take this thought with you. Come tomorrow, I intend to beat you at a game of bowls."

"Your Majesty may indulge in vain dreams," Brett said, bowing. "But with all due respect, I must tell you that you have not the slightest chance of beating me."

Laughing, Charles turned away. "We shall see. And speak to me not of respect, my lord Foxe. You know not the meaning of the word."

Chapter Eight

The tall manservant's eyes softened with appreciation as he looked at the girl standing before him. She was an enchanting sight in her wide-skirted pale-blue costume. The short, tight-fitting jacket was piped with cream satin. Bright hair gleamed beneath a provocative blue bonnet embellished with a curling darker blue feather. Her eyes seemed to the man to have a bright golden glow, and her creamy skin was flushed at the high cheekbones with a faint rose color.

"Mistress Hartford," the man said, removing his fascinated eyes. "If you will wait here, I will see if my lady Foxefield is desirous of seeing you."

Meredith did not like the faint condescension in his voice. He might have been a duke, she thought, staring after him. Certainly he looked very grand in his well-tailored black breeches and the long-skirted brass-buttoned jacket. When he had addressed her, he had sounded like someone who spoke to a servant or an undesirable. It was like my lord Foxe to employ such a man. It would not occur to him that the easily flustered Lady Sarah would detest such a superior personage in her home.

Meredith dismissed the servant from her mind and began to think of the real issue. The truth was that she was worried about Lady Sarah. Most of that lady's ailments, she knew, were largely imaginary, but the polluted air of London might well bring on a real ailment. Meredith's fingers played with her fringed purse. In her opinion, London, with its tall, tightly pressed and over-hanging houses, its miserable slums and its festering gutters, was no place for Lady Sarah. All day long and well into the night, the slimy cobblestoned and narrow streets were thronged with people. Summer brought great swarms of green flies to settle stickily on hot, perspiring bodies. In the winter the streets were rivers of mud. Sheets of mud from the constantly passing carriages sprayed the people from head to foot. The hawkers, heedless of the curses thrown their way, rushed up and down the streets crying out their wares in loud, raucous voices and thrusting their goods beneath the noses of the annoyed people.

Meredith could not believe that it was Lady Sarah's desire to live in London. She could not prefer this dirty, smoky city and her existence in this cramped house in Bonneville Place to the pleasant spaciousness of Foxefield Hall. Foxefield Hall looked out upon fragrant clover-studded green fields and leaf-burdened trees. Winter, summer, or spring the liquid caroling of the birds could be heard. Thinking of Foxefield Hall, Meredith felt a wave of homesickness. In London, one could never catch the sound of birdsong. There was only the never-ending clatter of iron-rimmed carriage wheels, the snorting and neighing of horses, and in the very early morning, when the city lay quiet for a short period, the persistent tuneless twitter of dingy brown sparrows. Instead of the fragrance of hedgerows and wild flowers, there hung over the city the poisonous effluvium of ordure and decay.

Returning, the manservant wondered at the deep frown of the beautiful Mistress Hartford.

"Well," Meredith said, in imitation of the man's pompous voice, "Is my lady Foxefield desirous of seeing me?"

"She is, Mistress Hartford. My lady has expressed a great desire to see you."

Surprised, Meredith saw the twinkle in the man's eyes. "I am gratified to hear it," she said, smiling.

Following the man along a white-paneled and brown carpeted hall, Meredith thought of Brett. Seven months since that disastrous moment when she had witnessed the Queen held in his arms. Since that time, she had seen little of Brett. When they did meet, it was usually by accident. Brett, curse him, would be icily polite, nothing more. Why could he not unbend a little? And yet, despite his icy manner, there were times when she could have sworn she read something in his eyes that did not match his stiff exterior. Last week, for instance, when, passing him with her head high, she had stumbled. His hand had shot out to steady her. Angry with herself for her clumsiness, she had said haughtily, "Thank you, my lord. I regret that I have troubled you."

His hand still gripped her arm. "Troubled me?" he said in a thoughtful voice. "Aye, perhaps that is the crux of the matter. You do trouble me constantly."

"Indeed, my lord. I have endeavored to keep out of your way as much as possible. You see very little of me."

"I do not have to see you. There are other places where you may be." He dropped her arm. "Mistress Hartford, you are looking at a fool." Without another word, he strode away. Bewildered, flushed with a sudden excitement, she stared after him. What did he mean? For those few moments his eyes had been warm. Did he like her just a little? Or was it all in her longing imagination?

Sometimes she wondered if Brett remembered that hard and insulting kiss he had given her? How many times since then had she longed for him to repeat the insult. He had dared to treat her lightly, and yet, when the Court had returned to Whitehall Palace, she had been foolish enough to hope that things might be different between them. But Brett seemed to go out of his way to avoid her. She sighed. Time had slipped by on wings. They were in a new year, and the King was shortly to be crowned. The King was happy, she knew, despite some matrimonial troubles, and the disastrous ending of the Parliament, which had reconvened on August the first of last year. The Queen was happy too. She glowed with love for her husband, and because of that happiness, she treated her servants almost graciously. Everyone was happy, it seemed, Meredith thought. But she herself was wretchedly miserable.

"Mistress Hartford," a patient voice said, "if you will stand aside from the door, I will announce you."

Startled out of her deep thought, she said in some confusion, "Of course. I am sorry." She moved to one side.

The man inclined his head. Opening the door, he announced in a loud, clear voice, "Mistress Hartford, my lady."

Meredith stepped past him into a room that was all white and gold. Even the furniture was upholstered in a white gold-threaded brocade. Pale January sunlight lay on the thick white carpet, on the jumble of small ornaments that crowded every available space, and lit up a myriad of whirling dust motes. Lady Sarah, in a pale-pink wrapper, was reclining on the couch, her back supported by a nest of vividly colored cushions.

"Meredith, my love!" Lady Sarah exclaimed in her fluting voice. She held out fragile hands. "How good it is to see you at last." Smiling, she received Meredith's kiss upon her delicately tinted cheek. "It has been such ages since I saw you," she added with a hint of reproach. She looked at the manservant. "You may tell Mary Elizabeth to serve refreshments, Brompton."

"Yes, my lady." Brompton left the room majestically.

Meredith had caught the faint note of apology in Lady Sarah's voice when she addressed Brompton. Seating herself, she pulled off her gloves. "The man is here to serve you, Sarah," she said. "You sounded almost apologetic."

Lady Sarah looked at her with an expression of poignant sadness. "I cannot help it, my love. I vow that the great creature quite makes me tremble. Even if Brett did insist that my own servants were deserving of a holiday, I wish that I had brought them with me." She smiled at Meredith. "But there, you must

148

not worry about me and my little troubles. I realize that I am of small account. The world has passed me by. I am past all help, past all happiness." She gave a trembling sigh. "It matters little what becomes of me. Doubtless there are some who will be vastly relieved to hear of my death."

Meredith, who had heard it all before, smiled at her affectionately. Lady Sarah obviously had a grievance she was dying to impart, and sooner or later she would do so. But for all her dramatic affectations there was no more harm in her than in a kitten. "I hope you do not mean that I am one of those who would be relieved, Sarah," she said gently. "If you do, I assure you that you are quite wrong. Now let us have done with such dismal talk. Your well-being matters to a great many people, and you know it."

Lady Sarah, who had been waiting to hear this, mustered a faint smile. "Then perhaps you can tell me, my love," she said, her jeweled fingers resting ominously near the region of her heart, "why my son has only been to this dreadful house on two occasions? I arrived in London four weeks ago, you know. I am only his mother, and a troublesome invalid at that, and must not expect any real consideration. But there, I shall be out of his life soon enough. I have no doubt that he will celebrate on that day."

"Sarah!" Meredith exclaimed, shocked. "How can you be so cruel?"

Lady Sarah's eyes opened wide. "Cruel? But, my love, I do but think of my son and the burden I must be to him."

"Nonsense, Sarah! My lord Foxe, though personally I consider him to be a loathesome man, is a very good son. If he has not been here to see you, then I am sure that he must have a very good reason."

Lady Sarah's fingers began to massage her heart. "Do not be so brusque of manner, dear Meredith, it makes you sound so hard. Indeed you sound exactly like Brett." She lifted a chiding finger. "It is wrong of you to call my dear son loathesome. And you must not call him my lord Foxe. You know well that he would not like it."

"I have told you repeatedly, Sarah, that I care nothing at all for his displeasure."

"I think you like him more than you are prepared to admit," Lady Sarah said archly.

Meredith's face flushed crimson. "I do not. I detest him!"

"I do not understand my children." Lady Sarah gave a little moan. "And you know, Meredith, I consider you to be my own child. Why can you not love one another? Poor Brett! The last time I saw him, I know that he was very upset by your attitude of hostility."

Meredith, knowing that this was only a ploy, said nothing.

Disappointed with her reaction, Lady Sarah said pitifully, "You have tried to excuse my son's neglect of my wretched self. But what of you? What is your excuse, my love?"

"I have sent you notes, Sarah, and gifts," Meredith said in an exasperated voice. "I have explained to you that my duties to the Queen keep me very busy. The Queen is a demanding lady, and can rarely be prevailed upon to grant a leave of absence. This is the first opportunity I have had to get away."

A tap sounded on the door. "Come in," Lady Sarah called in feeble accents.

A short, rosy-cheeked girl clad in a black gown, a stiff white apron, and an oversized mobcap that hid most of her hair, entered the room carrying a tray. With a shy smile at Meredith, she set the tray down on a table beside the couch. "A pleasant good afternoon to you, Mistress," she said.

"And to you," Meredith answered, returning the girl's smile. "You need not wait. I will pour the wine."

The girl bobbed an awkward curtsey, and departed hurriedly.

Lifting the decanter from the tray, Meredith poured wine into two fragile crystal glasses. "There, Sarah," she said, handing her a glass. "Drink it down. It will do you good."

"Thank you, my love." Lady Sarah gave a suffering smile. "But I fear that there is little in this world that will do me good."

"You must not exaggerate," Meredith said bracingly.

Lady Sarah had recourse to her heart. "You would scarcely

believe the palpitations I endure, my love. My only wonder is that they have not killed me off long ago."

"The wine will strengthen you."

Lady Sarah sipped delicately at the wine. Then, in quite a placid voice, she said, "My days are numbered, let me tell you."

"Oh, Sarah!"

"There," Lady Sarah said soothingly, "we will not talk of it since it distresses you. What were we talking about before Mary Elizabeth interrupted us?"

Meredith smiled. "I was about to tell you that I have wanted to see you very much. I have missed you."

"It is kind of you to say so." Lady Sarah smiled at her wistfully. "But who misses an old woman? You must know, dear Meredith, that I am quite old and useless."

Meredith said nothing.

"Am I not, my love?" Lady Sarah persisted.

"You are neither old nor useless, Sarah."

"My dear! Do not bark at me. My nerves cannot endure it. Really, Meredith, you—you sound so masculine."

"I am sorry," Meredith said wearily.

"Have you really missed me, Meredith." She sighed. "I am sure that I would like to believe you."

"Sarah!"

"My love." Lady Sarah recoiled in alarm. "What can I have possibly said to distress you so?"

Meredith set down her glass with a little bang. "I am not distressed, I am angry."

Lady Sarah's lower lip trembled. "I—I do not understand." She shrank back. "My love, pray do not be angry with me. It seems that I always say the wrong thing. Perhaps it would be better if I closed my mouth and never opened it again. That way, you cannot be angry with me."

Meredith's hand clenched on the arm of her chair. She looked at the fragile little lady with smouldering eyes. "Why must you be forever saying such wounding things, Sarah?"

"I did not mean to wound you, my love." Lady Sarah's eyes

filled with tears. Drawing her pink wrapper closely about her throat, she clutched at it with a tense hand. "Pray say that you forgive me!"

"Of course I do, Sarah. I am sorry that I was angry. But, little though you may think it, I happen to love you."

Lady Sarah's face changed, and Meredith had a flashing glimpse of the real woman beneath that pretty, silly façade. "I know you do, Meredith," she said, looking at her with genuine emotion. "I have always known that." She held out her hand. "And I love you. Please believe me."

Meredith clasped her hand, and then released it gently. "I believe you, Sarah." She sat back in her chair. "And you must believe me when I tell you that I have truly been unable to get away. The Queen, owing to considerations of religion, will not be crowned with the King. As for my lord Foxe, he has been kept busy with preparations for the King's coronation."

Meredith looked at her expectantly, but Lady Sarah had retreated once more behind her façade. With startling abruptness, she burst into tears. "Oh, my love!" she sobbed. "I am s—such a wicked old w—woman. I had completely forgotten about the King's coronation. I fear that I—I have m—misjudged my dear son."

So distraught was Lady Sarah, and so anxious to comfort was Meredith, that they failed to hear the bustle of arrival outside.

Brompton, for once failing to move with the majestic step that had irritated Meredith, hastened to open the big front door. "Good afternoon, my lord," he said as the Earl of Foxefield entered the hall.

Brett nodded. "Good afternoon, Brompton. How is my mother?"

"She is well, I believe, my lord. She has a visitor."

"Oh. Who is the visitor?"

"Mistress Hartford, my lord."

"Mistress Hartford?" Brett's black brows drew together. He was silent for a moment, then he said abruptly, "I will not disturb them for a while. I will be in the library. Bring wine, please." He strode away.

Brompton did not immediately move. So it was that way with his lordship, he thought, smiling. My lord might frown all he pleased at the mention of Mistress Hartford, but he had not failed to recognize that certain look in his eyes which told him that his aloof master had a tenderness for the lady. Still smiling, he went on his way.

Brett sat down in the big chair by the window. So the wench was here, he thought, drumming his fingers on the arm of the chair. He was annoyed to find that he was eager to see her. Since that day in his bedchamber, when he had kissed her by force, he had not been able to get her out of his mind. He was constantly thinking of her, and remembering the feel of her lips beneath his own. The wench even invaded his dreams. He thought of one particular time when he had encountered her during his waking hours. He had been talking to Charles, when Mcredith had come toward them. She swept a curtsey to the King and passed on. Charles had looked at him with smiling eyes. "My lord Foxe," he said, "whether you are aware of it or not, your eyes are very revealing when they rest upon Mistress Hartford."

"Revealing? What is Your Majesty's meaning?"

Charles laughed. "Be not so formal, my lord, to your friend. And do not seek to hold me at a distance. I know every twist and turn of your mind. You have fallen in love with that little lass."

"Nonsense, Charles! The wench annoys me."

"She may annoy you, but you are in love with her just the same."

He had not answered Charles. But, as they walked toward their horses, he felt a sense of utter confusion. Was it true? Did he indeed love the plaguy wench?

Only one more remark had Charles made before dismissing the subject. "Lie to others, my friend, if you must. But do not lie to me. More important, do not lie to yourself."

Now, seated in the library, he asked himself the same question. Did he love the wench? Did he love that thorn in the flesh who had ever tried her best to drive him insane with rage? His frown deepened. He did not want to be in love. He did not want to feel himself bound to any woman. Do not lie to yourself, Charles had said. His hand clenched as he faced the truth. Very well, he would not lie. It was true. For his sins, he had fallen in love with her. What a damnable plaguy thing was this love business. It stole upon you unaware, and before you knew it, you were deep in its toils. He smiled bitterly. Love her or not, he had little chance with her. The wench hated him. She had made that abundantly clear. Speaking of Mistress Hartford, Henrietta Maria had said, ''She is in love with you. Did you know that?'' In love with him. What nonsense! Nay, he would never make a fool of himself by declaring his love. Were he to do so, the bloody pig-headed, mealy-mouthed little bitch would laugh in his face.

Brett rose abruptly. Annoyed with himself, but nonetheless impelled to see her, he strode from the room.

When Brett entered his mother's room, he found Meredith stooped over the couch trying to comfort the bitterly sobbing Lady Sarah.

Meredith started violently as she saw him. ''My lord,'' she said, bright color flooding her face, ''I had not thought to see you here.''

He gave her an unsmiling nod, then he went to his mother's side. ''Mother!'' he laid a hand upon the heaving shoulders. ''What is it? Why the devil are you crying?'' Turning his head, he glared at Meredith. ''I might have known,'' he said harshly. ''Wherever you are, trouble follows. What have you said to upset her so?''

Recovering from the shock of his unexpected appearance, Meredith faced him indignantly. Her eyes took in his appearance. His black riding clothes were dust covered, as was the black and red cloak swinging from his shoulders. Her eyes dwelt meaningly on his dust-filmed boots, then she looked at him again. Ignoring his previous remark, she said in an accusing voice. ''No matter how busy you may be, my lord Foxe, I see that you still find

154

plenty of time to go riding. It might be as well were you to devote a little of your time to your mother.''

The knife-tongued bitch! Why had he the misfortune to love her? He suddenly felt very sorry for himself. Determined to show no emotion, unless it be anger, Brett tossed his leather gloves and his plumed hat onto the couch. "You will mind your own business, Mistress Hartford. What I do with my timo is scarcely your affair. What have you been doing to my mother?''

Lady Sarah found her voice. "Brett, my dear boy!'' she wailed. Picking up his hat and his gloves, she clutched them tightly to her bosom. She looked at him appealingly, her lips trembling in her tear-streaked face. "Pray do not enrage yourself, love. Meredith has done nothing.''

Knowing his mother and her nervous storms, Brett had no difficulty in believing her. But his fury, because he could not dislodge his love and his desire for Meredith, overcame him now. "Do not try to protect her mother,'' he said in a hard voice. "I intend to hear what this mischief-making chit has been saying. Well, Mistress Hartford, I am waiting.''

Meredith trembled with anger. The great black-browed bully! How dare he call her names. Forcing herself to ignore the wild appeal that, even in her anger, he made to her senses, she smiled at him scornfully. "Could it be that your conscience is troubling you, my lord? What is it you fear that I have told Sarah?''

Whatever reply he had expected her to make, it was not this. Even in her scorn and defiance, she looked so damned beautiful! He suppressed a desire to go to her and take her in his arms. Carefully nursing his anger, he said, "I will ask the questions, Mistress Hartford. What have you been saying to my mother? Out with it!''

It was easy to sustain his anger, he found, when she said nothing, but merely allowed the scornful smile to widen slightly. Curse her, he would like to strangle her! A pulse in his temple began to beat violently. "Do you intend to stand there grinning at me like a cursed loon, Mistress Hartford? Have you nothing to say for yourself?''

"Indeed, my lord, I have something to say. Has it never occurred to the awesome my lord Foxe that his mother might be weeping because of his callous indifference?"

Lady Sarah took one look at her son's blazing eyes, then, with a moan, she collapsed against the cushions. "Oh, Meredith, my love," she cried, "you must not say such things. You will only anger him the m—more!"

"Will I?" Meredith's calm collapsed. "I care nothing for his anger. To the devil with him, I say! I do not fear this bullying lout!"

"Lout?" Lady Sarah's hands fluttered in frantic appeal. "My dears, you must not quarrel! Can you not love each other, as does any normal brother and sister?"

Brett seethed inwardly. He wanted to shout at her, but she is not my sister, I am not her brother, that is the trouble. He looked at his mother coldly. He should be grateful that his love for this abominable shrew was not apparent to her. He said in a goaded voice, "Pray be silent, Mother. Allow Mistress Puritan to explain herself to me, if she can."

"If you are waiting for me to explain to you, my lord Foxe," Meredith said haughtily, "I fear that you will have a long wait."

"Will I so, Mistress Hartford," Brett said, taking a menacing step toward her. "Nay, I think not. If I have to shake words out of you, I will do so."

He was capable of anything, Meredith thought with a touch of fear. Ignoring the danger signals she saw in his eyes, she said in a high, breathless voice, "You are mistaken if you think you can intimidate me, my lord. What right have you to ask anything of me, you who are nothing but a lecher, and a false friend to the King? You have managed to wheedle your way back into his good graces, have you not? But the fact remains that you did betray him!"

Brett lost his head completely. "You slut! You evil-minded little bitch! I ask you how you dare to come here and pour your dirty little stories in my mother's ears?"

"Aye," Meredith shouted, "I have told Lady Sarah all. And if the stories be dirty, it is you and your lechery to blame. Is that what you wanted to hear me say, is it? Shall I tell her more? Perhaps she would like to hear of the disgusting picture you made when you stood in your bedchamber with the Queen in your arms. How dared you kiss that French whore, how dared you!"

"No! No!" Lady Sarah shrieked out in horror and despair. "It is not true, Brett. Meredith has told me nothing. Oh, my dear boy, can you not understand that she is but trying to anger you the more?" Her eyes turned to Meredith. "Say no more, Meredith, I implore you. Indeed you must not say such things about my poor innocent boy!"

Brett did not hear her. Much of his anger had been feigned for his own self-protection, and he had not really believed that Meredith had told his mother about that particular incident. But she had told her. She had admitted it. He was conscious of a sharp disappointment in her. He loved her, he admitted it freely. No matter what she might say or do, he knew that he would always love her. But for all that, he had no illusions about her. She was willful, stubborn, often bad-tempered, and she could be foolishly carried away by a persuasive tongue spouting new doctrines or ideas. But he had not thought her to be capable of this malicious tale-bearing. Anything else he might have expected, but never that! His anger was genuine now. God rot her malicious tongue and her unforgiving heart!

"Well, my lord Foxe?" Meredith's sharp tone stung him back to awareness. "What have you to say to me now?"

Despite the sharp voice, he saw that her mocking smile had returned. He lunged toward her, letting his fury and disappointment dictate his actions. Lifting his hand, he struck her hard on the cheek. "That is what I have to say, Mistress Hartford!"

Lady Sarah screamed. "Oh, pray do not, Brett! A gentleman must not strike a lady!"

Meredith, who had swayed with the force of the blow, recovered herself. Her cheek stung and burned and her eyes watered. With a choked exclamation, she struck him in return. "I hate you!" Hysteria seized her, and she continued to strike him. "I hate you! Hate you!"

Brett grabbed her roughly. "You damned little hellcat! Don't you know that I could break you in two, if I so desired?"

Panting, she struggled to break his hold. "Then do so, my lord Foxe, if it pleases you! By God, you swine. Were I a man, I would run you through!"

"Would you?" he said through gritted teeth.

Her eyes dilated as he thrust his face close to hers. With his glittering eyes and his black scowl, he looked mad. "Do you intend to kiss me again, my lord Foxe?" she shouted. "Do you, for the second time, intend to demonstrate the contempt in which you hold me? Go on, then. You know that I have not the strength to stop you. But know this. I care nothing at all for your opinion of me!"

His fingers tightened painfully on her arms. "Be silent!"

"Why do you not silence me, then? Force is the only way you can do it. Go on, kiss me as you would a cheap whore. As you would the Queen. But she is deserving of it. She is a whore!"

His eyes were narrowed and cruel. "You are strangely insistent, Mistress Hartford," he said in a rough voice, pulling her closer. "One would almost think you wanted me to kiss you."

"You? I had sooner kiss a snake! You revolt me! I warn you, my lord, if you kiss me, I shall—"

"I know," he interrupted, "you would vomit. You told me that once before. Remember?"

Remember! How could she ever forget? She had thought and dreamed of nothing but his kiss. He was laughing at her! She was suddenly afraid that those eyes of his could penetrate into her head and lay bare her pitiful and hopeless love for him. Tears filled her eyes and ran down her cheeks. "It is true," she said in a shaking voice. "I would vomit!"

The sight of her tears drained the last of his anger away. The trembling of her mouth unmanned him. He would kiss her, but not in contempt. She hated him, but he would have this one kiss to remember, he groaned inwardly. This was love? This melting feeling, this desire to hold her gently and beg for her forgiveness? Were all men made into weak fools by love, or only he?

She was bewildered by the change in his face. Why did he look at her in that strange way? His head came closer, his breath fanning her mouth. Tomorrow, she thought, she would have black bruises on her arms. The bruises would be a momento of his violence, of the desire he had to punish her. She tried to speak, to close her eyes against him, but she could only stand there staring at him, the tears still running down her cheeks.

"Do not cry," Brett said in a hoarse, strained voice. Other words clamored to be spoken, and he found he could not prevent them. "Please, love, do not cry. Forgive me!"

Meredith's eyes flew wide with shock. He could not have called her that little endearing name. Her ears must be deceiving her. "Wh-what did you s—say?"

His hand came up to touch her tumbled hair, then he drew a caressing finger gently down her cheek. "I am asking you to forgive me. I am saying something I vowed never to say, for I know well that you hate me. I am saying that I love you. Laugh if you will, and that will be my punishment. But it is true."

She began to tremble, and she felt his arms tighten about her. Had he guessed that she loved him? Was he playing some cruel game with her? "I forgive you, my lord Foxe. I hope that you will also forgive me."

She had spoken stiffly, but there was something in her eyes that made his heart beat wildly, a softness, a glowing. Was that love he saw in them? Impossible! She hated him! "Merry!" Again the words seemed to be forced from him. "Merry, answer me truthfully. Do you love me?"

"My lord"—her voice dropped to a whisper—"pray do not continue with this jest."

"It is no jest. A thousand times or more I have cursed myself for a fool, but it would seem that I cannot help loving you."

"My lord!" Surely it was truth she heard in his voice? Even he would not be this cruel.

"I ask you again, Merry. Do you love me?"

Her mouth opened to deny it, but she could not. "Yes," she whispered. "Yes, my lord."

"What did you say? I did not hear you."

"Yes!" she shouted. "Yes, yes, yes! Laugh if you will. But I do!"

"I will not laugh, my love, my darling! Oh, Merry, my Merry!"

Lady Sarah shrieked a protest as she saw Brett bend his head and press his lips to Meredith's. "Oh, Brett, pray do not! I know you are angry, but you must not treat Meredith so cheaply! Brett, stop!"

Brett lifted his head and looked into Meredith's eyes. "It is true?" he said in an unsteady voice. "You would not play with me, Merry? You do love me?"

Now she could no longer doubt. "Oh, yes, Brett, yes! I have always loved you!"

"Always? But I thought—"

She stopped the words with her hand. "Always," she said. "But I could not let you know it. I was afraid that you would laugh at me."

Lady Sarah was deaf to their words. Completely distraught, she wrung her hands together. Meredith had said, "Kiss me as you would a whore." And he had done so. He was still doing so. Brett had many faults, but until this day she had always believed him to be a gentleman. She pressed a quivering hand to her forehead. "Oh, please!" she cried. "My nerves cannot stand much more. Brett, you must not continue to insult her. You must not kiss her again!"

Meredith heard her. "Did you hear, my darling?" she said, smiling at him. "Lady Sarah has forbidden you to kiss me. Do you intend to obey that command?"

"Never!"

"It is as well, for I would never have forgiven you."

He kissed her again, then crushed her closely into his arms.

"Why the devil did I have to fall in love with a cursed bold-tongued shrew? Will you answer me that?"

She clung to him. How was it possible to be this happy? "I am not a shrew. I am very sweet and docile."

"Bah!" He kissed the tip of her nose. "Your many faults stagger the imagination. I know that women have a propensity to mold their mates nearer to their hearts' desire, so what of you? What do you hope to make of me?"

"Their mates?" She stared at him. "Are you asking me to marry you?"

"Nay. I want you for my mistress."

"My lord!"

He laughed. "Of course I am asking you to marry me, and you know it. Come now, answer my question."

"What answer can I give you? You would not allow me to mold you. And I assure you that I have no desire to do so."

"You arc wise. I love you, Merry, never doubt it. But I would not allow you to rule me. Remember that."

"Are you threatening me, my lord Foxe?"

"Warning you that I will stand no nonsense. You need a firm hand, wench."

She was too happy to be indignant. "But, my lord," she said demurely, "may I not be allowed to rule you now and again?"

He laughed down at her. "Aye, love, as long as you confine your rule to the bedchamber."

Lady Sarah lay back and closed her eyes. What were they whispering about? If she could rely upon the evidence of her ears, Brett had used Meredith cheaply, and yet they were both laughing. What was the world coming to? Meredith had been insulted. The least the wretched girl could have done was to have screamed, or fainted. Aye, fainted. That would have been the best. But no! With the degenerate morality of these modern times, she stood calmly in Brett's arms, laughing like a strumpet. They hated each other, as both had assured her repeatedly. Had it not been for that, she might have believed them to be in love. In love! Only a short while ago they had been glaring at each other with such hatred that she had feared it would bring on her palpitations.

"Mother," Brett's voice said. "What is it? Are you ill?"

Startled, she opened her eyes and looked up into his face. Then, sighing, she directed a reproachful look at Meredith, who stood by his side. "Small wonder if I were ill," she said bitterly. "But at least I have been spared that calamity. If you wish the truth, I am distraught."

"But why, Sarah?" Meredith said anxiously.

Lady Sarah gave vent to a burst of hysterical laughter. "You ask me why I am distraught?" she said passionately. "You can actually stand there and ask me that? How is a mother supposed to feel when her son strikes a defenseless female in the face? What is she supposed to think when her ward invites her attacker to—to kiss her like a whore?" She shuddered. "Shameless! I am ashamed of both of you!"

"Mother," Brett said, laughing, "you have not been using your ears."

"You were whispering. I tremble to think of what you might have been saying to each other, indeed I do. To think that you, Meredith, a delicately reared girl, and a Puritan, could laugh and condone my son's disgraceful conduct!"

Meredith could not believe that this spirited woman was the gently complaining Lady Sarah. If a butterfly had flown through the window and bitten her, she could not have been more astonished. There was vivid color in her cheeks, her eyes were glittering with anger, and she was displaying more life than she had done for years.

Meredith glanced at Brett, then looked quickly away. "There was nothing disgraceful about it, Sarah," she said gently. Then, on a purely mischievous impulse, she added, "I really quite enjoyed it."

The spirited Lady Sarah fled. "Enjoyed it!" She uttered a quivering shriek. "Oh, this is too much! Meredith, I greatly fear that you are immoral. It is the influence of that man Cromwell, I know it. I should have put a stop to it from the very beginning!''

''What has Oliver Cromwell got to do with anything?'' Brett put in, half amused, half impatient. ''I want you to listen to me, Mother. Meredith and I are going to—''

''No!'' Lady Sarah put her hands over her ears. ''I refuse to listen.''

''Why the devil not?'' Brett said, annoyed. ''I do not understand your attitude, Mother.''

''Mine?''

''Yours. Though how you can be said to have an attitude if you will not listen, I do not know.''

Lady Sarah turned apprehensive eyes to Meredith. ''Why is he angry with me? Should I not be the one to be angry?''

Meredith knelt by the couch and took Lady Sarah's hand in hers. ''I hope, instead of being angry, that you will be happy for us. Brett and I are going to be married. There, you see, I am not immoral, am I?''

Lady Sarah's jaw dropped. ''You are—are going to be married?'' She looked from one to the other. ''You and—and Brett?''

''Yes.'' Meredith smiled and glanced up at Brett, pure love in her eyes. ''It is no wonder you are astonished, Sarah. I can scarcely believe it myself.''

''But you hate each other!''

''No, Sarah. I have always loved Brett.''

Lady Sarah turned her bewildered eyes to her son. ''And you, Brett, have you always loved Meredith?''

''I suppose that I must have done, Mother. It took me a long time to realize it.''

''I see,'' Lady Sarah said. She put her hand to her head. ''No, no, I do not see! Well, I have always wanted a marriage between you. But it seemed that you could never meet without quarreling. I simply do not understand how this has happened.''

''But it has happened,'' Brett said, smiling at her. ''So be glad for us. In any case, I have no doubt that we will always quarrel.''

Lady Sarah blinked anxiously at Brett. "But, my dears, what will your life be like if you are always fighting?"

"Very stimulating," Brett said. "You are a fraud, Mother. You know well that you fought with my father all the time."

A tender smile touched Lady Sarah's lips. "Yes, Brett, we did fight. That was because my darling always insisted upon having his own way."

"And you wanted your way, Mother?"

"Yes. But it usually ended with your father having his."

"In this marriage, Mother, I shall have my way."

Meredith snorted. "We shall see, my fine m'lord."

"You have made me very happy," Lady Sarah said with her wistful smile. "A little while ago, I thought I was going to be ill, for I had some alarming symptoms, but now I feel much better."

"Of course you do," Brett encouraged her. "You have no time to be ill, Mother. There are preparations to make. I want to marry Meredith as soon as the King has been crowned."

Lady Sarah looked very pretty in her flushed excitement. "The sooner the better, my darling boy. And when the wedding is over, may I stay on at Foxefield Hall?"

"Of course. You have no need to ask permission. You are not a prisoner."

"I know that. Pray do not be angry with me, darling."

Brett sighed. "When have I ever been angry with you?"

"Many times, my darling."

Brett brushed this aside. "Well, I am not angry now. You should have told me that you wanted to go home. I thought that you wished to live in London."

"I thought I did, Brett. But Foxefield Hall is filled with memories of your father. Those memories often bring me pain, but I would not exchange one of them. No, not if the whole of London was offered to me."

"I understand, Mother. If you wish, you may go back before the wedding."

"Before? But surely you will be married from Foxefield Hall?"

Brett laughed. "Where else? I was waiting for you to suggest it."

"But why? Naturally you will be married from there." She glanced at his smiling face. "Oh, I see. You were teasing me."

"Only a little."

Lady Sarah settled back happily. "It is going to be a wonderful wedding! Do you know, children, I believe that I can die happy now."

Brett frowned and moved uneasily. "Let there be no talk of dying, please."

"Oh, no, not if you do not wish it." Lady Sarah beamed upon them both. "I feel so much better, it would not surprise me if I were to recover my health completely."

Meeting Meredith' smiling eyes, Brett lifted an eyebrow. "Amen to that, Mother," he said.

"Now, Brett," Lady Sarah said with a trace of reproach, "there is no need to employ sarcasm. You know well that I am in very delicate health."

"Nonsense!" Brett began. "You are perfectly well aware that—"

Meredith darted him a warning look, and said hastily, "Brett did not mean that, Sarah. It is simply that he does not like to think of you being ill. But we both know that your health is precarious. Do we not, Brett?"

"In any case, Mother," Brett said, evading the question, "I was not being sarcastic. I was expressing a fervent hope."

Lady Sarah said doubtfully, "As long as you understand my extreme delicacy, I forgive you."

"Thank you, Mother."

Lady Sarah gave him a sharp look. But evidently deciding to overlook the dry tone, she smiled at Meredith. "Are you not ashamed of the names you have called my son? I am so glad you have come to realize what a dear boy he is."

"The blindness of a mother," Brett murmured.

Meredith laughed. "Aye, my lord, 'tis fortunate for you, is it not?"

"What do you mean, Meredith, my love?" Lady Sarah said indignantly. "I would have you know that Brett is a very good boy."

"Mother, please!"

"Well, it is true, is it not, Meredith?"

"No," Meredith said firmly. "He is very bad tempered, and can, at times, be excessively disagreeable."

"My love!"

"It is true, Sarah. But despite his faults, I love him."

Lady Sarah's smile returned. "In that case, my love, there is nothing to worry about, is there?"

Chapter Nine

Attended by his retinue, the King passed into the huge hall of Westminster Palace. A coldness that had nothing to do with the weather or the atmosphere of the hall crept over him. He gripped his fingers firmly together hoping to hide his trembling hands. His lips felt dry, and his heart was behaving so erratically that it seemed to him to be shaking his body. The smothering fear he had felt in the early hours of the morning was with him again, attacking with renewed intensity. For it was on this day, this day of pale sunshine, with an unusually soft wind that held the first faint scents of the approaching spring, that he was to be crowned King of England. How would the generations to come view this solemn moment in their history? Would they look back on this date, Thursday, February 2nd, 1626, and curse it? he asked himself, or would they bless his name? Would they say of him that he had been a good King, a King who had loved his people and had, to the best of his ability, been scrupulous in his sworn duty toward them? Or would they say he had been a scourge, and that England had been well rid of him?

He closed his eyes momentarily, trying to compose himself. Despair mingled with his fear. A King was but a mortal man, he made mistakes. But often the people did not think of him as a man with human weaknesses. He must be above reproach, and certainly he was not allowed to make mistakes. He must deliver the country from pestilence, from enemies who menaced its shores, from famine, and from economic disaster. He must, in short, be able to inspire his people and to create miracles. But what if he failed them! Oh God, don't let me fail! Help me to do Your work, and through You, to uphold, strengthen, and to carry my country and my people on to a glorious mark in history! I would be to them more than a King, I would be father and mother also. Help me, I pray You!

Soon now, he would be entering Westminster Abbey, that place that was a monument to beauty as well as to England's glory. Where kings had been crowned since the reign of William I. Where kings and great men lay entombed in the incense-perfumed silence. He thought of the great lofty nave vault, more than 102 feet in height, under which he would shortly stand, of the Abbey's lancet arches, the great clear story windows, and the magnificent fan vault. He had always thought the fan vault the most beautiful of the Abbey's many attractions. It had a delicate lacelike design from which hung pendants, looking like frozen tears. When he was a child, he had thought of that elaborately beautiful ceiling as a huge web spun by magic spiders. The hanging pendants had been the tears of the spiders' victims. He felt a touch of awe when he thought of the fact that one of the churches on the Abbey's grounds was said to have been built in the year 616. And when he thought of the men who had designed such beauty as the Abbey contained, he was awed afresh, for upon such men God had surely laid His hand.

The King's thoughts came to an abrupt end. His eyes widened, and his breath caught in his throat. A violent shudder went through his body. It was as though he had seen a sudden vista of blackness, certainly he had experienced a chill premonition of disaster and tragedy. He could not know what the future held for him, it was not given to man to know, but it was almost as if God, hearing his prayer, had delivered a warning to him.

Buckingham had a favorite expression. "I feel as though somebody is walking over my grave." It had felt like that in a way, Charles thought, and yet more as if the shadow of God hovered over his grave. Did that shadow linger in pity, or in wrath?

Charles shook his head to clear it. He saw my lord Foxe and my lord Buckingham standing nearby. His eyes roved about the hall. He was surrounded by a formidable company of nobles, the Peers of England, and his own personal servants, and yet he had this frightening feeling of being completely alone. What was the matter with him? Was he then so weak that he must find himself a prey to these odd vapors and superstitious premonitions? He lifted his head high. He was Charles Stuart, King of England. He believed that he had much to give his people. With the help of Almighty God, he would rule wisely and well, and he would no longer allow doubts to crush him. He had a destiny to fulfill, and he would fulfill it, so help him God!

Charles caught my lord Foxe's concerned eyes upon him. At sight of this old friend, Charles's smile was spontaneous, and he nodded his head reassuringly. But that same smile became fixed as the newly created Knights of the Bath came forward to lead him to the prepared throne in the center of the hall. As always, the glistening purple satin of their robes brought back the poignant memory of the time he had witnessed the elevation of Henry, his much loved brother, to Prince of Wales. You should be here now, Henry, he thought, not I. You would have made the better King. The people loved you. I pray that they will learn to love me too.

Seated, Charles greeted the Archbishop of Canterbury and the other church dignitaries. He received into his hands, clasping them briefly, before returning them to the Duke of Buckingham, Constable of England, the sacred ornaments long used in the crowning of the Kings of England. But even as he held them, he could not seem to concentrate his mind on the reality and significance of the moment.

One by one they came to him, kissing his hand and bowing before him. Some clad in vivid robes of silk, satin, or velvet, some in dignified black with gold crosses glinting against the somber background, others in copes and surplices with great lawn sleeves lavishly trimmed with lace. He greeted them automatically, but all he could think of was his father's reign, and the mistakes he had made.

King James's Court, the people said, had been corrupt. They whispered that he had many times attempted to play off one powerful country against another, not for his people's gain, but for his own. He had been weak and vacillating, they said, too easily led astray by his pampered favorites, and far too extravagant, for the comfort of those favorites, with England's coffers. But Charles did not believe this of his father. Despite all evidence to the contrary, he believed that James had been sincere, and that he had meant well by his people. Perhaps he was blind to their needs, he thought, but let me not be equally blind. Let me profit and learn from his mistakes.

Absently, Charles acknowledged William Laud, the Bishop of St. David's. There had been many great men in his father's time, his thoughts roved on, and there were great men in his own. He remembered how his father had mourned the passing of William Shakespeare. The great Elizabethan poet had outlived his Queen, Elizabeth I. He had died in his home at Stratford-on-Avon, on April 23rd, 1616. Charles remembered Will well. The poet, clad in dusty velvet robes, his quill perpetually stuck behind his ear, his blue eyes far away, his lips moving as fresh ideas entered his head, had sometimes condescended to play with him. Will had not been very good at play, though. In the middle of being a horse, or some other animal, he would suddenly topple his young rider from his back, while his lean finger feverishly wrote words in the dust. Words that he would later transcribe on parchment. At James's command, Will had come often to Court, but he was never at ease there. He was not awed by the King, and many times told him quite sharply that the atmosphere at Court stunted his ability to write. But nothing could stunt Will's genius,

Charles thought, his claim was merely a ruse to escape to the green beauty of the Stratford-on-Avon countryside. Another of the Elizabethans, Sir Walter Raleigh, had been executed in James's reign, supposedly for treason, in the year 1618. And Francis Bacon, Lord Chancellor of England, had been arrested on a charge of corruption.

Unaware of the speculative glances cast his way, Charles's thoughts drifted to his mother. He had a sudden longing for her sturdy and invigorating presence. Unlike his wife, Henrietta Maria, who, though proclaimed Queen on June 21st, 1625, had refused to take part in the coronation because the service was Church of England, she would have upheld him in this awesome and rather frightening time. But his mother, Queen Anne, was dead. She had died at Hampton Court on March 2nd, 1619.

He remembered vividly the night before her death. He had been seated in a chair beside her bed, holding one of her wasted hands. "Go home, my son," the Queen had said, her eyes bright and imploring. "My time has come. I love you dearly, yet I would not wish to carry the memory of your grief to my grave. Go home! Go home!"

It was because of the life in her eyes that he could not believe she was dying. "I will not go," he had answered her. "I have come to wait upon Your Majesty, and here will I stay. In all save this one thing, I am, as ever, your devoted servant."

"My servant?" Queen Anne had managed a faint smile. "I am an enchantingly pretty piece to wait upon, am I not, my servant?"

The only other words he had heard her say were, "Commend me to your sister. Tell her that I ever loved her and held her dear to my heart."

He would remember his mother always, Charles thought, for he had loved her dearly. She had been pretty and flighty, for so he had often heard his father complain, but she had matured into a good wife, a good Queen, and a loving mother. Would it be so with Henrietta Maria? They quarreled less now, and there was love between them, but she was still headstrong and intent upon

171

gaining her own way. Once she had made up her mind, nothing, it seemed, could move her. As in this instance, when she had refused to enter the Abbey, and, if not take part in it, at least witness his coronation. He had been very angry with her, and he was still angry.

"Your Majesty," Buckingham's voice said, "pray come with us now."

Charles rose to his feet. There was no more time for memories, he told himself, as he walked from the hall. The moment was upon him, and he must now, once and for all, conquer his fears and apprehensions.

The morning sun was warm upon his velvet-clad shoulders as he and his royal procession walked along a path covered for the occasion with a thick blue and silver carpet. Just as they entered the doors of Westminster Abbey, he heard the great clock of Westminster striking the hour of ten.

Before the King went his marshals and his trumpeters, the Aldermen of London, the Knights of the Bath, the Barons of the kingdom, heralds, the Lord Archbishop; the Earl of Montgomery, bearing the spurs, the sceptre, by the Earl of Salisbury, the sword of Temporal Justice, by the Earl of Kent. Bishops clad in scarlet, their rich robes trimmed with fur; Viscounts in velvet coronation robes, holding in their hands their caps and coronets. There was the portly crimson-clad figure of the Lord Mayor of London, holding firmly to his mace. Rainbow-colored light from the Abbey windows glittered on the sword called Curtana of Mercy, held by the Earl of Essex, on the crown of St. Edward, borne by the Earl of Pembroke, and on the sapphire and gold of St. Edward's chalice, carried in the hands of Doctor George Monteigne, the Bishop of London.

With the singing of the gentlemen of the chapel sounding in his ears, the King walked beneath a canopy of scarlet and gold, held by the Barons of the Cinque Ports. He was supported on either side by the Bishop of Bath and Wells, and the Bishop of Durham. His train of purple velvet, which was more than six yards in length, was held by the Earl of Warwick and Lord Maltravers.

Entering into the church, Charles paused for a moment to greet the Prebends of Westminster. Bishop Laud now came forward. His thin face was grave as he placed into the King's hands the staff of King Edward the Confessor. The anthem sung by the choir sounding throughout the church, the King made his slow way to the throne.

The service began with the commanding voice of the Lord Archbishop, who presented the King to the Lords and Commons, to the nobles on the east side of the Abbey, the clergy on the west side, and the people on the north and south.

"Do you now consent to the coronation of King Charles, who is your lawful sovereign?" the Lord Archbishop cried out challengingly.

There was a moment of silence. Charles wondered what would happen to this awesome ceremony should they refuse. Then the silence was split asunder. Four times the shouted consent thundered forth. "God save King Charles!"

The first oblation was made. Feeling as though he walked in a dream, the King made his offering before the altar of a pall and a pound of gold.

Listening to the sermon, movingly delivered by Doctor Richard Senhouse, who had been his chaplain when he was Prince of Wales, the King was painfully aware of the concentrated gaze of many eyes. He had always been shy, and a hot flush stained his cheeks. He had so many things to learn, not only how to be a fair and a good King, but smaller things, like controlling his shyness and conquering his slight stammer.

Despite all his efforts, the doubts attacked him again as he rose to his feet and went to stand before the Archbishop. He felt insignificant and unworthy as the coronation oath was read out in the Archbishop's loud clear voice. Following immediately after the Archbishop, John Buckridge, the Bishop of Rochester, read the "Admonition of the Bishops for the privileges of the church."

Charles moved to the high altar. Making his oath, he thought that his voice sounded weak and unsteady. "I will observe my promises. I will be as every good King in his kingdom ought to be. I will be the true Protector and Defender of the Bishops and the churches under their government.'' He placed his cold trembling hand upon the great gold-bound bible. ''The things which I have here promised, I shall perform and keep. So help me God!''

The ceremony seemed to Charles to go on and on endlessly. He was aware of the beginning of a headache as he listened to the litany and the prayers. Once more he rose from his chair. In accordance with the ritual, he went to his chair of state on the north side of the Abbey, where he seated himself.

An inclination of the head from the Earl of Worcester, brought him to his feet again. Standing before the altar, he was divested of his outer clothing. He stood there before his people, a slim, almost boyish figure in his white satin doublet and hose, his dark curling hair touching his shoulders.

A slight querying murmur went up at the sight of the King clad in white satin. It had always been the custom of Kings at their coronations to wear the royal purple, and this departure from the normal had surprised and disconcerted the assembled people. ''The white King,'' the Earl of Fulton whispered to his neighbor.

The murmur died as the Lord Archbishop took the left arm of the King, and the Bishop of St. David's his right, and led him to the coronation chair. The anointing of the King was about to begin.

The King received the silky coolness of the holy oil into the palms of his hands. With bowed head, he listened to the lengthy prayer that followed, and to the sweet singing of the anthem in the background. At the conclusion of the prayer, the oil was touched to his breast, between his shoulders, on both shoulders, the crown of his head, and the hollows of both arms.

The Bishop of St. David's, smiling with affection upon the King, took up a fine white linen cloth, and, except for the head and the hands, dried the places of anointing. This done, he carefully closed the King's doublet.

More prayers followed. Then the linen coif was placed upon

174

the head of the kneeling King. His arms were raised and long linen gloves were drawn on. Clasping his hands together, Charles made his reverence before the altar. Then he was assisted to his feet, and he was clothed in the robes of King Edward the Confessor.

The prayers of the Arhbishop followed after the King, and the singing rose to the great vaulted roof as he moved once more to the chair below the altar. The King sat upright, his eyes looking straight ahead, as the hose of cloth of gold were put on him, and his feet fitted into cloth of gold sandals. The Duke of Buckingham, Master of the King's Horse, knelt at his feet and put on the spurs.

Once more the King rose and went to the altar, where the Archbishop placed into his hands the sword. A Peer moved forward. Taking the sword from the King's hands, he girded it about his sovereign's waist. Archbishop Laud placed the stole about the King's neck, and draped his shoulders with the mantle.

His heavy robes trailing, the King returned to his chair, the chair wherein reposed the traditional Stone of Jacob. The crown was now placed upon the altar, and the Archbishop intoned a prayer. Picking up the crown in both hands, the Archbishop moved over to the King. Stooping, his lips still moving in prayer, he carefully placed the heavy crown upon the King's head.

"God save the King," the choir sang in an ecstasy. "God save the King!"

Now the cry was taken up by the people, and it rose above the singing of the choir. "God save King Charles! Long may he reign over us!"

Tears of emotion standing bright in his eyes, the King watched the flurry of movement as Viscounts and Earls rose in their richly canopied stalls and put on their scarlet velvet caps circled with a coronet. He saw my lord Foxe standing tall and straight, the cap and coronet upon his dark head. He looked, Charles thought, with his grave handsome face and his tall imposing figure, more like a King than he did himself.

Now the King was invested with the ring. It was placed upon

the fourth finger of his right hand. Again he rose and went to the altar, where he offered up his sword. A Peer, redeeming it, took it from the altar. The blade flashed as he drew it forth from the gold-embroidered scabbard and held it before his face. During the rest of the ceremony he would hold it in that way and carry it before the King.

The Archbishop, turning from the altar, placed the sceptre in the King's right hand, and the Earl of Pembroke came forward to support his arm. The rod was put into the King's left hand. Holding them, he was assisted to kneel before the altar.

There was a buzzing in Charles's head as he listened to the Archbishop pronouncing the blessing. This was he, Charles Stuart, crowned and anointed in sight of his people, kneeling before the Archbishop.

His dreamlike state increased as he was helped to his feet and led to the throne by the Peers of the Realm. He heard the choir begin the *Te Deum*, and he did not realize that there were tears upon his cheeks.

The singing ended. "Your Majesty!" somebody spoke with quiet urgency.

Recalled to his duty, the King drew forth a parchment from his robes and handed it to the Lord Keeper. Coventry, the Lord Keeper, read it aloud, stating that the King, under his seal, offered a pardon to all of his subjects, no matter their crime, if they were disposed to take it.

When the Lord Keeper's voice faded into silence, the drums and the trumpets began to sound forth. "God save King Charles!" the people cried in ringing voices, and above the tumult there rose once more the clear triumphant chanting of the choir. "God save the King! God save the King!"

The smell of incense was heavy in the King's nostrils. The vivid colors of the robes, the flash and glitter of jewels met and merged together, swirling before his eyes. For a panic-stricken moment, he thought he was about to faint. He drew a deep breath, and was relieved to feel the weakness passing.

Smiling, he received his subjects. They came to him one by

one, kneeling at his feet to offer him their reverence and devotion. When they rose again, he inclined his left cheek for their kiss of duty.

"Well done, my liege," a familiar voice whispered in his ear.

Charles acknowledged my lord Foxe's comment with a faint smile.

Except for the high Mass, the second oblation, and the communion, the coronation was over. Now, indeed, in the eyes of God and of his people, he was truly King of England.

"Behold, God, our Defender," sang the choir, "look Ye upon the face of Thine anointed—"

Aye, look upon my face, dear Lord! Charles prayed silently. Aid me in my task that I may prove worthy, a true servant to this sacred earth, this glorious realm, this England! My England! And when my days are ended, let it be said of me that I served my people well. But know this. I will serve Thee first, and England next. Always and forever I will serve Thee first!

Chapter Ten

The year 1626 had been a disastrous year for the King of England. Starting with his coronation, which had been all that he desired, he had felt armored by the love of his people. But February 6th, four days after the coronation, had been the beginning of the disasters, for Parliament had once more assembled.

The parliamentary session had started badly. The committee for the Commons had drawn up a list of many grievances and abuses, which, they said, were detrimental to the rights and liberties of the people. Chief of these grievances was the levying of tonnage and poundage without the proper consent and authority of Parliament.

Charles, bewildered and stunned by their vehemence, by the odd temper that seemed to be prevailing throughout the House, had replied to these charges. But it seemed that they did not want answers, it was more as if they demanded vengeance for a great many abuses, both real and imaginary. There was uproar in the House. The members shouted passionately against the leniency toward Roman Catholics, declaring it to be a disgrace in a Protestant country that had suffered many times under the despotic heel of Catholicism. Why should not the penal laws against Catholics be increased in severity? If this was not done England might again, to her everlasting humiliation, to say nothing of the terror of her subjects, come once more under the dominance of Catholicism. Such a thing would result in a witch hunt of loyal Protestant citizens, in a tragic blood bath, such as had been experienced in the reign of Mary Tudor.

From this, they went on to an attack against the Duke of Buckingham. That evil, traitorous, and disloyal man, who was, they said, the instigator and the cause of many of the evils now attacking the country. Red-faced, determined to be heard, tempers steadily mounting, the members roared their denunciations against him. Buckingham, who gave evil and misleading advice. Advice that, while it brought the country to a sorry pass, greatly enriched the pockets of the gentleman himself. Buckingham, who had the King's ear, but cared nothing for England itself.

Things came to a pitch when, in May, Sir Dudley Diggs and Sir John Eliot gave to the House of Peers their carefully drawn-up papers of impeachment against the Duke of Buckingham for that House's scrutiny and judgment.

The King, upset and angry, had gone before the House of Lords. He had told them in no uncertain terms that "My lord Buckingham has done nothing that does not carry with it the express seal of my approval. My lord of Buckingham is an honorable man. He is a man who greatly honors his King and loves his country. My lords, you must look elsewhere for a victim, and for the author of these ills of which you speak. For I assure you that my lord Buckingham is in no way at fault."

"Who, then, Sire?" he was asked politely. "And may we respectfully remind Your Majesty that we do not seek a victim. We seek only to uproot the evil at England's heart."

Reigning in his temper with some considerable effort, the King had replied, "My lords, I would say this to you. Speaking for myself, my reign has just begun. There is much that I must do.

Much that must be corrected and improved upon. But in the matter of my lord Buckingham, grant me the wisdom to recognize duplicity in the men that serve me, if duplicity there be. But I tell you now that duplicity and self-seeking are no part of this man's character. After God, England and the welfare of my subjects are first with me. Think you that I would let any man stand in the way of that? I hold my lord Buckingham in great affection and esteem. But not even he would I allow to lead me from the path of my sworn duty. No, my lords, he has made mistakes, as do we all. But there is no evil in him.''

But the papers of impeachment stated that the Duke of Buckingham was guilty of the mismanagement of the affairs at present in his extremely incompetent hands. That he had been allowed to give support to France. Support that had resulted in the murder and the suppression of a great many innocent Huguenots: thus bringing about much grief and calamity; and strengthening the grip of Catholicism. That he was involved too in the buying and selling of important offices. And therefore the King's reply to these charges against the Duke, his taking to himself the blame for Buckingham's crimes against the country, and his vigorous attempts to paint Buckingham as an innocent and greatly misunderstood man had brought about a resultant coldness from both Houses toward their monarch.

"God rot it!" Diggs had shouted, quite beside himself and apparently forgetful of the King's presence. "The man is a traitorous swine! A knave! A cur!"

" 'Tis truth he speaks," Sir John Eliot supported him. "Had I my way, Buckingham would be flung in prison, there to await a traitor's fate!"

Looking about him the King saw hostility in all their faces. Only one man, my lord Butler, seemed unmoved. He was writing on a paper before him. It was as though he had no part in the uproar. He looked up at that moment. Seeing that the King looked his way, he studied him intently with his grave dark eyes, then he smiled a slow, charming smile.

The King knew something of my lord Butler's history. He had a reputation for being a great scholar. He was a man who seemed curiously withdrawn from the world about him. Who displayed no particular interest in his seat in the House, or in the political issues that constantly raged. He was handsome, though somewhat severe of countenance. It was said that he longed for a son. But with his whore of a wife, the Lady Mary Butler, it was doubtful if she ever stayed with him long enough for him to plant his seed in her perpetually unslaked body. Lady Mary scorned her husband's attentions, for apparently she despised him. My lord Butler, on the other hand, despite every shame she had brought upon his name, was reputed to adore her.

The King returned my lord Butler's smile. The Earl nodded in answer, then looked down once more at the paper before him. But the small incident served to hearten the King. He felt that he had found a friend, and he determined to further his acquaintance with the Earl of Butler.

The King, perhaps too aware of his dignity, saw in the attack upon Buckingham an indirect attack upon himself. He therefore issued a command that Sir Dudley Diggs and Sir John Eliot were to be arrested and imprisoned in the Tower. However, they spent less than a week in the grim confines of the Tower, for the Commons refused to admit that they had shown disloyal behavior, or used language that might be offensive to the King's ears. To show their determination, the Commons then vowed that they would refuse to continue the session until such time as Sir John and Sir Dudley were set free. The King perforce assented to their release.

Not until the month of June did the Duke of Buckingham make his answer to the charges brought by the Commons. They listened to him, their faces cold. He could not tell if he had reached them or not.

He was soon to find out. Sir Richard Deerborne, gray-haired, massive of figure, and choleric of temper, lumbered heavily to his feet. "Gentlemen," his voice rang through the House, "I demand that we draw up a paper petitioning the King to remove the Duke of Buckingham from all offices at present held by him!''

Sir Richard met the Duke's incredulous eyes. His full lips curved into a disagreeable smile, showing small stained teeth. ''Aye, my lord Buckingham, that is my demand.''

Wincing a little, Sir Richard rested one hand on his massive stomach. ''A little indigestion, gentlemen,'' he said, making a tame attempt at a joke. His hand rubbed his stomach in a circular movement. ''I further demand,'' he went on, ''that, until this scoundrel be removed, we issue a flat refusal to His Majesty to grant him any further monies to carry on this foolish war with Spain.''

A gasp went up from the assembled company. Sir Richard's words bordered on treason. Nevertheless, when silence was once more established, his demands were considered, and, finally, approved.

The King could not believe it. How dared they! He came once more to Parliament. ''My lords, gentlemen,'' he addressed them, his head lifted in arrogant rebuke, ''to show my trust in my lord Buckingham, I have this day recommended that he be given the office of chancellor of the University of Cambridge.''

He looked into their lowering faces. ''Further to that, I declare this Parliament to be dissolved.''

''Your Majesty!'' Lord Ravenscroft, together with the other lords of the council, rose to his feet. ''Sire, might there not be a delay in the dissolution of this Parliament? We have been assembled a scant four months. There is much business to conduct. Necessary business to do with the good of the kingdom.''

Charles looked at him stonily. ''I would delay, were it for the good of my kingdom,'' he answered. ''But it is not, my lord, I can see no point in these bitter and senseless wranglings over much-needed money.'' He rested his hands in the bar before him. ''And I will listen no longer to these lying charges against my lord Buckingham, who is one of my most trusted subjects.''

''Your Majesty!''

182

Charles's eyes were drawn once more to the Earl of Butler. For some reason that he could not define, he felt an affinity with him. The gentleman was, as usual, unflustered, and he seemed to be engrossed in something that lay just outside the window to his left. The King and the noisily protesting members might not have been there for all the notice he was taking. And yet the King thought he could sense the Earl's unspoken sympathy. He shrugged. Doubtless it was all in his imagination. He faced erstwhile loyal subjects who had somehow inexplicably become enemies. Whether their enmity would last he did not know. But he had no intention of humbling Buckingham and stripping him of his posts of honor. He trusted him and believed in his good intentions toward all. In the matter of the Earl of Butler, it was simply that he felt the need of a friend in the enemy camp. Butler might be that friend, or there might be yet another enemy behind that impassive face. Who could tell?

The King raised a hand to quell a further protest from Lord Ravenscroft. "Nay, my lord, not for one moment will I countenance a further delay. This Parliament is herewith dissolved."

The great doors were flung open. As the King strode from the chamber, the Earl of Butler's eyes followed him. He felt pity for Charles Stuart, who had been forced to assume the heavy burden of troubles left behind by King James. And a greater pity that Charles, who was obviously sincere, could believe in the integrity of such a man as Buckingham. The Stuarts were a stubborn breed, he knew. Once their loyalty and friendship was given, it was given for all time. An admirable trait no doubt, but one that was apt to blind them to a present danger.

From the King, the Earl's thoughts drifted to his wife. At the moment Mary was in residence in Milford Manor. What was she doing now? What man lay in her great canopied bed and spent himself within her lovely body? O Christ, a plague on the whore! If only he could stop loving her. If only he could forget how it had once been before the seeds of her unquenchable hunger for sex, sex with any man save himself, had taken root. He had not understood when her illness had first begun, for he could only think of it as an illness. He had raged at her, struck her, and had finally been reduced to pleading. Because of his lack of understanding, Mary was unforgiving. Driven by her bodily hunger, she remembered only his cold refusal to sleep with her until such time as her sordid cravings left her.

She had laughed when he pleaded, high, shrill laughter. "Nay, my lord," she had said, "you are too holy for me. My sordid cravings, as you choose to call them, will never leave me." Hands on her hips, she deliberately swayed her body. "See what you have given up, my lord. When first you refused to come to my bed, I swore that I would never again allow you to touch me. I despise you, holy man!"

"You cannot mean what you are saying, Mary. I will forget your past infidelities. It will be as it once was."

"Pray leave my bedchamber, my lord. I wish to disrobe."

"Other men have seen you disrobe," he could not resist the bitter sneer, "so why not your own husband?" He hesitated, then he heard himself apologizing. "I did not mean to say that. Pray to forgive me."

"Why should you not say it?" she answered him calmly. "It is true."

She stepped out of her gown. Beneath it she wore nothing. He stared hungrily at her small breasts, and then was sickened to see that she had painted her nipples a bright red. It was the trademark of the London whores.

She revolved slowly before him. "Look well, my lord," she taunted. She stopped before him, her eyes gleaming. "Are my breasts not soft and white?" she said, cupping them with her hands. "Dost remember how you once kissed them?"

"Stop it!" he shouted. "Can we not talk together, mayhap arrive at some solution? You must know that I want a son."

Her eyes opened wide in pretended amazement. "A son? Do you really, John?"

"Yes, yes! What man does not?"

Her eyes were bright with mockery as she answered him.

"Then you must take that holy body of yours and sire your whelp upon another woman, for it will not be me. Tonight I lie with another John. John Bascome, who, you have ever assured me, is one of your greatest friends." Her small teeth gleamed in a smile as she moved nearer to him. "John has a great lusty body, he will satisfy me for an hour or two. But never you, my lord, for you are but a pale shadow of a man." She spread her legs apart. "What would you not give to enter me, you priest! You monk!"

He had hit her then, knocking her to the floor. Then true madness seized him, and he flung himself upon her and began to beat her savagely. Dear Christ! That beating had aroused in her a frenzy of desire. Her hips arched upward invitingly. "You can be a man, then," she panted. "Take me! I won't fight you. Take me!" She took his head in her hands and tried to drag it down to her breasts. "Come, fool! What are you waiting for?"

Breaking her hold, he rose to his feet and looked down at her writhing body with sick eyes. "May God strike me dead if I ever touch you again!"

On hands and knees now, whimpering like the sick animal she was, she begged him. "You can't leave me like this! In the name of the Virgin, have pity!"

"Be silent! 'Tis profanity on your lips."

"My body is burning. Oh, God, you do not know what it is like! I must have ease!"

"I have told you to be silent."

"I will give you your son. Anything! Marcus, you told me you wished to call him. Help me, John, please. I am in torment!"

He could not speak. He turned from her and left the room. Her frenzied screams seemed to fill the house.

"My lord Butler?" a harsh voice scattered memory.

He looked up to see Sir Richard Deerborne bending over him. "Yes," he said in a thick voice. "What is it?"

Sir Richard frowned at him. "I know not why you trouble yourself to attend the sessions, my lord. Are you by any chance aware that the King has adjourned Parliament?"

"Naturally I am aware of it."

"I would not have thought so, my lord. If you please, may we now have your full attention? There are certain matters we must talk over." Sir Richard looked at him curiously. "You were not in this chamber with us, John, that I know. Of what were you thinking?"

"Of a woman. A whore."

Sir Richard smiled. "A likely piece, is she?"

"A very likely piece. You would be quite enchanted."

"Then you must give me an introduction to this enchanting doxie." Sir Richard put a plump hand on John's shoulder. "And now to business, my friend."

Words eddied and flowed. Concentrating, John managed to forget Mary and his barren life. He heard acid recriminations against Buckingham, against the King. Their dissatisfaction with the present state of England's affairs became more pointed.

Invited to speak, John said in his quiet voice, "My faith is not in my lord Buckingham, I think I have made that clear. But I have much faith in our King. I feel sure that he will, eventually, see Buckingham in his true light."

"He is bedazzled by the man!" somebody shouted angrily.

"His Majesty has had cause to remind us that his reign has only just begun," John went on calmly. "Might I suggest that we give him a chance to show his worth?"

Eliot jumped to his feet. "With Buckingham hanging on his coattails?" he exploded. He clenched his hands together. "By Christ, but the Stuarts are a feckless lot! Mark me well. King Charles will be just such another as his late and unlamented father, King James."

John's dark brows rose. "You speak treason," he said coldly.

"Then by Christ's bleeding wounds, my lord, if I speak treason, let it be so recorded. I'll not recant one word. I will stick to my belief!"

"And so will I," John answered, smiling slightly. He met Eliot's blazing eyes. "I will not record your treasonable speech. 'Tis a matter for your own conscience. You are entitled to your

186

beliefs, but I am likewise entitled to mine. I say before you all that I believe Charles Stuart will be a good and a wise King."

Seated in his barge, on his way back to Whitehall Palace, the King scarcely listened to the conversation of his gentlemen. Trying to swerve his mind from what he considered to be the blind stubbornness of the gentlemen of the Parliament, he thought instead of John Milford, the Earl of Butler. He believed that Butler would be a good man to have at one's side, and he made up his mind to send for him.

Two days later, he did so. The Earl of Butler, unlike Buckingham, who was away on the King's business, had little to say to his King. Certainly he made no attempt to fawn or to flatter him. But there was something in his calm manner and in his way of looking at him that gave Charles a new confidence in his own abilities. Together with my lord Foxe, who had taken an unusual and immediate liking to the Earl, the three men spent much time together. Temporarily, at least, Charles forgot his troubles. Now and again the chill premonition he had felt in Westminster Hall returned to plague him, but he nonetheless felt full of optimism for the future.

This optimism was somewhat quenched by a series of domestic quarrels with the Queen. Henrietta Maria sincerely loved Charles, but she was not above hurting him. And then too, she was too often goaded into indiscretions by the malicious promptings of her French attendants. Love had not gentled her tongue. Her imperious demands became so excessive that they bordered on the ridiculous. All must attend Mass, whether or not they were of her faith. All must be plagued by priests, whose duty it was to turn them from their souls' blindness to the glory of the True Faith. And Henrietta Maria must have three new gowns for every day of the year. She must have plumed hats to go with her morning gowns; feathers, ribands, perfumed gloves. And she must not be disturbed from her pleasures to solace the King in any troubles pertaining to England. She loved him. But the country and its stubborn, stiff-necked, and aggressive people were no concern of hers. Her country was France. True, she was Queen of England, but in her opinion that did not mean she must learn to love the country, or understand its people. She saw no reason either why she should master the English language and, consequently, did not make the smallest effort to do so. Her conversations with the King, or anyone else who came within her orbit, were conducted in French. Should anyone venture a few words in English, she would look at them with deliberately blank eyes, a petulant frown creasing her smooth forehead.

One evening, while dining, Charles came at last to a firm decision. The Queen, not troubling to hide her displeasure, had begun to upbraid the King in a shrill voice for some trifling fault. She was heedless of her husband's smouldering anger, or of the embarrassed faces about the board. Her voice went on and on, getting shriller by the second, until the King, rising and taking his departure, stopped the words on her lips.

When the Duke of Buckingham returned to the palace in late July, the King ordered him to make arrangements to ship the French retainers back to their own country.

"But, Sire," Buckingham said warningly, "would it not be better to wait until I have thought of a plan? You would not wish to be in violation of the agreement you made with the French."

"I care nothing for that," the King snapped. "I will be rid of them once and for all." His face flushing, for not even to Buckingham could the King speak with ease on this delicate matter, he went on, "I feel that the Queen and I could be very happy were it not for the cursed French. They constantly make mischief and incite the Queen to fresh displays of petulance and bad manners. It will not do. I must be rid of them!"

Buckingham complied. On August 8th, the French, except for two priests and a few of the French servants who had no real place of importance, and therefore no influence over the Queen's mind, sailed for France. Some, who had missed their homeland, were eager to be on their way. Others, who saw their cherished ambitions of a high place of honor in the English Court receding, were sullen in their manner and threatening of speech. To all of this Buckingham turned a deaf ear. Regardless of possible consequences from an irate Louis XIII, he herded them aboard as if they had been, as the King had more than once remarked, so many wild beasts to be driven away from England's shores.

Charles was never to forget the night when he went to the Queen and told her that she must now say farewell to her French retainers.

At the King's request, Henrietta Maria was alone in her apartments. At first she had not believed him. She stood before him, her dark eyes flirtatiously inviting, her face slightly flushed. She was lovely in her gown of emerald-green satin with its lacy gold overskirt. Diamonds sparkled from the gold rosettes adorning her green satin slippers. More diamonds flashed from her ears, and from the wide collar about her throat. Her childishly rounded arms jingled with gold bracelets set with diamonds, rubies, and emeralds.

"Oh, no, my husband," she answered his announcement. "You know well that we have spoken of this before. You agreed that my servants should stay."

"No, Henrietta, you are mistaken. I would never have agreed to such a thing."

"Well, perhaps you did not exactly agree. But it was understood between us, was it not?"

"Not by me, Madam. Henrietta, I mean what I am saying."

Now she believed him. "But—but you cannot do this. What of the promises you made, the marriage treaty you signed? Would you break faith with my brother, the King?"

"To secure one's happiness from the interference of foreigners is not, in my opinion, breaking faith."

"Foreigners!" she spat the word at him. "How English you are. How contemptuously you say that word. The arrogant Englishman who expects all others to crawl at his feet! It is as if all who are not English are scarce worthy of your regard. That is your opinion, is it not?"

It was not now and had never been his opinion, but her rising voice annoyed him sufficiently to goad him to sarcastic retort. "Well are they?" he answered in a cool voice.

"Why you—! How dare you!" she shouted. "I am a foreigner! Hast forgot?"

"So you are. But you must not let that distress you. You are my wife, and the Queen of this land."

"Damn you! As for this land, this miserable fog-bound land, I hope it sinks into the sea! 'Tis true that I am your wife, 'tis true that I am the Queen. But that does not make me English, and never think that I do not thank the good God for that!"

If she saw him as a bigoted Englishman aware only of his own importance and that of his country, then she did not know Charles Stuart. But he was angry enough now to foster the idea. Curse the little shrew! Let her think as she pleased. "Even foreigners," he replied, ignoring the rest of her words, "can in time, no doubt, be molded nearer to the heart's desire."

She did not see that he was deliberately goading her, and she shouted at the top of her voice, "I am French! French! Never will you make me into one of your grim and humorless English-women. For that is your heart's desire, isn't it?"

"But of course." He smiled. "It is a very strange thing, but foreigners usually believe that the English are not possessed of a sense of humor. Quite the contrary, we have a pronounced humor. But perhaps, though, it is a little too subtle for their taste."

"You—you arrogant man!" She clapped her hands over her ears. "I will not listen to another word. And I tell you once and for all that I will not, under any circumstances, part with my servants!"

"And you say that I am arrogant, Madam? However, so that you will be under no delusion, I will make it clear to you that the arrangements have already been made. They go. That is my last word on the subject."

"No, no!" She burst into loud hysterical sobbing. "I—I will n—not live in this Court s—surrounded only by your ab—abominable English."

He had scarcely understood her words, so distorted and tumbling were they, but she was hysterical, and the hysteria must be stopped before she created another unfortunate scene. He lifted his hand and slapped her smartly across the face. "That, Madam, should put a stop to any further hysteria," he said coldly. "I will go now. When I judge that sufficient time has passed to enable you to come to your senses, I will return."

Her body still racked with sobs, she stared at him unbelievingly. Then her face distorted into a mask of pure rage. Eyes blazing, she flew at him. She was like an angry cat. Her pointed nails raked at his face, leaving long, angry furrows, her small feet kicked hard and savagely at his legs. "I will kill you for that, you—you thrice accursed English pig! I spit on you! I spit on your country!"

He grabbed at her hands and forced them downward. Wrapping his arms about her, he held her so tightly that she was unable to move. "I am pleased to know your opinion, Madam. But if you utter one more word I will break your damned neck!"

His arms were like a vise about her, she could scarcely breathe. "You have no right to speak to me like that!" she managed to gasp.

"Not another word!"

Without warning, she rested her head against his breast in defeat. "Oh, Ch—Charles, you have used me ill! How could you do it, when you—you know how much I love you?"

"Love is not shown in screaming abuse, Henrietta." He loosened his arms and held her more gently. "Love is shown in a desire to make the other happy."

"But—but you have m—made me very unhappy. I wish my servants to—to s—stay."

"Their departure is for your good as well as mine."

"Do you—do you still love m—me?"

"I will always love you, dear heart."

"And you do not mind that I am a f—f—foreigner?"

He laughed softly. "Oh, sweetheart, I would love you were

your skin as black as ebony. Come now, let us not indulge in such silly talk.''

"I am g—glad you love me.''

She began to sob like a heartbroken child, her body shaking in his arms. He was adamant. He would not give in, he dared not give in, not if they were to have any kind of life together. Henrietta Maria must cease to be the spoiled and petted child. If she could not love him as a woman, then it were better not to have her love at all.

Perhaps Henrietta Maria sensed this thought. For, after weeks of crying and pleading, she suddenly changed. There were still the occasional bursts of temper, but on the whole she was reasonable. The King, knowing her so well, was suspicious of the meekness she displayed. He suspected it was a surface meekness that might at any moment erupt into violent rage and shouted accusations.

If Henrietta Maria had changed in her attitude toward the King, she had not done so toward the Duke of Buckingham. She believed, not altogether without cause, that the man had too great a hold on her husband, and that his influence was greater than her own. So, consequently, she did not trouble to hide her hatred. She wished him dead, and she said so loudly and publicly.

When the King remonstrated with her, Henrietta Maria said defiantly, ''Sire, am I not allowed to have my likes and dislikes?'' Without waiting for an answer, she had gone on quickly. ''I tell you to your face that I loathe and despise my lord Buckingham.''

So the year had worn to its end. The only bright spots being the coronation of the King, and the wedding, in July, of the Earl of Foxefield and Mistress Meredith Hartford.

As a further token of her new and astonishingly good behavior, Henrietta Maria had been eager to accompany the King in his attendance upon the wedding at Foxefield Hall. Clad in white silk embroidered all over with pearls, her dark hair piled high and circled with a slender coronet of diamonds and pearls, the Queen, with her vivid brunette beauty, rivaled the new Lady Foxefield.

Meredith had been robed in white satin, the bodice covered with silver lace, the sleeves slashed with cloth of silver. Her bronze hair was threaded through with emeralds and pearls. If the Queen's eyes dwelt rather wistfully on the tall bridegroom clad in dark-blue velvet, she did not allow her secret thoughts to show. The King had been very proud of her that day. She held herself with dignity, as befitted a Queen, and she was gracious to everybody.

Only one small incident had marred the occasion for the King. My lord Foxe, accompanied by a churlish-looking fellow, had approached him. "Your Majesty," Brett said, bowing, "may I present to you a near neighbor of mine, Mr. Oliver Cromwell."

There had been a wry twist to Brett's mouth as he spoke, and the King concluded that he did not like the man.

"I trust, Mr. Cromwell," the King said when the man had straightened from his bow, "that you are enjoying this festive occasion?"

The man had answered politely enough, but his words were strange and disagreeable to the King's ears: and there had been an expression in the light-blue eyes that he could not like. "I thank Your Majesty for your graciousness. I feel sure you will forgive me if I answer you with truth. I am honored and pleased to attend this wedding, but I would not have done so had it not been for the urgings of my frivolous wife. There is too much feasting, too much imbibing of wine to suit my tastes. And, forgive my frankness, Sire, too much touching and caressing."

Seeing the King's cold blank stare, Cromwell had added hastily, " 'Twas not my intention to offend Your Majesty. But with my own eyes I have seen couples clutched together in rooms where they should not be."

"And where you should not be, Mr. Cromwell," the King could not resist the remark.

"I crave Your Majesty's pardon. I am a bluntly spoken man, I know."

"You are dismissed, Mr. Cromwell."

Bowing, Cromwell had backed away, and the King turned to

give his attention to Brett, who was smiling with unconcealed amusement. "Is he not a self-righteous worm, Charles?" Brett said in a low voice. "I thought an encounter with the Puritan Mr. Cromwell might amuse Your Majesty."

But the King had not been amused. To his great annoyance and bewilderment, the memory of Cromwell's cold blue eyes had haunted him for weeks afterwards. He could not seem to drive the man from his mind. There had been an aura about him, an aura that was threatening and dangerous, that had made him feel that he personally was threatened.

He might have put it down to an overactive imagination had not Henrietta Maria, some time afterwards, exclaimed, "Charles, I keep thinking of that man Oliver Cromwell. I spoke to him for a few moments, you know, and I did not like him at all." She was silent for a moment, then she added, "Why should I think of him, a man like that? I know it is very silly of me, but there was something about him that quite frightened me. He was smiling, yet methought I detected menace in his eyes. Why should I fear him, Charles? How can he, who is naught but a country bumpkin, harm me?"

"Dear heart," Charles had consoled her, "you are not likely to see him again. You know well that it is your custom to make mountains out of molehills, and it will not do. Mr. Cromwell, I have no doubt, is a very ordinary and hard-working man, and scarcely worth such concentrated attention. His manner was not overgracious, though he did strive to be polite, but that, as far as I know, is all that is against him."

"Perhaps you are right, Charles. It was simply that, for some reason that I cannot fathom, he struck me as a very dangerous man."

A dangerous man, the Queen had said. He himself had called him an ordinary man. But Oliver Cromwell was no ordinary man, and the King, even as he had said it, had somehow known that. But since he had not nor ever could have any part in his life, he refused to brood more upon the matter. He told himself that there were those in this life who made an instant impression. Mr.

Cromwell had done that. A cold and disagreeable impression, it was true, but nonetheless an impression. And that, the King told himself firmly, was all there was to it.

Oliver Cromwell was forgotten as the troubles of England began to occupy the King's mind more and more. England was not only at war with Spain, but trembling on the brink of a war with France. Parliament remained adamant. The King, in his stubborn loyalty to the Duke of Buckingham, remained fully as adamant as they, and he continued to try to raise money by any means available to him. He was desperate. Money he must have in order to prosecute the war, a war that had not been started by him, but which he was honor bound to carry on. So far, Parliament had refused to grant their King one penny, and, for the present moment, it was stalemate.

The King, though he hated the necessity, for the members of the Commons had deeply offended him, knew that he must recall Parliament. He had not yet fixed the date in his mind, but call them he must. With as much patience as he could muster, he would lay his case, their country's case before them once more. If they still refused to grant him the sorely needed money, then he must think of further schemes whereby he might obtain it. He did not intend to see England forced to her knees in humiliating surrender. Surely, he told himself, the Commons would come to see it that way too.

Chapter Eleven

Seated in the carriage beside Brett, Meredith glanced surreptitiously at his absorbed profile. She was finding this silent journey to Foxefield Hall excessively boring. But, with rare discretion, she kept her tongue still. Doubtless Brett was thinking of the King and his obstinate Parliament, for nothing else could bring that particular look to his face. Or it might be that he was pondering on what would be the outcome of the parliamentary session the King intended to call on March 17th. She herself was concerned with recent happenings. There was an uneasy air at Court. The Queen, unconsciously responding to the prevailing uneasiness, was more difficult than ever before. What would this year of 1628 bring? Meredith wondered. Would it bring yet more troubles, or would the storm clouds that seemed to be gathering slowly and inexorably about the King disperse?

Meredith frowned. As yet the King's troubles had no definite form, but something was wrong. Whenever he appeared in public he was acclaimed wildly. Why then did she have this feeling that there seemed to be a spreading and sullen undercurrent of discontent among the people gathered there to cheer him? Did the King sense it too? Her frown deepened. Perhaps he did. Since that first and second Parliament there seemed to have been a subtle change in him. It was as though, somehow, he had grown immeasurably older and much graver. His smile was not so much in evidence these days, and his dark eyes were increasingly mournful. More and more he relied on the comfort of his friendship with Brett, my lord Butler, and the detestable Duke of Buckingham, whom, Meredith could not but feel, was the cause of the trouble. Although he had never said so, she was certain that Brett felt the same way about the Duke. But there was nothing Brett could do about that particular relationship. Not even he could persuade the King to relinquish his friendship with Buckingham, or to curtail some of the man's power. The King's affections, once given, were deep and enduring. He was loyal to Buckingham, and though the nurturing of such a friendship might lead to disaster, he would continue to be loyal. Buckingham, the King believed, was more sinned against than sinning.

Gripping her hands together inside her brown fur muff in an attempt to thaw them, Meredith settled herself more comfortably against the padded backrest. Perhaps, if she remained quiet, Brett would come far enough out of his abstraction to address a few words to her.

A smile touched her lips as she thought of the quarrel they had had last night. They had been married almost two years now, and, even as Lady Sarah had foretold, they quarreled often and violently. There were times when Brett, who, she had found, was no gentleman when his temper was stirred to boiling point, was even provoked to physical violence, which she returned in full measure. But the quarrels were part of their life, they added the spice, while their love added the sweet. They were both strong willed, both determined to have their own way, but they knew that nothing would ever kill the love between them.

The quarrel last night had been because of her insistence that they both request permission from the King and Queen to retire permanently from Court life. Brett had been equally determined not to be swayed from his duty to the King.

"Why will you not listen?" Meredith had cried. "I do not care for Court life."

Looking at her coldly, he had said in that quelling voice that always infuriated her, "You may request permission from the Queen to be released from your duties, if it please you to do so. But do not expect me to do likewise."

"Aye, my lord Foxe," she shouted, "you would like that, would you not?"

"What the devil are you shouting about? And what do you mean by that remark?"

"I mean that if I am away from Court, you need only trouble yourself to see me on the rare occasion!"

"Madam," Brett answered her, "if it please you to think so, then that is your affair."

"For the last time. Will you request the King's permission?"

"I will not." Seeing that she was about to make a furious rejoinder, he added curtly, "I know not what is happening about the King, Meredith, but these are uneasy times. Even if I wished to do so, I would not desert him now."

"Who speaks of desertion? 'Twill only be that you will not be so much about him."

"The matter is closed. If you wish, and if the Queen grants permission, I will find you a house in London." He smiled sarcastically. "In that way, my lady Foxe, I will not stray too far from your side."

"London!" She thrust out her underlip sullenly. " 'Tis not the place I had thought to bring up our child."

"When we have a child," he said, turning away from her, "I will give the matter more serious consideration."

Staring at his broad back beneath the well-cut wine-red velvet jacket, her anger had been replaced by a surge of love. It was not the way she had planned to tell him, but she let the words come. "My dearest lord Foxe," she said softly, "perhaps you should consider it seriously now."

He stiffened. "What do you mean?" he said, turning quickly to face her. "Merry, are you"—he broke off to stare at her incredulously—"Merry, are you with child?"

"I am, my lord Foxe. Your child."

"So I should hope." He ran his fingers through his dark hair, at a loss for further words.

She looked at his unsmiling face in dismay. "Are you not pleased, my lord?"

"What cursed rot are you babbling now? Of course I am pleased, you addle-pated wench! But you are too young to be with child. I cannot allow it."

"You cannot allow it! Oh, my lord!" she broke into laughter. "I am neither too young nor too addle-pated to bear a child, and there is certainly nothing you may do to forbid its birth."

He looked at her helplessly. "Merry, 'tis a hazardous thing to bear a child. Women have been—been known to die from the strain of the birth."

She ran to him. "Come, my lord Gloomy, you need have no fears for me." She put her arms about his neck. "I will not die, I promise you."

He drew her close to him. "If you do, my lady Foxe, know you now that I will never forgive you."

"Nay, I shall still be here to plague you. But, m'lord, will you not speak a few words of welcome to our child? He is scarce alive as yet, but I doubt not that he will make shift to hear his father's voice."

Her words seemed to galvanize him into action. With a swift movement he swept her up into his arms. "You must not stand too long, 'tis dangerous. If women were to rest more, 'twould not be such a dangerous time at the birthing."

Trying to control her laughter, she wriggled in his arms. "Nay, love, put me down."

"Are you laughing at me?" he asked her in an ominous voice.

"Aye," she confessed, "just a little."

He was astounded, outraged. "Laughing! I am distracted on your behalf, and you are laughing at me!"

She touched his dark scowling face with a caressing hand. "Come now, my lord, you know well that you are more distracted on your own behalf. Is it not so?"

He did not answer, and she went on coaxingly, "Pray put me down. I will come to no harm, my darling, I promise you. 'Tis my belief, you see, that when a woman is with child, she should walk regularly."

He stared at her as if she had been stricken with madness. "Walk! Nay, I forbid you to stir a step. Now indeed you must seek your release from the Queen's service."

She could not believe that this was her strong, self-contained Brett. It took her a long time to calm his most unusual fears, and she had reminded herself that it was, for him, a most unusual situation. Eventually she had managed to persuade him that disaster would not instantly dog her footsteps if she indulged in a daily walk. But then nothing would do for him but that he must carry her off at once to Foxefield Hall. Lady Sarah would be delighted with her news. And there, at the Hall, she must bide for a few weeks to get some good fresh air. "It will be excellent for the child as well as yourself," he had concluded firmly.

Dismayed, she had cried out in vehement protest that she would not leave him. "And anyway," she had added, thinking to triumph, "the Queen will never give her permission for me to be gone for so long."

Brett was adamant. "You may safely leave it to me. I will arrange all."

To her disappointment, he had arranged it. The Queen had even called her into her presence. Henrietta Maria, dressed in a vivid yellow gown, a wreath of satin-petaled diamond-hearted buttercups adorning her dark hair, had shown her first kindness to her English lady-in-waiting. "My lady Foxefield," the Queen cried in great excitement, "this is wonderful news I hear." Impulsively, she had kissed Meredith's cheek. "So there is to be a little my lord Foxe, yes?"

Meredith could scarcely believe that this was the same Henrietta Maria who had treated her with spite and a total disregard for her feelings. Her eyes were warm, her smile kind. "Your Majesty is gracious," she answered.

"I will be more so," Henrietta Maria said, gesturing with her jeweled fingers. "If you will allow it, I will be godmother to your child."

Meredith bowed her head, hoping to hide her amazement. "I would be so honored, Madam."

Pleased with her, the Queen kissed her cheek again. "Then it is settled. Mayhap, my lady, you will pray that I too may soon be blessed with a child?"

"I will indeed, Madam."

"There, run along. You must reassure your anxious husband, must you not?"

So here they were on their way to Foxefield Hall. Meredith sighed. She would have to stay for a few days, of course. But weeks? No, nothing could keep her from Brett's side for that long.

Meredith glanced at Brett again. He was still engrossed in his thoughts. She smiled to herself. How like him to display such frantic anxiety on her behalf at one moment, and on the next to behave as though he were completely alone in the carriage. The news she had given him had, for her sake rather than his own, she guessed, temporarily stunned and alarmed him, but now he was himself again. My lord Foxe would deal with any situation, whether it be a pregnant wife, an ill turn in the fortunes of the King, pestilence, or sudden war, in his usual cool and competent way. Only she, it seemed, could shake him from that composure. And only she, she thought with a touch of pleasurable smugness, who knew the man of violence and fire hidden beneath his rather austere exterior. Even the King was unacquainted with that side of his friend.

Shivering in a gust of wind, Meredith looked through the window at the passing scene. England in its infinite variety, she thought. Though the air was chill, the pale-blue sky was bright with thin March sunshine. Small fleecy clouds, pursued by a boisterous wind, skittered across the sky like playful lambs.

Meredith craned her head to look at a cart just ahead of them. The cart, drawn by a wearily plodding black and white horse, was piled high with dead branches. The driver, clad in a brown smock, a shapeless hat drawn down low over his eyes, suddenly drew the cart to a stop. Jumping down from his perch, he gathered the reins in his hand and led the horse along.

The carriage passed the cart in a whirl of fine brown dust. Meredith grinned as she heard the carter's shouted curses. She saw cottages with low, thatched roofs that looked like frowning brows above white-painted walls. Little gardens that were bright with flowers. Flowers bloomed along the sides of the rutted road, too. In a tangle of daffodils, crocus, the butter-yellow of cow-slips, the more vibrant yellow of buttercups, and the virgin-white and green-veined delicacy of snowdrops. The wind-tossed trees were clothed in the bright green of leaves just unfurled. Lilac trees were tightly budded and not yet ready to release their perfume, but Meredith, with that flying lift of the spirits occasioned by the season, imagined that it was borne to her on the wind. It would not be too long before the trees would be heavy with the hanging purple and white clusters of blossoms, and the air redolent with their piercingly sweet fragrance.

"You are very quiet," Brett's voice said in her ear. " 'Tis most unusual in one who is forever plaguing my ears with her shrew's tongue." He prodded her lightly with his cane. "What are you gaping at?"

Laughing, she turned to him. "I would have you know, my lord Foxe, that I am no shrew. Save, of course, for those times when you aggravate me into being so."

"What nonsense. Were I a man of good sense, I would have you permanently clapped into a scold's bridle. But what did you see that so occupied your attention?"

"Gaping, was the word I think you used, my romantic husband. Since you have not seen fit to speak to me, and have generally behaved as though I were quite invisible, I have been admiring the day, and gaping, as you call it, at the beauty of the flowers."

Brett sat back, his face beneath his wide-brimmed plume-laden hat thoughtful. Meredith believed that he was about to make an important pronouncement. Instead, he said calmly, "Though you be a strumpet and a troublesome wench, yet you have behaved yourself. I believe, yes I really believe that I will condescend to speak to you."

"Pray do not trouble yourself, my lord. I am quite happy in my solitude."

"Are you, by God!" The jeweled buttons on his crimson velvet tunic flashed in the sun as he leaned forward to grab her. "That is treasonable talk, my wench." He pulled her roughly across his knees. "But you are happier this way," he said, smiling down at her. "Come now, confess."

"I will do nothing of the sort," she said, avoiding the smiling blue eyes. She straightened her green bonnet which had been knocked awry. "Very much against my will, my lord, you have decided to banish me. Why, then, should I be expected to feed your conceit in yourself?"

"I am the most modest of men." He pushed back the bonnet she had just straightened. "That's better. I like to see your hair."

Happily, she settled against him. "If you do not mind me turning up at Foxefield Hall looking like a gypsy wench, then I'm sure I don't care."

He pulled her up until her head rested against his shoulder. " 'Tis better to look like a gypsy wench than a long-faced Puritan."

"Since I no longer have Puritan leanings, my lord, I would thank you not to mention it again."

He laughed. "Dost remember facing me with that atrocious bonnet on your head? God's soul, but you looked a fine fright!"

"Enough!" she cried indignantly. "And what of yourself? Your face like a thundercloud, your hands itching to tear the garments from my body."

"What!"

" 'Tis true. For though you assumed the role of stern guardian, you were aching even then to see my body."

"I will have no more of this indecent talk!"

"Ah!" she taunted. "Who is the Puritan now?"

He was silent for a moment. Then he said in a completely different voice, "Dost know that Oliver Cromwell will now sit in Parliament? He has been returned as the member for Huntingdon."

"No!" she answered, startled and surprised. "How could I know? In my circle, there is little talk of politics. Lately, though, it has seemed to me that the Queen is taking an increasing interest in such things. I wonder if she knows that Oliver Cromwell will be seated in the third Parliament? She will not like it, though it can make no difference to her. She met him briefly at Foxefield Hall and took an instant dislike to him."

"Aye, I understand that Cromwell made a disagreeable impression on their Majesties," Brett said, stroking her hair. "I confess that I am not surprised. At first I thought the man merely a fool and a canting hypocrite. But, since that first impression, I have met him several times, and now I am not so sure."

"If you ask me," Meredith said sharply, " 'tis a great pother about nothing at all. Why should you sound so serious and troubled over Mr. Cromwell, who is surely of very little importance?"

"Unimportant at the moment. But I have an uncomfortable feeling about him."

"You do?" Meredith frowned. "What feeling?"

"That's just it," Brett said, with an exasperated laugh. "I cannot put it into words. But this I could swear to. He is a hard, ambitious, and ruthless man."

"What of it? What has he to do with us?"

"With us, nothing. But with the King and the country, who knows?"

She put a hand to his forehead. "Have you a fever, my lord?"

"Certainly not." He brushed her hand away impatiently. "Why do you ask?"

"If you have not a fever, then your wits have gone a-wandering. Mr. Cromwell is quite unimportant."

"Aye, you're right. Forgive me, it is unlike me to indulge in such foolish babble. I usually leave such things to you."

The carriage swayed as it lurched over a humpbacked bridge.

"Overlooking your remark," Meredith said, "with my usual charity, I would remind you that we are almost at the gates of Foxefield Hall. And if we may now have done with Mr. Cromwell, I have something to say to you."

"Have you so. I like not your tone, wench."

"I care not, my lord. I have something to say, and say it I will."

"Then pray do so."

"We are now in March. The babe will not be born until late November. I—"

"I am aware of that, Merry."

"I wished to say," she went on, ignoring the interruption, "that I only intend to stay a few days at Foxefield Hall. The rest of the time will be spent with you."

"I am flattered," he remarked dryly. "However, you will stay at Foxefield Hall until September."

"What!" She glared at him. "I will do nothing of the sort."

"You will. I will see you frequently, of course."

" 'Tis good of you," she exclaimed, her voice rising. "But hast forgot that I am still in the Queen's service?"

"Nay, wench, I have not forgotten. Her Majesty, I know, will be happy to release you."

"I will not stay!"

"You will stay," he repeated calmly.

"Why should I?" Her eyes narrowed with sudden suspicion. "You are trying to rid yourself of me!"

He nodded his head. "I had hoped you would not guess. But the real truth of the matter is that I do not want you in London while the plague is rife."

"There is no plague."

"There will be. There are always a few cases during the summer months. Hast forgotten the last epidemic?"

"What has that to do with anything?" Meredith's jaw set mutinously. "You may say what you please, but I will not stay above a few days." She rose from his lap and set herself beside him.

He looked at her stiffly upright figure. "The matter, my dear, is no longer open to discussion."

"Tyrant!"

"If it pleases you to think so."

"We shall see!" she muttered. "We shall see, my lord."

The carriage turned to the right and entered the gates of Foxefield Hall. It bowled smoothly along the winding drive, and came to a halt before the great carved doors.

"Might I suggest," Brett said, as he assisted Meredith to alight, "that you remove that sullen look from your face. My mother, as you know, is inclined to take easy alarm."

"I am not surprised," Meredith said, tossing her head. "Had I such an overbearing bully of a son, I too would take alarm."

"Your time will come, madam. You are about to bear just such another as I."

"I pray not."

Brett turned to the coachman. "You may take the carriage to the stables. Pray see to it that the horses are groomed and fed."

"Aye, m'lord."

The man sprang up on his perch, and the carriage rumbled away.

Brett frowned at the closed doors. "Our arrival, I believe, was quite noisy. Where the devil are the servants?"

Her ill humor temporarily forgotten, Meredith grinned at him. "Doubtless they caught a glimpse of you, and the poor, frightened souls are now in hiding. I cannot say that I blame them."

Brett did not answer her. His eyes were on the doors, which were slowly opening. Surprised, he saw that instead of Jarvis, the butler, Mistress Elizabeth Cromwell stood there. Her eyes were heavy, as though she had been weeping a great deal, her mouth was quivering, and locks of hair straggled untidily from beneath her starched white cap.

"Good day to you, Mistress Cromwell." Brett spoke more sharply than he had intended. "Where is Jarvis?"

Mistress Cromwell twisted her apron between her reddened hands. "The servants are busy about the house, my lord," she explained. "There is—is a general turmoil. I told Jarvis that I would greet you and explain."

Brett's dark brows drew together. "Explain what, Mistress Cromwell?"

Meredith felt her heart beginning to thump uncomfortably. Unable to explain her sudden sense of apprehension, she moved closer to Brett's side.

A tear ran down the woman's cheek, and was quickly followed by another. "M—my Lord—" her voice cracked.

"You must forgive my abruptness, Mistress Cromwell," Brett said as patiently as possible, trying to stifle his agitation. "I do not have to tell you that you are always welcome at Foxefield Hall. But you seem quite distressed. What is wrong?"

"Oh, my lord! I thank the good God that He brought you here in time. 'Tis your mother. She is very ill."

Brett's heart leaped. "My mother?"

"Aye, my lord. 'Tis feared that she is dying. I—I came to see if I could aid in any way."

Brett stared at the woman with hard eyes, as though he were silently accusing her of lying, but the color had faded from his face. "What nonsense is this, Mistress Cromwell? I was with my mother only a few days ago. She was in excellent health."

"I'm sorry, my lord."

"Come, love," Meredith said, putting her hand on Brett's rigid arm. "'Twill serve best if we see for ourselves what's amiss."

"What ails her?" Brett shot the question at Mistress Cromwell.

"The physician tells me that 'tis her heart."

"Her heart!" Brett turned blindly to Meredith. "Nay! Surely it cannot be. I have ofttimes told her, when she complained, that there was nothing wrong with her heart. Just to think, Merry, that

I, in my superiority and my infinite wisdom, told her that!''

She heard the pain and the bitter self-reproach in his voice. ''I have often told her the same thing.'' She took his hand in hers and held it tightly. ''But do not let us become unduly alarmed,'' she went on comfortingly. ''It may be that Mistress Cromwell, without meaning to do so, exaggerates.''

Mistress Cromwell sighed. ''Aye,'' she said, looking at Meredith with understanding. ''Mayhap I do. But whatever the way of it, my lady, you have only to call on me if there is aught I may do for you.'' She moved down the wide steps, hesitated, then went heavily on her way.

''Come, love,'' Meredith said. ''Let us go into the house.''

In the cool dim hall, Brett recovered himself. He drew his hand from Meredith's, and turned on her a face so haggard, so devoid of expression, that she drew back in alarm. ''Brett!''

''Will you come with me?'' Brett said in a toneless voice. ''If you do not wish to do so, I will understand.''

''I love Sarah! Such a question is scarcely necessary!'' Meredith's own fear tinged her voice with anger.

''I'm sorry.'' He made an effort at a smile. ''Depend upon it,'' he said in that same toneless voice, ''this will be—will be merely another of my mother's coils. Doubtless she has quite convinced the physician that she had not long to live.''

Meredith winced before the tortured look in his eyes and the slightly unsteady note in his voice. He was, she knew, blaming himself for all the times he had treated Lady Sarah's complaints with casual indifference. He knew that Mistress Cromwell had spoken the truth, but for the moment he could not bring himself to accept it.

''Don't, my darling,'' she answered him in a low voice. ''You must not make it harder for yourself!''

They climbed the stairs together. Brett's hand gripped the carved banister rail as though he feared, if he let go, that he would fall.

Outside the door of Lady Sarah's bedchamber, they were met by Sir Brian Lancey, Lady Sarah's chief physician. Standing beside him was Mistress Tabitha Wellwood, Brett's onetime nurse, now the housekeeper at Foxefield Hall. Her seamed face was streaked with tears, and sobs shook her body.

The harassed Sir Brian cast an irritable look at the weeping woman. "No doubt my lord Foxefield and his lady would like some refreshments. I pray you to pull yourself together, Mistress Wellwood, and go about your duties."

Mistress Wellwood ignored him. With the familiarity of an old and trusted servant, she stumbled forward and threw herself into Brett's arms. "Oh, m'lord, I know not how you come to be here, for 'tis not long since I sent Jem Hawkins posting after you." She drew a deep sobbing breath. "But you are here, praise be to God! M'lady has been asking for you."

Brett's hands tightened convulsively on her plump shaking shoulders, then he released himself from her clutching arms. "Plague take you, Tabby, will you stop that damned caterwauling! Run along and do as you were bid."

His voice was so harsh that Mistress Wellwood started in alarm. "Aye, m'lord." She straightened her cap with trembling fingers. "I don't doubt that we'll all be needing something to sustain us before this day is past."

Giving Meredith a watery uncertain smile, she went toward the stairs. Stumbling down them, her eyes blinded with fresh tears, she almost fell headlong.

"Well?" Brett turned back to Sir Brian. "What is this nonsense I hear?" His mouth tightened. "My mother cannot be dying!"

"Would to God it were nonsense, Brett. But I'm afraid it is all too true."

"But there must be something you can do!"

Sir Brian's brown eyes were pitying. "I have done all that may be done. Lady Sarah simply does not respond. It is almost as though she does not want to live."

Brett looked at the gray-haired physician with hostile eyes. "That is an easy excuse. What of the times you assured me that there was nothing wrong with my mother?"

"To the best of my knowledge, Brett, I spoke truth. This attack was entirely unexpected."

"To the best of your knowledge, you say? Well, I say that you are an incompetent fool! Why are you not with her?"

Sir Brian was not offended. He knew that it was suffering that put the rough edge to Brett's tongue. His round, ruddy face registered that sad understanding as he said gently, "Though there is nothing more I can do for her, I was about to return to the room. But perhaps it would be best if you and your lady went to her instead."

Brett's hands clenched. "You have not tried to save her," he accused the physician in a low, taut voice. "There must be something else you can do!"

"Do you think I would not have done it? Have you forgotten that I love Sarah? 'Tis true she would have none of me, though God knows I tried many times to change her mind. I have used every skill at my command, but I am powerless. Only God can work the needed miracle!"

"I am sorry." Brett did not look at him, his eyes were on the door that led into the bedchamber. "I am sorry," he said again.

"So am I." Under the plum-colored ribbed silk of his jacket, Sir Brian's shoulders slumped in defeat. "All that are left to us are prayers. Go to her now. If you have need of me I will be just outside the door."

Lady Sarah's figure made a very slight mound beneath the white sheet and the sapphire-blue velvet bedcover. The padded crimson headrest, and the heavy crimson and gold bed curtains were in vivid contrast to her starkly white face. There were deep shadows beneath her closed eyes. Someone had drawn back her hair from her face and tied it with a black ribbon; the golden-brown ends, as yet untouched with gray, rested on her white-clad shoulders.

She looked, Meredith thought, bending over her, like a gaunt-faced and exhausted child.

"Mother!" Brett sat down on the side of the bed and took one of her small, limp hands in his. "Mother!"

Lady Sarah's girlishly long eyelashes fluttered. Brett had the flashing illogical thought he had had many times since his father's death. While his father had lived, his mother had been a warm and vital woman. But the woman left behind was not quite real to him. Pretty, fretful, gentle, hiding behind a determined invalidism, she was as insubstantial as a butterfly, and like the butterfly, she had now come to the end of her too-short span. "Mother!" he said again.

Lady Sarah's eyes opened slowly. For a moment she did not seem to see him. Then, on a caught breath, she whispered, "I knew you would come, Brett. I knew it!"

"Aye, I am here. There is nothing more to worry about."

Lady Sarah's pale lips smiled. "No, Brett, there is no more to worry about. Nor is there anything you can do for me."

Brett stared at her. She sounded almost triumphant. "I will not let you die, Mother!"

Sighing, Lady Sarah looked at him with love. "But there is nothing I wish you to do for me. Try to understand, I pray you!"

"The only thing I understand is that you must fight. Merry and I will be here with you." His fingers tightened on hers. "Surely you wish to get well," he added desperately.

"No." The single word was uncompromising, leaving him temporarily bereft of argument. "Meredith," Lady Sarah said, "hold my hand, child."

Meredith sat down on the other side of the bed and took her hand. She could not accept Lady Sarah's answer, or the look in her brown eyes that asked for understanding. She said warmly, bracingly, "Come now, you must not give up. We will help you to get well."

A slight shake of the head answered her. "I have given up, and so very gladly. I want to die."

Brett made a muffled exclamation. "Stop it! I refuse to listen to such talk!"

Now at last Meredith understood and accepted. Lady Sarah was eager to be gone. Brett's harsh dictatorial voice had been meant, she knew, to inspire a fighting spirit in his mother. But

211

Lady Sarah had long ago wearied of the fight. Brett could not hold her now. She was going happily.

Lady Sarah's eyes were fixed on Meredith. Almost as if Meredith had spoken, she nodded her head. "You love my son?" she asked.

"I do, Sarah. Very much!"

"You will help him? You will try to make him understand why I am glad to go?"

"I will. I promise."

"Thank you."

"Mother!" Brett's voice again. "You must try to make an effort."

"Please!" Lady Sarah's mouth trembled. "I want to be with my Hugh. I am so lonely without him!"

Meredith bit her lip and blinked her eyes fiercely to hold back the tears. It was the cry of a lost and lonely child. Poor Lady Sarah, who desired so passionately to put aside this life. To be free again, joyful again. Scarcely realizing what she was doing, she pressed her lips to the hand she held. "You must not worry, Sarah. The waiting is almost over. You will be with him very soon."

"Meredith!"

Lady Sarah did not hear Brett's wildly protesting cry. "You really believe that, Meredith. You really believe that my Hugh will be waiting for me?"

"Don't you, Sarah?"

"I do. I do indeed!"

"Then I believe it too. He will be there, Sarah."

"I'm so glad to hear you say so." A radiant smile lit her face to a momentary and vivid life. "Hugh!" she whispered. "Hugh!"

Meredith stared down at the face against the lace-trimmed pillow, not quite able to believe the change she saw there. It was as though, with the saying of her husband's name, the aging years had released their hold on her. She had always been pretty, but now she was beautiful, ageless, and, in this fight with death, the conqueror rather than the conquered. Was he here? Was Hugh

Foxefield here in this room? Was that the reason for Lady Sarah's radiance, for that look of triumphant joy?

"Tell her about the child." Brett's voice cut into the dazed moment.

Meredith started. "The child?" she looked at him blankly.

"Her grandchild." Brett's voice was hoarse with agony. "Tell her. Mayhap it will help her to live."

Meredith nodded. Lady Sarah did not seem to hear her quickly spoken words, her shining eyes looked beyond them. But she had heard, for after a moment she said on a sighing breath, "We are both so glad for you. But now you must let me go, my son."

"Mother!" Brett leaned forward and swept the little figure into his arms. "Mother!"

"Say good-bye, my lad," Lady Sarah whispered. "My dear son!"

"First you will tell me that you forgive me for the times when I have been harsh and unreasonable," Brett said in a choked voice.

"There is nothing to forgive. You have always been the best of sons."

Gently, he laid her back against the pillows. "You are a very lovely, very obstinate little creature." He touched his hand to her cheek. "I love you very much."

"And I you. I love you both."

Brett bent to kiss her forehead. "Good-bye, my mother."

Lady Sarah smiled. "Good-bye," she whispered.

Brett stared at her for a long moment, then he said in a dull voice, "She's dead, Meredith."

Meredith went to him and put her arms about him. "I know, love. We must be glad for her."

"But she's dead! Don't you understand? My mother is dead!"

Her arms tightened about him. "No, darling, she's alive. Try to look at it in that way. For the first time since your father died, she is really alive!"

Chapter Twelve

The August day was dreary. Along the open seafront, unshielded by houses or other buildings, there was a raw bite in the air that was reminiscent of winter rather than high summer. The sun, as if reluctantly aware of its duty, occasionally struggled through the shrouding mists produced by last night's rain to throw long lances of light across the Portsmouth sands, turning them from a dirty yellowish-brown to dark gold. The heaving gray sea, catching those fugitive gleams, transformed itself into rearing blue rollers sparked with emerald and coquettishly capped with frothy white.

Brett Foxefield, Meredith beside him, sat on the damp, low seawall. The twined green and white plumes on his black hat streamed in the salt-laden wind, and his green-collared black cloak flapped behind him like the wings of a giant bird.

"Damn!" Brett clutched the cloak to his throat with a gloved hand. "It's cursed cold. What other country but England could produce such plaguy weather in the middle of August?"

Meredith did not hear his complaint. Her eyes were fixed on

the tall black riggings of the Duke of Buckingham's now useless fleet. The great ships bobbed on the water, their sails lashed securely to the masts, circled by screeching gulls. The name of the ship nearest to her was *The Albatross.*

The Albatross? Meredith mused. She had heard somewhere that albatrosses were supposed to be associated with bad luck. She did not like the Duke of Buckingham, but she had to admit that the man, these days, certainly had bad luck. Public feeling was higher than ever against him. And now, having assembled his glorious fleet in order that he might carry out the King's command and sail triumphantly to the relief of the beleaguered Rochelle, word had now come to him that his expedition was unnecessary. Rochelle had already been relieved.

A faint cynical smile touched Meredith's lips. It must be bitterly galling for the Duke to know that the orders he had so very persistently beseeched his reluctant King to give were now useless. The King had been loathe to send the Duke, knowing that anything Buckingham attempted would be looked upon with hostile suspicion by the people. But Buckingham, as usual, the most powerful man in England, had won the day. No doubt, as the savior of Rochelle, he had expected to come back to a suitably grateful country. Himself covered with glory, the people having conveniently forgotten past grudges, and the country ringing with the name of great Buckingham.

Brett studied Meredith's absorbed face. Beneath her white, blue-lined bonnet, her bronze hair was blown into untidy wisps. Her face was pinched with the cold, and the tip of her nose was red. Under the blue cloak her slender body was swollen with five months' pregnancy. What sex would the child be? he wondered. Meredith hoped for a son. But he, unlike most men, wished for a daughter.

"Well?" He touched her cold nose with the tip of his finger. "What are you thinking about?"

Meredith looked at him. His face had grown much thinner since the death of his mother. The hollows in his cheeks were more accentuated, his mouth had taken on a sterner set, and his dark-blue eyes seldom smiled. She had not thought him to be a man who would wear a mental hair shirt, but she had been wrong. Brett continued to believe that he had killed his mother with his callous indifference to her various ailments. In consequence, he was increasingly watchful of herself. At the King's request, who seemed to believe that Buckingham, in view of his increasing unpopularity, stood in need of an extra watchdog, Brett, together with the Duke's other gentlemen, had accompanied him to Portsmouth. But she, Meredith, must go with him. He did not trust her out of his sight. He did not trust her to take care of herself. Was the spectre of Lady Sarah always to walk with them? Would he never stop blaming himself? Meredith frowned. It was nice to be cared for and protected, but it grew a little irksome to be overprotected.

"Have you lost the use of your tongue?" Brett spoke sharply. "I have addressed you twice."

"Nay, love." She smiled at him. "And don't be giving me that frosty look, my lord Foxe. 'Tis cold enough without that. I was thinking of my lord Buckingham's great disappointment."

Brett shrugged. "He will get over it."

Meredith moved closer to him. "Put your arm about me. I'm cold."

"Perhaps we should be getting back," he said, complying. "You will take a chill."

"Oh, Brett, be not so concerned for me. I am strong and healthy, and I am enjoying the fresh air." She smiled up at him. "I like not this new m'lord Foxe. I would have you as you were before."

"Callous, you mean," he said, his black brows drawing together. "Careless, and criminally indifferent?"

"Nay, m'lord, nothing of the sort. Rough, you sometimes were, and, at times, brutal, but you were always loving."

"I love you." His arm tightened about her. "It is because I love you that I must be careful."

"But—"

He cut her off, it was an old argument between them. "We will not discuss it."

Meredith's lips tightened. Her inclination was to flare out at him, to tell him roundly that she was a woman, not a piece of glass to shatter at a careless touch. But that would come later, after the child was born, if he should still persist in this brooding and unceasing anxiety on her behalf. She wanted to be to him the woman she really was, passionate and full of love. She wanted to have him bed her, to be able to express herself without fear of being smothered beneath his concern. She hoped to bear him other children, but she would do it as a true woman, not as the semi-invalid he was unknowingly trying to make of her.

Sighing, Meredith rested her head lightly against his shoulder. Lady Sarah's death seemed to have changed his whole personality. He had always been inclined to be austere, sometimes coldly remote, but now he was more so, and he seldom smiled. He watched her all the time, and sometimes she felt guilty and uneasy beneath that concentrated attention. Even the King had noticed the change. Once, when Brett had rebuked her harshly for wandering in the grounds without a cloak to cover her thin gown, and had refused to listen to her excuse that it was a warm night, the King had smiled at her sympathetically.

"You must not mind, my lady Foxe," the King said, when Brett's attention had been claimed by my lord of Basely. "As the shock of his mother's death diminishes, so too will his anxiety on your behalf." The King pressed her hand. "Anxiety for the loved one is quite understandable, but too much becomes a burden. Is it not so?"

"Your Majesty is gracious to concern yourself."

"I will always concern myself with my friends, my lady Foxe."

Desperately, Meredith had looked the King in the eyes. "I pray Your Majesty to forgive me if I presume. I love my husband very much, but he is smothering me, trying to make me what I am not. It would be kind indeed in you, Sire, were you to speak to him. Mayhap he will listen to you." Assured of the King's sympathy, she was emboldened to go on. "I wish him to be my husband, not my gaoler!"

"Gaoler?"

"Aye, Sire. A kind and considerate gaoler, too kind, too considerate, but nonetheless a gaoler. I would have back the man I married."

"His concern is not for himself, you know."

"Would that it were, Sire. Mayhap he would take less chances with himself. My lord thinks nothing of duelling, or riding a horse at such speed that 'tis a wonder to me he is not thrown. Last week he was thrown, and, when I reached his side, he lay at such an angle that I felt sure his neck was broken."

"I know," the King had soothed her. "I promise you, my lady Foxe, that I will speak with him."

Whether the King had spoken or not, Meredith had no way of knowing. With brooding eyes she looked along the seafront. A little distance from them, a man sat crouched on the seawall. He wore a tall hat adorned with a shiny buckle, and he was muffled in a caped coat. Just beyond him, a group of sailors, careless of the wet sand, lay sprawled at their ease. Their voices, interspersed with laughter, drifted toward her. Farther along the beach, one or two couples who had decided to brave the wind, walked slowly along, cloaks sailing out behind them.

Meredith's attention came back to the lone man. There was something odd about his slumped posture, something despairing. "Look at that man," she said, glancing at Brett. "He stares so intently at the sea that one might almost think he were contemplating hurling himself in."

"His name is John Felton," Brett said.

"You know him, then?"

"Not exactly. Last night, after you retired, he approached me and introduced himself. He is from Suffolk. He desired an interview with Buckingham."

"Why?"

"It seems that he has taken upon his own shoulders the grievances of the country. He is a one-man avenger, and his mission is to persuade Buckingham to release the army pay owing to so many soldiers.''

Meredith laughed lightly. ''A laudable ambition, surely. I wonder if my lord Buckingham will see it in the same light?''

''He does not. Felton, without my aid, managed to see Buckingham. Apparently he did not put his case well. According to my lord Buckingham, he is naught but a ranting fanatic.''

Meredith made a face. ''In that case, I am automatically on the side of Master John Felton.'' She looked at the man again. ''I wonder if my lord Buckingham took the time to assure him that things will improve now that Parliament has granted the King his subsidies?''

''I doubt it. Buckingham has an unfortunately high-handed manner which does nothing to endear him to those who have a genuine grievance.'' Brett was silent for a moment, then he went on slowly, ''The subsidies granted by Parliament only amounted to three hundred and seventy thousand pounds.''

''A fortune!'' Meredith cried.

''Not when you think of all that must be done with it. And that was only granted because the King decided to sign the Petition of Right. 'Twas a piece of very sophisticated blackmail, that.''

''Aye, but I like well its terms.'' With her eyes on the huddled man, Meredith quoted: '' 'A freeman shall not be required to give gift, loan, or tax without the consent of Parliament. He shall not be imprisoned or detained unless it be in full accordance with the law of the land. If he be soldier or sailor, he shall not be lodged in private houses. Soldiers and sailors shall not be punished by martial law.' Why, Brett, I think 'tis noble!''

''So too did the King. It was simply that he did not like to be coerced. Had the Bill been presented to him in full courtesy, there would doubtless have been less delay in the signing. But no man, especially if he be King, likes to be bullied and threatened and blackmailed with the threat of subsidies permanently cut off. I sometimes think Parliament take too much upon themselves. They should deal with the King as the King, and not as a puppet who must be made to dance at their command. I know Charles. 'Tis the wrong way to deal with him. He can be stubborn, very stubborn, but give him the respect to which he is entitled, and they will find him reasonable and amenable.''

Meredith nodded. ''Dost remember the rejoicing when the King signed the Bill? The bonfires, the dancing?''

''I remember.'' Brett took his arm away and rose to his feet. ''Come,'' he said, holding out his hand, ''we are to breakfast with Buckingham.''

''Must we?'' Meredith allowed him to pull her to her feet. ''I had far rather we breakfasted alone.''

Brett smiled faintly. ''I too. But this breakfast is in the nature of a conference. Buckingham is persuaded that the news of Rochelle's relief is but a wily trick on the part of the enemy.''

''Do you believe that, Brett?''

''I do not.''

Meredith hung back. ''I do not care to breakfast with Buckingham and his officers. 'Tis no place for a woman. Pray allow me to breakfast in my apartments.''

''Nay,'' Brett answered, pulling her along. ''We will suffer together.''

''My presence will be resented.''

''It matters not. Where I go you go.''

''Am I never to be allowed to be alone?'' Meredith kicked pettishly at the sand. ''Am I never to be trusted again?''

''I cannot trust to your common sense to look after yourself properly,'' Brett said calmly. He paused a moment to draw up the collar of her cloak. ''There, that is better.'' He looked at her sullen face. ''Why do you resent my care of you, Merry?''

''Because I—'' She drew a deep breath. ''Because I am a woman, not a child. Oh, pray stop fiddling with my cloak, you are choking me!'' She struck his hands away. ''You can stop worrying, my lord Foxe. I am not going to die. You will not have me on your conscience!''

At the stricken look on his face, she was appalled. ''Oh, Brett, my darling, pray forgive me! I did not mean to say that.''

220

His face went blank. "You will please to lower your voice, madam. You are attracting attention." He extended his arm. "Shall we go?"

"Brett?" She took his arm and walked slowly along beside him. "I did not mean what I said, indeed I did not!"

"You meant it, Meredith. I understand your irritation. But I believe that you do not understand."

"I am not your mother, Brett," she pleaded. "I am very healthy. I am not full of imaginary aches and pains like Sarah. And, more important, I have no wish to die."

"We will not discuss my mother, if you please."

At the freezing note in his voice, her heart sank. They walked in silence, and Meredith found that she could not bear that withdrawn look on his face.

A sound from behind her made her look over her shoulder, and she saw that John Felton was walking a few paces behind. That fleeting glance showed her that the face beneath the tall hat was fair and very young, but there was something about the expression of the face that caused her heartbeat to accelerate. Suddenly she was frightened.

"Brett!" Her fingers pinched nervously at his arm. "That man, John Felton," she said in a low voice. "I am sure he is following us."

Brett glanced round casually. "Nonsense," he reassured her. "If it pleases him to do so, he is entitled to walk in the same direction. Doubtless he has decided that the wind is too cutting."

Meredith was slightly cheered by the warmer note in his voice, but she found that fear, in the person of that soft-footed follower, still went with her. She could not explain her panic over a harmless young man. She quickened her steps, annoyed to find that her legs were beginning to tremble.

The Duke of Buckingham was in a peevish mood when they joined him in his apartment. He was still being groomed, and his loud, hectoring voice filled the room.

Catching sight of Meredith, the Duke gave her a sour look,

221

then turned his attention to Brett. "You are late, my lord," he snapped.

"Am I?" Brett looked pointedly at the valet who was hovering anxiously. Brush in hand, the man awaited the Duke's permission to give a final brushing to the wide-skirted scarlet jacket and the tautly drawn black pantaloons that disappeared into high black shiny boots embellished with gold tassels.

The Duke intercepted his glance. "The fool has brushed me three times already. 'Twas but a way to pass the time until you decided to make your appearance." The gold buttons on the scarlet jacket gleamed in the light from the window as he turned irritably to the valet. "Get away from me with your infernal brush. And let me not see that rat's face of yours for some hours to come."

"Yes, Your Grace." The man could not altogether hide his resentment, but, obviously relieved to be dismissed, he scuttled from the room.

"I see you have your lady with you, Foxefield," the Duke said, a hard note in his voice.

Brett turned his head as Buckingham's officers came in silently from the inner room. "As usual, my lord Buckingham," Brett answered smoothly, "your eyesight does you credit."

Buckingham flushed angrily at the grin on a junior officer's face. Then, looking at Meredith again, he attempted a smile. " 'Twill be no place for a lady, Foxefield. Rough soldiers' talk, you know, is not fitted for delicate ears."

Brett ignored Meredith's pleading look. "I feel sure that the soldiers present will moderate their conversation."

Buckingham shrugged. "Very well." He walked over to the door. "We are breakfasting with the Earl of Lindford. There are a few things that must be discussed, then I must ride directly to the King with the news that Rochelle has already been relieved."

There was such disbelief in his voice that Brett smiled. But Meredith, following on Brett's arm, was unconscious of anything save her own embarrassment. Perhaps if she told Brett that people were noting and laughing at his absurd caution over his wife, it might give him pause to think.

Hidden in a dark recess, John Felton watched the Duke advance along the covered passageway. Just behind him was the tall dark man he had spoken to the night before, my lord Foxe, as he was popularly known. On his arm was the pretty girl with the lovely hair, whom he had seen sitting on the seawall. My lord Foxe's wife, perhaps?

Following after them came Buckingham's officers. In their bright red tunics, red pantaloons striped at the outer seam with black satin, high tasseled boots, black red-lined cloaks, and black shakos adorned with a red feather, set precisely on their heads, they made a brave display.

Felton was sweating under his heavy coat. Now that the moment was upon him, he could not control his fear. His limbs were shaking, and a sour bile rose in his throat. Swallowing, he drew himself up stiffly. Now was the time to call upon all his courage. It was not given to every man to strike the blow that would aid in righting the wrongs of a nation. He, John Felton, was the chosen of God. Was he then, because of his miserable cowardice, to ignore God's command? Buckingham, that evil man, must die! Was he not responsible for all the ills of the country? Did he not lead good King Charles by the hand, forcing him to follow after him in his wicked designs? Buckingham was responsible for the tragedy of the seamen and the soldiers, who, having given of their best for England, were now ignored, starving for want of their just pay.

Felton's cold fingers touched the knife in his pocket. He grasped it firmly. He would strike in the name of God, in the name of England, his beloved country, held firmly beneath the heel of a tyrant and a traitor. "Foxe," the King called the dark man. What then did he call the Duke of Buckingham? "Weasel!" The name rose up in Felton's mind. "Weasel! Weasel!" And the time had come for the weasel to be exterminated.

223

The Duke was very near now. Blood drummed in Felton's ears, his heart was pounding painfully, and there was a searing pain in his head. Through a wavering mist he saw the Duke's face, the light, cold eyes, the implacable line of the mouth, the cheeks flushed with the healthy color of good, full living.

"I feel sure that I can convince the King," the Duke was saying. "He will see, as I do, that the reports of the relief of Rochelle are merely a trick of the enemy to catch us off guard." He laughed. "Are we children, to be so deceived?"

Hot savage talons of pain were clawing at Felton's head, and he could feel the bile rising in his throat again. "Now, Felton, you coward! Strike now, now!" God's stern voice thundering in his ears. "Why do you wait?"

Screaming, Felton sprang from his cover. It was like a grotesque tableau. The wild-eyed man, the knife in his hand, the people frozen into position, Buckingham, slack-jawed, fear in his eyes.

"Weasel!" Felton shrieked. "Traitor!" His hand moved; the knife flew like a bright streak to bury itself in Buckingham's breast.

Buckingham made a hoarse coughing sound. He retched violently. Blood spewed from his mouth and spattered his jacket. A moment he stood there, swaying like a tall tree, then he crashed heavily to the ground.

"Christ!" Brett sprang over Buckingham's body. His fist crashing against Felton's jaw threw the man back against the wall. Felton was laughing as he began to slide downward, a high, tittering, crazed sound.

The paralyzed officers moved. Pulling Felton to his feet, they pinioned his arms behind him. One officer drew his sword and struck the laughing man on the side of the head.

"Stay with him," Lord Edgemont addressed Brett. "My God! What a thing to happen!" With one last horrified look at Buckingham, Edgemont hurried after the men who were leading the assassin away.

Meredith was crouched beside Buckingham, his head in her

lap. "My lord Buckingham," she said through shaking lips. "Oh, my lord!"

Buckingham was not quite dead. "M—my wife," he muttered in a thick, difficult voice. "My s—s—son. I—I want—" His hand clawed feebly at the air.

"Be still, my lord. You must not move."

A spasm seized Buckingham and his body arched. His throat swelled and he retched painfully and continuously, until the retching was silenced by the blood pouring from his gaping mouth. It stained Meredith's pale-blue cloak, and she felt the sticky warmth soaking through to her gown. He made one last strangled sound, then he was still.

Meredith looked dazedly at Brett. He was kneeling beside her. Gently he removed Buckingham's head from her lap. She watched with dilated eyes as he straightened Buckingham's body and closed the staring eyes. She was unaware of the crowd gathered at the other end of the passage as she cried out in a stricken voice, "Brett! He can't be dead!"

Brett rose and helped her to her feet. "He's dead," he said quietly.

Meredith's face was drained of color. She stared down at the blood on her cloak. "He—he spoke of a son. I did not know he had a son."

"Aye. The child was born this year." Brett spoke in the same quiet voice, hoping to quell her rising agitation.

"Poor little boy!" Meredith swayed. She put her hands to her stomach in an unconsciously protective gesture. "He will never know his father."

"Are you all right?" Brett said, sharply alert. "Shall I escort you to our apartments?"

"Nay, Brett. 'Twould be cruel to leave him alone."

"Someone will be here in a moment."

Meredith shook her head. "Stay with him until they return. I am well able to go by myself. Besides, I think I would like to be alone for a little while."

Surprisingly, considering the shock she had undergone, Brett made no demur. ''I understand.'' He touched her shoulder, squeezing it gently, then he let her go.

Meredith walked along the passage. The crowd gaped at the white-faced girl, at the blood on her hands, on her cloak, and on the cream gown beneath it. Silently, they parted to let her through. As she passed on, the silence was broken by a man's rough voice, '' 'Tis Buckingham lying there. I'd know the bastard anywhere!'' Somebody else laughed. ''Aye, 'tis him all right. He deserved to die!''

Meredith's footsteps faltered. Tears streamed down her cheeks. How cruel! she thought. A man lies dead, and they can find nothing good to say of him. I did not like him myself, but whatever Buckingham has been, does he not deserve better than the laughter of the crowd and their callous comments? What of Buckingham's newborn son? She had once heard the Duke say that if he ever had a son he would name the boy after himself. Well, he had his son. Another George Villiers, Duke of Buckingham. What would life hold for the boy? Would he be just such another as his father, or would he be cast in a gentler mold? She shivered. The Buckinghams! Somehow, wherever a Buckingham led, there followed a tale of treachery and disaster.

Chapter Thirteen

The Queen had dismissed her ladies. She sat perched on the window seat, her dark head bent over her embroidery hoop, seemingly absorbed in pulling the colored silk through the tautly drawn linen. It was an occupation she detested. It was unsuited to her restless nature, and she found nothing soothing in it as did her ladies. Her stitches were not only crooked but they made no attempt to follow the pattern. Her mind was with her husband, who had joined her some moments ago. Since entering the room and greeting her, the King had not uttered a word. He sat stiffly upright in his chair, his hands gripping the padded armrests, his dark mournful eyes staring unseeingly at the silk-hung walls.

The Queen's needle stabbed angrily through the linen, taking several large careless stitches. She paused to stare down at her work. She had given the lion a green mane, and the child, standing beside him, a yellow mouth. She frowned. Well, she cared naught for such fiddle-faddling nonsense.

She glanced at the King again. Doubtless, she thought bitterly, he was thinking of Buckingham again. 'Twould seem that he thought of little else these days. Five months, she fumed, five months since Buckingham's death, and he grieved as if it had been only yesterday! Bah! She had no patience with him. The people, at least, were grateful for Buckingham's death. On the day he had been buried there had been bonfires in the streets, big celebrations. She had once heard it said that the measure of a man's success was the hole he left in people's hearts. Buckingham had left no hole. There was only a wild joy at his passing.

It was this callousness that had so embittered Charles. He could see no fault in Buckingham, and he clung tenaciously to his memories. Even his ministers had been unable to hide their joy when the news of the assassination of Buckingham had reached them. One by one they had come to the King, their lips expressing their sympathy for His Majesty's loss. But Henrietta Maria, seated on Charles's right, had seen the same look in every eye. A look of triumph. An obstacle, a very dangerous obstacle, had been removed from their path.

Henrietta Maria took another haphazard stitch. Recalling that moment when Oliver Cromwell, newly elected to Parliament, had come forward to kneel before the King, she felt suddenly cold.

"Your Majesty would honor me if you would accept my sympathy for the loss of the noble Duke of Buckingham," Cromwell had said. His light piercing eyes had looked into the King's face. "But 'tis God's will. I cannot but feel that 'twould greatly comfort Your Majesty were you to accept it as such."

Cromwell's words had been conventional enough. Yet, whenever she recalled the man, she found herself shivering. What was it about him that so terrified her? Charles, sunk in the apathy of his grief, had been unmoved. But she had felt an even stronger return of the revulsion and fear Cromwell had inspired in her on that first meeting at Foxefield Hall. Her fear was the more acute because she did not understand it. She had always been superstitious, and she felt that this man had an evil part to

228

play in their destiny; now that he had been elected to Parliament, the unknown terror had moved one step nearer. She was tired of trying to laugh away her fear. Tired of trying to reason it away. She only knew it was there, and it stabbed painfully like an irremovable thorn in her flesh.

Henrietta Maria rested the embroidery hoop on her lap. She herself had been wrong to take the news of Buckingham's death so calmly. Charles had expected her sympathy, not her unmoved reception of the news. Perhaps if she had at least assumed grief, Charles would not have withdrawn from her so completely. She would always remember what he had said to her that day. "You are glad of the death of my lord Buckingham, Madam. I can see it in your eyes. You rejoice that this fine man, who has been to me as a father and a brother, lies dead by the knife of an assassin!"

Angry and jealous at the all too evident signs of his grief, she had answered with her usual impetuous folly. "Buckingham has ever been more to you than your own wife. Aye, I am glad he is dead!"

"So I thought, Madam." He had turned and left her. She had indulged in a storm of hysterical tears. Since that time, he had spoken to her only when necessity dictated. His visit today had been entirely unexpected. These days, it was unlike Charles to seek her company.

Something stirred inside her. A feeling that was so warm and melting that it brought the quick tears to her eyes. Poor Charles! He looked so lost and lonely sitting there. It was no wonder he thought constantly of Buckingham. There was joy all about him at the death of his friend. There was only he and, perhaps, my lady Buckingham to mourn the man. He had retired into himself. Not even the company of my lord Foxe or my lord Butler could lighten his grief.

Henrietta Maria said with unaccustomed gentleness, "My lord King, is it not today that my lord and lady Foxefield are to present their son to you?"

Charles's head turned slowly. "It is," he answered.

229

"And have they not decided to name him Anthony Charles?" Henreitta Maria prompted, hoping that he would take up the thread of conversation.

"They have."

"I have seen him, you know."

"So I understand."

Henrietta Maria bit her lip, but she persevered. "Aye. He is a beautiful child. He has golden eyes, like his mother, and black curly hair, like his father." She laughed. "There is not much of it as yet. The hair, I mean. But, except for the eyes, he promises to become remarkably like my lord Foxe."

Charles looked at her coldly. "I have never before known you to express an interest in children, Madam."

She felt as though he had stabbed her. Did he not know that she prayed for a child? Though, with the way he had been avoiding her bed, it was doubtful if she would conceive at all. The warm melting feeling left her. She said spitefully, "Surely 'tis your own indifference to children that speaks, Sire. Were you to come to my bed, it might be that I would bear you a child. We would see then, would we not, who has a genuine interest in children?"

"I will come to your bed when I am ready, Madam, not before. However, since you are displaying such remarkable interest, you might like to know that my lord Buckingham's son, George, is to be educated with Master Anthony Foxefield."

Buckingham again! Curse Buckingham! But he expected her anger, so she would disappoint him. In any case, it was the chance she had been waiting for. She would show him how warmly sympathetic she could be.

Putting her embroidery hoop from her, she rose to her feet. Her red silk skirts rustled as she ran to his side. "Charles." She covered his hand with hers. "I am very sorry about the tragic death of my lord Buckingham. I have been wanting to tell you so this long time. 'Twas a mistake on your part to believe me unfeeling."

His hand was tense beneath the pressure of her small jeweled fingers. So lovely, he thought, but without a genuine emotion. She had said that she loved him, yet she had made no attempt to help him bear his grief. Like the others, she had greeted the news of Buckingham's demise with indifference that was tinged with a cruel joy. Now she stood before him in her red gown, her white breasts almost fully revealed above the daringly cut silver-laced bodice, her shining dark curls caught up and threaded through with a rope of pearls, and hoped to seduce him from the memory of her callous behavior.

Charles pulled his hand away. He answered her with resentment and anger. "You lie, Madam. Your feelings toward my lord Buckingham are well known to me."

Seeing that he was about to rise, Henrietta Maria promptly seated herself upon his lap. Her heart was beating very fast as she wound her arms about his neck and pressed her face to his. If he snubbed her, she would die! "Charles," she whispered, "I am sorry he is dead, if only because it has hurt you so." Her soft lips touched his cheek. "Does it really matter that I disliked him? You did not, and that is all that counts. Surely it cannot matter to you what others think? Oh, Charles, I love you so much! Pray do not keep me at a distance, for I cannot bear it!"

He could smell the apple-blossom fragrance of her hair, and he felt himself weakening. Damn her! She was seducing him with ease. He forgot Buckingham, forgot everything but the soft perfumed body in his arms. He loved her, he wanted to give in. It had been so long since he had lain with her. Remembering the heart-jolting passion of her response to his love-making, he weakened still further. It was his duty to present England with a Prince.

"Charles!" She lifted his hand and guided it to her breast. "I want you! Touch me, make love to me!"

Inside her bodice, his hand closed about her breast. "W— when did you request your l—ladies to return?" he asked in a hoarse, shaken voice.

"They will not return until I bid them do so."

"Get up, Madam," Charles said, releasing her breast.

"Charles!" She drew back and stared at him in dismay. "Surely you will not leave me now?"

It was the old Charles who answered. "Madam, if you do not immediately rise and get yourself to your bedchamber, I will surely do so."

Henrietta Maria sprang from his lap. "My lord King, I am but a woman. I have not the strength to restrain your going. But should you take one step toward that door, just one single step, then I promise you, my dear Sire, that you will be very sorry."

Laughing, she ran toward the bedchamber. "Come!" she called. "Hurry, my darling!"

Chapter Fourteen

Standing before the King, the Earl of Butler seemed to be at his ease. His stance was nonchalant, and his dark eyes held their usual cool gleam. It was only his nervous fingers that betrayed him. First pushing back a lock of dark hair that had fallen over his forehead, then touching the lace at his throat, flicking a speck of dust from his plum-colored velvet jacket, and twisting the heavy gold ring on the middle finger of his left hand, all these small movements spoke of an inner agitation.

The King looked with some amusement at the Earl of Foxefield, who stood by his side. "Our friend seems nervous, does he not?"

"Somewhat, Sire," Brett agreed.

"John," the King addressed the Earl of Butler. "I have twice requested that you be seated."

The Earl seated himself at once. "I beg Your Majesty's pardon. I did not hear you."

"That is obvious." He looked at Brett. "Will you also be

seated, my lord Foxe. It is obvious to me, my lord Butler, that you have much on your mind." He lifted questioning eyebrows.

"The same thing that is on Your Majesty's mind," the Earl answered. He clasped his hands loosely together. "Parliament casts a long shadow these days. I am at a loss to know which way they intend to jump."

The frown that seemed to have settled permanently between the King's eyes deepened. "And so, my lord? Knowing you, I am assured that you have more to say."

"I have, Sire. Your Majesty is fully aware that for some time I have not been at ease with the machinations of Parliament. And now, more than ever, I wish myself well away from the whole mess."

Brett's eyes were suddenly intent. But the King seemed to be unmoved by the Earl's words. "I see," he said quietly. "Go on."

"Even were I at ease," Butler resumed, "I would not wish to be associated with Your Majesty's enemies."

Charles drew in a sharp breath. "Christ's wounds! You use strong terms, Butler."

"I do, Sire, but not, I believe, without cause. 'Tis my earnest belief that they are your enemies." He paused, then went on quickly. "Believing this, I ask Your Majesty's permission to resign my seat."

Charles leaned back in his chair. "It can be arranged, my lord. I will arrange it." His fingers tapped the brocaded armrests. "Seated in Parliament," he said, smiling faintly, "you have ever seemed to me to be a fish out of water. You are a scholar, not a politician. But tell me, what are the latest rumblings from my dissatisfied Parliament?"

Butler hesitated. "You will not like it, Sire," he warned.

"I am sure of that," Charles said dryly. "But we are more than King and subject, we are friends." His quick smile included the Earl of Foxefield. "You have my permission to speak freely."

"It is believed that Her Majesty the Queen has too great an influence over you, Sire," the Earl said uncomfortably.

Charles swore beneath his breath. "So they said of Buckingham. I am nobody's puppet. I am and have always been my own man. Pray go on."

"It is feared that the Queen will corrupt you to Catholicism. And the country, in its turn, will be forced to yield to popery."

Charles stared at him in astonishment. "I am the last man to turn Catholic. My Christ! It would be funny were it not so damned tragic. What else, Butler?"

"There are murmurings against the Bishop of London. In many eyes, and in the eyes of the Puritans in particular, the High Church Service is thought to be too reminiscent of Rome."

Charles sighed heavily. The strain he had undergone these many months showed in the deep shadows beneath his eyes and in the lines graven at the sides of his mouth. "So now my bishop, my trusted William Laud, is under fire too." The King's eyes sharpened. "Speaking of Puritans, was I wrong in believing that man, Oliver Cromwell, to be a potential troublemaker?"

"You were not wrong, Sire. Cromwell is a rabble-rouser. He has an uncanny ability to hypnotize his audience. Already he has made several speeches. In them, he condemns those men most trusted by Your Majesty, saying that he suspects them of preaching popery. So far as Cromwell is concerned the divines, when preaching to their flock, must tread a very wary line. And he is the same man who has spoken out so heatedly against religious intolerance!" Color tinged the Earl's cheeks. "To my mind, Cromwell is a narrow-minded bigot. He is incapable of seeing a point of view other than his own. He is also one of that party who view with dark suspicion Your Majesty's favoring of Thomas Wentworth."

Charles's mouth tightened, and for a moment his eyes held an ominous gleam. "They go too far! There is no favoring about it. Thomas Wentworth is a man to be trusted. The only man to take my lord Buckingham's place. He has been so appointed by me. There is no more to be said on the matter." He glanced at Brett. "You are very quiet, my Lord Foxe. What have you to say?"

Brett smiled, but his blue eyes looked hot and angry. "I say that Your Majesty has been subjected to too many humiliations.''

"I agree with you," Charles answered mildly. "But I dislike that warlike gleam in your eyes, my lord Foxe. There must be a middle path I can take whereby I may satisfy Parliament and yet keep intact my dignity.''

Brett shrugged. "If Your Majesty knows of this path, I would be happy to tread it with you.''

"And I," my lord Butler said.

"I am fortunate in my friends." Charles's face darkened. "I would to God that Buckingham were with us now.''

Brett did not answer. On that one point he could not agree with the King. The manner of Buckingham's death had been deplorable, but he could not help the feeling that the King was better off without him. He looked at the Earl of Butler and saw from the expression on his face that he agreed with him. Buckingham had been unpopular with everyone but the King.

"What now?" Charles's voice broke the silence that had fallen.

"Tomorrow," my lord Butler said, deliberately evading the question, "I shall have to take my seat in the House.''

The King laughed. "Aye, my lord, you will. Your resignation may not be effected so soon." He paused, then added significantly, "However, since the House is far from attending to business, and are resolved instead to air what they consider to be their many grievances, my only recourse is to once more dissolve Parliament. So it may be that you will not suffer overlong.''

My lord Butler's dark brows drew together thoughtfully. "Your Majesty will, I hope, forgive me, but might it not be wise to allow Parliament to continue for a while longer? There is much dissatisfaction. Whether it be real or imaginary, I feel that it would be folly to give them yet one more grievance to prate upon.''

"They will look upon me as a tyrant, you mean. Nay, I stand firm on this, John. If they cannot agree among themselves, if they cannot put aside their grievances in the service of their country, then 'tis useless to go on."

The last day he sat in Parliament, on March 10th, 1629, was a day that the Earl of Butler was to remember for the rest of his life. For it was then, so it seemed to him, that the fortunes of Charles Stuart took that final and sinister turn that was to lead him to the scaffold.

The temper of the House was high. Oliver Cromwell stood up and made a further speech on the subject of religious intolerance. He stood there stiffly, his pale eyes flashing, beads of perspiration standing out on his forehead as he thundered his denunciations. When he sat down again the members seemed to take this as their cue to go from one indiscretion to another. After a great deal of impassioned shouting, in which more than one member was openly insulting to the King and Queen, the House seemed to settle down.

It was ironical, therefore, in view of Cromwell's speech against the evils of religious intolerance, that Sir John Eliot should choose to say in his loud, carrying voice, "I demand that anybody who attempts to bring popery into this land, anybody even remotely suspected of preaching such a gospel, shall be looked upon as a capital enemy!"

A roar of approval answered him. Thrusting his hands into his pockets, Sir John went on confidently, "On the question of taxation, taxation that is unauthorized by Parliament, anyone advising such a course shall likewise be looked upon as a capital enemy of this kingdom."

Sir John turned to the Speaker, Sir John Finch. "Despite the Petition of Right, this disastrous course continues to be followed by His Majesty the King. Therefore, Mr. Speaker, I pray you to put to the House the question of these our complaints."

Sir John Finch rose shakily to his feet. He was a short man of meager frame. Today, with his shoulders slumped with the intensity of his despair, he looked smaller than ever. His face pale but resolute, he said firmly, "Your meaning is not even thinly disguised, Sir John. You speak slander against His Majesty. I refuse to put these complaints to the House. I must also tell you that I have this day received an order from His Majesty to adjourn the House."

Sir John Eliot's face went purple, and his eyes glared with rage. As Sir John Finch turned to make his way from the House, Eliot roared, "Lock the doors! I will not allow this man to leave while these questions remain unresolved!"

Sir John Finch stared in disbelief as the bolts were slid into place. "Stand away from those doors!" he shouted. "This House is adjourned. I act under the direct command of His Majesty the King!"

Eliot ignored him. "Denzil, Valentine, restrain this man!"

Denzil and Valentine sprang forward and gripped the Speaker's arms. Ruthlessly they wrestled the struggling man back to his chair and held him there by force.

Eliot called for silence, but it was a long time before his voice was heard. When the members finally settled down, they looked furtively about them while Eliot shouted his resolutions into their ears. "Whosoever shall tamper with the religion of this country, thus bringing about in the natural course of events grave strife and bloodshed, shall be named an enemy of the people of this kingdom. Whosoever brings about the levying of tonnage and poundage without proper consent of Parliament shall be likewise named. Whosoever ignores the properly instituted laws of this land and pays the duties wrongfully imposed upon him shall be called an enemy too!"

Valentine relaxed his grip upon the stunned Sir John Finch's arm, and put the resolutions to the House.

There was a momentary silence. Then, with the exception of one or two, the members rose like one man and bellowed out their assent.

They had no sooner settled back into their seats than a thunderous knocking sounded upon the locked doors. "Open!" a voice demanded. "Open in the name of the King!"

Undismayed, laughing at the consternation reflected in the faces of the other members, Eliot rose to his feet again. "Let them do as they will!" he cried. "We are within our rights. I declare this House to be adjourned for the space of seven days. Open the doors!"

The doors were unbolted and pulled wide. Eliot, his shoulders squared, thrust his way forward, followed by the other members. Black Rod, he whose voice had demanded entrance, was thrown back roughly against the wall by the press of men.

Captain Thornby, marching along Whitehall at the head of the King's guard, saw the members as they emerged into the street.

"Halt!" the captain cried to his troop.

"Sir." Saluting, Captain Thornby approached Eliot, who seemed to be leading the men in a triumphant progress. He saluted again when they stopped to face him. "Sir, by the King's orders, I am come to carry away the Mace."

Eliot smiled. "Your name?"

"Captain William Thornby, sir. At your service."

Eliot's smile turned into a sneer. "At my service?" he said. Encouraged by the laughter of his companions, he went on boldly, "I doubt you will ever be at my service, captain. So you have come to carry away the Mace?"

"I have, sir. Such are my orders."

"The orders of a tyrant," Oliver Cromwell put in.

"Aye," Eliot agreed after a momentary hesitation. "A tyrant."

Captain Thornby's face froze. He looked at the black-clad Cromwell, disliking his narrow, pale face with its spattering of freckles, the cold eyes, and the thin mouth. "Sirs," the captain said, his eyes turning once more to the florid-complexioned Eliot, "you speak treason."

"And you will duly report it, I suppose, Captain Thornby?"

Driven from the refuge of his official calm, Thornby snapped, "You may be assured of it, sir."

"Ah! Then I must expect to be lodged in the Tower, eh?"

Damn the man, he was deliberately baiting him! Steadying

himself, Thornby answered with admirable calm, "I believe that must be the expectation of all traitors, sir."

"Are you calling me a traitor, captain?"

"That is not for me to say, sir. I would say, however, that by your own words you have so branded yourself." Thornby drew himself stiffly to attention. Looking at a point just beyond Eliot, he said coldly, "The Mace must be delivered into my hands."

"That will not be," Eliot answered with equal coldness. "Since His Majesty is so anxious to obtain this insignia, you must enter and remove it for yourself."

A faint contemptuous smile touched the captain's lips. "So be it, sir. I wish you good day."

Eliot watched as the captain marched his men toward the House. He had not liked the man's smile, or the note of dignified rebuke in his voice. "Puffed-up pompous little toad!" he grunted. "Damned King's man!"

"And are you not also a King's man, Sir John?" a quiet voice said from behind him.

Eliot swung round and glared ferociously at the tall man in the caped gray cloak. "Ah, so now at last we hear from you, Butler. I do not recall hearing from you a while ago."

"Possibly because I had nothing to say. Your beliefs are not mine, just as your ambitions, whatever they may be, are not mine." The Earl of Butler touched Eliot's shoulder lightly with the small cane he carried. "But if matters continue to progress at their present ugly pace, you will most certainly hear from me. And, for that matter, from a great many of the King's men. It may be that the manner in which you hear will not be to your liking."

Oliver Cromwell, unable to contain his anger, thrust himself forward. "And you will hear from us, my lord," he spat out the words. "You and your like will curse the day you crossed swords with us!"

"Me and my like? Now I wonder, I really do wonder what you can mean by that."

"You know, King's man, oh, you know!"

Eliot shifted uneasily. "Guard your tongue, Cromwell. You go too far."

"Nay, not far enough," Cromwell snarled. "Not yet! But the day will come. Something must be done about the desperate situation in which England finds herself!"

The Earl looked faintly amused. "And you, I suppose, have constituted yourself the leader of the opposition, Mr. Cromwell?"

"If by opposition, my lord Butler, you mean those who have the courage and the purity of purpose to oppose the King, then the answer is yes. Right willingly will I oppose His Majesty's harsh and unjust methods of extracting money from the country. I'll not have it, when I know that 'tis to feed his selfish pleasures and his cursed unnecessary wars!"

The Earl's brows rose. "Unnecessary, Mr. Cromwell?"

"That is what I said, my lord. Unnecessary! If such an office should be thrust upon me, I will willingly lead the opposition."

"So heated, Mr. Cromwell," the Earl said, sounding bored. "Such boiling of the blood is surely bad for the veins. As for the office of which you speak, I doubt if that or any other office will be thrust upon you. It may not have occurred to you, but to oppose the King as gravely as you suggest might well result in a civil war. Hast given thought to that?"

"I have. If need be, you will find me ready and willing to follow even that drastic course."

The uncomfortable shufflings and the shocked murmurings of the other men caused Eliot to break in hastily. "My lord, Mr. Cromwell is obviously not himself. His words are empty. They mean nothing."

Spots of angry color glowed in Cromwell's pale cheeks. "Speak not for me, Sir John!"

The Earl studied Cromwell closely, and he glowered beneath that cool gaze. "I think I have your measure now, my good Cromwell," the Earl said, his smile mocking. "When you have decided to declare war against the King, pray be so good as to

inform me. It is certain to add a touch of amusement to my day.''
He touched his plumed hat with his cane. "A good day to you,
gentlemen.''

"Royalist Swine!" Cromwell muttered, glaring after him.
"So it will add a touch of amusement to his day, will it! 'Tis he
and his kind who sap England's strength. We must be rid of them!
We will be rid of them!''

Eliot, relieved to see that the Earl was out of earshot, rounded
on the fuming Cromwell. "You fool! Are we not all good
royalists? We do but demand justice, not violence. What possessed you to say such things? Who of us here talks of war?''

Cromwell's eyes were still sullen with the anger awakened by
the Earl. "I do. If I think 'tis the only way to save my country,
then I will work to that end.''

"Then you will work alone. We stand for fairness and for
equality. We, too, are willing to oppose the King, but it must be
done lawfully. We'll have naught to do with any of your mad
plans.''

"But in the end, Sir John, my plans will be your plans. You
will see.''

"You are insane!''

"Nay, not I. If you look for true insanity, look to the King.
'Tis he, with his extravagance, his callous disregard of our laws,
his smug assumption of the divine right of kings, who leads us
ever onward to disaster. Civil war may not come for many years,
but, while Charles sits on the throne of England, it cannot fail to
come. You may be assured of that.''

Eliot flinched before the look in those light eyes. He glanced at
John Hampden, who was regarding his cousin with something
like awe. "You seem set on violence, Mr. Cromwell. And who
will declare this war? You?''

Cromwell smiled. "I? Nay, I am but an insignificant part of
the whole. But in time, Sir John, you will remember my words on
this day. For then we will all be of the same mind.''

"Not I,'' Eliot blustered. "Never think it!''

"Then there is no more to be said, is there, Sir John? And now,

242

like the so exquisitely polite my lord Butler, I bid you good day, gentlemen.''

Cromwell motioned to John Hampden to follow him, then, with a fair imitation of the Earl's long, lazy stride, he went on his way, leaving the others gaping after him.

"That man is dangerous!" Thomas Hazeltine spluttered, finally breaking the silence that had fallen. "I like not his words. I like not the purpose I sense behind them.''

Eliot pulled himself together. He said slowly and thoughtfully, "Aye, Cromwell is dangerous, but there is great power in him too. He would be a leader, never a follower. He is a ruthless, an unlikable man, and yet, pondering on his words and on yours, Thomas, I ask myself who is the most dangerous? Is it the King? Or is it Oliver Cromwell?''

Peter Dickinwell gaped at him. "Never say you are of one mind with Cromwell!''

"No man makes up my mind for me," Eliot assured him. "But I will tell you this. If it would cause the wind to blow fair for England, I might well turn my mind and my heart to war.''

Peter Dickinwell, about to answer him, closed his mouth and stared at the figure of Thomas Wentworth, who was coming along the street toward them.

Thomas Wentworth nodded pleasantly as he drew near. It was obvious from his manner that he knew nothing of the recent events in the House.

"Well, gentlemen," Wentworth stopped before them, "we are well met.''

"Say you so?" John Pym said, looking at him resentfully.

Wentworth smiled agreeably. "Aye. Since I have left you for the service of the King, I had hoped to meet with you again.''

Pym looked at him with smouldering eyes. "It may be that you have left us, sir. But be assured, traitor, that we will never forget you! When the time comes we will know how to deal with you.''

Wentworth stiffened, his smile fading. "The King called me to his side. I did but answer the call. I am no traitor.''

"Mr. Wentworth," Pym said, "we do not wish to bandy

words with such as you. You may best serve us by leaving us.''

"So be it." Wentworth bowed. "Despite your hard words, John, I am still your friend."

Pym did not answer. He turned his back as Wentworth walked away.

Chubby Sir Cedric Oliver frowned at Pym. "Another damned fire-eater. Blessed if all this pother and brawling doesn't make a man wish he'd never left his bed!" He turned up the collar of his cloak. "The wind grows cold," he grumbled. " 'Tis time we were away to our homes."

"Aye," Eliot agreed, "let us disperse. But 'tis not the wind that grows cold, Oliver. Say rather that it is the times in which we live that cause a man to feel an inner and outer chill."

"Plagued if I know what the devil you're talking about, Eliot. But then you always did talk in cursed riddles."

Peter Dickinwell's round blue eyes clouded. "I hope, gentlemen, that we have not been too impetuous this day." He shivered. "You may say what you please about the weather, but 'tis colder still in the Tower."

Eliot ignored his remark. "We will meet again in seven days, gentlemen."

They were not destined to meet in seven days. Sir John Eliot and several of his companions, who, strangely, did not include the outspoken Cromwell, were sent to the Tower.

The King came to the Lords. He did not call on the Commons. In a speech that was both moving and dignified, he acquainted the Lords with his intention of dissolving Parliament at once.

His lips colorless with the force of his emotion, his dark eyes bright with the sheen of tears, the King said to the grave-faced men, "For inasmuch as we cannot see eye to eye on the problems besetting our country, 'tis useless to go on. For the good of England I would gladly die. And I will have done with this hurly-burly and confusion that does nobody any good, least of all my England. I am the King, yet my ministers turn the faces of enemies upon me. When I seek to do good, they impede my way

244

with all their might. Whether it be from mistaken ideals, or simple contrariness to the wishes of the Crown, I know not. Now I declare unto you, good gentlemen, that I will rule England without the aid of my ministers." He looked from one face to another. "It is not without much heart-searching that I have come to this conclusion, that it will be a long time before I call Parliament together again. If indeed I ever do."

Oliver Cromwell, that most malignant of the King's enemies, was allowed to return to the peace of his country home. His eyes brooding, his lips forever moving with his inner thoughts, he took up his tasks again.

Elizabeth Cromwell, unable to sleep because of her husband's restless movements, would hear his oft repeated mumble, "The King! That popinjay! We will chop off his head while the crown is yet upon it! They will see. They will all see!"

She feared for her husband's sanity, and yet when he awoke from his feverish dreams, where he wandered she knew not. He seemed sane enough. He had always been surly of manner, but he had at least made some small attempt to bridle his speech. But now, on his infrequent encounters with his neighbors, the Earl of Foxefield and his lady, he was brusque and belligerent of speech. To Meredith, whom he had once considered his protégé, he would scarcely address a word. He felt that, in succumbing to a life of pampered luxury, she had gone over to the side of the devil. Her uncovered hair shone brazenly in the sun, her fingers sparkled with jewels, and her high, firm breasts were sinfully exposed, so that the scanty covering of her bodice, that sought to partially conceal them, became naught but a mockery and a useless and absurd sop to convention. So Cromwell became yet harsher with his wife. If one small strand of hair showed beneath her starched bonnet, he would slap her face, and then spend much time in raving about the indelicacy of women who sought to flaunt their charms.

Elizabeth Cromwell remembered with acute embarrassment the day when her husband had been shown the Foxefield heir. She herself had held Anthony Foxefield and looked upon the little face with tenderness. But her husband, after one disgusted look, had said, "Another one to grow up in the King's shadow. Another child to absorb his baseness, his false ideals, and to mimic the lying hypocrisy of his tongue!"

He had turned and stumped away. Elizabeth Cromwell saw the ominous blaze in my lord Foxe's eyes, and the way his hand had jumped to his sword. She said pleadingly, "I pray you, my lord Foxefield, to forgive my husband. He has not been well of late, and I know that he does not mean what he says."

"Madam," Brett answered her curtly, "Mr. Cromwell hath a dangerous tongue. 'Tis not wise to speak treason against the King in a loyal man's presence, and least of all in mine."

"I will speak with him, my lord Foxefield. But pray to forgive him for this one time."

Perhaps pitying her embarrassed confusion, my lady Foxefield had spoken out, "Do not bully Mistress Cromwell, my lord. 'Tis no fault of hers."

The severity of my lord Foxefield's face relaxed into a charming smile. "Forgive me, Mistress Cromwell, 'Twas not my intention to bully you."

"I know it. Thank you, my lord Foxe." Elizabeth Cromwell's face had flushed scarlet as she realized her slip. "Forgive me again. I should have said Foxefield."

Brett laughed. "So long as you do not accuse me of resembling the wily creature, you may call me Foxe as often as you please."

"Oh no," Elizabeth stammered, "th—there is no resemblance a—at all."

"Yes there is," the outrageous Lady Foxefield said calmly. "In my opinion he is like unto a fox."

"My lady!"

"You will pay no attention to my wife, Mistress Cromwell. 'Tis the fiery color of her hair that bakes her brain."

Meredith laughed. *"Touché*, my lord."

A sound from behind made her turn. "Ah, here is Mistress Pampton bearing my temporary charge."

Not understanding, Mistress Cromwell looked at the smiling nurse and the small bundle she cradled.

Meredith handed her son to Brett, then took the bundle from the nurse. "Mistress Cromwell," she said, "may I present to you His Grace, the Duke of Buckingham."

Mistress Cromwell stared down into the small face, and her eyes clouded with pity. "Poor little fatherless mite," she said. She looked up at Meredith. "I was most distressed to hear of his father's death."

" 'Tis generous in you to say so, Mistress Cromwell," Brett said gently. "There are few who mourn him."

She would like to have asked him if he mourned the Duke of Buckingham, but she lacked the courage. Instead, she said, "I believe, my lord Foxe, that the Duke was not a good man. Yet for all that, I do not like to think of his violent death." She looked down at the blond baby again. "Mayhap the child will grow up to bring glory to the name of Buckingham." She smiled. "He is a pretty child, is he not?"

"Aye," Meredith answered her, "but not as pretty as my Anthony."

"Pretty, madam?" Brett looked at her vivid face with tender eyes. "I had thought you considered that our son greatly resembled myself."

"Why, so he does." Meredith's laughing eyes opened wide as she said mockingly, "My lord, have I neglected to tell you that you also are excessively pretty?"

"Pretty! What a word! Get you to the house, madam. My patience with you is finally exhausted."

Watching them go, Elizabeth Cromwell had envied Meredith. My lord Foxe appeared, to a stranger's eyes, to be stern and somewhat unapproachable, yet she could see that there was joy and laughter between them. It must indeed be wonderful to be able to expand with one's husband. To be one's true self. Lovely, too, to be able to wear pretty gowns and sparkling jewels, to let your hair blow free in the wind. Mayhap, one day, Oliver would forsake his austere ideas and allow her to wear silk now and again. Even as she thought it, she knew it was a forlorn hope. Were she to wear colored silk, Oliver would think her a very sinful woman who had fallen for the blandishments of the devil. Nay, she would be forced to go on wearing her thick uncomfortable black gown with its wide white collar that crackled with starch and set up a painful inflammation of the neck. No doubt, she thought mournfully, she would also be buried in it. She forced herself to remember that, for all his irritating ways and his sometimes frightening severity, she loved Oliver devotedly. Which was a very good thing, or she would long ago have rebelled at the constant child-bearing and the restrictions of her life.

Approaching the house, she remembered the thrilling news that my lady Foxefield, drawing her to one side, had confided in her. At least it was something new to tell Oliver, and perhaps it might distract him and give him something other than the King and his perpetual worries over the fate of the nation to think about.

Cromwell looked round as she entered the house. He greeted her with a nod of the head and a grunt.

"Oliver, I have something to tell you."

"That can wait. Sit down, Elizabeth. I wish to speak to you upon a certain matter."

Seating herself, she gave him a quick, furtive glance. His pale eyes were gleaming, and his mouth was twitching. She gripped her hands together in her lap. Why, she thought in amazement, I am afraid of him! She concentrated her attention upon him. What had she done this time? Or was it the children? If so, if the children had angered him, she hoped the culprit was not Richard. Richard seemed to particularly irritate Oliver. He was always saying that the boy was a weakling now, and that he would grow into a weakling man.

"Now, Elizabeth, I want you to listen carefully," Cromwell said, coming to stand before her. "I wish you to cease taking your walks along the Elmtree Way. There are other walks fully as pleasant.''

"But why?" her words were a whisper. But she knew why. She braced herself and waited for the tirade that was sure to follow.

"Because I wish for no more encounters with my lord Foxe, or with that strumpet he calls wife. The man is a friend of the King, and because of this fact I verily believe he thinks himself superior to all others.''

"Oh, no, Oliver," Elizabeth ventured. "I am sure you are wrong.''

His control deserted him. "I am not wrong!" he shouted. "Have you not seen the way he looks at me? As though I were a clod of earth beneath his feet. Someone scarcely worth his attention.''

"I like him, and I like my lady Foxefield." She was immediately horrified at her words. He would be so angry with her!

"So you like them, do you!" He ground out the words, his face flushing a deep red. "I might have known that the meek obedience of your attitude is only a guise to deceive me. Beneath it, you are as sinful and as frivolous as all women.''

"I—I try not to be sinful. But my lord and lady Foxefield have done us no harm.''

"That kind do harm with every breath they draw. They harm England with their extravagances, their popish ideals. Can you not see that, you fool woman?''

"But they—they are not Catholics.''

He swept this aside. "Are you attempting to defy me?''

"Oh, no. Indeed not!''

"Then you will do as I say. Soon we will be moving away from this district, but until that time you will have nothing further to do with the Foxefields of Foxefield Hall.''

Elizabeth's eyes filled with tears. She enjoyed meeting the Foxefields. Her own life was drab, and they were fascinating in

249

her eyes. But Oliver had decreed it, and she must obey. She nodded slightly.

"You will not attempt to disobey me?" he said, his narrowed eyes on her face.

"Have I not always obeyed you, Oliver?" She made an attempt at a bright smile. "But before we close the subject, I must tell you that my lady Foxefield today gave me some thrilling news."

"I have no interest in any news that trumpery bitch may have to impart."

She was shocked. Of late, with the other changes that had beset him, his tongue had coarsened. "I think you will be interested in this news."

He hesitated. "Well, what is it?"

"The Queen is with child." She looked at him closely, hoping to see a softening in his grim expression. "Is it not exciting?"

He regarded her unsmilingly. "And there is another whore," was his comment. " 'Twould not surprise me to learn that the child she bears in her body springs from another man's seed."

"Oliver, don't!" She could not bear to hear him speak so. His hatred and resentment of the King and all who were associated with him festered inside him and crippled him spiritually. Oliver was a good man, she reminded herself desperately, and it broke her heart to have to stand by while he slowly destroyed himself with hatred, fanaticism to what he believed to be a pure and holy cause, and undying malice toward his sovereign.

At her shocked look, he shrugged his shoulders. "I have work to do; I cannot idle about the house like a woman. If you have more to say, then 'tis best to say it now."

Now it was she who felt resentment. Idle about the house! She? Her hours were depressingly full with the care of the children, her baking, her housecleaning and her constant washing. Swallowing her indignation, she said quietly, "There is little more to tell, save that the infant Duke of Buckingham is at present residing at Foxefield Hall."

She heard the swift intake of his breath. "So," he said, and there was that certain note in his voice she had come to dread, "and now the viper's son is come amongst us."

"Nay, Oliver, be not so uncharitable. He cannot help the sins of his father. He is naught but a harmless child."

"I give charity where charity is deserved. The child is Buckingham's son. He will grow into just such another viper as his father before him. Than that, no more needs to be said."

Chapter Fifteen

Anthony Van Dyck's brows drew together in a frown as he regarded the slim dark-haired boy who sat so restlessly before him. A very ugly lad, he thought. Certainly he could not seem to sit still at all.

The boy was unconscious of Van Dyck's displeasure. His eyes were fixed with wistful longing on the partly opened window, where there drifted through to him the voices and laughter of his sisters and his brother at play. Why could he not be with them, he thought crossly. He and James, together with Anthony Foxefield and George Villiers, had arranged to play a splendid game. Foxefield and Villiers were going to represent Parliament, he himself would be the King, and James, after much persuasion, had agreed to play the part of the Queen. It had been little use for James to argue that Mary or Elizabeth could take the part of the Queen, for he knew well that girls were not allowed to take part. Females were stupid and given to crying, and they did not play well.

252

He scowled as a fresh burst of laughter came through the window. It was all very well for them to enjoy themselves, but what about him? He must sit still for hours while this bad-tempered Belgian painter daubed at his stupid canvas. He did not want Van Dyck to paint his portrait. He had told his father and mother so. His father had listened to his arguments, then had told him coolly that it was his wish that he should sit for his portrait. His mother, on the other hand, had been very angry with him. She had said that if he did not wish Van Dyck to immortalize him, then he was very stupid. She had added that he was as obstinate as a pig, but, since God had seen fit to burden her with such a son, she must carry her cross with Christian patience. Remembering that scene, he grinned to himself. He paid little attention to Mam. She was always losing her temper. When she was not losing her temper, she was striving behind his father's back to turn him and his sisters and his brother into good Catholics.

"Your Highness." Van Dyck's cold voice cut into his thoughts. "I am aware that this sitting is extremely boring for you. Might I suggest, if you could contrive to sit still, that it will be over the sooner."

Charles, Prince of Wales, turned innocent dark eyes on the speaker. Van Dyck's face, adorned with a little pointed black beard, seemed paler than usual, and his hands were trembling. Charles, when not annoyed by these interminable sittings, was a warm-hearted boy. He said impulsively, "Are you unwell, Sir Anthony?"

"Your Highness is gracious to inquire," Van Dyck said dryly. "However, I am perfectly well. Pray to sit still now, and I can promise that I will release you within the hour. If Your Highness will straighten your collar and fold your hands in your lap, as I previously arranged them, it will be an inestimable help to me."

Charles pulled the wide white lace collar straight. Folding his hands in his red velvet-clad lap, he gave himself up to dreams. Mayhap his father could be persuaded to allow him to go with Anthony Foxefield and George Villiers on a visit to Milford Manor. The Earl of Butler had already spoken to his father about the visit. He had the feeling that he might agree to let him go. Of course James, his brother, would wish to go too, but the two of them must not be absent at the same time. James was Mam's favorite son. Nay, she would not dream of letting him go. He shot a swift look at his father and mother, who were seated at the other end of the room. They had wished to be present at this sitting. Neither of them were speaking. Sir Anthony, the temperamental, would not allow speech at the sittings. Even with the King and Queen, he insisted upon and got silence. His mother was busy with her embroidery, in which he well knew she took no interest at all. She had been working on that same cloth these many months. His father seemed to be lost in thought. He hoped that he was perhaps thinking of and approving the visit to Milford Manor. It was true that he was the Prince of Wales, and special care must be taken of the heir to the throne, but might he not, for this one time, be simply a boy? Young Charles's thoughts wandered on. The Earl of Butler had a son who was the same age as himself. Marcus, he was called. But since the Earl never spoke of the boy, it was almost as though he had no son at all.

"Eyes looking straight ahead, Your Highness," Van Dyck's commanding voice.

Charles turned his eyes obediently. Why did the Earl never speak of his son? Was he crippled? Deformed? Disfigured? He would like very much to meet this mysterious Marcus Milford. He would befriend him, whatever ailed him. Could it be that the Earl was ashamed of his son? Nay, he would have to be an unnatural monster, and the soft-spoken, gentle Earl was certainly not that. Charles frowned, his dark brows drawing together in a straight line. He liked the Earl very much, and it made him uneasy to know that his father was worried over his health.

Van Dyck added a touch to the canvas. Was this to be his last painting? he wondered mournfully. Of late he had been feeling very ill indeed. He was only forty-one years of age, but mayhap he too was doomed to die young. It was a fate that had overtaken many of the male members of his family.

Van Dyck stared at the face of the boy on the canvas. It was an odd face, he thought. And, for one so young, with a strangely cynical twist to the mouth. The lad was ten years old, but that mouth made him look much older. There were some, he knew, who were said to be born old. Mayhap young Charles Stuart was one of them.

He touched his brush to the dark brows. If this should prove to be his last painting, he had the consolation of knowing that it was his best to date. He had another consolation too. In the King's gallery were hung the paintings of Guido, Titian, Raphael, and Correggio, but it was the works of Van Dyck the King reverenced and admired the most. When he had taken up his residence in England, in 1632, the King had been then and had remained his friend. He had been granted a knighthood, a home at Eltham Palace, and a pension of two hundred and fifty pounds. He had been responsible for most of the royal paintings. Often, when he was in his studio at Blackfriars, he was honored by visits from the King. His hand began to tremble so much that the brush fell from his fingers. Stooping to pick it up, he thought with anguish, Why must I die! My life is pleasant, my work is all that I ever prayed it would be, and I have the sincere friendship of the King, whom I love and admire. Yet I cannot help knowing that I will die, and soon! There are so many signs. How can I help knowing?

The King looked at his son, remembering the moment, ten years ago, when Charles had been placed in his arms. May 29th, 1630, he had been born, and he would always remember that date. Each birth was wonderful to him. Mary, born on November 4th, 1631. James in November too, in 1633, and Elizabeth, in the December of 1635. His eyes saddened as he thought of his other two daughters. Little Anne, whose life was despaired of, and Catherine, who had not lived very long. Now Henrietta was with child again. In three months' time she would present him with what he hoped would be another son. He loved all his children, and he sorrowed with the Queen over the fragility of Anne, but with his first-born, Charles, that had been the most wonderful moment.

He glanced at the Queen. She was looking very attractive in the white and silver gown she had designed herself. The cleverly cut garment successfully disguised the advanced state of her pregnancy. Her dark curls were piled high in her favorite style and threaded through with silver ribbon, and there was a delicate color in her cheeks. She looked very far from her thirty years, and, in his loving eyes, she had changed very little from the fifteen-year-old girl who had come so reluctantly from France to be his bride. She had matured in many of her ways, though not sufficiently so. She was still hot-tempered, still given to making embarrassing scenes; she was sublimely selfish, unreasonable, and, where her religion was concerned, steadily growing more and more fanatical.

Charles smiled to himself. Faults she had in plenty, as did he, but he loved her to distraction. He was made happier too by the knowledge that she returned his love in abundance. He knew, though she did not think he knew, that she was constantly trying to turn Charles's heart to her own religion. It was the same with all her children, for in Henrietta Maria's eyes her children were damned unless they forsook the religion of their father and turned to the comforting and safe haven of Catholicism. But with Charles, their eldest son, she tried harder. Doubtless she thought that England, under Charles II, a Catholic monarch, would revert to what she called the true religion.

Charles rubbed his hand across his aching eyes. The ache in his eyes matched the constant ache in his heart, he thought wryly. He had often wondered how so much disaster could afflict one man, but so it had turned out. Restlessly, unwilling to dwell on his troubles, he tried to force his mind back to his wife. Henrietta Maria, as always, was blind where she did not wish to see. She continued to dream of a strong and Catholic England, and she completely disregarded the many warring religious factions in the country, among which the Puritan party stood firm and strong, gaining in strength every day. Nay, her dream would never be realized, the calamity with Scotland should have told her that.

Scotland! So now his mind was back to worrying at his troubles. It seemed that he could not forget, not even for a few brief moments. His position was perilous, and, unlike Henrietta Maria, he could not blind himself to unpleasant facts. Indeed things were steadily going from bad to worse. Lying in his bed at nights, unable to sleep, he would wonder what course of action he might take to avert the disaster that daily loomed ever more dark and dreadful over himself and his family.

It had been eleven long years since he had dismissed Parliament. But now events had conspired to force him to call them back. So, reluctantly, he had summoned them back. On April 13th, of this year of 1640, they would once more take their seats in the House. He hoped that some of their insulting arrogance might have left them, that they would perhaps be reasonable, cool-headed, and prepared to listen with open and generous hearts to their King.

Charles's mind moved rapidly over the sequence of events since his angry dismissal of Parliament. He had hoped the dismissal would be final, but it was not to be. At that time he had been determined to rule his people wisely and well. He believed, despite rebellion and open warefare from the hostile Scots, that he had done so.

He had started well. First, in the April of 1630, he had made peace with France. In the following November of the same year, peace had been made with Spain. It had seemed to him, with the peace he had brought about, that he was giving a precious gift not only to his country, but to Charles, his first-born son. With England finally at peace there had come an increase in prosperity. His chief advisors had worked well with him. Thomas Coventry, the Lord Keeper; Thomas Wentworth, the Lord President of his northern states; Richard Weston, Lord Treasurer; William Noy, Attorney-General; and William Laud, the Bishop of London. The efforts these men had put in had been commendable, but when disaster came they had been powerless to avert it.

Despite the increased prosperity and the improved living conditions of his people, there had been a thin thread of dissatisfaction throughout the country. He had understood the cause. They were dissatisfied because he had been forced to levy fines to obtain the money so desperately needed for the running of the country, the maintenance of the royal fleet, and the securing of the coast from possible invasion. Besides these fines for major and minor offences, he had issued a writ for ship-money from the seaport towns, and later a second writ destined to apply to the whole country. There had been much resentment, but why could his people not see that he had had no choice? He did not waste their money, spend it on luxury, or to indulge favorites, as had his father before him. No other way had been open to him. The money he must have if his country was to stand proudly with the rest of the world.

Charles thought of John Hampden, cousin of Oliver Cromwell. The man had refused to pay ship-money. For this direct defiance to the King, who stood for the ultimate good of the country, Hampden was tried. The judgment had gone against him, but the storm he had stirred up still lingered. But it was in Scotland that the real challenge to the King's authority had been issued.

Charles sighed heavily. He did not see Henrietta Maria's sharp glance in his direction, or the worried frown between her brows. He was back to that day in 1633 when, in sight of the Scots, he had once more been crowned a king. The ceremony had taken place at Holyrood Church in Edinburgh, and the air had been filled with the frenzied acclamations of the people. How was he to know on that pleasant June day, while their cheers yet rang in his ears, that the Scots remembered the religious changes brought about by his father with furious hatred and resentment, and, though perhaps not consciously at the time, were now preparing to transfer that hatred and resentment to the son.

In April 1636, believing that his father, King James, in changing the Church of Scotland from Presbyterianism to Episcopacy, had done well and to the complete satisfaction of the people, he had issued a proclamation calling for a Book of Canons and a new liturgy, and it was then that the people's smouldering anger had exploded into outright rebellion. On the day the new liturgy was introduced in the churches, the riots began in earnest. The Scots demanded from him the abolition of the Court of High Commission, the withdrawal of the Canons and the Liturgy, a free Parliament and a free Assembly. Naturally he could not be expected to overlook this bold challenge to his authority. There was only one course open to him and he had taken it. He had prepared for war. Even as he prepared, he was fully aware that the Scots were doing likewise. He tried to tell himself that things would right themselves, that he would not be forced to make war on his own people, but it was not to be. The Covenanters, as the Scots called themselves, went from one audacity to another. They took the fortresses of Douglas, Dumbarton, Edinburgh, and Dalkeith. He knew then that he must meet the challenge or lose face not only with the Scots but with all England.

On May 8th, with his troop of twenty-four thousand foot soldiers, most of whom were little better than raw recruits, he had marched into the north, and had finally camped a scant two miles from Berwick by Tweed. There he had made preparations to oppose thirty thousand trained Scottish veterans.

Charles felt the familiar puzzled sickness as he thought of that first venture. Neither side, it seemed, wished to make the first move, and so there had been no fighting. The Scots waited, dour-faced men, impassive of expression. They were secure in their own strength. Their food was plentiful, and they had the added strength of knowing that their troops were paid with French money. French money to aid rebellion, to encourage war against their King! The Scots, observing the King, were aware that his food supplies were fast dwindling. That many of his men, restless with the cold, short rations, and the interminable waiting for the battle to begin, were beginning to desert. They could afford to wait, the Scots told themselves.

As they sat through another long day and night, my lord Foxe, who was beginning to show impatience and whose resentment against the smug Scots was rapidly growing, said sharply, "Your Majesty, if we do not attack soon we will find ourselves without troops to do battle. Let us rally our men. Let us take the enemy by surprise." He had laid his hand in its fine leather glove on Charles's arm, the pressure of his fingers urgent. "Sire, I beg of you! Their insolence, their jeering goes beyond bounds. We are all men here, are we not? How much can we reasonably be expected to take?"

Looking into that dark frowning face, Charles had known that no disrespect to himself had been intended. My lord Foxe's words were indiscreet, but then he was no courtier. "Nay, Brett," Charles answered, shaking his head firmly. "I still think of them as my people. I cannot believe they are really my enemies. They must make the first move, not I. I will not have that on my conscience."

"A plague on conscience!" Brett exploded. "The swine are laughing at us!"

Seated on Charles's other side, Lord Butler had said quietly, "My Lord Foxe is as impulsive as ever, Sire, but nonetheless I can appreciate his feelings." He smiled. "Likewise I can appreciate Your Majesty's words and the sentiment that inspires them. But, Sire, we are in a bad position. Should the Scots decide upon an attack, we will have few men with which to face them. Those who remain have, I assure you, but little heart for battle." He looked at Brett, his tired, worn face expressing sympathy. "So you see, my lord Foxe, your surprise attack is simply not possible."

Charles did not hear my lord Foxe's reply. He sat there silently, his shoulders slumped. He was conscious of a black despair and he tasted the bitterness of defeat. He had not wanted to make war on the Scots, but neither had he wanted the venture to end so ignominiously. He was the King, and yet not a true king to these wild northern people. They would grant him his crown and his right to rule, provided that he ruled their way and did not by any word or action scratch at their touchy pride. Obviously, then, he would be forced to meet their arrogant demands.

"Charles." My lord Foxe's voice, softer now and full of concern, came to his ears. "Have you no word for us?"

He turned his head and looked into the dark-blue eyes regarding him so intently. "Aye," he answered, and the bitterness he felt was in his voice, "I have a word for you, Brett, several words in fact. I regret this blow to your fighting spirit, but seemingly there is nothing left to do but enter into negotiations with the Scots."

To his surprise Brett had laughed, and it did not occur to him until much later that the laugh and the easy reply were designed to save him further humiliation. "God's beard, Sire," Brett drawled, "look not as though your world has crashed about you. Let us then enter into these cursed negotiations. Anything that will get us away from this plaguy place."

So the officers of the two armies had met. The Scots promised to disband their army, and Charles, in his turn, promised that his fleet would withdraw from the waters of the Forth.

"Your Majesty's fortresses will be restored to you," the Scottish officer said, standing at rigid attention before the King. "In return we ask of Your Majesty a free General Assembly, to meet at a reasonable date from now. Likewise a Parliament."

Charles had tried to meet the man's eyes, but he was staring resolutely beyond him. He could not tell the officer's heart. It might be that he agreed with the principles he apparently stood for, or perhaps violently disagreed. It was impossible to tell, for there was not a flicker of expression on his broad face. "Granted," Charles said quietly.

"I thank Your Majesty, but there are yet more conditions."

Charles felt a flash of rage. Quickly, using all his control, he suppressed it. "More?" he answered coldly. "State these conditions, sir."

His tone implied that the Scots with their conditions were insufferably insolent, and he had the satisfaction of seeing a faint flush appear in the wooden face. "The conditions are these, Sire," the man said loudly. "That Your Majesty's subjects shall have that liberty to which they are accustomed restored to them. That their—"

"I was not aware that they had been deprived of their liberty, sir," Charles had interrupted smoothly.

As though the King had not spoken, the officer went on in the same loud voice—"That their lands and houses and goods shall be restored to them, and the means with which to support themselves."

Brett, his hands clenched at his sides, took a quick step forward, his mouth opening on speech. Charles frowned, flashing him a warning look. "Granted, sir," Charles answered the officer in a weary voice.

The peace sat uneasily upon both English and Scot, but at last the negotiations were concluded. Scarcely had Charles, with his small army, set foot in England, when he learned that the Scottish Parliament had made all haste to hold their meeting in Edinburgh. One of their first acts had been to do away with the Episcopalian religion.

Charles could never remember being so angry before. War against the Scots, despite his reluctance to shed Scottish blood, must come, it would seem. He had met all their demands, but this, this destruction of the Church he could not and would not allow! In preparation for this war, he had sent for Thomas Wentworth, who was now the Lord Deputy of Ireland. Wentworth, hurrying from Ireland, was delighted to be in England again. When he returned once more to Ireland, he went as the newly created Earl of Strafford, and left behind him a promise to aid Charles in any way he could.

Charles smiled, remembering how well the Earl of Strafford had fulfilled his promise. Strafford had succeeded in causing the Irish Parliament to grant subsidies and troops to aid the King in the coming war with the Scots. It was because of this unrest, because of his desire to settle things with the Scottish rebels, that Charles had broken the eleven-year silence and once more recalled Parliament.

"Your Majesty," a soft voice with a faintly foreign intonation said. "I have released His Highness from bondage."

Charles smiled at Van Dyck. "Bondage, Sir Anthony?"

The painter smiled. "So I feel sure His Highness views it."

The King gestured to the boy, who was standing uncertainly beside Van Dyck. "I know you are anxious to resume your play, Charles, but you will remain for a few moments longer."

The boy bowed. He smiled at his mother, then settled on a seat beside her.

Anthony Van Dyck, seeing that smile light the dark face, wondered why he had ever considered the boy ugly. When he smiled he appeared to be a very handsome lad. He had a great longing to destroy his half completed painting and to present to England the face of a smiling Stuart. Gravity did not become the lad half so well.

While the King accompanied Van Dyck to the door, the Prince turned his dark eyes on the embroidery in his mother's hands. "Why, Mam," he said in an amused voice, "your work is monstrous dirty. Why do you continue to stitch on that piece when you know well that you hate to embroider?"

Henrietta Maria looked up. Studying her son, she became conscious of a familiar anger. Charles had always irritated her. Nothing he could say or do could stir her to the same tenderness she felt for James, her younger son. Charles was but ten years old, and yet she had the feeling that it was a cynically amused man who looked from his eyes. Those eyes seemed to see right through her. They told her that she was a vain silly creature and scarcely worthy of the love the King bestowed upon her. She had spoken of her feelings to the King, but he had only laughed and accused her of an overvivid imagination. "The boy is young to inspire such strange and strong feeling. You are his mother, why cannot you love him?" he had rebuked her.

Henrietta Maria's mouth tightened now, and she answered the boy with her accustomed sharpness. "What I choose to do is scarcely your concern, Charles." She looked at him critically. "Your face is dirty and your jacket is wrinkled." She put the embroidery to one side and reached a rough hand to his hair. "Disgracefully untidy! You should be ashamed to go about in such condition. James is always neat. I would have you follow his example."

The Prince's face darkened. "I am sorry that I do not please you, Mam. I am myself. I cannot be like James."

There was an expression in his eyes that momentarily disconcerted her. Had she not known better she would have sworn that she had seen a film of tears. He was looking down at the floor now, and she told herself that she had been mistaken. If only James had been heir to the throne instead of Charles. James was so bright and handsome. But Charles, in contrast, was distressingly dark and sallow and ugly. Her brow wrinkled in genuine perplexity as she thought of the adoration Mary had for her brother Charles. As for little Elizabeth, she was only content when he was near. But James, her darling, for all his looks, seemed unable to inspire that same love and devotion. It was especially irritating when one realized that careless Charles made no effort to attract his sister's love, it was just there, whether he willed it or no. Even her ladies, the very serving wenches, favored Charles over her handsome James. Serving wenches? Henrietta Maria's teeth gritted together with rage as she thought of a tale related to her only this morning. Alice Davies, Countess of Elwoode, and one of the few English ladies she counted as friend, had come to her, and had said with much laughter and blushing, "Madam, I saw it with my own eyes. The wench was dusting the furniture in the Prince's bedchamber. The door was open for all to see when the Prince advanced upon her stealthily and raised her skirts." Alice had gone into a further flurry of giggles as she met the Queen's eyes. "Aye, 'tis true. Oh, Madam, His Highness is such a charming boy, so manly. One forgets his extreme youth when he smiles upon one. I declare, that smile of his quite has me in a flutter!"

Coldly angry, Henrietta Maria had dismissed the woman. As the door closed behind her, she wondered that she had ever looked upon the Countess as a friend.

The Prince was watching her, speculation in his dark eyes. "Has something angered you, Mam?"

He spoke in a tone of such innocent inquiry that Henrietta Maria's rage burst its bounds. Forgetting the presence of the

King, who had just closed the door behind Van Dyck, she shouted, "Aye, something has angered me. 'Tis the dirty tales I hear about you!"

"Dirty tales?" The Prince shrank back, viewing her working face with some alarm. "I—I do not understand, Mam."

"Do you not? Will you deny that you were seen lifting the skirts of a serving wench? Will you deny that you fondled her legs, and afterwards bent to place a kiss upon them?"

The Prince stared at her for a moment, then he broke into nervous laughter. "But, Mam, 'twas only Felicity. She doesn't mind, she likes it."

"What!"

"Besides, 'twas because of a dare. George bet me that I would not lift her skirts. He said that were I to do so, I would find her skin remarkably silky and well worthy of a kiss."

"Buckingham? That little monster!"

"Oh, come, Mam, Buckingham is a good sport and great fun." The Prince laughed again. "Felicity didn't mind, truly." His swarthy skin flushed faintly, and he looked shyly pleased. "Afterwards, when I dropped her skirts, she asked me to kiss her. So I—so I did. She said that I kissed just like a real man."

Henrietta Maria gave vent to a small outraged scream. "You beast! How dare you tell me such things!"

The Prince glanced at his father, who was listening with a grave face. "But—but there was nothing so terrible about it, Mam. I found it to be a very pleasant sensation. I enjoyed it." His shy look vanished and his lower lip jutted sullenly. "If she asks me to kiss her again, I will do so. I—I quite liked it."

"Next, you vile boy, you will be bedding the wench, I suppose?"

"Henrietta Maria!" There was a warning note in the King's voice.

She rushed on regardless. "Do you not see? He is not as other boys. He is evil!"

"Henrietta Maria, you will please be silent!"

The Prince had not cried in a long time, but he did so now.

Tears welled into his eyes and fell down his cheeks, marking the red velvet of his jacket. "I d—do not mean to be e—evil," he faltered. " 'Twas naught but a h—harmless prank. If you do not l—like me to kiss her I w—will not do so again." He moved nearer to his mother. "Mam," he held out a pleading hand. "I w—would be happy if you were to l—love me as you do J—James." He placed his hand on her arm, squeezing it pleadingly. "Please, M—M—Mam!"

Henrietta Maria pushed his hand away roughly. "What do you mean? I do love you. You are just being absurd!"

He shook his head and the tears jetted from the corners of his eyes. "No, Mam, you do not." His voice broke. "Y—you have never l—loved me, though I have t—tried to make you d—do so."

The sight of his tear-filled eyes and mournful face drove Henrietta Maria into a guilty frenzy. Without fully realizing what she was doing she lifted her hand and struck him hard across the face. "Idiot! I am your mother, am I not? If I say I love you, then do not dare to argue with me!"

The sound of the boy's choked sobs was too much for the King. He crossed the room in three strides and took the shaking boy in his arms. "There, my son, there! Mam did not mean to strike you. She is not feeling well today."

"I am perfectly well," Henrietta Maria screamed. "The boy annoys me, he has always annoyed me. He is a fool!"

Over the Prince's head the King looked at her, and she had never seen his face so cold and forbidding, so utterly devoid of that tenderness she had grown accustomed to seeing. It was almost as though he hated her. "I suggest you call your ladies to attend you, Madam," he said in a hard voice. "You are obviously distraught and in need of their care."

"I will stay here!"

"No, Madam, you will go, if you please. I have things that I wish to say to my son."

"He is my son too!"

"So he is. But you surprise me, Madam. I had thought you had forgotten that very important point."

Frightened by the look in his eyes, Henrietta Maria cried out wildly, "Do not hate me, my husband!" Her hands clenched on the folds of her skirt. "Pray do not hate me! I cannot help my feeling for the boy. I have tried to love him, but I cannot! I cannot!"

A shudder convulsed the Prince's body. His arms crept up about his father's neck, tightened and clung desperately. "You have said more than enough, Madam. If you do not go at once, I myself will put you out!" The King's eyes turned to the door. "Your ladies are without. I trust they have not heard your words."

Henrietta Maria stared at him for a long moment, then, with a muffled cry, she rushed to the door.

The King waited until it had closed behind her, then he said softly, " 'Tis the child your mother carries in her body that causes her to speak so. She loves you, Charles, I pray you to believe me!"

The Prince's arms loosened. After a moment he nodded, but the shuddering of his body continued.

Gently the King freed himself and held the boy away from him. Stroking the dark hair away from the hot face, he went on, "You do believe that Mam loves you, do you not?"

"If—if you say so, Papa."

"That is not an answer, Charles."

"The truth, Papa?"

"The truth."

"Then, no. I—I do not believe it." Charles's head drooped again. "You love me, do you not, Papa?"

"Oh, my son!" The King's arms drew the boy close. "Aye, I love you," he muttered, stroking the boy's hair. "So much more than I can ever tell you!"

"Then I can be happy again." Remembering his father's reserved nature and his horror of emotional scenes, he added quietly, "Would you like me to promise you never to cry again?"

The King was silent for a moment, struggling to control his own emotion, then he said in a shaken voice, "No, Charles, I would not like such a promise from you. We must all cry at times. Even grown men have been known to cry, did you not know that?"

"I have never thought about it. Have you ever cried, Papa? Now that you are grown, I mean?"

"Aye, sometimes. And doubtless will do so many times before I die."

"I hope not. I don't want you to cry. I want you to be happy." The Prince drew away from him and sat up straight. "I want that very much, Papa."

"The fact that you are my son makes me happy." The King smiled. "You are strong and tall, a son with many fine qualities. You make me proud, Charles."

"Thank you, Papa. But I—I am not handsome like James. I am very ugly, I fear."

"Are you? The serving wenches do not think so."

Seeing the twinkle in the King's eyes, the boy, his heartbreak forgotten for the moment, grinned widely. "Aye, Felicity says that I am a very exciting boy." His brow wrinkled. "Papa, which is better, to be handsome, or to be exciting?"

The King laughed. " 'Twould be nice to be both, son. But if one must choose, then I would say 'tis better to be exciting."

"Why?"

" 'Tis a little hard to explain," the King said hastily. "But when you are a man you will realize the truth of my words."

"Will the ladies like me as much as they will James?"

The King studied him intently. "More, I believe, Charles," he said slowly. "Much more."

"Why?"

"Why, why! How you do overwork that word, my son." He shrugged. "I cannot answer you. It is something I feel."

The Prince nodded, accepting this. "Papa, you do not believe I did an evil thing when I lifted Felicity's skirts?"

"Not evil, no. As you said, 'twas a harmless prank. However, you are the Prince of Wales. 'Twould perhaps be best to give a thought to your dignity now and again."

"But is it not better to have fun than to be dignified?"

"Perhaps a mingling of both," the King suggested.

"I like fun best."

"Aye, Charles, and I believe you always will. No matter, you have a natural dignity. Much will be forgiven you." He smiled. "And now, if we may change the subject, I have pleasant news for you. I have decided to allow the visit to Milford Manor."

"Papa!" Charles clasped his hands together in ecstasy. "We will have such a good time. George is going too, and Tony Foxefield. We will meet my lord Butler's son. Have you ever met him?"

The King's face sobered. "No, Charles, I have not met the lad."

There it was again, the Prince thought, that strange look that appeared on the adult's faces whenever my lord Butler's son was mentioned. "Papa," he began diffidently, "is there something wrong with this Marcus? Is he—is he perhaps an invalid?"

The King's mouth tightened to a straight line as he thought of the scandalous tales concerning the lady Mary Butler. Tales of her neglect of her son, born a month after Charles. Tales of her callous disregard of her husband's feelings. It was said that the boy, Marcus, was not the son of my lord Butler, but of one of the lady's numerous lovers. Butler himself did not seem to doubt his paternity. When, on rare occasions he spoke of the boy, there was however a certain restraint in his manner. It was as if he could not bring himself to enthuse as would a normal father. So perhaps, after all, though he did not doubt that Butler loved the boy, he did entertain certain doubts. Becoming aware that Charles was watching him, the King answered reluctantly. "There is nothing wrong as far as I know. I understand that the boy is very shy. He has not mingled with boys of his own age before. It may be that he will be a little hard to know.''

"Is that all!'' Charles exclaimed. "I have been imagining all sorts of things. I will soon bring him out of his shyness. I am not hard to know, am I, Papa?''

"No, indeed you are not. You have a gift for putting others immediately at their ease.''

"Do I?'' Charles looked pleased. "Do you have that gift?''

"No.'' The King smiled ruefully. "I have not your open and friendly nature.''

"Would you like me to teach you?''

"It is not something that can be taught, Charles. It is there or it is not there.''

"Papa, will I meet my lady Butler?''

"You will not,'' the King answered quickly. "The lady is paying an extended visit to friends in London.''

"I don't mind that.'' Charles's face took on a look of enthusiasm. "We will be able to play the better for not being watched all the time, and perhaps scolded for playing games that are too rough, or for soiling our clothes.''

"I understand and sympathize with your point of view,'' the King said with some amusement. "But it is only fair to warn you that you will not be entirely unsupervised. There are servants in the house. There is also Mrs. Thomas, Marcus's nurse. She can be, I understand, quite a dragon. There will also be my lady Foxefield.''

"Lady Foxe!'' Charles cried. "She's great fun. I like her. She never scolds. She's pretty too. Sometimes, when we allow it, she joins in our games.''

"There will also be your guard,'' the King reminded him.

"But why must I have a guard? My lord Butler will be there, will he not?''

"He will. Nevertheless a guard you must have.''

Charles dropped the informal "Papa.'' "Sire,'' he said, striving for dignity, "if you will dispense with the guard, I will promise to behave and to conduct myself as you would wish.''

"The guards are not there to supervise your behavior, my son. There is always a certain amount of danger surrounding a royal personage, and we cannot risk harm coming to you."

"No harm will come to me."

"I hope not. But we must be sure. If it will make you any happier, I will instruct the guards to remain within hearing but out of sight."

Charles sighed. "It is better than nothing, I suppose."

"It most certainly is." The King laughed and ruffled the boy's long dark hair. "Run along, Charles. I am expecting my lord Butler and my lord Foxe shortly."

Charles jumped to his feet and ran to the door, then, remembering his manners, he came back and bowed low. "A very good day to Your Majesty," he said.

"And a very good day to Your Highness," the King answered with suitable gravity.

After Charles had left, the King thought over the situation at Milford Manor. My lord Foxe, who had met Marcus Milford on one or two occasions, had said of John's heir, "He is a strange and lonely little creature. Not having had many in his life, I suspect, he is suspicious of friendly overtures. He adores his father, but not even with him does he behave as a normal boy. It is as though he fears to fully reveal himself, in case of a rebuff."

"You make him sound old beyond his years," Charles had answered.

"That he is, Sire. Once, when my lady Butler was present, the boy came into the room. When he looked at his mother, there was terror in his face. And yet, when she turned to address a remark to him, he answered her with dignity, but so coldly that I confess I was taken aback. His manner, that of a mature man, did not match the terrified expression I had previously seen."

"Why should he fear his mother?"

Brett's jaw set grimly. "That is something I should like to find out. I detest cruelty to children."

"Is Marcus always so self-contained?"

"I saw him crumble once. His father called him to his side, and the boy stood there quietly and waited for his father to speak, those sad, dark eyes of his intent. My lord Butler sighed and frowned, then he said to him, 'Why do you look at me like that, Marcus? You need not fear me, you know. I have sent for you because I desire your company. When I have to be away for long periods at a time, I miss you very much.' At first the boy said nothing, then, as though something long suppressed had broken, he hurled himself forward. I saw his knuckles whiten as he clung to his father, and told him over and over again that he loved him. I was so damned moved, Sire, that I had to turn away.''

Thinking of that conversation, Charles frowned. Marcus Milford did not sound at all like a normal boy. He could not help wondering if he had been wise to allow this visit to Milford Manor and the strange atmosphere there. The lady of the manor was naught but a brazen whore, her son apparently haunted and terrified. Should he allow young Charles to be exposed to all this? Each time when my lord Butler paid a visit to the manor, he returned looking more ill and worn than before, and considerably thinner. Butler was older than his wife, but still a comparatively young man. He should not be looking quite so old as he did.

Charles got up and wandered restlessly to the window. Staring down into the courtyard, he firmly dismissed the worry from his mind. He had promised Charles that he should go on the visit, and he would keep his promise. His son was not as level-headed as he would like him to be, though, if he put his mind to it, he could be. Might it not be that far from harm coming to Charles, he could do some good? Perhaps he could draw Marcus Milford from his unchildlike shell of reserve. Charles was a very kind boy, and he had great charm. Most people responded to him.

The King's hand clenched on the satin drapes. Most people, but not his mother. Aye, poor Charles had his troubles too. The responsibility of his heritage, which would become heavier as he grew older. A mother who did not love him, and was cruel enough to say so. And an idle and pleasure-loving nature to conquer and shape to his position in life.

The King turned away from the window. Because he could not help loving Henrietta Maria, he had tended to overlook the streak of cruelty in her nature. But he would not allow her to hurt Charles. He thought of the stricken look on the boy's face, and his anger welled up anew. He could not force Henrietta Maria to love her son, but she must be made to treat him in a pleasant and civilized way.

His brooding thoughts scattered as the door opened and my lord Butler and my lord Foxe were announced. Greeting them, Charles thought again how terribly ill Butler looked. "Come, come, John," he said, as the man made to kneel before him, "I do not wish you to kneel. Be seated, gentlemen."

When the King gave his consent to the visit of the Prince of Wales to Milford Manor, he was touched to see his friend's tired, lined face light up with pleasure. "I promise you that I will take very good care of His Highness," he eagerly assured Charles. "He and Tony and George will be companions for my son. In accordance with your wish and the Prince's, there is to be no formality. Marcus knows he is to have visitors, but I did not tell him that one of those visitors will be the Prince. I wished to give him a pleasant surprise."

"Is Marcus looking forward to playing with companions of his own age?" the King said in a gentle voice.

John Butler's face changed. "I have no way of knowing, Sire. I can never tell what Marcus is thinking or feeling." He glanced at Brett, who was lounging back in his chair. Then his eyes turned again to the King. "I fear that I am a poor father, Sire. Something has hurt my boy terribly, and yet I cannot seem to find out what it might be. Sometimes I have thought—" he stopped, his face turning a fiery red. Swallowing hard, he went on firmly. "Sometimes I have thought that he might have heard the gossip about— about his mother. But then I tell myself that even if he had, it would mean nothing to him." His eyes went pleadingly from one face to another. "He is surely too young to understand the implication of such gossip. Do you not think so?"

273

Brett did not think so. He glanced helplessly at the King, then, by way of answer, he gave John a faint, warm smile. Charles looked at Butler's flushed, gaunt face and his trembling hands. Seeing him stripped of his normal cool reserve, he was greatly distressed. Leaning forward, he laid his hand over the Earl's twitching fingers. "John," the King began hesitantly, "you do not think that the boy has seen Lady Mary with—" Meeting the Earl's shadowed eyes, he stopped in confusion.

"In bed with her lovers, Sire," the Earl finished for him. It seemed that now he had broken his silence that he was determined to conceal nothing. "No, I think not. Not even she would be that careless."

Charles nodded. Taking his hand away, he leaned back in his chair. "Forgive me, John, but I must confess that the thought had crossed my mind."

The Earl's trembling increased. "I would kill her, if I thought for one moment that she would allow the boy to witness such an act! Aye, I would kill her!" After a moment, in which he visibly struggled for calm, he said in a toneless voice, "I ask your pardon, Sire. Such a parade of naked emotion is quite unforgivable." He gave a tight smile. "I will not offend again."

"You know well that there is nothing to forgive."

"Plague take you, John!" Brett cut in. "For the Lord's sake don't climb on your high horse again. What do you think friends are for, if not to listen, and to help if possible?"

"Thank you, Brett, but I'm afraid you cannot help me. I am weak, I fear, or I would have helped myself long ere this. The devil of it is that I loathe her for what she is, and yet I cannot stop loving her. Can you possibly understand that?" Febrile color stained his cheeks. "I could have broken free, but when it came to it, I hadn't the will or the desire." The Earl fell silent, and it was as though he had forgotten where he was. He leaned back in his chair, his eyes closed, the sound of his labored breathing filling the room.

He is dying! Charles thought. Dying by slowly tortured inches!

His eyes met Brett's, and he knew that the same thought was in his mind. He bit his lip. His two friends. The old friend of his boyhood, and the new and equally precious friend. He had known Butler intimately for only a few years, but in some ways it was as though he had known him forever. He had lost Buckingham, and he could not bear to think of losing Butler also. His fear showed in his voice, as he said sharply, "My lord Butler, pray to attend. Although there is to be no formality on this visit to Milford Manor, there are nonetheless still some things we must talk over."

The Earl opened his eyes and gave him a dazed look. "Forgive me for closing my eyes, Sire. It is just that I am so very tired."

"I understand, my lord," the King said in a softer voice. "But I fear you are ill. Under the circumstances, do you think the Prince's visit is wise?"

"Nay, Sire, I assure you I am not ill," the Earl said, betraying signs of that unusual agitation. "I am very well." He met the King's serious eyes. "Sometimes," he went on unwillingly, "I have a little difficulty with my breathing. But I beg you to believe me when I tell you that it is nothing."

"Does the visit mean so much to you, John?"

"I am always happy to welcome the Prince." The Earl's hands were tense on the arms of his chair. "It is not for myself that I earnestly desire this visit, but for my boy. For—for Marcus. The Prince will be well cared for. No harm shall come to him, I swear it!"

"No need, John. I would willingly place Charles's life in your hands and know it to be perfectly safe."

"Thank you, Sire."

"Very well, then. The matter is settled."

The Earl gave a deep, relieved sigh. Brett, pitying him, said easily, "That's all very well, but my sympathies are with the Prince and with Marcus, to say nothing of Tony and George. Hast forgotten that my lady will be there to keep order?"

Charles smiled. "I had thought, from the reputation my lord Butler has given her, that the formidable Mrs. Thomas deserves the reputation of dragon, not my lady Foxe."

"Ah, but the two of them together will be a terrible and daunting combination," Brett answered with a smile.

"Mrs. Thomas?" the Earl said hoarsely. "I fear I have misled you, Sire. I thank God for her!" He gave a strained smile that sought to make light of his vehemence. "Dragon though I might have unwittingly painted her, to Marcus she is a very kind and loving dragon. She has been with the boy since the day he was born. I truly believe that she would give her life for him."

"Then young Marcus is fortunate in such devotion," the King answered.

"Fortunate indeed, Sire, since he has not his mother's love."

The King thought of Charles and the painful scene that had occurred. He had that much at least in common with Marcus. Neither of them possessed their mother's love. Mayhap they would discover a mutual sympathy. The King started out of his abstraction. "Come, gentlemen, let us talk of other things."

The conversation turned to the Scotch uprising, and the means by which they might satisfy the Scots and quell the rebellion once and for all. The King then went on to speak of the coming Parliamentary session and his hopes of finding a new and amicable relationship with his Ministers. Surely, if reason and loyalty prevailed, they must find a common meeting ground?

The Earl listened intently and occasionally put in a shrewd word. He seemed to have recovered his poise. The tormented look had left his eyes, and they now wore their accustomed sleepily smiling expression.

When they rose to take their leave, the clasp of John Butler's hand was firm and reassuring to Charles. He must have been mistaken in believing him ill, Charles thought. He thought of Butler as a rock, stern, strong, and unwavering, but he should have remembered that there were times when even the strongest of men broke down. He comforted himself with the thought that

Butler, though obviously not a well man, was very far from dying.

Left alone, Charles bethought himself of Henrietta Maria. After a while, he went in search of her. This time, he told himself, he would be very firm with her. If he should find himself weakening and giving in to her wheedling, he had only to recall his son's tear-stained face and his piteously trembling mouth.

Chapter Sixteen

Mrs. Thomas sank wearily into her comfortable chair. From her position by the window, she could see the broad, winding drive with its edging of wind-swept oak trees. Stretching out for some distance on either side of the great oaks were velvety lawns bordered with lilac shrubs bearing starry burdens of purple blossom and white blossom. The smooth, green expanse of the lawns was broken here and there with long beds and circular beds of bright and fragile spring flowers.

Mrs. Thomas sighed, unable to take her usual pleasure in the view. For the twentieth time she asked herself what more she could have done to avert disaster? Last night, as soon as she had recovered from the shock of my lady Butler's unexpected arrival, she had sent a messenger posting off to my lord Butler to acquaint him with the dismaying news. But she greatly feared that the messenger would be too late. Doubtless Lord John and his young visitors were already on their way. What would be my lord's reaction when he found his wife here, occupying the master bedroom with her latest lover?

Closing her eyes, Mrs. Thomas relived last night's scene. Lady Mary, her eyes bright, her full lips smiling, had swept into Milford Manor. She was beautiful in a habit of scarlet velvet. Dark curls fell from beneath a man's velvet bonnet stuck with three curling white plumes. Her mouth was painted as brightly as her habit. The man accompanying her was Sir Jeremy Forster, whom she had brought to the manor several times before. Of all Lady Mary's men, Mrs. Thomas hated Sir Jeremy the most. He had small cruel blue eyes, a fleshy mouth, and a habit of fixing one with a bold and penetrating stare.

"Well?" Lady Mary had said, seeing her obvious agitation. "Why are you gaping at me like an idiot, Thomas? Have you no fond greeting for your mistress?" Turning to Sir Jeremy, she broke into high-pitched laughter. "The woman absolutely adores me, Jerry. 'Tis true, is it not, Thomas?"

Even with Lady Mary's mocking eyes upon her, Mrs. Thomas, because it was her way, spoke the truth. "No, my lady," she answered, a grim note in her voice, "I have no fondness for you."

"Ah! Because of your precious Marcus, eh?"

"Because of Marcus and many other things, my lady."

"Take care, Thomas, lest you be parted from Marcus."

"But I will not be parted from him, my lady," she answered, ignoring the threatening tone. "Lord John would not countenance my dismissal."

"Do not be too sure."

Mrs. Thomas took a deep breath. "I am very sure of that, my lady. There—there is something I must tell you. Lord John is expected here on the morrow. He is bringing with him some young guests. They are to spend a few days with Master Marcus."

Lady Mary's dark eyes narrowed. "So the monk is coming, is he? Who are these guests he brings?"

"I know not. My lady, he will not expect to find you here."

"Then it will be an added pleasure for him. As for you, Thomas, I find you too outspoken for your own good. From your tone and your general bearing, I gather that you would like me to leave?''

It had taken courage to answer, but she had done so. Looking at Sir Jeremy meaningly, she said bluntly, ''It might be best, my lady.''

''But then I never do the best thing. You should know that by now. No, Thomas, much as I regret to disappoint you, I must be here to greet my lord. You know well that the holy man would not have it any other way.''

Laughing at the expression on the woman's face, Lady Mary turned away and walked over to the stairs. She was followed by the grinning Sir Jeremy. ''By the way, Thomas,'' she said, pausing, ''instruct a servant to bring dinner for two to my bed-chamber. After we have dined, you will bring my son to me.''

''No!'' Mrs. Thomas uttered the word loudly and defiantly. ''I will not be bringing him to you. I will not have that poor boy upset again.''

Lady Mary stared at her. ''You have a bold tongue, but I feel sure you know better than to defy me. You will do as you are bid. Marcus will present himself to me. Do you understand?''

Mrs. Thomas tasted despair. It was Sir Jeremy who unwittingly came to her aid. ''Let the boy alone for tonight, Mary. I wish your attention to be all for me.''

Lady Mary hesitated. Then, her mouth sullen, she said reluctantly, ''Very well, Jeremy, if you wish it so. As for you, Thomas, I promise you that you have not heard the last of this.'' Mrs. Thomas opened her eyes. No, she had not heard the last of it. Lady Mary, if she knew her, would have her way. But perhaps she could appeal to Lord John. She would say that she feared for the lad. That Lady Mary was callous and cruel to Marcus. She shuddered. What would it do to him, poor man? But if there was no other way out, she would do it. She thought of Marcus after one of those sessions with his mother, his eyes big in his pale, sick face. Trembling, terribly afraid, after the mental torture he had been forced to endure. He would fall asleep briefly, only to start up again in the grip of his recurring nightmare. Mrs. Thomas put her hand to her unsteady mouth. What did the woman do to the boy? Did she strike him when she made those cruel and scathing remarks about his father? Perhaps she herself had not fought as hard as she might for Marcus. She had not been strong enough or bold enough. But there must be some way she could counter Lady Mary. There had to be, for his sake, her dearest Master Marcus. What of Lord John? Was he even now on his way? She leaned forward, her eyes searching the distance. Or had the messenger managed to intercept him?

"Thomas! Thomas!" the frenzied screaming of her name brought her quickly to her feet.

"I'm coming, Master Marcus!" Her heart hammering, she tore open the door and ran into the wide hall. She stopped short, staring.

His face hidden in his hands, Marcus was huddled at the top of the stairs. A laughing Lady Mary stood over him. Her thin blue robe, open at the front, exposed her naked body and the brightly tinted nipples of her breasts, prominent now with the excitement that possessed her. "You shall listen to me, Marcus!" she said. Her long black hair spilled forward as she reached down to grasp the boy's arm. "Your father is no man, he is a bloody monk. I hope he dies soon, do you hear me? I hope he dies!"

Marcus managed to jerk his arm free. "I hate you, you bad, nasty woman!" he screamed. "I hate you!"

Lady Mary grabbed at him and pulled him to his feet. "You don't hate me, you love me. You want to be with me, admit it. Say instead that you hate the man you call father, and I will give you anything you desire. Say it, you little swine!"

Marcus's dark eyes blazed from his pale face. "I wish you would die! Let me go! I want Thomas."

His use of her name brought Mrs. Thomas out of the paralysis that had bound her. Gathering her skirts in her hands, she rushed up the stairs. "Let him go, my lady! Let him go!"

Sheer amazement caused Lady Mary to release the boy. She stepped back a pace, staring at the tall, angular woman with the fiery blue eyes. She found her voice. "How dare you, Thomas!

Your audacity goes beyond all bounds. You are Marcus's nurse, not his mother!''

Mrs. Thomas ignored her. "Go, Master Marcus. Go on. Don't be afraid, my lovie.''

She watched Marcus stumble down the stairs, run across the hall, and fumble blindly with the latch of the great carved door. Only when he was safely outside, did she turn to look at Lady Mary. "Never touch him again, my lady, or seek to influence him against his father,'' she said harshly. "If you persist, I will go to Lord John.''

Studying her, Lady Mary began to laugh. "You may tell him what you choose, but it will accomplish nothing.''

"It will. He will stop you. I swear that you are driving my poor boy insane!''

"My lord will do nothing, I tell you. He is a weak fool.''

Filled with the dismal certainty that Lady Mary spoke the simple truth, Mrs. Thomas looked away. Lord John had always been a strong and reliable man. But where this woman was concerned, he was lamentably weak. But surely he would make some effort to defend his son.

Lady Mary seemed to be reading her mind. "Oh, he will warn me, Thomas. But then he will tell himself that he has done his duty. You see, he is only concerned with his own misery and longing.''

"Nay! Lord John is not like that!''

"I believe he was a strong man once, but now he is a nothing. My God, I cannot bear him! I would not have Marcus grow up to be such a weak fool. He is not the man I married. He has changed beyond all recognition.''

"And if he has changed,'' Mrs. Thomas cried, "if he has become less than he was, whose fault is that? How can he be the same man when he does not know in whose bed his wife might be lying? When he does not know when that wife might descend upon him to humiliate him once more with her lovers? Why, he cannot even be sure that Master Marcus is his own son!''

A faint amused smile touched Lady Mary's lips. "I should be

very angry with you, Thomas, but strangely enough I am not. On the contrary, I think I rather admire your courage." The smile abruptly disappeared. "Tell me, Thomas, how old are you?"

"What has my age to do with anything?"

"How old, Thomas?"

"I am—I am thirty-two."

"Thirty-two. It is not young, is it? Your age might not be in your favor, should you have to seek a new position."

Mrs. Thomas felt suddenly chilled. Her reply lacked its former confidence. "Lord John will not consent to letting me go."

"And I have told you not to be too sure. If I wish it so, you will be dismissed." She turned away and strolled to the open door of her bedchamber. "My advice to you, Thomas, if you wish to keep your position, is to curb your tongue. Also to look the other way when I send for my son."

A trembling seized Mrs. Thomas. "So that you may have the freedom to distort his mind?" she shouted. "Aye, my lady, I'll curb my tongue, but I will never look the other way! 'Tis useless for you to ask such a thing of me!"

But Lady Mary had swept away. The slam of the bedchamber door was her only answer. Through the door, Mrs. Thomas could hear the rumble of Sir Jeremy's voice, followed by Lady Mary's high laughter. Turning, she went slowly and heavily down the stairs.

In the cool dimness of the stable, always his retreat in times of mental anguish, Marcus lay flat on his stomach with his hot face resting against a bale of hay. The sweet dry smell of the hay was strong in his nostrils. He sneezed. Behind him, a chestnut mare, startled by the abrupt sound, curvetted nervously and gave a soft, plaintive whinny.

"Maggie May." Marcus rose to his feet and approached the mare. Stroking her soft nose, he spoke to her in a voice that was still hoarse with tears. "I love you, Maggie May. You and Thomas are the only two ladies I shall ever love. I swear that I will never marry! Ladies are cruel, and they can make men cry.

Because of my mother, I have seen my father cry. But I will never, never cry over a lady!''

Maggie May responded with another whinny. Lowering her head, she began to snuffle his pocket. "You are a greedy wench, Maggie May," Marcus said, laughing shakily. "I have nothing for you at the moment. But I will bring you something later, I promise.''

Maggie May lifted her head again. She stood quietly while Marcus stroked her mane, and her large, velvet brown eyes appeared to study him. Marcus laughed again, for he had the comforting conviction that she understood what he was saying. "My father will be coming soon, Maggie May," he went on. "He is bringing some boys with him. They are to be companions for me. But I do not want companions. I wanted my father to come alone, for I do not like to share him with others. Do you know, Maggie May, there are times when I think my father really loves me? But then there are those other times, when I am sure that he does not." Marcus's eyes took on a bleak expression. "I see little enough of him as it is. Why should I share him? If he makes a bigger fuss over those boys than he does over me, I shall fight them and knock them down. My father will see then that he and I only need each other.''

An hour passed before Lord John arrived with his party. In that time, Marcus's angry jealous resentment grew stronger. "I do not want companions," he told Mrs. Thomas. "I wish to be alone with my father.''

Mrs. Thomas studied him with loving but worried eyes. Marcus was a tall boy for his age, with a muscular but slender build. With his thickly curling black hair, his dark eyes, and his strong, well-cut features, Mrs. Thomas thought that he would grow into a remarkably handsome man. But for one so young, his expression was decidedly austere. She imagined that it would become more so as he grew older. It was not really the face of a boy, it was too mature, too sad. Answering him, she strove to make her voice placid. "It will do you good to have some young friends, Master Marcus. You have been too much alone.''

His mouth was obstinate. "I don't want friends, Thomas. I am happy as I am."

He was happy! She longed to draw him into her arms and hold him close. But when he wore that particular expression, she knew that he did not want to be touched. There was something very aloof about him, and, absurd as it might seem, something forbidding. "Master Marcus," she said in an unsteady voice, "I have warned you before about that jealous streak in your nature. It will get you into trouble one day, I warn you. You are too possessive."

He ran his fingers through his thick hair in an angry and impatient gesture. "I am jealous, you say, I am possessive. What other faults have I, Thomas?"

"Many." She gave a slight smile. "But they are too numerous to mention in one day."

He gave her a suspicious look. "Do you speak truth, or are you teasing me?"

"Of course I am teasing."

He shrugged. "Anyway, I am not possessive. It is simply that I do not care to share my father with others."

"And what is yours, Master Marcus, you and you alone will hold? You see, you are condemned out of your own mouth."

"Very well. But it is how I feel."

She laughed. "You are very grown up and dignified today, love."

"Certainly," he said indignantly. "I am ten years old, almost eleven. And I would have you know—" He broke off, listening with strained attention. He heard the sound of hooves striking stone, jingling harness, voices and laughter. Subconsciously, he realized, he had been hearing the sounds for some time. "Look, Thomas," he said loudly, "my father is just turning into the gates. He and those boys are here. There are a lot of other men too."

He moved closer to the window and pressed his nose against the glass. My lord Butler, astride a big black horse, headed the procession. Save for the red and white plumes in his hat, he was

285

dressed all in black. To Marcus's fond eyes, he looked very handsome and imposing. Behind him, rode a slender dark boy. He was splendidly mounted on a white horse with red trappings. He was clad in jacket and breeches of emerald-green velvet. A short black cloak fluttered from his shoulders, and his face was shadowed by a broad-brimmed black hat adorned with a green feather. The sunlight glinted on the curling ends of his long black hair, giving it a blue-black sheen. Behind him rode two other boys. One was dark-haired, with a good-looking, open countenance, dressed in sapphire-blue with white trimmings. The other boy, burly of frame and blond of hair, wore red velvet. His jacket was slashed at the wide, padded sleeves with twined black and white satin. Farther along, Marcus could see my lady Foxefield. From beneath a big blue hat loaded with white plumes her bright hair fell to her shoulders. It looked, Marcus thought, like curling flames licking at the white velvet of her gown. He had met Lady Foxefield on several occasions. She had always been kind to him, but his guarded and withdrawn nature had not yet accepted her for what she seemed to be. Too often, as in the case of his mother, kindness could quickly turn into a blow or a curse. My lady Foxefield had asked him to call her Meredith, but thus far, he was still formal with her. One of those boys, he supposed, would be Anthony Foxefield, her son. He rather thought that he might be the boy in blue.

The procession had stopped. They were dismounting and preparing to enter the house. Marcus could hear the excited voices of the servants and the running feet of the grooms. He stiffened suddenly as he saw his father aid the boy in green to dismount. He did not care for the way his father was smiling at the boy, or the friendly arm about his shoulders.

Standing beside him, Mrs. Thomas cast a quick look at his frowning face. She guessed what Marcus would say. He said it. "My father has never been so friendly to me. I am his son, but he rarely smiles at me."

"Could it be that your manner does not encourage him, Master Marcus?" Mrs. Thomas laid a hand on his stiff shoulder. "You do not often smile yourself, you know. Even an adult needs a little encouragement."

He turned his head to look at her. "What do you mean? He must know that I love him."

"Have you ever told him so?"

"Yes, once." Marcus remembered the time when, confused and angry with his mixed emotions, he had clung to his father, sobbing, and telling him over and over again of his love for him. Since that time, Lord John had returned only once to the manor. He had been kind but aloof, with no perceptible difference in his attitude. Marcus told himself now that the reason there had been no difference, was because his father did not love him, would never love him! He had never looked at him as he had at the boy in green. Hot, stabbing jealousy pierced him, and he gave a muffled cry.

Mrs. Thomas stared in dismay as he whirled about and made for the opposite window. "Where are you going?" she cried. "Come back, Master Marcus! You must be present to greet your father and his guests."

Marcus did not answer. Opening the window, he clambered through and dropped to the ground. Making his way to the stable that housed Maggie May, he remembered thankfully that the grooms would be settling the horses in the other stables. For a little while he would be undisturbed. He had not the wish or the inclination to greet his father just yet. Thinking of the boy in green, he scowled. He hated that boy for being the recipient of his father's smiles, and for his easy and assured manner, which he himself longed to achieve. Because he had no trust in proffered friendship or kind words, his manner became yet more awkward and sullen. When he tried to smile easily, as that boy had done, his lips would not obey his will.

Mrs. Thomas closed the window. She shook her head sadly. She knew where Marcus had gone. Likely he would stay in that stable for hours. Poor lad! He wanted so much to love and to be loved in return. Lady Mary had much to answer for! It was she, with the constant mental torture she inflicted upon him, who had stunted Marcus's emotions and made of him the suspicious and wary little being he was today.

Her thoughts turned to Lord John. She walked over to the door and stood there uncertainly. As Marcus's nurse, it was not really her place to go forward and greet Lord John. That was for Mrs. Phelps, the housekeeper, to do. But she must see Lord John. This was no time to think of the order of precedence. She would go into the hall. It might be that she would be able to catch his eye. If he should come upon Lady Mary unexpectedly it would prove a very painful and disagreeable shock. In all the time she had known him, never had Lord John entertained guests when Lady Mary was in residence. He knew only too well how his lady delighted in humiliating him.

Driven by a sense of urgency, Mrs. Thomas lifted the latch. Opening the door, she stepped into the hall. Oh, God! she thought. What if Lady Mary should come down the stairs. She might come down stark naked, if the mood moved her. She would put nothing past the hateful woman!

Lord John was standing in the center of the hall. Next to him were the three boys and Lady Foxefield. The men who had accompanied them were standing by the door, drawn up at stiff attention. Mrs. Thomas glanced at them with fleeting curiosity. They were dressed as civilians but they looked like soldiers.

"Now, Your Highness," Lord John was saying in an indulgent voice, "I am sure the Prince of Wales has been taught patience. Marcus, I am quite sure, will be here at any moment."

The Prince! Mrs. Thomas's eyes widened in dismay. The boy clad in green was the Prince of Wales! But that made matters worse than ever. She took a quick step forward, all thoughts of keeping her place forgotten. She must speak to Lord John at once. She must warn him of Lady Mary's presence.

Lady Foxefield saw her first. A smile lit her face. "Mrs. Thomas," she exclaimed. " 'Tis good to see you again."

"My lady." Mrs. Thomas inclined her head respectfully.

"So you are Mrs. Thomas." Smiling, the Prince came toward

her. "I have heard much about you. Tony, George, give greetings to Marcus's Mrs. Thomas."

At any other time Mrs. Thomas would have been both charmed and flattered by the Prince's unexpectedly friendly attitude to one he had never met before, but now she was agitated. Smiling at him absently, she dropped him a quick curtsey. "Welcome, Your Highness."

Lord John looked keenly at Mrs. Thomas, and his light-hearted manner dropped away. "What is it?" he asked her. "Is something wrong?"

Mrs. Thomas moistened her lips. "If I—I might have a moment of your time, my lord."

"Of course." He took a quick step forward. "You are not going to tell me Marcus is ill?"

Mrs. Thomas wished that Marcus could see that look of intense anxiety on his father's face, then he could never again doubt that he was loved. "Nay, Master Marcus is not ill," she reassured him. "It is on another matter that I wish to speak." Unconsciously, she gave him a beseeching look.

Lord John hesitated for another moment, then he said in a heavy voice, "Very well. But where is my son, Mrs. Thomas? The Prince is anxious to meet him. I had expected to see him before this."

"I am quite sure that Master Marcus is unaware of your arrival, my lord," she murmured, evading his searching eyes.

"Indeed. Where is he?"

Unable to help herself, Mrs. Thomas turned anxious eyes toward the stairs. "I—he is with Maggie May, my lord. I feel certain that he will be here in a few moments."

"And who is Maggie May?" the Prince queried.

Again Mrs. Thomas gave the boy a faint, absent smile. "His horse, Your Highness. Master Marcus is tending her. And a spoiled and vain creature she is."

Charles grinned. "Maggie May? I like her name. And I like Marcus for caring enough to spoil her. I love horses, and I believe that nothing is too good for them. I will go to the stables and make the acquaintance of Marcus and Maggie May.''

The men lined up at the door stiffened as the Prince started forward. ''Rest easy, gentlemen,'' Charles said, giving them an impatient look. ''I will be perfectly safe, I assure you. Pray stay where you are, for I imagine that quarters will shortly be allotted to you.''

Sir Peter Fordyce, a dapper red-faced man with a shock of graying hair, stepped forward smartly. ''But Your Highness well knows that we must accompany you. Your safety, after all, is our main concern.''

''Aye,'' Charles said hotly, scowling at him, ''and mayhap you think a worm will make off with me, or a bird, with evil intent.''

Sir Peter gave him an indulgent look. ''If we might follow at a distance, Your Highness,'' he suggested. ''I can safely guarantee that you will not be aware of us.''

''Plague take it! 'Tis foolishness.''

''His Majesty's orders,'' Sir Peter said placatingly.

Charles shrugged. ''If you must, then. But for my part, I find it very wearisome.''

Meredith, who had quickly become aware of the urgency in Mrs. Thomas's manner, said, ''Your Highness, shall I show you the way to Maggie May's stable?''

''I will find it for myself, my lady. After all, if you are to find the strength to scold us on the morrow, you will have need of rest.''

Meredith gave him an affectionate smile. ''But Your Highness knows that I would not so presume.''

''I know no such thing. Pray call me Charles, Lady Foxe. Or hast forgotten that we promised to drop all formality?''

''No, Charles, I remember well. But since we are being so informal, won't you call me Meredith?''

''I will, my lady, with pleasure.'' Charles glanced at the other boys. ''You two stay here with Meredith,'' he ordered.

"But I don't want to stay with mother," Tony Foxefield protested. "George and I wish to come with you."

"Aye," the young Duke of Buckingham put in. "We'll come with you."

Charles shook his head. "No, you won't. I have long wished to meet Marcus, and I have a fancy to do so alone."

Marcus, standing by Maggie May and talking to her in a low voice, did not hear the approaching footsteps.

Charles stopped in the doorway, looking curiously at the tall boy with the untidy black hair. Marcus was dressed in jacket and breeches of a very dark purple. The suit was elegant, but untrimmed, and there was no lace at the wide cuffs. Charles, who had a love of finery, decided that he did not like such plain garb. At that moment Marcus turned, and Charles abruptly changed his mind. He might not like the suit for himself, but it most certainly suited this boy.

"Hello, Marcus," Charles said softly.

Marcus stared back at him with hostile eyes. He disliked the green velvet finery of his visitor, his face, everything about him. "Well," he snapped, "what do you want? Can't you see that I'm busy?"

Charles smiled at him. "No, I can't see that. You're only talking to Maggie May. That's not being busy, is it?"

"How did you know her name?"

"Mrs. Thomas told me."

"Oh." Marcus hesitated. "Did—did my father ask for me?"

"I don't remember. Still, I expect John will be searching for you in a little while. At this moment he's talking to Mrs. Thomas."

Charles was startled at the blaze in the other boy's eyes. "John!" Marcus gasped. "You dare to call my father John, you—you dressed up monkey!"

Charles's good humor deserted him. He stepped forward, his fists clenching. "Don't you dare to call me a dressed up monkey! As for your father, I will call him John at any time I please. We

291

have decided to drop formality, and I have his permission to do so. Now, then, you unmannerly lout, you take back what you called me."

"I will not. You are an ugly dressed-up monkey. And you are not to call my father by his name. I won't allow it!"

"You! You won't allow it!" Thoroughly roused, Charles stared at him in outrage. "I will call him what I please. John! John! John!"

Marcus's anger and jealous resentment engulfed him in a burning wave. Fists swinging, he rushed forward. One hard fist caught Charles on the nose, the other drove into his stomach.

Gasping, Charles went down. He tried to fight back, but Marcus was on top of him, pummeling savagely. After a few desperate moments, Charles managed to wriggle free. He drove his fist into Marcus's face, and had the satisfaction of hearing him gasp. "Dressed-up monkey, am I?" Charles shouted. "You'll take that back, or I'll know the reason why!"

"I will never take it back!"

"Why, you—you—!"

"Your Highness!" a voice said sternly. A hand grasped his arm. "What has happened? Did this boy actually dare to strike you?"

" 'Tis no business of yours," Charles said defiantly, annoyed with the man's forbidding expression. "Anyway, we struck each other at the same time."

"Forgive me, Your Highness, I cannot believe it started that way. Who struck the first blow?"

"Oh, what does it matter? He called me a dressed-up monkey. I didn't like it, so we started to fight." Rubbing his throbbing nose, Charles grinned. "It was a good fight. I enjoyed it."

Staring at Sir Peter, Marcus jerked his thumb at Charles. "What did you call him?"

Charles answered. "He called me 'Your Highness.' I am Charles Stuart, Prince of Wales. But you may call me Charles."

"Oh," Marcus said, looking slightly taken aback. "Well," he

said after a moment, "I don't care if you are the Prince of Wales, I'll not retract one word. You are an ugly monkey."

"A dressed-up one, you have forgotten that." At the outrage in Sir Peter's face, Charles began to laugh. "If you could only see your expression, Sir Peter!"

"I find nothing amusing in the situation, Your Highness," Sir Peter said coldly. "The boy is impertinent. It is my duty to report his conduct to my lord Butler."

"You will do no such thing." Charles's voice was as cold as his. "A plague on your report! I can take care of myself."

"But, Your Highness, he fought with you. He insulted you."

"I fought with him too. And I say that he may call me anything he pleases. We are going to be friends. And now, Sir Peter, if you don't mind, please leave us. We have things we wish to discuss."

After Sir Peter had departed unwillingly, Marcus broke the silence that had fallen. "You might as well go too. I have nothing to discuss with you, and certainly we are not going to be friends. I do not like you."

"Oh? Why not?"

"How do I know? I just don't."

"I like you, Marcus, though you are a sullen fellow. I am going to be your friend whether you like it or not."

"Why?" Marcus said, glowering at him suspiciously. "Why should you wish to be my friend? I hit you. I called you names."

"I did the same to you," Charles said on a note of irritation. "I like you. That is all there is to it."

"I don't want you for a friend. I will not have you."

"You can't stop me. You may go around hating me, if it pleases you, but you can't stop me."

Marcus gave him a baffled look. "I don't understand."

"It is because I like you, and because you fight jolly well."

A faint smile touched Marcus's lips, then almost instantly vanished. "Well?" Charles urged. "What do you say?"

Marcus looked him over carefully. "You've got straw in your hair, and there's mud on that green velvet thing."

"You look a bit bedraggled yourself," Charles answered with a delighted grin. "I think you are going to have a swollen eye."

Marcus looked pleased. "Oh, am I? What about you? Do you think I broke your nose?"

"Nearly. Shall we be friends, Marcus?"

"I don't know. Let me think about it."

Charles whistled. "Well! Have you no respect for your Prince?"

Marcus looked seriously into the laughing eyes. "I'm not certain I will like you. But if I do, it will be because you are Charles, not the Prince of Wales."

"That is direct enough." Charles held out his hand. "Agreed, my friend. Stop scowling at me and shake hands."

Marcus felt a growing warmth inside him. Charles's words gave him a strange but pleasant feeling. Yes, he would like to be this boy's friend. Almost shyly, he took Charles's hand.

Charles wrung his hand enthusiastically. "Come," he said softly, as if afraid to spoil the moment, "let us go back to the house. My lord Butler is doubtless wondering where you are."

Marcus nodded. Walking by Charles's side, he said abruptly, "If my father has given you permission to use his first name, I will withdraw my objection."

"Thank you," Charles said meekly. His dark brows drew together thoughtfully as he sought to work out his feeling of instant comradeship with Marcus Milford. He could not fathom it, but it was there. Already he had a warmer feeling for this strange boy than ever he had had for Tony or George. He did not understand it at all. Characteristically, he thrust deeper thought aside. As was his way, he simply accepted. His laughter rising again, he thrust his arm through Marcus's. "And how, my friend, are we going to explain our appearance?"

Marcus shrugged. "That is easy. You may tell my father that I struck you first."

"But you wouldn't like me to do that, would you?" Charles said shrewdly.

"No," Marcus answered him honestly. "But it is the truth."

"Bah! We will let them guess."

Marcus seemed to feel than an explanation was required. "I'm not afraid of my father, understand," he said hastily. "But I would rather he did not think ill of me."

"I feel like that about my father."

Marcus stopped walking. "Thank you, Charles! Thank you for everything!"

Struck by the fervent note in his voice, Charles said slowly, "For what are you thanking me, Marcus?"

Marcus shook his head. "Just thank you."

"You are a strange one, Marcus Milford, but no doubt, in time, I'll come to understand you."

Marcus's dark eyes studied him, and then, for the first time, he smiled. That smile, robbing him of his unnatural gravity, made him look entirely different. "I was mistaken when I called you ugly, Charles. Now I come to really look at you, I see that you are not ugly at all. Forgive me for my words."

Charles stared. Never had he come across a boy so formal of manner. "I fear you were not mistaken, Marcus. I know I'm ugly, but I really don't mind."

"You are wrong," Marcus insisted. "I think, when one gets to know you, that you cannot be considered ugly."

"Can I not? Do you know me, Marcus?"

"I think so," Marcus said thoughtfully. Then, in a firmer voice. "Aye, Charles, I am sure that I know you."

"I have the same feeling about you, Marcus. But what think you makes for the difference in my appearance?"

"I don't know," Marcus said in a puzzled voice. "It is when you talk and smile, I think." Thus Marcus Milford tried to reason out Charles Stuart's potent charm.

Dismissing his words, Charles said enthusiastically, "Let's be friends forever, Marcus!"

"But I have not yet said that I will be your friend."

"I know. But you will, won't you?"

After a long pause, during which Charles grew surprisingly anxious, Marcus said slowly, "Aye, I'll be your friend."

295

Charles's face lit up. "Forever?" he urged. "Come hell or high water? You must swear it."

Marcus gave in. "Forever," he said simply. "Come hell or high water. I swear it, Charles."

Charles Stuart and Marcus Milford clasped hands in genuine friendship. And with that handclasp, they sealed a pact that was to last a lifetime.

They turned a corner and came within sight of the house. A scene of confusion met their eyes. Mrs. Thomas stood on the broad front steps of the manor. Standing beside her was Lord John, his face drawn, his hand clutching at his heart. A carriage was drawn up by the steps. And, as the two boys began to make their way forward, a woman was brought out of the house. Her arms were clasped on either side by two footmen. She screamed out in a hysterical voice, "You'll pay for this, you bloody holy man! I swear to God that you will!"

Lord John seemed to lose his head completely. "Get into the carriage, you whore!" he shouted. "Go on, get in beside your lover!"

"If I'm to be banished, John, I will take Marcus with me!"

"I wish to God that I could banish you. But the moment my back is turned, you'll come creeping back! As for my son, he stays here with me!"

"Your son! Your son! How you do love to prate those words. He is not your son, you holy swine! You know it."

"Push her into the carriage," Lord John instructed the footmen. "Do anything you must to get her out of my sight!"

Marcus had stopped short. For a moment he stood there transfixed, his body trembling so violently that Charles thought he might fall. Then, with a choked sound of anguish, he ran straight to his father. "Say it is not true!" he shouted, clutching at Lord John's arm. "Say it! Say it!"

"Be quiet!" Lord John pulled free. "I know not any more what is true or false. Go to your room, Marcus. Stay there until I come to you."

Marcus turned stricken eyes to Mrs. Thomas. "Thomas!" he faltered.

"Don't look like that, my lovie!" she exclaimed, pulling him into her arms. "Of course it is not true, darling!"

"You heard me, Marcus!" Lord John thundered. "Go to your room."

"Please, my lord," Mrs. Thomas pleaded, "let him stay with me. The poor lamb is very upset."

"Do not interfere, Mrs. Thomas. I will be obeyed in this."

"But, my lord, he has done nothing."

Lord John sagged back against the door. He was gasping painfully, and there was a faint blue line about his mouth. He struggled to bring out words. "I will go to him I—later. I w—will try to explain. Oh, my God, woman, don't look at me like that! Do you think I want to hurt him?"

"No, my lord." Mrs. Thomas released the boy. "Go to your room," she said gently. "Don't worry, my darling, everything will be all right."

Marcus went past her and into the hall. He backed slowly to the stairs, his wounded eyes never once leaving his father's face. Reaching the stairs, he turned blindly. He rushed up the stairs headlong, and those assembled in the hall heard the little moaning sounds he made.

For the first time, Lord John seemed to see Charles. "Your Highness," he said hoarsely, trying to force a smile, "I ask your pardon for—for the scene you have just witnessed. Later, if you permit, I will try to explain."

Charles felt momentarily at a loss, and he wondered what he could possibly say to comfort this suffering man. He assumed a casual voice. "There is no need for explanation. But you, my lord, you are ill. Should not someone be tending to you?"

"I will do that, Your Highness." Mrs. Thomas bobbed a curtsey, and then turned to her employer. "Come with me, my lord."

Lord John shook his head. "Nay. Call my man, please. He knows what to do for me."

"I daresay. But Palmer has not yet arrived, my lord, though I daresay he will be here directly. In the meantime, I pray you to come with me."

Lord John looked curiously like a beaten and bewildered child as he allowed her to lead him away.

"Charles!" the Duke of Buckingham ran to the Prince's side. "Where have you been? You have been missing all the fun!"

"I would not call it fun, George," Charles said coldly. He looked at Meredith, who had her arm about a pale-faced Tony. "Do you know which room Marcus occupies, Meredith?"

"Aye. The first door to your right, on the second floor. But, Charles, you must not go to him. He is a very strange boy. I think it would be best to leave him alone for a while. It might be that he would not welcome you."

"He will welcome me," Charles said with confidence. "Aye, he will. And someone should be with him."

"Then perhaps I," Meredith suggested reluctantly. "He will not thank me for my presence, but I will try. I cannot seem to reach him."

"You have to understand him first."

Meredith smiled at him affectionately. "And you think you understand Marcus?"

"I do. I did so almost immediately." Charles touched his nose. "Aye," he repeated, "almost immediately."

Meredith said with mock admiration, "But how wonderful is Your Highness."

Charles ignored the sarcasm. "I felt an immediate kinship with him," he explained. "We are the best of friends. I will go to him now."

"I must confess that I do not understand this quick friendship," Meredith said. Her eyes narrowed as she took in his battered face and his soiled clothing. "What on earth have you been doing to yourself, Charles?"

Charles smiled. "I should have thought it was obvious. I had my first encounter with Marcus, of course."

Leaving her speechless, he turned away and began to mount the stairs.

"What did he mean, Mother?" Tony asked.

"I really don't know, darling. The Prince has chosen to be cryptic."

Jealousy flared into the Duke of Buckingham's eyes. "I doubt His Majesty will allow the Prince to befriend a bastard," he snapped.

Meredith looked at him with dislike. "Be silent, George!"

"It is true. He is a bastard!"

"George!"

"I don't care. It is true!"

"You must not say that. You know nothing of the matter."

The Duke gave Meredith a resentful look. "I came here to enjoy myself," he said angrily, "not to get mixed up in family squabbles. I can tell you that the King would not like it, were he to know what awaited the Prince on his arrival at Milford Manor."

Meredith frowned. "I will not tell him," she said sharply. "Will you?"

"I make no promises." Scowling, the Duke walked across the hall and vanished through the still open front door.

Tony turned to his mother. "Sometimes, though I don't know why, I find myself quite disliking George."

"I also, Tony," Meredith said, sighing, "though I should not say so."

Marcus lay on his bed, his head resting on his folded arms. "Go away!" he said, as the Prince entered the room.

"Save your breath," Charles said, walking over to seat himself on the edge of the bed, "for I'll not go away." He laid his hand on Marcus's quivering shoulder. "Come, you dolt! It is not true."

"What is not true?" Marcus muttered, refusing to look at him. "Look, why don't you just go away and leave me alone!"

"I will not. We swore a vow, Marcus, remember? Come hell or high water."

Marcus was silent for a moment. Then, a belligerent note in his voice. "I could throw you out!"

"It would be a waste of energy, my friend. I should only return."

Marcus appeared to accept this. He said in a calmer voice, "Stay then, if you insist. Tell me, Charles, what did you mean just now? What is not true?"

"What you are thinking. My lord Butler is your father."

"And how could you possibly know that?"

"Because I am not blind, that is how. You each share a similarity of eyes and features. If you have any brains, Marcus, which I am beginning to doubt, then I beg you to use them."

"What do you mean by that?" Marcus said fiercely. "I have as many brains as you. Maybe more!"

Charles did not answer this challenge. When Marcus fell silent, he sat there patiently. He started as he heard a choked sound, and the shoulder beneath his hand began to shake. Gently, trying to impart comfort, Charles patted and squeezed the shoulder.

"Don't pat me!" Marcus cried out at last in a strangled voice. "If you think I am crying, you are quite mistaken!"

"Of course you are crying. And why not? I often do it myself. There is certainly no need for you to feel shame." Remembering his father's words, he brought them out triumphantly. "We must all cry at times, you know. Even grown men do."

"I know that, stupid!"

"I didn't know, not until my father told me. But now I come to think of it, why shouldn't adults cry if they feel like it?"

"Whether you know it or not, Your Highness," a voice said from the doorway, "you are very wise and very kind. Those qualities are not often found in one so young."

Charles looked at the man standing there. "I did not hear you, my lord Butler. Are you quite recovered?"

"Aye, I'm feeling much better now." Lord John, looking

paler than ever, deeply graven lines about his mouth and a strained look in his eyes, advanced into the room. "Mrs. Thomas's noxious potions must contain some kind of magic, for it was not long before she had me feeling easier." He looked at Charles pleadingly. "Your Highness, I know that you are deserving of an explanation, but I am not at all sure that I can make you understand."

"You need tell me nothing, my lord. But should you have the wish to do so, then I hope I will have sufficient intelligence to understand."

Lord John nodded. "I had forgotten your strict training, Charles. It has made you grow up very quickly. It is apparent to me that you think like a man rather than a boy." He crossed over to the bed and stood there looking down at his son with tender eyes. "Marcus, too, thinks like a man. But I fear that his enforced growing up springs from quite another reason."

"Aye, my lord. So I would think."

"I am glad you have made friends with my boy, Charles."

Charles smiled. "We have made a pact to be friends forever. Have we not, Marcus?"

Marcus did not move or speak, but his head nodded in agreement.

"I am glad," Lord John said. "I could wish Marcus no better friend. But for now, Charles, if you will excuse me, I would like to be alone with my son."

"Of course." Charles rose swiftly to his feet and went over to the door. "Call if you have need of me, Marcus."

"All right," Marcus muttered.

When the door closed behind the Prince, Lord John sat down on the bed. "Marcus," he said softly, "please sit up and look at me."

Slowly, unwillingly, Marcus raised himself. At the sight of his drawn face and his tear-blinded eyes, Lord John gave a cry of distress. "Marcus!" With a swift movement, he drew the boy into his arms and held him tightly. "Your mother lied. You are my son! My dearly loved son!"

"I want to believe that, Father."

"Believe it, Marcus, believe it!"

"Why did mother lie?"

Lord John stroked Marcus's thick curly hair. "It was to hurt me, lad. Only that. I would like you to believe me."

Marcus drew back to look into his face. "But I know that for a moment you believed her. I saw it in your expression." He hesitated, then burst out, "If I found I were not your son, I think I should die!"

"Hush! You belong to me, and I am very proud of you. If I seemed to believe your mother, Marcus, it was only for a moment. Oh, my boy! Surely you can forgive me for a moment's stupidity."

Marcus's hand tightened on Lord John's arm. "Of course I forgive you, Father. But what would you have done if I had proved to be not your son?"

Lord John's mouth quivered, and he looked away so that the boy should not see the tears in his eyes. "I should have gone on loving you, my son, as I have ever done."

"You love me?"

"Very dearly. Never doubt it!"

"That makes me happy, Father." Marcus went limp against him. His next words were jerked out in some embarrassment. "And I love you! I had rather be your son than the son of the King of England. But I hate Mother! I wish she would die!" His voice rose. "I'd like to kill her with my own hands!"

Lord John's heartbeat quickened. He knew quite well that this was no childish outburst. There was truth in Marcus's hysterical voice. God help Mary if she ever had to deal with an adult Marcus. For he could sense the implacable quality in him. The hatred his strumpet mother had fostered in him was very strong. Oh, Christ! What had she done to Marcus? How terrible was the intensity of his hatred! Hoping to still the violent trembling of Marcus's body, he said in a low voice, "You must not say such things, lad."

"But if I feel them," Marcus cried, pulling away from him

"why not?" His eyes grew hard with accusation. "How can you love her, Father? How can you possibly go on loving that—that woman!"

Just for a moment Lord John felt a desperate wish to withdraw into that cold reserve that had shielded him on numerous painful occasions. He pushed the wish firmly from him, and said in a gentle voice, "I know it is hard for you to understand. If I could solve the mystery of my continuing love for her, I would indeed be a very wise man. But I want there to be truth between us from now on, Marcus. Aye, I love her, and I fear it will be my misfortune to love her forever." He gave a shaky laugh. "But come, we should not be talking like this."

Marcus was looking at him steadily, and Lord John saw the dawning warmth in his eyes. "Poor Father!" Marcus said in a soft voice. "You must talk to someone, so why not to me?"

"You are too young to understand, Marcus."

"But you said yourself that she has forced me to grow up quickly."

"That is true. For my sake, Marcus, will you try to love her? It would please me immensely if you would make the effort."

The warmth left Marcus's eyes, and his mouth twisted in bitter scorn. "Love her! I had sooner love a snake or a toad. I pray that she will die!"

"Marcus! Oh, for God's sake, don't look like that!"

"How do you expect me to look?" Marcus cried wildly. "If all women are like her, I will never marry. I will never be so foolish as to allow myself to fall in love, that I promise you!"

"You will change your mind one day, my boy."

"Never! Women are not to be trusted. My own mother has proved that to me."

"All women are not the same, Marcus."

"I don't believe it. Of course they are."

"You don't hate all women. For instance, you love Mrs. Thomas."

"I love her," Marcus conceded unwillingly.

"She is a woman."

"But we are not talking about Thomas. She is quite different."

"You are arguing against yourself," Lord John said, smiling.

"Thomas loves me!"

"I see. And when you are grown, if a woman should come along and tell you that she loves you, what then?"

"I would not believe her."

"One day, believe me, Marcus, you will fall in love. Then you will tell yourself that the woman you love, like Thomas, is different from all others."

"I will not," Marcus said obstinately. "If she talks some nonsense about love to me, and expects me to believe her, I shall—I shall spit in her face!"

At this typically childish response, Lord John breathed a sigh of relief. So he had not entirely lost Marcus to the overshadowing man. It would seem that somewhere amidst that terrible welter of bitterness, the little boy still lingered. He said light-heartedly, "Very well, for the moment you may have it your way. And now let us talk of other things."

Feeling oddly relieved, Marcus settled back against the pillows. "All right. What shall we talk about?"

"The Prince for one. Do you like him?"

A smile brightened Marcus's solemn face. "He's all right. We had a fight in Maggie May's stable. I nearly broke his nose. He said I did." Proudly he touched his swollen eye. "And he gave me this. He defended himself well, I thought. I don't mind being his friend, since he wants it so much."

Lord John could not help smiling at the condescension in the young voice. "I should reprove you for fighting with the Prince. But I won't. I won't even ask you how the fight started. You have evidently settled things between yourselves. Marcus, I have a thought. When you are older, would you like a place at Court?"

Marcus gave the question his serious consideration. "Well," he said after a moment, "I don't believe I would like all that bowing and scraping. But if Charles and I are to continue friends, then I suppose I should be where he is. But for all that, he need not expect me to take orders from him."

"Knowing you and knowing the Prince," Lord John said dryly, "I imagine you will order each other about in equal proportion. Charles is a friendly and warm-hearted boy, but he is certainly not an angel. There are times when he can be very arrogant and imperious. But then, Marcus, so can you."

Marcus looked surprised. "I? Nay!"

"Yes, Marcus, you. If you do not manage to curb the tendency while you are young, you will grow up to be a very arrogant man."

Marcus sighed. "Thomas tells me that I am jealous and possessive. You say that I will be arrogant and imperious. I must indeed be a very disagreeable character."

Lord John laughed. "You must not look so woebegone," he said consolingly. "It is not that bad. I think that I can guarantee that you will be a very interesting man. I have no doubt that the despised ladies will find you quite irresistible."

"Oh?" Marcus's face darkened. "Let them, and the more fool they. I shall take no notice of them." He changed the subject. "Father, do you think that Charles will be an interesting man?"

Lord John's eyes twinkled. "There is no doubt about that. The difference between you will be this. Charles Stuart will take too much notice of the ladies, and you too little."

"How do you know?" Marcus asked, smiling.

"Charles's character is altogether different from yours, my son. Even at his early age, he already shows signs of the weakness for women that will undoubtedly be his."

"Does he?" Marcus said, looking surprised but interested. "How odd of him to take pleasure in their company."

"Nay, natural. But, Marcus, you sadden me. I know that most young boys tend to scorn and disregard females; I did myself. But you have such a bitterness against the sex, and you are too young for such a mature emotion."

"I'm not bitter, Father. I just don't like them."

"I trust you will find yourself softening as you grow older."

Wishing to smooth away his father's frown, Marcus said quickly, "Mayhap I will, if I find a wench like Thomas."

"I hope you will find someone to love. Someone who can convince you that she loves you in return. I want so much for you to be happy, my son!"

Happy? Marcus thought. He could never remember being happy. Thinking of the woman his father hoped would love him, his thoughts inevitably went to his mother. His mouth hardened. "You must not worry about me, Father," he muttered. "Somehow, some way, I will be happy."

Lord John was pained by the cynical look in the boy's dark eyes. Oh, Marcus! he thought. It must be something more than your mother's reputation that has hurt you. I must speak with Mrs. Thomas. It might be that she can tell me what has caused this shock and horror and loathing, this terrible bitterness against the female sex. Again he hastened to turn the subject. "How do your studies go, Marcus?"

The brooding look instantly vanished from Marcus's face. "I think I would like to be a writer, Father. I have been told that I have the gift and the imagination. I have written some short pieces, you know."

"I did not know. Will you show me some of your work?"

"Aye, if you promise not to laugh."

"I won't laugh."

"I would like to become a famous writer."

"I believe you have it in you to become anything you wish to be."

"I showed Thomas my latest piece." He laughed. "She gets very cross when I make her sit still and listen. Or at least she pretends to be cross. All the same, I know she is pleased with the piece. She said it made her want to laugh and yet to cry."

"Then you must certainly show it to me."

"I will. I promise."

Lord John ruffled the boy's hair with an affectionate hand. In that moment he felt very close to Marcus, and hopeful for the future. "I must go," he said. "I have my duties as a host. You also, Marcus, so do not let me down."

At the thought of facing those boys who had witnessed his

father's humiliation, and his own, Marcus flushed hotly. But if his father could face it, he told himself, so could he. "I will try my best, Father," he said quietly.

After Lord John had left, Marcus lay for some time staring out of the window. Sun touched the gauzy drapes and turned them into nets of gold. His mind whirled with a confused jumble of impressions. The look on his mother's face when she was ejected from Milford Manor, and her screaming threats. The fight with Charles, Maggie May in the background, stamping and snorting her disapproval. Charles calling him "friend," and the rapid friendship that had bewilderingly developed almost on the heels of the battle. He thought of the other two boys, the one dressed in blue, the blond boy in red. He wondered what they were like to know. He heard again the gasping sounds of his father's labored breathing as his mother was forced into the carriage. Charles's entry into his bedroom, the smile, the comforting hand upon his shoulder. Marcus's face softened. He could not deny that he liked Charles, but he would not keep telling him so. There was no sense in giving him a bigger head than he already had. Nay, if Charles desired compliments from him, he would have to work very hard to get them. Even then they would be doled out sparingly, for he was not given to soft words. Thomas was forever telling him that he should strive to be more amiable and friendly. But how could he? It was not his way. He thought of the oath he and Charles had made. Come hell or high water. Forever. Aye, Marcus told himself, he rather thought the friendship would turn out that way. There was something about Charles Stuart, something that drew him despite himself. Vague thoughts of loyalty to the Prince swirled through his head. Loyalty, he reminded himself fiercely, not subservience. Never that! His thoughts turned now to the conversation with his father, and the new understanding they had seemed to reach. His heart warmed, and a feeling that might have been happiness touched him. One torturing doubt was removed from his mind. He was loved by his father. But was he really his father?

Marcus turned over on his stomach. He would believe he was

the son of my lord Butler, because if he did not, he felt that he could not survive such misery. Charles had assured him that he and his father were alike. Nevertheless, he knew well that he and Lord John were not really alike in appearance. That had been a kindly lie, designed to comfort him. Marcus's hands clenched. He would refuse to let himself doubt. It might be that he would never know the truth, therefore he would make his own truth.

"I am Marcus Milford," he said aloud. "I am the son of my lord Butler. One day, though I pray that that time may be far off, I will be Marcus Milford, the fourth Earl of Butler."

The words seemed to bounce back at him from the walls, and he found them oddly comforting and convincing. Just before he drifted off to sleep, he thought of the color of my lady Foxefield's hair. It was such a beautiful bright color. Were he a painter, his one desire would be to get that lovely bronze sheen on canvas.

Chapter Seventeen

The shouts and screams of the horrified onlookers outside, and those of the worshipers inside, rent the air, mingling in shrill cadence with the hoarse triumphant yells of the marauding English soldiers who came bursting into St. Agnes's Church.

The soldiers took no notice of the frightened people huddled in the pews. It was doubtful if they even noticed them, so intent were they upon destruction. These troops were on their way back from the north, where they had gone originally to give half-hearted battle to the Scots, who, in direct defiance to the King and his troops, were intent upon occupying Newcastle. The English soldiers, who were in sympathy with the Scots and antagonistic to the King, had finally abandoned the fighting and left the enemy to its occupation. Now, on their long journey back to their London barracks, and unrestrained by their officers, they had, by way of diversion, although they and their officers called it by the nobler sounding name of "doing God's work," amused themselves by pillaging all the churches on their route. St. Agnes's was the last church before entering London.

The soldiers, driven by their Puritanical zeal, told themselves that all these churches with their High Services, their jeweled relics, lace-bordered cloths, the rich copes and surplices of the priests, and the incense-laden atmosphere were an insult to the Almighty, and fit only for destruction by God-fearing men. There could be no charge of sacrilege against them. Did they not avenge for Him, who was surely outraged by these popish services held regularly, in defiance of the new and simpler and nearer to God religion now sweeping England? Puritanism was on the upsurge, and rapidly going from strength to strength. So it was down with popery. Down with the Episcopalian religion, which was, in their opinion, little better than popery. The people who worshiped in this church and in those others they had destroyed, were doubtless secret Catholics, for all they called themselves Episcopalians. So, too, they were sure, was the King. How could he be otherwise, when he was constantly harried by that French trollop, whom they were forced to recognize as the Queen of England? She was constantly after him, so the gossip went, to turn Catholic. But they'd not have a Catholic King. And if he practised Catholicism in secret, the secret would soon out, and then it was down with him too.

Damnation to the King! was the thought in their minds as they burst into the church. They had not wanted to fight his cursed war with the Scots. They did not want to see their border cousins defeated, not when the war was on the issue of religion. They had abandoned Newcastle and Durham to the Scots without a qualm, nor any feeling of disloyalty. They had a right to worship as they pleased, and if the King wanted to make war upon them, then let him fight it out, with his bloody nobles for support. Let my lord Foxe, that swaggering cutthroat on whom it seemed the King placed so much dependence, lead the charge. They would have no part in it!

It did not occur to the soldiers, as they began their destructive work, that if the Scots had a right to worship as they pleased, so did these others, whose church they now defiled. The priest was nowhere in sight. The people watched, their eyes angry and hopeless. They could do nothing against the invading horde, and they knew it. Besides, these days, with England in a state of turmoil, it was dangerous to speak one's mind, or to take violent action.

The great golden cross glittered above the altar. "God be praised!" a soldier cried, as he took it down and hurled it to the floor. It was instantly grabbed up by the more avaricious, and a squabble for possession broke out. Jeweled communion cups were stuffed into rucksacks, sacred relics were torn from the walls, spat upon, and then likewise stowed away. "God be praised!" they shouted with each fresh act. "Glory unto His name!"

One soldier urinated on the floor. His action brought a gasp of horror from his captive audience, but no movement was made toward him. His menacing look as he rebuttoned his breeches held them still. Another, having previously armed himself with several heavy stones, heaved them one by one at the stained-glass windows. He laughed loudly when the windows shattered and showered the church floor with a deluge of rainbow-colored shards. Still others, their Puritan spirit burning fiercely, chopped with sharp axes at the communion rails. The rails splintered apart, and the soldiers, whooping their triumph, tore them free. As they rushed outside to burn them, they paused for a moment to pull down the costly and beautiful tapestries adorning the walls. "God be praised!" Bundling the tapestries under their arms, they took them too for burning. As they worked, the thought came into their minds that they would enjoy burning this Godless church to the ground.

A gray-haired woman, a black lace shawl slipping from her head, cowered low in her pew. She looked on with distended eyes, her limbs trembling in an agony of frustration, grief, and anger. A wild wailing sound issued from her lips as the soldiers ripped off the scarlet- and gold-fringed altar cloth and trampled it beneath their muddy boots. She watched, tears starting to her eyes, as they removed the altar from its place against the wall and placed it instead in the middle of the church.

311

"God be praised!" came their shouts. "Glory unto His name! No popery! No bowing down to idols!"

Anger conquered fear. Howling with rage, the woman jumped from her seat and went rushing toward the soldiers. Cheers and approving cries drifted after her, but no one else rose to follow her example.

"You heathens!" the woman shouted at the soldiers. "You filthy vile heathens! How dare you destroy God's house. I pray that He may strike you dead!"

"Now, mother," a young soldier jeered, "that's not a very Christian spirit, is it? Know you not that God is to be found in simple places, places where men of good heart and simple spirit pray? You will certainly never find Him in this jeweled and perfumed mockery. Why, 'tis more fitted for whorehouse than church."

"Hypocrite, liar, vandal!" She stared into his glittering gray eyes. "You lie! God is to be found wherever men gather together in His name." Her lips trembled and her face began to work with the violence of her emotion. Overcome by frenzy, she raised clenched fists and pounded them against his chest. "Get out, all of you! Don't you dare to touch another thing!"

The soldier, his jaw falling, gaped at her for a moment, then he began to laugh. Placing his big hand in the middle of her forehead, he heaved her from him roughly, sending her sprawling on the muddied marble inlaid floor. "Come see," he shouted to his companions. "Come see the old bawd who seeks to stop us from our sacred work. Shall we teach her a lesson? Shall we give her a good dousing in that stuff she calls holy water?"

Distracted, willing to join in this new game, those nearest to him rushed to do his bidding. Standing in a laughing group about the woman, who was trying to get to her feet, they poured the water over her hair, her upturned face, her garments, saturating her to the skin. "Now you're holy, old mother! Now you're cleansed of all your sins!"

"Let's take her outside and burn her with the communion rails," a soldier suggested in a loud voice.

"Let's burn her! Burn her!"

It was their idea of humor. Her terror amused them, and they laughed aloud as she began to scream and entreat them for mercy. Ignoring her continuing screams, some of them holding back the people who had risen to their feet as though to go to her aid, they carried her from the church and threw her down beside the roaring fire.

"Christ have mercy!" the woman sobbed, trying to curl herself into a ball. "Lord, look down upon Thy daughter! Holy Mother, pity me, succor me!"

The soldiers reached down, their hands tearing at her clothes, exposing her heavy woolen underwear, ripping away her bodice so that her thin, pendulous breasts fell loosely. One pulled the pins from her hair, sending it tumbling in a still beautiful silvery mass about her shrinking shoulders."

"Ain't she nice?" they bellowed, delighting in their sport. "Ain't she a pretty sight? Look at them lovely breasts o' hers. How'd you like to kiss 'em, eh?"

The onlookers stared dumbly. Some, who made a tentative move toward her, stopped as they caught the menacing looks of the soldiers. Soon, however, the soldiers tired of tormenting her. Turning away, they ran back into the church, elbowing aside the people crowding the doorway.

The woman seemed unconscious of her audience. Tears jetting from her eyes, she got shakily to her feet, trying to cover her breasts with her hands. She brushed aside the people who were now moving forward to offer their aid. Her head shaking as though in the grip of a palsy, she turned and began to stumble away.

It was Lord Foxefield, who was riding beside the King at the head of a column of soldiers, who first saw the fire. He stared hard at the woman stumbling toward them. Apparently she did not see the horses, or hear the feet of the men stamping to a halt, for she did not glance in their direction. Just as Lord Foxefield spurred his horse toward her, she lost her footing and went sprawling to her hands and knees.

The thunder of the hooves penetrated the woman's ears, and she turned her head. She screamed in superstitious fear as she saw the horseman. Astride his big white horse, long black hair falling to his shoulders from beneath a broad-brimmed plumed hat, a red cloak streaming from his shoulders, she had the confused impression that here was the avenging fury for which she had been praying.

She jumped quickly to her feet, a bubbling sound of fear issuing from her throat as he came straight toward her. She held out her hands, entreating mercy, but the horseman, leaning sideways in his saddle, scooped her up and placed her before him. The ruddy light from the burning communion rails flickered over his dark features and glowed in his eyes. "Have mercy!" the woman whimpered, struggling to free herself. "Let me go! I have done nothing! 'Tis not I who should be punished, but those soldiers who are pillaging our church."

Brett stiffened. "Christ's wounds!" he exclaimed. "Another church!" Recovering himself, he added, "You have nothing to fear from me, mistress." He began to ride slowly toward the King. "Cease thy struggling," he bade her. "You are quite safe with me. I will put you on the way to your home."

"But the soldiers! What of the soldiers?"

"You may safely leave the soldiers to us."

"My lord Foxe," the King said, as the horse came to a stop. "What is happening? Is the woman hurt?"

"I will see to her comfort in a moment, Your Majesty." He jerked his head toward the church. "It would seem that St. Agnes's has fallen to the vandals, Sire. This woman, if I mistake not, was a victim of the soldiers."

The King turned his head. "Sir Terence," he snapped. "You will take some of your men and clear the church. Place the soldiers under arrest."

"Yes, Sire." Sir Terence Carter wheeled about and shouted an order.

The woman had gone limp against Brett. She stared for a moment at the soldiers marching toward the church, headed by their officer, then she turned her head and looked up into Brett's face. "You are—you are my lord Foxe?" she gasped.

"I am, mistress."

"I have heard m—much of you. I cannot believe that I am actually speaking to you!"

"Yet you are." Brett smiled. "Will you now believe that I have no intention of harming you? Or does the mention of my name add new impetus to your fears."

"My lord," the woman faltered, "my lord! I know you will not harm me, and I—I can believe anything now!"

"Then will you likewise believe that you are in the presence of the King, whom you, madam, are ignoring?"

There was a hint of laughter in the words, but the woman did not hear it. "Is it—it really the King?" she whispered in an awed voice, without turning her head. "I heard you call him 'Your Majesty,' and yet I could not believe I was hearing aright!"

"Will you not look at me, madam," came Charles's gentle voice. "I assure you that I too am quite harmless."

As though pulled by a string, the woman's head jerked round and she stared straight into the King's dark eyes. "Your Majesty!" she gasped. " 'Tis surely a dream I am having. I am—" She stopped short, flushing with embarrassment, one hand trying to clutch the rags of her bodice together. "I—I ask Your Majesty to forgive my appearance."

" 'Tis no fault of yours, madam." Charles put up a hand and released the strings of his cloak. Removing it, he leaned forward and draped it about the woman's shoulders. "Allow me," he said.

"Your cloak! You have given me your cloak!" She looked at him with awed eyes. "Oh, Your Majesty, I shall treasure it forever!"

Charles smiled his warm smile. "Where is your home?" he asked.

"M—my home?" The woman pointed with a shaking finger to the left. " 'Tis not far from here. Just beyond that stile is my cottage. Your Majesty can see th—the roof through those trees."

"Then my lord Foxe and I will escort you to your home. Mayhap, Mistress—" He hesitated and looked at her inquiringly.

"J—J—Joan Turnfield," she stammered.

"Then mayhap, Mistress Turnfield, you can find some refreshment for two weary travelers?"

"You would—you would honor my home?"

"The honor shall be mine, Mistress Turnfield. But I warn you that I am most monstrous thirsty. If I may have something for my parched throat, you will earn Charles Stuart's gratitude."

The woman sat up straighter. "My house and everything in it is yours, Your Majesty," she said proudly. "My food is not of the finest quality, and I have naught but cider to quench your thirst. But such as it is, you are thrice welcome."

"I have ever had a partiality for cider," Charles said, with that unconscious gallantry that was so much a part of his nature. "And food served by your hands could not be other than fine."

She looked at him with bedazzled eyes. "God bless Your Majesty. God bless the House of Stuart! I can render to you only this small service, but my desire would be to serve you in all ways."

Touched by her obvious sincerity, Charles said quietly, "Your goodwill heartens me, Mistress Turnfield." His face clouded momentarily. "The goodwill and the loyalty of my subjects is indeed precious to me." He looked at her steadily, his eyes puzzled. She was quite obviously an educated woman. He could not help but wonder what had befallen her that she should now be living in a cottage, apparently in humble circumstances.

It was as if she had caught his thought. "My husband was once in a position to serve," she said. "He held a commission in your late father's army. He died fighting for the King. After his death, naught was left to me. But I am content with my cottage. I have enough to live upon, and I also have my memories of more gracious times."

"I am sorry," Charles said softly.

"No need for sorrow, Your Majesty. I have had a good full

life." She smiled at him. "Do you know, I once saw King James. 'Twas on the advent of his coronation. Now I have had the honor of speaking with his son. I have also seen the Prince of Wales, bless him for a bonny friendly lad! He waved at me, did the Prince, and he smiled straight at me. Ah, that smile of his! I have never forgotten it. I have no doubt that many a lady will dream of that smile." She started, recalling herself. "But I must not ramble on. Your Majesty is hungry and thirsty." She nodded toward the remaining soldiers, who stood in attitudes of stiff attention. "I have not enough food to feed them all, but I have more than enough cider for your men, should they desire it."

"They will desire it," Charles assured her. "Soldiers get very thirsty when on the march." He listened for a moment to the confused uproar coming from the church. Above the uproar, Sir Terence's voice was raised in stentorian command. Then he turned to his men, saying in his easy, friendly way, "Two of you remain here to acquaint Sir Terence of our whereabouts. The rest of you follow after us."

Entering the cottage, Brett following, the King bumped his head on the low beams and staggered back a pace. Mistress Turnfield paled and stared at him with an appalled expression. "Your Majesty! I should have remembered to warn you."

"No matter," Charles said, rubbing his head, "the bump will be a reminder of your gracious hospitality." Seeing her face, he broke into laughter. "All is well," he soothed her. After a moment, infected by his laughter, and Brett's smiling eyes, she joined in.

When the woman hurried away to get food and drink, Brett grinned at the King affectionately. "That gallantry of yours will get you into trouble one day, Charles. You know well that you detest cider."

Charles leaned back in his chair. "Hold your tongue, rogue," he retorted. "When I am thirsty, I would have you know, all liquid becomes as nectar."

Brett waited until Mistress Turnfield had served them, seen to the comfort of the men, and then retired to her small bedroom, that they might have privacy, then he said quietly, "Is it the treaty with the Scots that is troubling you, Charles? Come, don't look away, I know that expression, and I know you."

"The treaty, Brett?" Charles gave a hard laugh. "Now why should the Treaty of Ripon worry me? Why should I feel anxiety because I am now forced to leave the counties of Durham and Northumberland in the hands of the Scots?"

Brett stretched a hand across the table and laid it briefly over Charles's thin, nervous fingers. " 'Tis bitter, I know, Sire. But what else could you do? The advance of the Scots had to be stopped, and 'tis, temporarily, at least, the only way."

"And the money I have had to pledge to the Scots, Brett, where is it to come from? Nine hundred pounds a day to maintain their armies, until such time as a more permanent treaty can be drawn up."

"The breakdown of the Parliament of April thirteenth must not cause you to despair, Charles. You have called another Parliament, have you not?"

"I have. The House will sit on November third." Charles shrugged. "But I have no great hope of reaching an understanding with my ministers."

"Charles, I like not to see you so downcast. An understanding will be reached."

"Will it? Can you guarantee it, Brett?"

"Nay, Charles, would that I could. But, unlike you at this moment, I am hopeful."

Charles looked at him with those mournful dark eyes that were so like to the Prince of Wales's. "Am I a weak man, Brett, a bad King?"

"Nay, Charles. You have made mistakes, but so do we all. You are a good King, you know it."

"Do I? If I am a good King, why are my ministers antagonistic? Why do they refuse to grant me the subsidies I need? Why do they block me at every turn?"

"Charles!" Brett said warningly. "Calm, Sire, calm."

Charles put a hand across his eyes, and turned his head away.

318

"Only with you or Butler am I able to speak in this way. With you two, I may be myself, and there is no shame if I occasionally let down my guard."

"Nay, no shame, Sire," Brett assured him. "There has never been pretense between you and me, nor ever will be. Say what you will, Charles. I am ever ready to listen."

Charles's hand dropped. He looked at Brett, tears in his eyes. "Dear God, Brett, my friend, what is happening to our England!" His voice shook. "I love my country, I love my people, yet lately, or so it seems to me, the faces of my people have turned into the hating faces of enemies. I have dreams, terrible dreams! And in those dreams I see the downfall of the House of Stuart."

"That shall never be," Brett said quickly. His heartbeat quickened slightly as he saw the look in Charles's eyes, so mournful, so tragic. "I do not believe in dreams, Charles. Forget them, and concentrate instead on the reality."

While he waited for Charles to answer, Brett thought bitterly of the Queen. There was no doubt in his mind that she loved her husband, but she was a fanatic, with a burning zeal to convert her husband and her husband's people to the Catholic religion. He felt that she, with her arrogance, her disregard of the people's will, her outspoken criticism of the King and the people, was responsible for much, if not all, of the King's present unpopularity. Half the things that Charles had done to put the people against him would not have been done without Henrietta Maria's constant urgings. No, he did not believe that Charles was a weak man, but he did believe that his love for his wife had weakened him in the things in which he should stand firm and strong.

"You would have me concentrate on the reality, Brett," Charles said slowly, the hard brittle note back in his voice. "Then this is the reality. Lambeth House was attacked by the Puritan party, St. Paul's was attacked. Insults were called after me, offered with threats of violence. Violence, that is the reality. I put down the unrest, 'tis true, but still the people murmur against me in the streets. I cannot forget that these things have

319

happened, and mayhap will happen again. The Puritan party work hard to convert the people to their religion, and, to add to their strength, they urge them on to revolt against their King, against all that England has stood for these many years. There is one other thing that I cannot forget, and that is that I, in order to ensure the safety of my family from the violence of the people, was forced to send them to Greenwich under the protection of a strong guard. There, Brett, there is your reality. What next, I wonder?''

Brett was silent. It was all true. He remembered the fighting in the streets, the great bonfires, the burning of Charles in effigy. The faces of the people, as Charles passed in his carriage. Hostile faces, faces twisted with hatred, sneering mouths that had spewed forth obscenities against their monarch. Yet, not too much later, those same faces had been wreathed in smiles for their King. They had shouted his name, roared their loyalty. Brett was conscious of an inner shudder as he thought of the party that worked so diligently to arouse the people to hatred. Would their love for their King be proof against the constant insinuations against him, the slander? Aware that Charles was waiting for him to speak, he said the first comforting thing that came into his head. "It will pass, Charles."

"Will it? Do you really believe that?"

"It must pass. I cannot conceive of the people of England turning permanently against their King. There is hostility, of course, but reason will prevail, I am sure. In any case, there is nothing we can do but wait and see."

Charles did not seem to have heard him. His eyes brooding, he said in a voice that was full of pain, "There is a spirit abroad in England these days. A spirit of menace and hatred. It grows like a poisonous root, a root that grows beneath the earth of this country, and one day it will split England asunder. I know it, I feel it!"

"God's body, Charles!" Brett exclaimed, "Enough! Go on like this and you will have me hanging myself from the beams." Despite the heat in his voice, there was a deep anxiety in his eyes as he regarded Charles. " 'Tis not long since you recovered from the lung fever. I would not have your worries tumble you into illness again. You know well that you feed upon your nerves, and this brooding cannot be other than harmful."

Charles forced a smile. "My health is of the best, I would have you know. But you are right, my friend, enough of despair and gloom. Let us speak of pleasanter things."

"Aye, let us. But do not think I have to be soothed like a child. If it will relieve your mind to talk of these things that trouble you, then by all means do so. As I have said, there must be no pretense between us."

"Nor will there be." Now it was Charles who was determined to change the subject. "But I find, in contemplation, that I grow too cursed gloomy for my own liking."

"In that case," Brett said, smiling at him, "we will certainly speak of pleasanter things." His voice softened to a mocking drawl. "And what shall the subject be? Shall we talk of the young Duke of Gloucester?"

The mournful look left Charles's eyes. "Now I wonder how you guessed. You have picked my favorite subject."

Henry, Duke of Gloucester, had been born in this year of 1640, on July 8th. And though Charles knew that his overwhelming paternal pride was a source of amusement to his friend, yet he could not resist speaking of the boy. "You know, Brett," he added, "he is almost two months old now."

"Yes, Sire," Brett's lips quirked. "You may have forgotten, but I am aware of the passage of time."

Charles laughed. "God rot you, Brett!" he cried. "Cannot a father speak of his son without bringing your sarcasm down on his head?"

"If Your Majesty would but confine yourself to speaking of him a dozen times a day, rather than a thousand, it would save much wear and tear on the nerves."

"But he is a bonny lad, you'll admit?" Charles said, grinning.

Brett sighed. "Aye, freely do I admit it, Charles. He is round and rosy and lusty, and with a bellow on him that goes like a cursed knife through the head." His dark brows rose. "Never

321

have I seen a finer child than Henry, save, of course, my own son.''

Charles waved a disparaging hand. ''Tony is well enough, but he cannot be compared with Henry.''

''Naturally not. But I beg you not to let my lady hear you say so. Where Tony is concerned, she is a veritable tigress.''

''And where you are concerned, my lord Foxe?''

Brett's face softened. ''Meredith is the bane of my life, but the wench loves me well.''

Charles said softly, ''And is my lord Foxe too proud or too secretive with his inner feelings to add that he also loves the lady well?''

Brett smiled. ''She is passable. It does not do to go about prating of one's love for a female. They get above themselves. Add that to the usual addle-pated condition of their brains, and where are you?'' Meeting Charles's eyes, he added casually, ''Aye, I love the wench. There, now you have heard it. Are you satisfied?''

''I am. Though I knew it all the time.''

''Speaking of sons,'' Brett said, changing the subject, ''now that you have at last met Butler's heir, what think you of him?''

''I like him,'' Charles said after a thoughtful moment. ''There is something frozen about the lad, something curiously withdrawn, which on first meeting I must confess disturbed me. It is not natural in a lad of his age. But when I saw Charles's enthusiasm for Marcus, I looked deeper.''

''And what did you find?''

''I found that beneath that frozen exterior there is a great deal of warmth. But, as in the case of his friendship with Charles, that warmth is shown sparingly. He is wary and suspicious of friendship. But methought I saw in those eyes of his a longing to be liked. A longing to give freely of friendship as well as to take. When I last saw him, I thought I detected a dropping of his guard and, in his relationship with Charles, an easing of manner.''

Brett frowned. He was remembering Meredith's account of that disastrous visit to Milford Manor, the events of which the

King knew nothing about. Small wonder that the boy was suspicious and withdrawn. "You are right, Charles," he said aloud. "At heart Marcus is a fine boy and I believe he will grow into a fine man. I have done some observing of my own, and I do not believe you need to worry about that particular friendship. Marcus, though he would die before he would admit it, is fully as devoted to Charles as Charles is to him."

"The boy certainly has a strong personality, else he would not occupy our thoughts so much." Charles's fingers curled about the beaker of cider before him. Raising it to his lips he drank, making a wry face. "I have a feeling that Marcus Milford will be very much a part of Charles's life." He put the beaker on the table. "But what of my Lord Butler?" he said, sobering. "You know, Brett, sometimes I have the uncomfortable feeling that our friend has not very long to live."

Brett, who knew that Charles had never fully recovered from Buckingham's violent death, was aware that Butler's failing health caused him great concern. Trying to reassure, he spoke bracingly. "Come, John was looking a great deal better when last I saw him. If he could but have a happy family life, I believe he would be entirely well."

"Aye, 'tis the fault of my lady Butler. That damnable woman, though it pains me to say it, is thoroughly evil."

Brett nodded agreement. "Her morals certainly leave much to be desired. She is a bitch in constant heat. However, at the moment she is not at Milford Manor, so there is nothing to plague John just now."

"Only the thought of what she might be doing," Charles said grimly. "She is in London, where I pray she will remain for a long time. As for John, I believe he will be greatly cheered by the knowledge that Marcus will shortly be returning to Milford Manor."

"So the two young royalists are to be parted, are they?"

"For a short while. If it should be a long parting, Charles will very soon make known his dissatisfaction. You said the two royalists. Is Marcus equally ardent in my cause?"

"He is indeed. It is not too much to say that Marcus is flamingly ardent. 'Tis the only way I can describe it."

Charles gave a pleased smile. "I am happy and relieved to hear it. In these uneasy days loyalties are liable to go either way." He laughed. "What a pity he is only a boy. I could use that loyalty."

"Little boys grow up, Charles. Should you have need of him when he is grown, though I pray not, I have no doubt that his sword will ever be at your service." Brett chuckled. "Young Marcus has a talent I am sure you will be able to use. I have observed them once or twice at their games of hide and seek. When 'tis Marcus's turn to hide, he does it very effectively. His Highness, search though he may, can never find him. Then out will stroll Marcus, and Charles will find, to his baffled fury, that Marcus has been hidden in one of those places he had previously so zealously searched. That boy seems to have quite a talent for that sort of thing. If a real enemy should be in pursuit, it could be damned useful."

"Aye." Charles laughed with him. "I can imagine that Charles would be furious. He does not like to be baulked. But Charles is a boy who is good nature itself, so I doubt his fury would last long."

"Nay, and especially not with Marcus." Brett paused, tempted to tell Charles of the fight upon the two boys first meeting. He decided against it. The incident had amused him, but it might not amuse Charles. He, unlike his lazy, good-tempered son, believed in the dignity of princes.

"My son admires Marcus so much," Charles was saying. " 'Tis strange this friendship, for never were two boys more unalike in character."

" 'Tis the attraction of opposites, I make no doubt. They will be good for each other."

Mistress Turnfield watched them through a crack in the door. She had not intended to eavesdrop, but merely to allow herself to take pleasure in the sight of the two young men, and to once more assure herself that the King of England was actually sheltered beneath her roof. She tried to stop her ears but she could not but

324

be aware that they were talking of the Prince of Wales. Mistress Turnfield smiled fondly. She remembered with pleasure the Prince's smile, his lazy way of walking. The way, when his eyes had met hers, he had made her feel that he had singled her out from the crowd for his attention. Only a boy it was true, but a boy with a most unique charm. There was something about him, a something that compelled. She found herself remembering him calling a remark to his companion. His warm voice, unusually deep for one of his age, had but added to the fascination. James, his brother, had been with him on that occasion. The little Duke of York was by far the handsomer of the two, but the eyes of the people had rested on him only fleetingly before being drawn back to the Prince. The Duke might not have been there, for all the attention they had paid him, but for the Prince they had cheered themselves hoarse. The Duke had jumped up and down in his excitement, waving both hands. But the Prince, the object of their adoration, had merely flapped a lazy hand and smiled, and that smile had caught them all.

Mistress Turnfield sighed sentimentally. One day that dark and ugly Prince, if she mistook not, would be responsible for a great many flutterings in the hearts of the ladies.

Her eyes turned now to the King. The Prince bore no resemblance to his father, who was a very handsome man. Black curling hair fell to his shoulders, his mouth had a tender expression, and those deep and very dark eyes of his were smiling. His black velvet coat, looped across the chest with gold braid, and his well-cut black breeches suited his thin elegant figure to perfection. A double ruffle of lace edged his cuffs, and his lace cravat was pierced through with a sapphire pin. On the middle finger of his left hand, he wore a heavy gold band set with diamonds, and on the middle finger of his right, a similar ring, but set with rubies. Aye, he was a handsome and attractive man. So too was the other gentleman, my lord Foxe. His hair was as black as the King's and curled fully as much, but his eyes were dark blue, enclosed in a heavy frame of unusually long black lashes. He too wore black, but his high collar and his cuffs were edged with scarlet, matching his cloak and the plume in his hat. His only adornment was a thick band of gold on his marriage finger, and Mistress Turnfield wondered if it had been placed there by his wife on the occasion of their wedding.

The King rose to his feet. Stretching his arms above his head, he yawned widely. "It has been pleasant to linger here," he said. "But I am grown so sleepy that I think 'tis best if we went on our way. If I do not make a move I shall fall asleep, and I doubt that would please our hostess."

Mistress Turnfield, entering the room in response to a hail from Lord Foxefield, curtsied low before the King. She would have liked to tell him that he could linger as long as he pleased. Aye, and sleep the day away if he so desired, but she had not the words. She could only gaze at him.

The expression in her eyes touched Charles. Taking her hand in his, he raised it to his lips. "Madam," he said in his soft voice, "I will ever remember with pleasure your most gracious hospitality."

"Your Majesty is more than welcome."

He smiled at her, his teeth very white against his dark skin. "You mean that, I know. Mayhap, if I should pass this way again, you will allow me to avail myself once more of your hospitality?"

Color flamed into her withered cheeks. "Your Majesty must know that such a prospect, even though it unfortunately be remote, will give me the greatest pleasure and joy to think upon."

"Thank you. I pray you to walk with me to the door." Charles put his arm about her thin shoulders, and the folds of his black cloak, which she had reluctantly returned to him, fell about her.

Catching sight of the look of dazed joy on the woman's face, Brett smiled to himself. That charm of yours, Charles, he thought, is a little too potent at times. It may not be as potent as that of the Prince, but it makes itself felt too cursed strongly for our hostess. She looks about to swoon. I have no doubt that she will remember this day for the rest of her life. I would to God that all your subjects were as devoted.

At the door, Charles removed his arm. "Madam," he said, once more untying the strings of his cloak, "the day is warm, and I have no need of a cloak." He handed it to her. "Pray keep it to remember me by."

"With or without it, I shall remember Your Majesty always. But it gives me the greatest pleasure that you would deprive yourself for me."

Taking to the road once more, Brett said in a laughing voice, "Charles, did you have to charm that woman quite so blatantly? She looked as if she were about to fall to her knees and kiss your feet."

Charles turned his head and looked at him in genuine puzzlement. "I understand you not. I thanked her for her hospitality, that is all."

"Is that what you think you did?" Brett laughed. "You are a Stuart. And though, as you say, you understand me not, I believe that says it all."

Chapter Eighteen

Henrietta Maria stared at the King with tragic eyes. Her face, except for the flaming spots of color in her cheeks, was stark white, and she had bitten her lips so hard that little spots of blood flecked her chin. "I will not go, Charles!" she burst out in a shaking voice. "I will not leave you! I care nothing for the malice of the people. I care nothing that you command me to leave your side. You cannot make me go!"

"I can," the King said wearily. "But for the moment let us not discuss it further."

"Charles, I pray you not to be so adamant!"

He shrugged, but made no answer. He watched her as she resumed her frenzied pacing of the room. Tears were tumbling down her cheeks now, and she was wringing her hands together. The frantic gesture was usually the preliminary to one of those screaming outbursts he so hated, but this time her extreme agitation was caused by grief rather than anger. She was so beautiful, he thought. Today she was all black and white. Black hair, white satin gown, the white slope of her shoulders and the graceful stem of her neck. The only touch of color was in her cheeks and her vivid lips.

"Charles!" Henrietta Maria stopped her pacing and whirled round to face him. "Oh, Charles, why have the people turned against us? Why do they snarl at us like wild beasts whenever we appear? There is such hatred in their eyes, that I cannot bear it!" She clutched at the region of her heart with her white jeweled fingers. "My heart is quite broken! And now, if I must leave you, how can I bear to go on living? I was born to tragedy, it seems, and you do but add to it!"

He was used to her extravagance of speech. Usually it made him smile, but now he found himself unbearably touched. He went to her and drew her stiff figure into his arms. "Henrietta Maria," he touched her hair with his lips. "Do not grieve, my darling, I beg of you. If parting there must be, 'twill only be for a little while. I feel sure that the people will come to their senses in time."

Fear for this beloved man who was her husband, and her grief that they must part, he to face the ever growing enmity of his people, and she to mourn their separation at Hampton Court, turned her tongue to vindictiveness. "So they will come to their senses in time!" She thrust him away from her. "You are a fool, Charles, a fool! Know you not that you are but a puppet to the Parliament? You are no longer the King, except in name. 'Tis Parliament who rule in your stead. The people do not want you, they do not want me, or our children. As for me, I am in worse case. They utter threats against my life. Aye, they wish to see me dead, these English pigs whom you call subjects! And if they cannot see me dead, they will seek to impeach me on a charge of high treason against this country." She laughed, a shrill, hysterical sound. "Is it not exquisitely funny, Sire? I, the Queen of England, to be charged with treason. And all because I tried to help that good man, the Earl of Strafford, escape the death those fiends had planned for him!"

"You will never be so charged, so cease your wailing,"

329

Charles answered her in a dull voice. "As for Strafford, he is dead. They cannot touch him more." His voice began to shake. "And t—to think it was I who s—sent him to his death! I signed the order for his execution. 'Tis true that I tried by all means within my power to save h—him, but in the end I signed it. I shall never be able to forgive myself, never be able to forget. I should have held out. I should have refused to sign the warrant. Oh God, why did I not refuse!"

"If it had not been for that traitor Brooks, who betrayed my plan to Parliament," Henrietta Maria went on as though he had not spoken, "we might have, together with the loyal army who came from Yorkshire to aid us, have captured those traitorous members of the Parliament, and effected my lord Strafford's release."

Charles shook his head. "You do but dream, my dear. It would never have worked. It was a foolhardy plan at best."

He turned away from her and went over to the couch. Seating himself, he stared unseeingly at the floor. Why was it, he wondered, that Henrietta Maria, though she loved him, always managed to fail him in his hours of greatest need? He became aware of a dull ache in his head and a pricking at the backs of his eyes. He swallowed hard. Perhaps it was just as well that she had failed him this time, he thought wryly. Had she come to him and put her arms about him, shown him that tenderness of which she was capable, he would doubtless have laid his head against her breast and disgraced himself by breaking down and crying like a child. Henrietta Maria would have been so alarmed, poor child.

He clenched his hands together. God, there was such pain in his heart! It was a pain, he knew, that was composed of a large measure of grief and an equally large measure of guilt. Guilt, because it was he who had signed the warrant that sent loyal Strafford to his death. Tom, forgive me if you can! I knew not what I did when I urged you to be present at the opening of Parliament. You had misgivings, and you spoke to me of them. But I am the King, and I thought I could protect you from the malice of the Parliamentary members. I thought that I, in my power and authority, could hold you safe. I, who am to all intents and purposes stripped of that authority. But I did not know it then. I was foolish, blind! Dear Christ, Tom, why could I not sense the danger into which I led you. But you, my good and faithful servant, you followed me uncomplainingly into that danger. The King must be obeyed, unthinkable to go against the royal will! That was how you thought, Tom, I know, then and always. Aye, you knew that they were preparing to spring the trap upon you. But when you tried to tell me, what did I do? I dismissed your fears as nonsense. I would not listen, for I believed that you made too much of it, and above all, I believed that I knew best. I, Judas that I proved myself to be, would not listen!

Charles put his hand to his mouth and bit savagely at his knuckles. He could never be happy again with this burden on his conscience. He was a haunted man. Always slender of build, he had grown very thin, almost painfully so. He ate little, he slept little. When he did fall into exhausted sleep, he would dream of Strafford. Strafford, dressed in unrelieved black, walking with slow dignified steps to the scaffold. Strafford, kneeling, refusing the binding for his eyes, laying his head upon the block. He would see the axe lift in the hands of the marked executioner, the swell of his muscles as it descended in a gleaming arc, and then the severed head would be lying in the straw. Blood! There was blood everywhere! Soaking the straw, seeming to spread out in an ever-widening pool until it covered the earth all about them. Blood, and the fixed grimace on Strafford's dead face! He would start up wide awake, his night clothes plastered to his body with perspiration. The sleep for which he prayed, but at the same time feared, would again desert him for many dragging hours. In vain had my lord Butler and my lord Foxefield, appalled by his appearance, remonstrated with him. They pointed out patiently that he could do no other than sign the death warrant. He was caught in a vise. Parliament howled at his heels, the people gathered together in mobs, threatening the life of his family if Strafford was allowed to escape. They clamored for Strafford's blood, calling him "vile traitor!" And if the King refused to sign the warrant, he too was a traitor. Better no King than a traitor.

"You know well that the life of the Queen and your children were endangered," Brett had patiently pointed out to the stunned King. "Your own life too was in danger."

Charles's face twisted in pain. "My life! What care I for that? Strafford is dead! I could have saved him by holding my hand, by resisting!"

"Nay, Charles," Butler had said. "I beg you not to flay yourself so mercilessly. Mayhap you hold your own life at little value, though it means much to us. But the lives of the Queen and your children were quite another matter to you. Even had you refused to sign the warrant, has it not occurred to you that they would have found some way to murder him? And did not my Lord Strafford himself write to you from the Tower, urging you to sign?"

Strafford's letter! He could not think of it without agony. Strafford, who had told him that he thought only of the happiness and safety of the King's sacred person. Who had said that his own miserable life was the only thing that stood between the King achieving happy understanding with his subjects. Who had told him that he, by giving his consent to the signing of the warrant, absolved his King from guilt to God and the world. And in return for the gift of a quiet conscience to his beloved King, had asked only that his four children should be cared for. "Treat them, I beg of you, my Liege," the letter had concluded, "with as much kindness and consideration as you have ever shown to their unfortunate father. And know this, Your Majesty, that though men may hold me guilty, God will judge me innocent."

The letter could not comfort him, the reasoning of his friends could not comfort him. It seemed to him, though much time had passed, only yesterday that the grim drama had been played out.

Charles had forgotten that Henrietta Maria was in the room. He closed his aching eyes against the bright sunlight streaming through the window. Memory, as he had feared it would do, instantly carried him back to that day, November 3rd, 1640, when the recalled Parliament had sat for the first session. He smelt again the mingling of dust, the dry distinctive odor of new parchment, ground ink and stale air, as, with the fearful but obedient Earl of Strafford walking by his side, he made his way into the chamber. What had he looked for then? Was it friendship, reason, or just simple respect for their monarch? He found instead that hard eyes surveyed him, blank faces and unsmiling mouths, and it was then, on Strafford's behalf, that he had known his first touch of uneasiness.

From the very first, in that memorable session, the Commons and the Lords showed their hostility. Biting attacks were made upon the King's loyal ministers, the charges against them being many and varied. Some of these charges were so fantastic, so wild and unfounded, that had not Charles developed a sudden acute intuition of the danger in which the Earl of Strafford stood, his dry humor might have come to his aid and caused him to laugh the charges aside as ridiculous. But by that time he had lost the power to laugh. He could scarcely believe the deadly malice, the implacable enmity his Parliament were showing. He could only stand there, his eyes on Strafford's paling face, which seemed to him to grow gaunter by the hour.

On November 12th, Parliament dropped all pretense. The Earl of Strafford was formally accused by the Commons on a charge of high treason. The King's passionate protest was swept to one side. They appeared to listen, yet he knew they did not. They waited only for his voice to cease, before placing Strafford under arrest. He was sent to the Tower to await trial. But that trial did not begin until March 22nd, 1641.

More was to follow the accusation and arrest of Strafford. In the month of December, 1640, William Laud, Archbishop of Canterbury, an old man now, a man who all his life had worked in the best interests of his King and country, was likewise accused of high treason.

The Archibishop stood before them at the bar, his eyes blinking in bewilderment, his lined face showing the first traces of the anguish that was to be his. He was accused of leading his sovereign into the ways of evil. By seditious and dangerous advice, he had urged on the said sovereign to the performance of acts that were against the kingly prerogative. That were, in fact, prejudicial to the rights and liberties of the King's subjects. "My Lord Archbishop, you have, from the eminence of your position, striven to set at naught the laws of this land. You have, like a creeping serpent, endeavored to force your religion on those who would worship God humbly, and who scorn the pomp and circumstance of your church."

"A lie!" the Archbishop cried, his voice trembling.

"You say you are no papist. Wherein lies the difference between your religion and Catholicism?"

Color surged into the old man's face. He drew himself up proudly. "Gentlemen, my lords," he cried, his eyes flashing, "is it my religion you detest, or my so-called treason?"

"Both. But the charge is treason."

"Then, if you have more charges, I pray you to recite them. But revile not my religion, and I promise that I will not attempt to revile yours."

Charles pressed his shaking hand against his pounding head. He had been so courageous, that proud and loyal old man. So armed in the knowledge of his own innocence, that he had answered them roundly, with a fiery spirit that Charles had not known he possessed. Of all the faces that had been turned to the Archbishop, one stood out in memory. The pale, freckled face of Oliver Cromwell. The man's light eyes had turned only once from the Archbishop. His eyes had stared straight into the King's. His slow smile was more of a sneer than a smile. It had seemed to Charles that all the malice surrounding him was concentrated in that one pair of eyes. Cromwell! Cromwell! The thought of the man nagged at him unceasingly. From that very first meeting in Foxefield Hall, he had somehow known that Oliver Cromwell was a man to be reckoned with. The man hated him, and that hatred had reached across the chamber to strike him like a physical blow.

Keeping his eyes firmly closed, the low sound of Henrietta

Maria's voice in his ears, Charles tried to make his memory a blank. He found that he could not do it. It was March 22nd, 1641, again. He, the Queen beside him, were entering the royal box in Westminster Hall. They were all assembled there to listen to the trial of the Earl of Strafford.

Strafford's face was thin and sharp and extremely pale. His long brown hair showed faint threads of gray that had not been there a few months ago. New lines showed beneath his eyes and about his mouth. But the real difference was evident in his clothes. He, who had always been so immaculate and fastidious, wore a dark-blue jacket and breeches, but the garments were so crumpled that one had the impression that he must have slept in them. Much of his wardrobe had been removed to the Tower, and provisions had been made for his grooming. This laxness on his part showed the King more than anything else might have done that he had lost heart.

It was too painful to look upon the Earl. Charles turned his face away. The Queen spoke to him several times. Ignoring her petulance at his neglect, he did not answer her. He tried to occupy his mind with other things, and he told himself that Strafford would be proved innocent, he must be proved so! He concentrated on the blur of sunshine gilding the dark head of Brett Foxefield, the lined and wasted face of my lord Butler, and the fly buzzing against the window, vainly seeking entry. But he found he could not shut out the voice that uttered such grave accusations against the Earl of Strafford. He was impeached on several charges, but the major one seemed to be that he had collected money from the Irish Parliament, hiding his nefarious intentions under a cloak of assumed candor and goodwill. This money, ostensibly to be used for the King's support in the war against the rebellious Scots, was, in reality, to be used for quite another purpose.

"Thomas Wentworth, my lord of Strafford," the accusing voice roared through the court. "Can you deny that you obtained that money from our Irish friends under false pretenses? Do you dare to stand there and deny that that money was to be used against the people of England? It was to humble them, was it not? It was to destroy their churches, to force upon them a religion they abhor. It was to bring them to their knees in spiritless and humble surrender. Deny it if you can!''

''I do deny it,'' Strafford said. ''To say that this was my design is to say that it was also the King's. It is to accuse the King of England. Gentlemen, I am guiltless of these charges, as is my sovereign lord.''

''What mean you by your babblings, my lord Strafford? Who of us here accuses the King?''

''You do!'' Strafford pointed a lean, accusing finger. ''If you find me guilty on such a charge, you do. You all do!''

All eyes were turned to the royal box. Henrietta Maria drew in her breath sharply. ''Insolence!'' she cried in her high arrogant voice. ''Do these fools dare to accuse Your Majesty?''

Charles's hand pressed hers in warning. Her hand struggled to free itself, but he held it firmly. ''Madam,'' he said in a low voice, ''as you love me, do not create a scene.''

Her cheeks scarlet, her eyes furious, she stared at him. ''They fear Catholicism, or so I gather from that idiot's bleatings,'' she said loudly. ''But, if they do not turn Catholic, they should fear more for their immortal souls. They will burn in hell's fire if they do not soon see the light. England needs a Catholic king, and Catholic heirs to follow, if it is to avoid God's wrath!''

Charles saw the narrowed eyes, the knowing, satisfied smiles of his enemies, and he groaned inwardly. By Christ, this woman would destroy him with her foolish tongue! For the first time he cursed the day when he had commanded Henrietta Maria to master the English language. Again his hand pressed hers, harder this time. ''You will be silent, Madam,'' he said in the same low voice. ''If you utter another word, I swear you will regret it!''

Henrietta Maria's head rose haughtily. She opened her mouth to reply, but, finding herself subdued by the dangerous light in his eyes, she closed it again and relapsed into sullen silence.

The trial resumed, but Charles knew that Henrietta Maria's outburst had done much harm. They could not shake Strafford, however. He defended himself and his policy so brilliantly that the impeachment charges began to take on an absurdity. The faces of his accusers grew grim as they realized that, despite the advantage gained by the Queen's reckless words, despite the wave of enmity they had inspired, sympathy was turning toward Strafford.

Day after day, the trial went on. But Strafford's enemies were not baffled for long. They might have failed to impeach the Earl, but they had turned their attention to a bill of attainder against him. When the bill was first introduced, the Lords hesitated to give their approval, but despite this it was passed on April 22nd.

Charles could not believe it. He wrote to the Earl, assuring him of his friendship, and of his intention, once the Earl was released, that his honor should not suffer, neither his fortune.

Once the Earl was released! Charles smiled bitterly. Aye, he had believed then that right and justice must triumph. He had worked diligently to obtain Strafford's release, refusing to let himself surrender to what seemed to be the inevitable. But every attempt he had made had been frustrated. He had even tried to rescue Strafford by force. But when he and his men had attempted to take the Tower, it had resulted in dismal failure, and humiliation for himself.

For once, he who was always so conscious of the dignity of princes, had scarcely cared, so filled with anxiety was he for the Earl. He had believed that Henrietta Maria's impetuous plan to gather the loyal Yorkshiremen together and overpower the Parliament was a foolish one. But it had been conceived for the sake of Strafford, so he had conceded. When the plan was betrayed by Gorton Brooks, the Queen's Chamberlain, his heart had sunk to a new depth. It had been a foolish plan certainly, but sometimes foolish plans succeeded. He had not realized how much he had been unconsciously counting on it until they were betrayed.

A new menace made itself felt. Charles, from his window, listened to the howling of the inflamed mob gathered about the palace. Fists were shaken, stones were thrown, and he had the feeling that were he to appear before them, they would tear him to

337

pieces. "Strafford must die!" came the shout. It was taken up by others until it swelled into a frightening roar. "Strafford must die! We want no traitors!" Then a new cry was set up. "Down with the Frenchwoman and her Catholic bastards! Kill the papist whore!"

Alarmed for his family, the King's long struggle with his conscience began. One by one his bishops came to him and told him that it was his duty to sacrifice the Earl for the safety of the throne. "What is one man, Sire, when so much depends upon his death? The people demand that he die. You, as their King, must listen to their voices. Your private conscience is another matter. You will have the comfort of knowing that it remains inviolate."

He held out against them, refusing to listen to their advice. His mouth grim, he rebuked them. "My lords, a man cannot have two consciences, for such is the idea you have tried to urge upon me. My private conscience may protest, you say, and condemn the injustice done to my lord Strafford. But my kingly conscience must let him die an undeserved death. Nay, gentlemen, I'll have none of it!"

It was shortly after that that Strafford's letter, urging him to sign the death warrant, had reached him. Even then he might have rejected this sacrifice on the Earl's part had not the threats of violence to his family reached new and alarming proportions. For himself, so involved was he, he scarcely cared. If he died, he would at least do so with honor. But Henrietta Maria and his children must not die. All that night, after Strafford's letter came, he lay awake. When the morning came, he had resolved to do what was best for his family. He signed the death warrant. And then, as though scarcely realizing what he was about, he signed another Bill that stated that the Parliament now existing could not be dissolved without its consent. This Bill limited still further his own powers, but he shrugged this aside.

He made one more desperate gamble to save Strafford. He sent his son, the Prince of Wales, with a letter to the House of Lords. In this letter, he begged them to show mercy to the Earl of Strafford. To punish him if they sincerely believed in his guilt, but not to take his life. "I cannot feel that even this would serve the ends of justice," his letter went on, "for I well know that the man is guiltless. Nonetheless, my lords, if you will comply with my request, you will earn my undying gratitude."

There was silence in the House after the letter had been read aloud. Eyes turned to the slim dark boy who stood before them. The Prince, who had never before encountered hostility, smiled at them. That smile softened, but it did not alter their resolve. Their only answer was to acquaint the King with the date of Strafford's death, which was to take place on May 12th, a Wednesday.

Charles was not present at the execution. But there were plenty to assure him that the Earl had died well and bravely, even his enemies had to concede this. But although Charles had not been present, he imagined the macabre scene, and his haunted dreams persisted in showing it to him over and over again. Tossing and turning in his bed, he would accuse himself of murder. For he was guilty of murder, he told himself.

Events followed fast on the heels of Strafford's death. The Princess Mary, just entering her twelfth year, was given in marriage to the Prince of Orange. In the celebrations that followed, there were two who were indifferent to the rejoicing all about them. Charles, wracked by his conscience and grieving for Strafford, and Mary, his daughter, who clung to her father and wept copiously, viewing her Dutch bridegroom not only with the greatest distaste but with sullen rebellion. She hated him, the ugly little man. Henrietta Maria, trying to soothe her daughter and bring her to a proper sense of duty, finally lost her patience and boxed the girl's ears soundly.

It was only the Prince of Wales who was able to comfort Mary and bring her some ease. But when Marcus Milford, whom Mary secretly adored, uttered a few brusque words of comfort, her tears flowed afresh. Thirteen-year-old Marcus, so handsome and aloof, so seemingly indifferent to her fair beauty, was the object of all her dreams. In her heart she knew that she would never have been allowed to marry him. A Princess of England could never

339

marry a commoner, yet this had not prevented her from dreaming and hoping. She found herself comparing the Prince of Orange with Marcus, to the Prince's obvious disadvantage.

When Marcus left the room, Mary turned once more to her brother. "Charles! Oh, Charles, what shall I do?" Clinging to him, her tears spotting the green velvet of his coat, she gasped out, "I can never love the Prince. I detest him! He has no manners. When he was walking with me yesterday, he cleared his throat and then spat upon the path. Oh, Charles, how can I be expected to love somebody like that!"

Charles stroked her long fair hair with a gentle hand. "It may be that you can learn to love him, Mary."

"No! I never will!"

" 'Tis Marcus whom you think you love, is it not, Mary? They would never have let you marry him, you know. It would have been quite impossible."

Mary's eyes were horrified. "Charles! If you have guessed so easily how I feel, then—then Marcus must also know."

Charles laughed. "Nay, not he. I was surprised when he made the attempt to comfort you. He detests females so much that he usually ignores them. Aye, Mary," he went on, guessing the question that trembled on her lips, "princesses are no exception."

"But when he spoke to me just now, his eyes were kind. It is the first time I have ever seen them so. Usually they are so cold."

"But you love him?" Charles teased.

"Oh, yes, I do! I am sure he likes me too, else he would not have looked at me so."

"He was sorry for you. Marcus is kind, though he does his best to hide it."

"But you, as his friend, have known his kindness?"

Charles nodded. "Aye, Marcus is devoted to me. I believe I am the only one to whom he has told his secret dreams and yearnings."

"Are you devoted to him, Charles?"

340

"I am. I would do anything for him."

"Tell me of his secret dreams."

"Nay. Would you have me betray his confidence?"

Mary sighed. "I suppose not. But I would like to be able to understand him."

"Oh, come, Mary! Od's fish, don't start crying again! Marcus is not and never will be for you. 'Tis better you realize that."

Mary continued to weep bitterly, but after a while the shaking of her body ceased. Handing Charles her kerchief, she allowed him to dry her tears. "But you see," she said in a forlorn voice, "having known Marcus, I greatly fear that I will never be able to forget him."

"Of course you will, Mary. You are but a child. This fancy will pass."

She sniffed. "You are only thirteen yourself. If I am a child, then so are you." She looked into his dark eyes. "But sometimes, Charles, you seem to me to be much older than your years."

He smiled that faintly cynical smile that had so puzzled and intrigued Anthony Van Dyck. "I have never felt or thought like a child. Perhaps that is your answer."

Taking her hand, Charles led her over to the couch. Seating himself, he pulled her down beside him. "I am going to miss you very much. I like my family about me."

Mary managed a small teasing smile. "With the exception of our mother, of course?"

"I have little cause to love Mam," he said. His face became brooding. "I know well that she does not love me."

"Charles, dearest, do not say such a thing! Of course she loves you."

"Nay, Mary. As I grow older her manner becomes more respectful, but that is because I am the future king. She does not love me. From her own lips have I heard it."

Mary was genuinely distressed. She adored Charles. She turned to him and took his face between her hands. "Then she

341

must be the only one that does not," she said, kissing him tenderly. "I love you, dear Charles. You are my favorite brother."

"Even though I called you a child, Mary?"

"Even so." Her hands fell away and she rested her head against his shoulder. "I do wish that I were not so unhappy. I shall miss my family so much. But you and Marcus I will miss most of all."

"Perhaps you would not be so unhappy if you could bring yourself to think of our father's troubles rather than your own. Sometimes, Mary, I am terribly afraid for him."

She sat up and looked at him. "What do you mean?"

"The Commons have introduced bills, their object being, I have heard, to curtail our father's free action and to restrict his powers."

Mary's eyes were apprehensive. "These—these bills have been passed?"

"They have. As has the bill abolishing Episcopacy. The Root and Branch Bill, it is called. It was introduced by that fellow, Oliver Cromwell."

Mary was very pale. "I do not understand what it all means. But it gives me a very cold feeling."

He nodded, his face sober. "I too."

"How do you know of this?"

"I keep my ears open. People often talk freely when they think you are not listening or could not possibly understand. The Commons also demanded that the military forces be placed in their hands, and that all Roman Catholics residing at Court, be banished." Charles's face darkened. "Now the military have surrendered to them. So far, however, the Catholics remain at Court. Can you imagine how Mam would scream were they to be banished? Her wailings and her frenzied outcries would pierce the ears of every citizen in London."

"I should not say this, I know," Mary said, her smooth brow puckering, "but she is so fervent where her religion is concerned that she makes me feel quite uncomfortable. In her eyes, if you are not Catholic, that is the gravest sin of all. I wish that she would not be forever fussing at me and trying to turn me to her beliefs." Mary looked at him, her deep-blue eyes asking his understanding. "Were one forced to listen to her continually, her very fervency could make you begin to dislike the thought of God." She gasped at the enormity of her words, and added quickly. "Have I shocked you, Charles?"

He laughed. "Nay, for I understand your meaning. God is the very spirit and embodiment of love, and so will I always believe. But when Mam speaks of Him, He becomes a God who breathes fire and vengeance, and who has no time to smile upon His children, or applaud their small virtues. However, you are not the only one Mam plagues. She tries continually to turn our father, James, and myself Catholic. But we all, to her great despair, remain adamant. I wonder that our father does not tire of her constant tears, her tantrums, and the scenes she is forever making. Had I a wife like that, I would cut my throat, or hers."

Mary giggled nervously. "Only you would say such things, Charles."

"I often wonder why there is not more tolerance," Charles went on thoughtfully. "It would be a very pleasant world if people were allowed to worship as they pleased, would it not? But no, it seems that people are determined to interfere with their neighbors' beliefs. I tell you, Mary, when I am King, I shall pass a law saying that people must be allowed free choice."

Mary nodded, but she was not really listening, her troubled thoughts had returned to her father. "The people should be pleased, should they not, Charles, that our father has brought about peace with Scotland?"

"But I have heard that it is no real peace," Charles answered. "And now, of course, with Ireland in rebellion, there is more trouble." Sensing her mood, he did not remind her of the London riots. They went on almost daily, and they were demonstrations against the King and all that he stood for. He was puzzled that this should be so, for he knew his father to be a gentle and good man. A man that had the good of his country at heart. He was not the monster they made him out to be. Charles's indignation rose when he thought of the slanders attached to his father's name. They said of him that he had taxed the country to breaking point. But what else could he do when Parliament refused all his demands for the necessary money to run the country. They said too that he and his French Queen were trying to enslave England once more under the yoke of Catholicism. That might be true of Mam, Charles thought, for, if she had her way, the whole world would turn Catholic. But it was not true of his father. He did not deserve the hatred of his people. At this last thought, tears came into Charles's eyes. Would he ever be able to understand what had happened? The people seemed to hate not only his father and mother, but all of them.

Mary's hand clutched his arm, and she spoke the thought that had been in his mind. "The people riot against us. Why, Charles? I thought they loved us. Although I have not spoken of it, I have been afraid this long time. And now that a bill has been passed abolishing Episcopacy, that can only mean—" She broke off, her eyes fearful.

He nodded. "I know what you would say, Mary. It means that we must now worship as we are told to worship. England, I have heard, with the exception of the still loyal subjects, is controlled by the Puritan party." Again that strangely mature but infinitely charming smile lit his face. "So you see there is not really that much difference between Mam and the Puritans. Both, in their own way, are equally fanatical and determined to make miserable all who do not see things their way." In an effort to banish the trouble he saw in her face, he said softly, "I do not like to tell you this, since you are already most disagreeably vain, but you are looking excessively pretty and extremely grown up."

Normally Mary would have preened herself at such a compliment, especially when it came from her beloved Charles, but now she hardly heard him. She smiled vaguely. The compliment was merited, for she did indeed look pretty in her gown of ivory silk. The bodice and the hem, which was ruffled with lace, were sewn with pearls. The neckline, in respect to her married status, had been lowered to reveal a glimpse of her immature breasts. Wide gold bracelets adorned both thin wrists, and delicate diamond drops, quivering on thin gold wires, dangled from her ears. On her left hand, worn very reluctantly, was her wedding band, and above it her betrothal ring, a huge ruby surrounded by small glittering diamonds, mounted on a slender gold band. Her long fair hair, with its slight hints of red, had been left loose, it was caught at both temples with golden bows.

"What are you thinking of?" Charles said.

Mary rose abruptly to her feet. "I am thinking that I should go to our father and ask him what means this unrest."

Charles grinned at her. "You may ask him, but I doubt he will consent to a discussion with a child."

"Oh, Charles, sometimes you can be so infuriating! If I am old enough to be married, then I am old enough to understand."

"Go to him, then. Doubtless it will please him to know you have concern for him."

"Aye, I will. And mayhap, if there are troubled times ahead, he will allow me to delay my sailing in order that I may stay by his side."

"If that is what you are hoping for, you hope in vain. To Holland you will go, to become the beloved of Orange."

Mary stamped her foot. "Be quiet! Why can you not try to understand my feelings?"

"I do, but there is not a bit of use to keep on moping and crying." Charles rose and put an arm about her shoulders. "Poor Mary! But Orange, though dull, seems kind. Mayhap it will not be so bad. Later, when they deem that I am old enough to travel, I will come and see you."

Mary's face lit up. "Oh, do, Charles! Pray promise me that you will do so."

"I promise."

"And will you bring Marcus with you?"

"Mayhap. But I warn you that I'll have no improper affairs going on under Orange's very nose."

"Charles!" Color stung her face. " 'Tis not proper to speak to me so.'' As suddenly as it had come, her confusion vanished. She smiled at him. ''But there, I think that all his life long, Charles Stuart will never be proper.''

''I have noticed that proper people can be very dull.''

''Like Orange?''

''Like Orange, minx. But if I know my Mary, she will very soon turn him merry.'' He took his arm away. ''Be off with you, and mind you behave yourself.''

Mary went straight to her father. She told him of the conversation she had had with Charles. But as her brother had prophesied, the King, though kind and endeavoring to soothe her fears, was disinclined to discuss his ever mounting troubles with her.

The King opened his eyes. Henrietta Maria had ceased her pacing. She was sitting in a chair opposite the couch, watching him.

''Charles, what were you thinking about? You were frowning so, and you looked so worried.''

''I was thinking of Strafford.''

''Again?'' She made an impatient movement. ''I, too, mourn him, but you must not allow the man to haunt you.''

''But he does. I cannot help it.''

''Bah! There are other things to be thought of.''

''If it will soothe you at all, I was also thinking about Mary.''

''Oh. What of Mary?''

''Of a conversation she had with her brother Charles, and which she came to me and reported. She was worried about me, and about the conditions existing in the country.''

Henrietta Maria's hands clenched and she began to breathe hard. ''Mary is safe in Holland, and I'll warrant she is not concerned with England now,'' she said shrilly. ''She has a happy life in a country where she is loved and reverenced.'' She beat her fist on her knee. ''But what of me? I am in a country I despise. I am hated, reviled!''

Charles saw the tears coming. He could not stand another

346

scene. "You are not hated by me," he said as gently as possible. "Are you then so sorry that you came to this country to be the bride of Charles Stuart?"

She changed immediately. "Oh, no, Charles, no! I love you so very much!" Rising from the chair, she dropped on her knees before him. "Dear, Charles, my dearest one!" she laid her head in his lap.

Charles's hand touched her hair. "If I seem brusque at times, dear heart, it is only because I have so much on my mind. You must know this."

She got to her feet and sat down beside him. Now she was all humbleness, all eagerness to please. "Do not apologize to me, my darling. I am a very wicked woman, and 'tis I who should apologize to you. I could kill myself when I think of the way I plague you!"

Charles smiled. Her words were genuine enough at this moment, but she was enjoying the little scene. Her love was genuine too, for despite the scenes she made, and the unrest she created, she had proved that love in many endearing ways. She was like a tempest, he thought, a whirling destructive tempest, and all must bow to the mood of the moment. Yet, for all that he was ofttimes offended and sickened by her posings and her histrionics, he could not do without her.

"Henrietta Maria," he said quietly, "I had rather a kiss from your lips than these reproaches you are heaping upon yourself."

"But I am a wicked woman. You are right to hate me. But please try not to, please try!"

"I do not hate you, I love you." He put his arms firmly about her. "And now, Madam, if you please, my kiss."

Her lips met his, clinging hungrily. Some moments later, she said huskily, "You see, we cannot be apart. Don't send me away, please, Charles!"

"Let us leave that matter for the moment. There are other things I would like to talk over."

"Yes, please, Charles. Talk to me!"

347

"You remember that I told you of the five members of the Commons, charged by my Attorney-General with high treason?"

"How could I forget!" She put his arms from her and sat up. He knew, from her heightened color and the angry sparkle in her eyes, that he had her full attention. "Those rogues!" Henrietta Maria cried in a rising voice. "They should be hung! To think that they have been in communication with those Scottish rebels, and that they hoped, with Scotch aid, to make war on Your Majesty! Had I my way, they would be hung drawn and quartered!"

"If you will not calm yourself, Madam, then this conversation must cease."

She looked at him with hurt eyes. "You are impatient with me, my Lord King? But why, what have I done? My anger was for you."

"I know it." He patted her hand apologetically. "But to resume. You also know that, when I sent my Sergeant-at-Arms to arrest those five members, he could elicit no response from them. They stared at him, he told me, but nobody moved from their seats. He might not have been there, for all the attention they paid to him. So today—"

"Those wicked men!" Henrietta Maria interrupted. "How dare they defy the King's Majesty! Something must be done about it. If things like this, such blatant acts of defiance, are allowed to go unpunished, we shall become the laughing stock of the world!"

"I intend to do something about it. Today I go to the House myself. I will demand that the five members be delivered to me."

Henrietta Maria's jaw dropped. "You, Charles?" Apprehension clouded her eyes. "You will not go alone, I trust?"

"I am not afraid to face them."

"Nay, Charles." She clutched at his arm. "I do not trust those men. It might be that they would not hesitate to attack you."

"They would not dare." He smiled. "But I see you are anxious for me. I like that."

"I love you," she cried indignantly. "Why would I not be anxious?"

"Forgive me, dear heart. I know you love me. It is merely that I like to hear you say so. Of course I shall not go alone. It would look rather strange, would it not, if the King were to march five men into the jail? Nay, I will take with me a small company of guards. My lord Foxe will also be with me."

Her face darkened. She told herself that she had long ago forgiven my lord Foxe, but the sight of him, the mention of his name, still brought back to her the memory of that humiliating encounter in his bedchamber. But she had been a green girl then, just fifteen years old. Today she was a poised and mature woman of thirty-two, and with no yearning for anyone but her husband.

Dismissing thoughts of my lord Foxe, she turned eagerly to Charles, her eyes beginning to sparkle. "When do you go, my love?"

"In a few moments. The guards have their orders. They will be awaiting me."

"We will show them, will we not? We will show them what it means to work against the King and to defy him. I tell you, they should be hung!"

"But I have not your bloodthirsty instincts, my dear." Smiling, Charles rose. "I seek to teach them a lesson, that much is true. But I do not ask their lives."

"I would! Oh, indeed I would!"

"Then they are fortunate that it is I they deal with." He reached for her hand and drew her to her feet. "If a little time elapse," he said, kissing her, "and you hear no disastrous news of me, then you will know, when next you see me, that I am once more the master of my kingdom."

Tears filled her eyes again, and she clung to him frantically. "I pray you will succeed, dear Charles. I pray that very soon we may all be happy again, and I no longer the Queen of tragedy!"

Henrietta Maria and her extravagant speech! Gently he released himself. "Rest easy in your mind, dear heart."

After he had gone, Henrietta Maria began to pace the room

again, her excitement mounting rapidly. At last, unable to bear to be alone, she sent for her ladies.

They curtsied before her, then, with a crisp rustling of their gowns, they settled in their places about the Queen. Although she now and again managed an absent-minded reply, Henrietta Maria was only half listening to their conversation. Her mind was with the King.

Lady Felicity Carr, a dark-haired young girl with soft doe eyes, and who had managed through adroit flattery to endear herself temporarily to the volatile Queen, looked up from her embroidery. "Your Majesty is well, I trust," she murmured in her timid, rather breathless little voice.

Henrietta Maria glanced at her. "Why do you ask? Do I look ill?"

"I thought you rather pale." Felicity smiled apologetically. "I trust I have not offended Your Majesty?"

"Nay, Felicity. 'Twas kind of you to inquire."

Felicity glanced at the Queen's tightly clasped hands. "Your Majesty appears agitated," she persisted. "Is there aught that I may do for you?"

Henrietta Maria met the soft smiling dark eyes, and she felt a wave of affection for the girl. She rose from her chair. Beckoning to Felicity to follow her, she walked to the other side of the room. She must tell somebody, or she would fly into little pieces. She could trust this nice child.

"Felicity," she said in a carefully lowered voice, "I have such wonderful news to impart!" She grasped both of the girl's hands, squeezing them in her excitement. "Oh, Felicity, be happy for me! When the King, my husband, returns once more to my side, I believe that he will again be the master of his kingdom!"

Felicity's eyes grew cold and wary, but the Queen did not notice. "I rejoice to hear it, Madam," she ventured.

Henrietta Maria, her cheeks glowing and her eyes shining, laughed aloud. Unaware of the speculative glances of her other ladies, she rushed on. "But I see that you are thoroughly bewildered. And why not, when I have not yet explained my meaning?"

"Nay, Madam, you have not. But I would indeed be honored if you would explain."

"Aye, I will, and with the greatest of joy in the telling." The Queen leaned toward her. "The King has gone to the House with a company of guards," she whispered. "By this time, Kimbolton, Pym, and their fellow rogues will have been arrested on a charge of high treason. All will be well once more, for all men will know that they cannot defy the crown with impunity." It did not occur to Henrietta Maria, imparting her thrilling secret into those alert ears, that the King had scarcely had time to reach his destination. She forgot too that the King was usually delayed by those who would beg a boon from him.

Felicity's eyes widened until they appeared enormous. "Madam!" she breathed. "Oh, dear Madam, I am so very happy for you!"

Henrietta Maria beamed upon her. "I knew that you would be. I have told you of this because I trust you. When the King returns, it will no longer be a secret, but will instead be joyous and triumphant news, for the King will have come into his own. But until that time, I ask you to keep your silence."

Felicity's dark lashes fluttered as she lowered her eyes. "Your Majesty has no need to ask. I am greatly honored by your confidence."

Felicity settled back in her chair. The bright embroidered birds on the square of linen blurred before her eyes as her brain worked rapidly. She must find some excuse to leave the room, but it would not do to arouse the Queen's suspicions. Nevertheless a way must be found. It was essential that the accused members be warned. Darting a quick look at the Queen, Felicity pulled her kerchief from her sleeve. Pressing it against her lips, she gave a moan.

Henrietta Maria looked at her sharply. "What is it? Are you ill?"

351

Felicity nodded. "I must beg Your Majesty to excuse me," she gasped. "I fear I am about to vomit."

"But of course you may be excused."

"I thank Your Majesty." Felicity jumped up from her chair and fled from the room.

The Queen smiled as she looked toward the door that had just banged behind Felicity. She is overcome with the news, she thought with indulgent affection. The dear child is as happy as I.

Chapter Nineteen

There was an ominous silence as the King, unheralded and attended only by Lord Foxefield, entered the House of Commons.

The Speaker glanced round wildly, but the set cold faces of the members did nothing to reassure him. He stared at the King for a moment, then, his face pale, his jowls quivering in agitation, he rose from his chair. "Your Majesty honors us with his unexpected appearance," he said in a thick difficult voice. His eyes flickered nervously as he gestured toward the chair he had just vacated. "I p—pray Your Majesty to be seated."

"Thank you, sir," the King said in his soft courteous voice. He sat down. "But I do not believe you can say in all truth that my appearance is entirely unexpected."

The slight smile and the direct glance of the King's eyes was too much for the Speaker. He fell to his knees. "Your Majesty," he began, uncomfortably conscious of the profound disapproval of the silent men, to whom his action must have seemed craven,

"I am but a servant who must do my duty as directed, and that direction comes from the House. Should I note injustice, I must pretend not to see, and certainly I am forced to keep my tongue still."

The King gestured to him to rise. "You know why I am come," he said, addressing the members. " 'Tis to demand the persons of those five men who sought to conspire against me."

My lord Foxe, bending to pick up an imaginary object from the floor, whispered, "Christ's body, Sire, but my eyes see not the traitors. 'Twould seem that all have scuttled to their holes."

Charles gave a barely perceptible nod. Anger rose like a hot tide, but he exerted himself to suppress it. His eyes roved, resting for a significant second on each empty seat. " 'Twould seem that these men lacked the courage to face their King," he said in an icy voice. "If it will help to resurrect their courage, you may assure them that I intend to proceed against them in the strictest legality. If they be proved guilty, I shall not ask that they die a traitor's death, but that they will sign a full and clear confession that they did conspire against the crown. You understand me, gentlemen?"

"And if they be innocent, Sire?" a voice shouted.

The King turned his head to look in the direction of the voice, but found his eyes arrested by Oliver Cromwell's face. There it was again, that expression of indescribable malice. The eyes gloated. They seemed to him to be saying, "All here are your enemies, Charles Stuart, but I most of all!"

Charles's face froze into an expression of extreme hauteur. He looked beyond Oliver Cromwell. "If they be innocent, they will be proved so. I have confidence in the laws of this land." Even as he said it, he thought of Strafford. He closed his mind firmly. The trial of these men would not be conducted in a spirit of animosity and prejudice, as had been Strafford's. Their friends would no doubt work diligently to save them. If anyone must fear injustice, it was he.

Oliver Cromwell leaned forward in his seat. "Even the King

has no right to dictate to the House," he cried in a ringing voice. "All of us here claim our age-old privilege!"

"To that, Mr. Cromwell," the King said, "I will return no answer. In the matter of these men, I leave it to your consciences." He looked straight at Cromwell. "If, indeed, after this disgraceful episode, you can be said to possess either conscience or loyalty."

The man's face flushed and fury blazed from his pale eyes. But when cries of "Privilege! Privilege!" came from all parts of the House, his faint sneering smile returned.

The King's eyes met Brett's. His heart contracted as he saw in that dark-blue gaze the same fear that had haunted him these many months. My lord Foxefield, who was usually so calm and sure and strong, was betraying that he saw only darkness ahead for the King. The next moment the expression had vanished, the eyes were serene and full of smiling encouragement.

Charles rose to his feet. His manner deliberately disdainful, he looked about him once more. "Since these absentee gentlemen must at some time return," he said in a clear voice, "I naturally expect you to send them to me at once. Should you fail to do so, then I must warn you that I will take stronger measures to enforce my will in this matter."

Turning his back on them, he placed his plumed hat upon his head and swung his caped cloak about his shoulders. "Gentlemen," he said, strolling toward the door, "I bid you a very good day."

The ushers knelt as he passed, but Charles scarcely noticed them, his eyes were fixed straight ahead. Following after him came again the cries of "Privilege!" He tried to close his ears, but he could not block out the sound. Even when they passed into the street, it seemed to him that he could still hear those shouts. In his imagination it became a mocking chorus that told him that he, Charles Stuart, had become as nothing to them.

Making their way back to the palace, the King spoke no word. Brett, after his first tentative efforts at conversation, lapsed into silence as he saw the despair in those dark eyes, and the droop of the shoulders that were usually proudly held. Charles! he thought, I fear for you, my friend. There are dark days ahead, I feel it!

Brett felt a vast relief when some of the still loyal people called greetings. "God save Your Majesty!" they cried enthusiastically. Then Charles came to life. He waved his gloved hand, smiling at them. He signaled to the guard to go on their way, in order that he might exchange a word here and there.

The guard marched away, led by two officers, their red coats brilliant in the pale sunshine. About the tall figures of the King and Brett Foxefield there milled a little group of smiling people. One woman, carrying a basket filled with market produce, was so flustered when the King smiled at her that she dropped it.

"Your Majesty!" she gasped, as he bent to retrieve the basket, "Let me be doing that."

"Nay, madam, 'tis my pleasure to aid you." He handed her the basket. Bending once more, he picked up a herring. "A little soiled by the dust, I fear," he said, plopping it into the basket. "But I doubt not 'twill make good eating."

The woman gaped at him, her round, pleasant face rosy with confusion. Then, as she saw the kindness in his eyes, her face split into a big grin. "Thank you, Your Majesty." Emboldened, she went on. "And has Your Majesty a fancy for the herring?"

Charles, who hated herrings, avoided Brett's eyes as he replied gravely, "Madam, they are my favorite food."

The woman beamed with delight. "I've two of 'em in my basket, if Your Majesty will honor me by accepting 'em." She put a hand in her capacious pocket. "And here's a clean kerchief to wrap 'em," she cried, drawing out a linen square.

Charles was equal to the occasion. "Mine is the honor, madam." Taking the wrapped fish from her, he handed them to Brett. "My lord Foxe would be vastly disappointed were he not allowed to carry this gift," he murmured. "Would you not, my friend?"

Brett held the odorous bundle cautiously. "Oh, immensely so,

Sire.'' Charles's hand rose to hide his smile, as Brett added, ''I cannot tell Your Majesty what your gracious condescension means to me.''

Realizing that they had not only the King in their midst but the famed Lord Foxe, the crowd pressed yet closer. They were delighted with the King's friendly attitude. The small jokes he made, his charm, the warmth of his smile, seemed to reach out to embrace them all. If the whole of the English population could but be exposed to Charles I personally, Brett thought, his troubles would be over. These people surrounding him, could not seem to have enough of their King. They laughed, they called their remarks in a loud voice, they reached out hands that they might touch him, and generally competed good-naturedly for a moment of his exclusive attention.

It was some time before they managed to break away, and the crowd saw them depart with extreme reluctance. ''God bless Your Majesty,'' the crowd called after the King enthusiastically. ''Long may you reign!''

''Charles,'' Brett said, when they were safely on their way, ''it does me good to see you smile. It has been some time since last I saw you do so.''

''There is so little to smile at these days,'' Charles answered, ''that I needs must welcome every small relief. If I find an occasion to smile, I embrace it heartily.'' His face clouded. ''But inside, I fear, there is much weeping.''

''Aye, Charles, I know.'' Unwilling to abandon the lightness of the moment to a return to grim reality, Brett added with a smile, ''I trust the sight of your loyal and devoted friend forced to carry these stinking fish affords Your Majesty relief?''

''Aye, my lord Foxe, I cannot deny that it helps.''

''I am so glad,'' Brett said with a touch of irony. He motioned with his head to the gutter running the length of the street, and already overflowing with a noisome burden. ''But Your Majesty will not mind, I am sure, if I now throw my bundle away?''

''But you are quite mistaken, my lord Foxe,'' there was the faintest twinkle in Charles's eyes, ''I would object most strongly.

Those fish are a gift from a loyal subject. I have learned to cherish such shows of loyalty.''

"The strength of Your Majesty's objection would have much ado to compete with the strength of the odor now plaguing my nostrils.'' Brett looked down at his gloves which were stained with the seepage from the linen, and grimaced with distaste. "A plague upon these fish, I say! 'Twould not surprise me were people to take me for a cursed hawker. But, if you will have it so, regardless of my feelings, then I must continue to suffer in silence.''

Charles gave him a laughing glance. "Hardly in silence, would you say, my lord?''

Brett laughed. "Aye, Charles, you are right. 'Tis not my nature to suffer in silence. But since it is by your will that I carry this bundle, then the least you can do is to give ear to my justly voiced complaints.''

Despite his words, little more conversation was exchanged between them. Charles lapsed into brooding silence, replying with absent-minded courtesy to Brett's occasional remarks. Brett guessed that he pondered upon the matter that exercised his own brain. How had the members of the House known that the King would descend upon them today? The absence of the accused members seemed to denote foreknowledge of the visit. Now he came to think of it, the stony silence of the members and the Speaker's extreme agitation, had not been compounded of surprise, as he had at first thought.

The Queen was uneasy. For all her excitable and temperamental qualities, she was normally a very astute woman. A fact which, deceived by her hysteria, many had found to their cost. For once the Queen had not given matters careful thought, and, forgetting her habitual distrust of Englishwomen, she had allowed herself to be carried away by Lady Carr's humble, meek, so very eager to serve her sovereign attitude, and now she was bitterly regretting that she had been moved to confide the King's plans to her. Lady Carr's sudden indisposition had not at first roused her suspicions, but, with the woman's absence grown overlong, and no message from her to excuse the length of time, suspicion, never far from the surface, was beginning to burgeon.

At last, unable to bear her increasing worry, the Queen sent one of her women to inquire after Lady Carr. Her alarm increased when Lady Fenbury, returning, reported that Lady Carr had left the palace.

"Left!" Henrietta Maria shrieked. "What do you mean, you fool? How dare you come to me and tell me that she has left the palace!"

Intimidated by the wild gleam in the Queen's eyes, Lady Fenbury backed away a step. "But 'tis true, Madam," she said hastily. "Lady Carr informed the guard that she was carrying a message fr—from Your Majesty."

"What! O Christ have mercy!" Henrietta Maria's face whitened, and the wildness in her eyes intensified. Now, when it was too late, she was remembering the rumors of Lady Carr's close friendship—some said love affair—with Allan Greenbury, a member of the House of Commons, who had more than once spoken out against the King's policy. Why had she been so unthinking, so foolishly trusting as to allow herself to confide in the wretched girl? Suspicion now jumped to full-fledged certainty. The King's plan to surprise the members and to demand the surrender of the five accused men had been betrayed. But was it her fault, the Queen tried to excuse herself, that she had been born with an open, friendly, and trusting nature? Carr, may the little strumpet be forever accursed, had deceived her with her sly ways. Finding no comfort in this self-defense, the Queen abandoned it. Why, she asked herself despairingly, could she not learn to keep a still tongue?

Moaning, Henrietta Maria dropped onto a chair. Obviously the girl would not be returning to her service. The sly little bitch would never dare to show her face again! Oh, if only she could get her hands on her for a few moments! Bending forward, she pressed her kerchief to her eyes and burst into a torrent of tears.

Her ladies eyed each other apprehensively. They were frankly afraid of the Queen in all her uncertain moods, but never had she shed tears before them. It was said that she had so indulged with her Frenchwomen, but never with them. Scenes she had made aplenty, and many of them had had their hair pulled, or had felt the sting of her hand across their faces, but this was entirely new. They did not know what to make of it. Not a few felt superior. Were they Queen, they told themselves, they would not so disgrace their position.

They flocked about the sobbing Queen, and for a time Henrietta Maria listened to the soothing or bracing sounds that they made, then she lost patience. She did not want the twittering fools with her, she must think! Balling her wet kerchief in her hand, she screamed at them, "Get out, all of you! Do you not have the sensitivity and imagination to understand that I wish to be alone?"

They went thankfully, telling themselves that she was surely quite mad. In their anxiety to be first through the door, they pushed roughly at each other.

When the door closed behind them, the Queen's tears began afresh. She sobbed, she moaned, she tore at her hair in a frenzy of self-reproach. Aloud, she cursed the day she had been born to plague and betray the dearest, kindest, the most patient and beloved man ever to walk the earth.

Entering the room some time later, Charles found her crouched on the floor, her face hidden in her hands and her body still wracked by sobs. Now what was afoot, he asked himself wearily? Had he not enough to bear? Bidding my lord Foxe wait, he closed the door. Crossing the room, he stood there for a moment looking down at her. "Henrietta Maria," he said, forcing warmth into his voice. He lifted her bodily to her feet. "Now, Madam, what means this? What has occurred to put you into such a state?"

At the first sound of his voice, she had screamed, cowering away as though certain he meant to strike her, but now she clung to him. "Charles! Oh, tell me that you have placed those traitors under arrest!"

"Would that I could." He looked at her with eyes grown bleak. "The men were not there when I reached the House. I know not how, dear heart, but quite obviously my plan was known."

"Oh!" Her hand went to her mouth. "Do not call me dear heart," she cried in a trembling voice. "I deserve not your endearments. Oh, Charles, my dearest, it was I who betrayed you!"

He held her away from him. He had seen her in many moods, but never before had she presented such a wild appearance. She seemed, he thought anxiously, almost demented. Her hair, usually so smooth and gleaming, was tangled; her gown was crumpled and her face so blotched and swollen that it appeared disfigured. "Be still, my love," he soothed her, seriously alarmed now. "You do not know what you are saying." He put a hand to her hot cheek. "You have a fever."

"I am not ill!" She pulled free and began to beat at her chest with clenched fists. "I tell you that it was I who betrayed you! I did not mean to do so, but I was so happy, and so I confided in Lady Carr. Shortly after that she pretended to an indisposition. And then, Charles, I found that she had left the palace. When I confided in her, I did not remember that she was a friend of that hateful Greenbury man! Oh, Charles, I deserve your hatred! You do not need to tell me that you will never be able to forgive me. I cannot blame you, for I can never forgive myself!"

He took those punishing fists and held them tightly, forcing her to calm. Greenbury? he thought. Greenbury and Lady Carr. It was well known that they were in love. Well known to everybody but the Queen. How had she come to be so careless? Aye, the news could have traveled through Lady Carr. She would have had plenty of time to reach the House before him, for he had been delayed several times on the way. The temptation was to lash out at Henrietta Maria, but he crushed down the bitterness and the words of reproach. Her conscience had already punished her enough, and he had no doubt that it would go on punishing her. When she said that she would never be able to forgive herself, she

361

had meant it with all the force of her stormy but penitent heart. Mayhap this indiscretion would teach her a valuable lesson.

"Henrietta Maria," Charles said softly. "Nay, dear heart, do not look at me so! I have no blame for you."

"But you must blame me, I demand it!" she cried out. "Oh, pray do not be kind to me, do not forgive me. I had rather you struck me, killed me, for I know well that I deserve it!"

He shook her slightly. "You must endeavor to compose yourself. I love you. I cannot hate you because you demand it."

She shook her head from side to side, the tears raining down her cheeks again. "But you must punish me, Sire, you must! Don't you understand? I am not fit to live, not fit to be your Queen! Indeed, Charles, I cannot bear your kindness."

"I am not kind," he said, trying to tease her away from this mood of hysterical self-reproach. "I am a surly, bad-tempered man, I am also very obstinate, which is why, despite your entreaties to me to desist, I shall go on loving you." He put his arms gently about her. "But if you insist upon punishment, you shall have it. I will kiss you, and that shall be your punishment."

"Oh, Charles! I do not deserve you. I am a very wicked woman! 'Twould have been better by far for you and for England had I entered a convent. At least there I could do no one any harm. I could have dedicated my life to God. Anything, anything, rather than that I should now have to face this knowledge that I, who love you beyond all things, except God, have ruined you!"

"Henrietta Maria, you are too impossibly dramatic, and I like it not." He smiled, but the smile was a little forced. If he did not manage to stop her now, she would rave on for days. In the end, exhausted mentally and physically, she would have to take to her bed. It had happened many times before, for she dramatized everything. Lately she had complained of pain, describing it as a gnawing sensation in her stomach. Apprehensive but interested, for he ever sought for a chance to add to his stock of knowledge, he had wondered if her stormy emotions, her anger and tension, her perpetual worry over the smallest thing, could indeed produce pain in that area. Now, seeing her sudden wince, he was worried. "Come, now," he went on, "you know well that 'twould not have done for you to enter a convent. It would not have served the best interests of our Good Lord, for He would then have been subjected to the full and exclusive tempests of my Henrietta Maria."

"Charles!" Her eyes went wide with shock. " 'Tis sacrilege to speak so. You make it sound as though—as though God were only an ordinary man!"

He watched her as she hastily crossed herself. "If I do indeed speak sacrilege," he said in a voice he strove to keep light, "then I feel sure that God will understand and forgive me. I have ever believed that God must have a remarkable sense of humor, and He has instilled that self-same spark into His creations. He has given us the ability to laugh at ourselves, lest we be inclined to take ourselves too seriously. He has even given to some of us the ability to laugh in the face of danger and disaster."

Henrietta Maria, whom Charles had sometimes thought was utterly devoid of humor, proved it now. "But, Charles," she said in a wondering voice, "that is a silly thing to say, is it not? No one in their right senses could bring themselves to laugh when danger and disaster threatened."

He wanted to tell her that he himself was doing just that. He was almost certain that it was her indiscretion to Lady Carr that had betrayed them, and would, he was certain, have set in train a chain of events that he did not care to contemplate. Had he succeeded in taking the accused men, it might have quenched the growing hostility of the House, and have forced them to feel a new respect for their King. But, as things now stood, they could only see him as an ineffectual figure who had tried to set himself against the might of Parliament.

"Charles, what are you thinking about?"

He started. "I was thinking of humor," he answered her hastily. "I was also thinking, or perhaps I should say hoping, that I would have that ability."

"What ability?" She had already forgotten the previous conversation, and her mind was once more occupied with her guilt.

"Why, to laugh in the face of disaster, my dear."

"Oh." She nodded gloomily. "Aye, and I have helped to bring about that disaster."

"Nonsense!" He tightened his arms about her. "I won't hear another word about it."

In the days that followed, Charles found that his premonition was to be proved right. His repeated demands that the five men be surrendered to him were refused. Mob violence, subtly encouraged by the Commons, prevented those in sympathy with the King from taking their seats in the House of Lords. Charles, forced to remonstrate with them, knew the bitterness of being openly defied. The Scots, encouraged to treason by the Commons, voiced their contempt for the King and for all that the existing British Constitution stood for. And always, or so it seemed to Charles, the voice of Oliver Cromwell sounding above the rest. Cromwell speaking words that inflamed and incited, words that sounded the clarion call to rebellion. Cromwell, gloating in the fact that, by unanimous vote of the Commons, Portsmouth, Hull, the Tower, had been secured for Parliament.

In this bitter time, the King's only comfort was the support of his true friends, and the knowledge that the Queen and his family were safe behind the protecting walls of Windsor Castle. Now that he no longer needed to worry about the safety of his family, he began to make his negotiations with a Parliament who were, seemingly, deaf, dumb, and blind to all reason.

On the day the King came once more to Parliament, the freezing January wind that bent the trees seemed to match the coldness in his heart. Attended by my lord Butler, my lord Foxe, and various other gentlemen, he paused before entering the House. His eyes scanned the leaden sky and the bare, wind-whipped branches of the trees. Shivering, he drew his cloak closely about him. The howl of the wind and its icy sting seemed to be inside him and all about him as he went forward to face those men who were no longer his loyal subjects, but who sat today for the sole purpose of rendering judgment upon Charles Stuart, King of England.

"My lords, gentlemen," Charles addressed himself in a clear carrying voice to the blank-faced men. "I have negotiated with you these many months, and all apparently in vain. I know not what you want," he smiled to give point to his little joke, "unless it be the head of Charles Stuart."

A shocked murmur went through the House. And now the blank faces registered strong disapproval. "Your Majesty is pleased to jest?" came the censorious voice of Sir Jonathon Beechampton.

"I do trust so." Charles, who had not expected to be taken seriously, was startled. He looked straight into the man's eyes. "Aye," he said in a musing voice, as though a new and unpleasant idea had presented itself to his mind, "I do indeed trust so."

Sir Jonathon, who was an earnest man with the good of his country at heart, had no personal animosity against the King. It was not so with many of his fellow members, he was uneasily aware, for they freely expressed their hatred of their sovereign. This malevolence that had begun to rob Sir Jonathon of his usual peaceful and dreamless sleep was typified by the hissing whisper of his neighbor, Oliver Cromwell.

"Look not so shocked, Sir Jonathon," Cromwell said, his eyes expressing the fire within him. "For I tell you now, had I my way, 'twould not be jest but reality. I have said many times that we will cut off his head while it yet wears the crown, and by God's sacred breath, I vow to you that the temper of the people is such that they will have it so!"

Sir Jonathon stared at him with such distaste, that Cromwell smiled grimly. "Worry not, King's man. We will save a lock of the Stuart's hair, for I doubt not you will wish to keep it as a sacred relic."

"You—you would not dare lay violent hands on the person of His Majesty!"

"Would we not? The time will come, you will see."

Sir Jonathon sat up stiffly, not looking at the man again. Sweet Jesus! he thought. If Cromwell's bold words reflect the people's will, then God help Charles Stuart!

"Therefore, gentlemen," Sir Jonathon heard the King say, "in my desire to be fair to all, and not to just a few, I bid you to draw up a full list of your grievances, to be presented to me at the earliest opportunity. If these grievances be such that they affect the welfare of my people, they shall be rectified." He paused, his eyes going from one face to another. "I further promise that they will be rectified without the delay of even one hour."

William Compton stood up. "And will Your Majesty agree that we have the right to appoint all officers to positions of command, not only to command of the Tower, but of the militia and the fortresses?"

"You will refer that question to me later, Mr. Compton," Charles said coldly. "I decline to answer you now."

Brett, who could so easily read the King's mind, knew that his answer would be a refusal. Brett's hands clenched at his sides. Curse the insolent fools! Did they seek to deprive the King of all power? It should not be, not while he had breath in his body. Those loyal to the King would rally to fight in his cause. He now had no doubt that, before the ills afflicting England could be cured, it would come to a fight. God help England! God save the King!

Chapter Twenty

Brett looked across at Meredith. She was seated on the couch, her eyes on the King. Charles, seated opposite to her, appeared to be sunk into a mood of the deepest depression, and Meredith's expression clearly showed her sympathy.

Like all women, Brett thought with a touch of impatience, she was ready to put the King's mood down to the departure of the Queen for Holland, on February 11th, to pay her daughter, Mary, a long-promised visit. Meredith was, for the moment, concerned only with the romance and the sadness of that parting at Dover, and she doubtless believed the King to be mooning after his lost love, because now, with England in turmoil, the parting might be long. She would not believe that the King might be concerned not with his wife but with the fact that England now trembled on the brink of civil war. The people no longer cheered when their King passed. There was only sullen silence, the silence quite often broken by riots and demonstrations against him. Even when the Queen had taken ship at Dover, there had been a crowd collected, a hostile crowd, who had shouted, "Go back to France, where you belong!"

When the soldiers had turned to arrest the agitators, the crowd had melted like magic, running before the pursuing soldiers, and shouting their insults as they ran. But the crowning insult for Charles, Brett thought, had been when he had ridden to Hull and demanded admittance into the town. The gates had been barred against him, and he had been refused entry by Sir John Hotham, the governor.

Meredith, could she have seen into Brett's mind, would have been indignant. She was not thinking of the parting of the King and Queen, but of the humiliations to which the King had been subjected, and of one humiliation in particular, the refusal of the governor, Sir John Hotham, to allow the King entry into the city of Hull. Furious, the King had written an indignant letter to Parliament, demanding the meaning of Sir John Hotham's unprecedented action, and asking that he be disciplined for this insult to the sovereign.

In their reply, Parliament had openly shown their contempt. "Sire," came the answer, "Sir John Hotham, having shown himself to be a good and loyal servant in all particulars, we do not feel that we can justly question his decision to disallow Your Majesty entry into the city of Hull. The reason that prompted his refusal is, unfortunately, not known to us. But we ask Your Majesty to believe that we have every confidence in him. This being so, we are therefore compelled not to question him, but to give his action our vote of confidence by awarding it our full approval."

Meredith moved restlessly. They did not know the reason that prompted Hotham's refusal! Poppycock! She had boiled with rage when Brett had quoted the letter to her, and she boiled now. She had completely forgotten her onetime adherence to Oliver Cromwell and his ideals. She seldom thought of the man now, but when she did, it was with distaste. Gone were the butterfly notions of her youth, at the age of thirty-four she remained steadfast in her loyalties and her convictions, and that loyalty was given for all time to the King. But her sudden violent rages had not left her. That smooth answer from Parliament, she decided, had been tantamount to a slap in the King's face. And shortly after that letter, had come a further blow to His Majesty. The Commons, without warning, had seized command of the Royal Fleet and had installed a Puritan admiral. This action was already known to the King when he had been asked to receive a party of commissioners representing Parliament.

Meredith had been present when the commissioners were brought into the King's presence. She had looked questioningly at Brett, and, seeing his slight nod of dismissal, she had curtsied to the King and then turned to leave.

"Nay," the King said, placing a restraining hand on her arm, "I pray you to stay, my lady Foxe, and you also, my lord Foxe. The gentlemen of my Parliament have, by their actions, made their future intentions quite clear. Therefore any words they may have to say cannot be secret in nature. I doubt not but that these words will seek to expand that which they have already done."

Sir Godfrey Fullerton, the spokesman for the group, looked decidedly uncomfortable. "Sire," he said stiffly, "we have traveled to Newmarket to make a direct request of Your Majesty. Perhaps it might be best if we made that request in private."

"Best?" Charles lifted a cynical eyebrow. "Best for whom? Surely, at this late hour, you do not pretend to consider the dignity and the feelings of your King?"

"Sire, I must protest! We are come hither in a spirit of friendship. All here have one thing in common, the good of England."

"The good of England?" Charles smiled slightly, but the smile was grim rather than amused. "However, Sir Godfrey, you may protest all you please, but it will avail you nothing. I will hear you in the presence of my loyal friends, or I will not hear you at all."

He laid such stress on the word "loyal," that Sir Godfrey's ruddy complexion deepened to a purplish hue. "Very well, Sire," he said abruptly, "if it be your pleasure to have it so. With the full approval of Commons, we are come here to request that Your Majesty deliver the command of the militia and that of all the fortified places into our hands.''

Charles had been expecting something like this, but nevertheless he appeared to be momentarily stunned. The rings on his fingers flashed as he lifted his hand in a gesture that was almost menacing. Then his hand dropped heavily to his side, but such a blaze of fury lit his dark eyes that Fullerton, taken aback, glanced uneasily at his companions. They looked startled, but they did not speak. "Sire," Fullerton began, "I—"

"You dare to ask this of me?" Charles rasped. "Even this!" His nervous and angry stammer impeded his next words, but he brought them out clearly enough. "Is—is there n—no end to y—your arrogant im—impertinence! B—by God, I am a m—mild-tempered m—man, but you go t—too far!"

Thoroughly alarmed, Sir Godfrey looked anywhere but at the King. "If Your Majesty would but listen, I will explain to you that Your Majesty's own actions have scarcely been conducive of—"

Again Charles cut him off. "You will be silent," he said, looking at him with contempt. He enunciated every word clearly in order that he might not stammer. "You have made your request. My answer is no! I have made many concessions, some of them against my will, wisdom, and conscience, but this one I will not make. I will surrender nothing more to your rapacious masters. I am the king of this land, and yet you have dared to ask that of me which would be intolerable to the king of any country. Get you gone, sirs, all of you! Your request is refused now and for all time. Tell those who sent you that Charles Stuart will no longer do destruction to his dignity and standing by treating with treasonable dogs!"

"Treasonable, Sire?" Sir Jeremy Ashbright rose to his feet and looked directly at the King. He stood there, tall, spare, his face stiff with offense; even the gray hairs at the back of his neck seemed to bristle with the force of his outrage. "I believe that Your Majesty must know that no treason may be imputed to myself, or to anyone here present. England founders beneath the misery inflicted upon her in the reign of your late father. By his many extravagances he brought her very low, and now it seems that you, Sire, seek to follow—''

"Be very careful, sir," Charles interrupted smoothly. "I could have you arrested for those words. If ever I have heard treason, I have heard it from your lips."

Undaunted, Sir Jeremy glared at him. "Do as you will, Sire, have me arrested."

"And make you a martyr to your cause? You would welcome that, would you not? Nay, you are free to go."

He stood there waiting, and when they made no move to depart, he added imperiously, "Perhaps you did not hear. You are dismissed."

"Is this your final answer, Sire?" Sir Godfrey Fullerton, though he was not aware of it, said almost pleadingly. "Might it not be wiser to reconsider?"

"I have not that much wisdom, Sir Godfrey, so I say away with your wisdom!" Charles gave him a long steady look, and Sir Godfrey, as though he could not bear what he read in those eyes, looked quickly away.

"Must I repeat," Charles said, "that you are dismissed?"

As he moved to the door after the others, Sir Godfrey was conscious of something like awe. His was a minor position in the House, and he had never thought that he might actually confront the King. He had tried to do his duty as instructed, for he had been proud of the trust placed in him, but when he had stood before this man whose character had persistently been torn to shreds by such men as Oliver Cromwell and his ilk, he was not so sure that the King's detractors were right. There was something about Charles Stuart, despite his alarming flash of anger, a dignity, a true kingliness that, quite suddenly, made the malice of the others seem like the petty tirades of jealous children. Stopping by the door, Sir Godfrey hesitated, then, turning, he bowed deeply. "Your Majesty," he heard his own words with dismay, " 'twas not my intention to offend. I pray you to forgive me."

Charles smiled. "I forgive you freely. You do the will of those in command, therefore I hold you blameless." He held out his hand. "I bid you good day, sir."

Sir Godfrey looked at the extended hand, then he stumbled forward. Falling to his knees before the King, he took the hand and pressed it to his lips. Something moved in his heart, prompting his next words. "Mayhap I have served the wrong masters, Sire."

"Mayhap." Charles gestured to him to rise. "But there is always an alternative, is there not?"

Sir Godfrey got to his feet. "An alternative, Sire? What mean you?"

"You may serve me instead."

"But, Sire, I—I could not."

"Very well, if you feel that you could not, then there is no more to be said."

Meredith smiled to herself. Sir Godfrey, a deeply bewildered man, had taken his departure, but, after less than ten minutes, he had returned.

Sir Godfrey, red-faced and earnest, had stood once more before the King. Drawing himself to an attitude of stiff attention, he said huskily, "Sire, accuse me if you will of loyalties that are blown by any wind, but I find that I have been mistaken. If you will have me, I would serve Your Majesty."

"With all your heart?" the King questioned gently.

"Aye, Sire, with all my heart, and with all my strength!"

"I believe you," Charles assured him. "But what has brought about this change of heart?"

Sir Godfrey's thick sandy brows drew together in a frown of genuine perplexity. "I know not, Sire, unless it be, recalling the duty I was sent to perform, I became conscious of revulsion." He looked straight into the King's eyes, and, because he was a blunt-spoken and almost painfully honest man, he added, "Even now I know not for a certainty which side be true, or which false. But I do know, that if you will have me, I have chosen the master I must serve."

"I believe that I understand you better than you understand yourself, Sir Godfrey," Charles said. "Right heartily do I welcome you."

"Then mayhap Your Majesty will one day find the time to teach me that same understanding," Sir Godfrey replied with dry humor, "for I must confess that my emotions do ofttimes bewilder me."

Since that time Sir Godfrey had more than proved his worth. Traveling with the King and his retinue to York, he became very active in the King's cause. He appeared to have a listening ear in every place of importance. He it was who brought the news that Parliament had taken a resolve to alert the kingdom, warning the citizens that they must prepare to defend themselves against Charles Stuart, King of England, their most dire and baleful enemy!

"M—my people m—must defend themselves against m—me, their King!" Charles had stammered in his distress. "Gracious God, d—do they believe m—me to be their enemy? This is too m—much. This is m—more than I can endure!"

Sir Godfrey looked for support to Brett, who had come forward to place a comforting hand on the King's shoulder. "You will endure, Sire, because you must!" Sir Godfrey had spoken abruptly, bracingly, and was rewarded by an approving nod from Brett. "But I have some good news too for Your Majesty. I have heard that many have withdrawn from the two Houses, and are even now on their way to York to join you."

Charles's eyes did not light up, as he had hoped. "How many?" he said in a dull voice.

"A hundred or more." Sir Godfrey smiled rather grimly. "I am sorry to have to add that certain Parliamentary commissioners will also be present in York. Their object being to spy on Your Majesty's movements. Parliament is alarmed by this exodus of those whom they believed to be their staunchest allies."

"I see." There was a faint animation in Charles's expression. "But tell me," he said curiously, "how the devil you manage to find out all these things?"

"I have my methods, Sire," Sir Godfrey answered, looking faintly smug. The King looked at him, inviting him to go on, but he did not elaborate.

Meredith swung her foot backward and forward, a restless movement that caused the diamond buckle on her green satin slipper to flash in a shaft of sunlight coming through the rose-tinted windows. It was for these defaulting members they waited now. She would not be present at that meeting, when the men would once more render their oath of loyalty to their sovereign, and she felt regret that she must be excluded. But Brett had already told her that she could not be present. He would make sure that she took her departure.

Her movements caught the King's eyes. "You are restless, my lady?"

Meredith rose to her feet. "Not restless, Sire," she answered, curtseying. She glanced at Brett from the corner of her eye. "Merely sad that my lord will not permit me to be present when Your Majesty's subjects repeat their oath of loyalty."

A snort from Brett answered this slyly couched appeal to the King's feelings. But Charles smiled. "By Gad, Brett," he said thoughtfully, "it might be called an historic occasion. Don't you think the lass might be present?"

"Only if you so command."

"Nay. 'Twas merely a suggestion."

"Then I say no, Charles," Brett said, strolling forward. "The wench is well enough, but she has no place at such a proceeding. The men will already be embarrassed because they have stood out against you. They will be more so, if my lady is present."

Charles looked thoughtful. "I fear, my lady, that your lord is right."

Meredith looked at Brett with kindling eyes. "You know well, my lord, that I would not dream of embarrassing them. Though," she concluded virtuously, "they deserve to be for their first disloyalty."

Brett gave an exasperated sigh. "The female mind! A man

must be either sinner or saint, there are no half measures. No allowance is made for the slightest deviation.''

Laughing, Charles looked at Meredith's stormy face. "You have not changed one whit, either of you. But that is how I would have it, my dear friends. When the dear and the familiar changes all about you, it is good to hear you quarreling as fiercely as ever.''

"Then I shall say no more to him, Sire," Meredith said haughtily. "I will not give him the satisfaction."

Brett grinned. "Thank God for that."

"I would have you know, my lord," Meredith began, "that if the King commands, you cannot presume to dictate to me."

"But the King has not commanded," Brett corrected her. "And another thing, you—" A knock at the door caused him to break off.

Charles rose slowly to his feet. Brett saw that his hands were clenched tightly at his sides. "Enter," Charles called.

Meredith, who had thought to take full advantage of this timely intervention, and relying on Brett's natural excitement, prepared to make herself as inconspicuous as possible. She was arrested by Brett's commanding eyes. " 'Tis little use to hide, my lady," he said quietly. "Pray leave us."

"Oh, you! Oh, very well," Meredith tossed her head. Seeing his unmoved grin, she sent him a furious glance. Drawing to one side, she waited until the men had filed into the room, then, with an angry flounce of her green skirts, she withdrew.

Edward Hyde, in the forefront of the group, took a step forward. He looked apprehensively at the sober-faced King, and his own fear of rejection was reflected in the eyes of the hundred and nine men behind him. "Your Majesty," Hyde bowed deeply. "I have been asked to speak for all present. I trust you will believe me when I tell you that we sincerely regret all that has occurred. If you feel that you can forgive us for past disloyalty, then I would ask if you have a welcome for us." He took a deep breath. "Though, until we discovered that we had embraced the wrong cause, we did not believe we were guilty of disloyalty. So perhaps we should merely say that we were mistaken.''

Another bluntly honest man, Charles thought. In many of his ways, Edward Hyde reminded him of Sir Godfrey Fullerton. And there were Colepepper, Spencer, Drambourne, and Falkland, all good men to have at one's side. His eyes went from one taut face to another. They were weary and travel-stained, uneasy in his presence, and obviously fearing his angry reproaches rather than anticipating his welcome. Some of them looked away, as though not daring to meet his eyes. In their nervousness they appeared almost furtive, yet he could not doubt their sincerity.

It was Charles's slow dawning smile that melted the tension that held them. They relaxed visibly, eagerly craning their heads forward when they saw that the King was about to speak. Brett, with Sir Godfrey, who had entered the room with the men, watched them. Their faces were moved, yet they appeared to be undergoing some strain. His eyes narrowed slightly. They all, Hyde especially, had the expression of those who were the bearers of bad news. Brett looked at Sir Godfrey, who shrugged and shook his head.

"My lords, gentlemen," Charles was saying, "I—I''— his voice choked in his throat for a moment —"I have not the words to tell you of my joy.'' He flung out both hands in an appealing gesture, as though asking them to help him out. "I welcome you! Aye, with all my heart!''

"God save the King!'' Somebody cried out in a ringing voice.

"God save the King!'' they cried together. One by one they dropped to their knees, and the cry was repeated over and over again.

The hubbub died, and in that pool of silence, Edward Hyde's voice was heard. "Again I speak for all, Sire. We swear that we will serve you with our hearts, our minds, our bodies. We will be faithful unto death! To you, our sovereign lord, do we pledge our allegiance and our everlasting loyalty!''

Although Hyde had spoken for all, the murmur of their voices

376

nonetheless accompanied him, repeating that oath that bound them once more to the King.

It was like a tableau, Brett thought, the tall elegant King, clad in scarlet, his long, dark hair falling to his shoulders, the kneeling men looking up at him, the bright fervor of their eyes, the renewed pride in their faces. They had strayed, that expression said, but they were back where they belonged. Their swords and their lives were the King's to command. It was an emotion-charged moment, and Brett was keenly aware of it, but still he could not control his sense of uneasiness. The men were sincere, he could not doubt that, but somehow he knew that they had more to say. They were rising to their feet, their eyes were turning to Edward Hyde, their spokesman. Brett took a quick step forward as Hyde opened his mouth to speak. He saw that the man's eyes were full of tears, and his forboding increased.

"Y—Your Majesty," Hyde said in a shaking voice. "I regret that I m—must be the bearer of this news—" He stopped, swallowing convulsively. "Your Majesty, both Houses have declared for—for civil war."

"War!" The color drained from the King's face. He swayed slightly. "Civil war! Brother against brother. Christ's wounds! What will become of my England?" In his anguish, he seemed to have forgotten the men.

It was Edward Hyde's voice that brought him back to the present. "We were not present at the session, Sire, for we had already resigned. Would to God we had been, for then we might have raised our voices in opposition. As it was, we heard that only two were opposed, and a very few doubtful."

Charles stared at him, the life gone from his eyes. "Civil war!" he whispered. "Before God," his voice rose, "I swear that I will not raise an army to fight against my own people! I cannot, I cannot!"

"Parliament have already raised an army against Your Majesty," Hyde said. "The Earl of Essex is in command."

"Essex? Essex, who knelt before me at my coronation. Who

laid his hands upon the crown and swore everlasting loyalty!''

"Aye." Hyde's voice rang loudly through the room. ''Your Majesty's enemies have finally declared themselves. Oliver Cromwell too, that scum, is likewise eager to march against you!''

The dazed look was leaving Charles's face, and anger was taking its place. It was as though the mention of Cromwell's name had released something inside him, something fierce and proud that rose to meet the challenge. ''May God forgive me, but it seems that I have no choice.''

Now voices rose to fever pitch. ''Declare for Charles!'' the men shouted. ''Charles! Charles! And damnation to his enemies!''

The men milled about the room, and Brett was swept forward. Charles saw him, and came quickly to his side. ''My people, Brett! Oh, my poor people!''

''Sire!'' In a surprising act of reverence, Brett took the King's hand and pressed his lips to it. ''Your enemies are my enemies, now and for all time!''

Charles looked at the humbly bent dark head, and a faint smile touched his lips. ''Art humble, Brett? Can this be my arrogant m'lord Foxe who speaks?''

Brett looked up. ''Even so, Sire. Where you go, I go. I can be humble if the cause be right, and your cause is right.'' There was a touch of anger in his eyes. ''Why so surprised? You do not question my loyalty, I trust?''

The King's face sobered. ''Don't be so confounded sensitive, Brett. I, question your loyalty? Never in this world!''

''Then, Charles, if I may advise you,'' Brett said eagerly. ''You must publish a declaration. You must tell the people of all the insolent and disloyal acts wrought against you. You must let them know that England's enemy is not Charles Stuart. Their true enemy is the Parliament, who have raised forces to attack Your Majesty, and to destroy the traditions and privileges for which England has long stood!''

Charles was fired by this enthusiasm. ''I will do more. I will declare them to be guilty of treason. I will forbid my subjects to aid them, or to render obedience in any way whatsoever.''

"And men, Charles,'' Brett continued to plan. "We must see that men are inspired to rally to your cause.''

Charles's spurt of eagerness died, leaving his face drawn and exhausted. "If men must be inspired, then how can they be said to believe in the King's cause?''

Brett shook his head impatiently. "Nay, Charles, I vow you are too harsh in your judgment. Men may believe whole-heartedly in something, but ofttimes they are apathetic until their fighting spirit has been ignited. They need drums and trumpets, the fluttering of the flag, the tramp of marching feet and the charge of the cavalry.''

"If I am harsh in judgment, my lord Foxe, you have, by your words, proved yourself to be a cynic.''

"I am no cynic, I merely face facts. There are times when we all need to be inspired. Hast forgotten that Prince Rupert is in England?'' Brett asked. "Now there is one who needs no inspiration.'' He smiled. "Think you that you can keep that headstrong nephew of yours from riding to your aid?''

Charles thought of his sister, the Queen of Bohemia, recalling the many times in Rupert's childhood when she had despaired of her son. But wild and handsome Rupert had grown up to be a credit to her. It was true, Rupert, that ardent royalist and dashing cavalry leader would come riding to his aid. He knew well that he could not be kept from his side once he heard the news. " 'Tis true, Brett,'' he said. "Rupert will be with me, and I doubt not that he will come with the blare of his own trumpets and a beating of drums.''

"Aye, and where Rupert leads, Maurice will not be far behind.''

Dusk was beginning to tinge the storm-whipped sky. The heat of the August day had vanished on the wings of a howling gale. Rain lashed down in blinding sheets, soaking the seven men who sat motionless astride their horses at the top of Castleford Hill. Two of them, the Prince of Wales and Marcus Milford, could hardly be said to be men, since they had not yet reached their fourteenth year. But the expression on their faces as they watched the rain-soaked ceremony of the raising of the Royal Standard bore the stamp of maturity.

Prince Rupert, his long, black hair blowing in the wind, took his eyes from the ceremony to observe the other men. The King looked gloomy. The Earl of Lindsey, beside him, stern. As for my lord Butler, who was shivering violently beneath his cloak, he looked definitely ill. Rupert felt a surge of impatience. "If Butler was ill, then he should not be here." Loyalty was all very well, but a sick man could prove to be a liability. As for the King, his Uncle Charles, he could not imagine why he did not burn with that same flame that consumed himself. In Nottingham, on this unseasonable August day, the Royal Standard was being raised. Why then this cursed gloom and despair? Young Charles and that stern-faced boy, Marcus Milford, showed far more enthusiasm. War! Rupert's nerves thrilled to the word. War in the King's cause. It had a glorious ring! His eyes met my lord Foxe's, and his heart lightened. Now there was a man more of his kidney. My lord Foxe was smiling at him understandingly, and Rupert felt for him a sudden warm kinship.

"Your Highness," Brett put his head close to Rupert's and shouted above the wind, "your feelings show all too plainly. 'Tis but the beginning, you know. You can scarcely blame the King for being despondent. Civil war is a terrible thing. How much more terrible must it be for the king of the afflicted land?"

"I understand that," Rupert shouted back. But Brett knew that he did not really understand, did not want to understand. "But we have become engaged in a glorious cause," Rupert went on. "My uncle should forget his scruples. He should enjoy the adventure."

Brett fought a longing to cuff the arrogant young man. Rupert was bold and fearless, qualities to be admired, but he had not the imagination or sensitivity to sense the King's problems. What did he know or understand of the King's agony that his people had taken up arms against each other? Brett answered Rupert mockingly, "But you see, to him it is not an adventure, 'tis a tragedy. But fear not, Your Highness, your time for blood and death and glory will surely come."

Unabashed, Rupert grinned. "Aye, it will, I'll see to that. But, Foxefield, I think you are making fun of me."

"How discerning of Your Highness. I was a little, but only in the kindliest way."

"Ah, a pox on you," Rupert grumbled good-naturedly. "And if you insist on calling me Your Highness, may the devil fly away with you."

"Then I will not insist, Rupert."

"Thank you. 'Tis better than all that plaguy formality."

The Prince of Wales stiffened in his saddle as the drums began to beat and the trumpets to blare. "See there, Marcus," he cried in a voice high with excitement, "the Standard is erected!"

Marcus stared downward. "Aye. But it would seem that few men have come in answer to the King's call."

His fascinated eyes on the fluttering Standard, Charles shrugged. "They will come," he said confidently. "The men have been called to arms. They will come!"

Marcus turned his head to look at his father. His expression grew somber. My lord Butler was slumped forward on his horse, and he looked to be in imminent danger of falling to the muddy ground. Marcus edged his horse alongside. "Father," he whispered urgently, "are you all right?"

Lord Butler nodded, and managed a smile. He was rewarded for this effort by Marcus's own rare smile. The boy was so handsome, the father thought proudly. Almost strikingly handsome when the too mature, too grim cast of his features relaxed. " 'Tis only that I am cold, lad," Lord Butler reassured him. "Do not waste time in worrying about me. Look, the Prince is beckoning to you."

Marcus hesitated, doubt in his eyes, then he nodded. With a last close look at his father, he pressed his horse to the Prince's side.

Lord Butler sighed, and stifled a cough. This was one of his bad days, and they were becoming all too frequent of late. But he must keep it from Marcus at all costs. Beneath his son's stiff exterior there was a gentle and remarkably sensitive nature. His love was given to few. If he had any suspicion that he might be losing one of those few, he would take it very hard.

Lord Butler began surreptitiously to massage the region of his heart. He was in pain, and his chest felt as though it were circled by an iron band which, slowly tightening, was squeezing the breath from his body. There was a history of heart trouble in his family, and knowing this, he was often concerned for his son. Pain struck at him again, deeper this time. Perhaps it would pass, he thought desperately, as it had always done before. But there were times when he could almost believe that he was dying. He did not really mind that, for in all truth he was weary of life. But he was concerned for Marcus and his baby daughter, Jessica. Jessica, he knew, was not really his daughter. She was the child of one of Mary's lovers. Nevertheless he had always thought of her as his daughter. Marcus, for all he knew, might not be his son. But he did not care, he love 1 the boy dearly. How could he leave his children defenseless, at the mercy of their mother? But Marcus was fast growing up. Lately, he had taken a firm new stand against his mother. He had not liked it at all when he had allowed Mary to return to Milford Manor in order to give birth to Jessica. He did not doubt Marcus's love for himself, but he felt that he had been contemptuous of the weakness he had displayed in allowing her to come to the manor to give birth to her bastard. Aye, it had hurt him to read contempt in Marcus's eyes. Yet why should it, when he knew well that he was a weak and contemptible fool where his wife Mary was concerned. Many times he had tried to stand against her, but it had never been any use. He loved her, he would always love her, and he could not change at this late date. But Marcus was changing. With each passing day he became stronger, more ruthless where Mary was concerned. He shuddered, thinking of Marcus's eyes whenever they chanced to rest on his mother. So cold, they were, so merciless. And Marcus, he knew, when he became the head of the family, would show her no mercy. He thought of his long ago interview with Mrs. Thomas. For the first time he had learned of the mental injuries Mary had inflicted upon her son. Oh, God! Even knowing that, he still could not help loving her, so what manner of man was he? But the time would come when Mary must deal with Marcus. And he, were he in a position to look on, would be able to feel no pity for her. Her lot would not be an enviable one, but whatever came to her she would deserve.

Lord Butler started out of his thoughts at the Earl of Lindsey's sudden shout. "Sire," the man cried, pointing down the hill, "the Standard has blown down!"

Lord Butler, well acquainted with the strongly superstitious streak in the King's nature, understood his obvious dismay. He placed a gentle hand on the King's arm. "Nay, Charles," he said soothingly, "You must not become the prey of superstition. 'Tis unfortunate that the wind has blown down the Standard, but you must not think of it as an ill omen."

Charles nodded at him and smiled, but he had not really taken in the words. Civil war! he was thinking with that now familiar horror. If only he had been called upon to fight any other war than this one. But Englishman against Englishman! May God find it in His heart to forgive him for accepting the challenge. May He likewise forgive those enemies who had forced this terrible necessity upon him! He looked down at the Standard lying upon the muddy ground, and at the startled faces of the men grouped about it, and his heart misgave him. How dare he ask God to forgive him? How could God do other than frown upon men who dared to take up arms against their brothers?

A wild yell of excitement came from the Prince of Wales as his cousin Rupert, spurring his horse to full gallop, went plunging down the hill. Mud sprayed from his animal's hooves as he rode straight toward the men at the bottom of the hill. Bringing his horse to a rearing halt, he leaned from his saddle and snatched up the Standard. Holding it aloft, Rupert shouted, "For England! For Charles, King of this realm! Victory to the King!"

"Victory to the King!" young Charles echoed the shout, and his lean dark face was ablaze with the thrill of the moment.

The King closed his eyes against pain. Victory? But did he want victory at such a bitter price?

Chapter
Twenty-One

Her eyes burning, her head throbbing with savage pain, the Queen lay still and straight in her narrow bed. This bed, in the cottage of a fisherman, was the only shelter she had been able to obtain. Most of the inhabitants of the cottages along the quay had turned their backs on the Queen, fearing, if they gave her shelter, that swift reprisals at the hands of the Roundhead soldiers would surely follow.

Mistress Bunkerton, the fisherman's wife, in whose cottage the Queen now lay, had been more courageous than the rest. Planting her hands on her ample hips, Mistress Bunkerton had shouted at her neighbors, "I ain't afraid o' Cromwell, let me tell you. Not him nor all his soldiers. Besides, he ain't nowhere near here." Her eyes surveyed them scornfully. "As for you lot, 'tis skulking cowards you are, who fear to give shelter to the Queen of England! Out o' my sight, all of you, or I'll be taking my broom to your backsides!"

Turning to the wet and shivering Queen, flanked by her

equally miserable ladies, Mistress Bunkerton had taken her arm in a firm, warm grip. "You come along o' me, dearie," she said in the tone of one soothing a child. "I'll soon have you warm and snug." She looked after her thankfully disappearing neighbors. "Folks!" she snorted. "Just ain't no accounting for 'em. But no one can say of Martha Bunkerton that she turned her own Queen from her doorstep." Her indignation returned. "Them cowards! The very idea! As for them Roundhead soldiers, just let any o' 'em come poking their noses in my affairs, an' I'll make 'em bloody sorry they was ever born, I will 'n' all!"

Her grip on the Queen's arm tightened. "Don't you be afraid, my dearie, I ain't going to let no one hurt you. Have a job to get past me, they would. Me an' my man are for the King and Queen, an' we don't care who knows it. Martha'll take care o' you, don't you fret."

Henrietta Maria, by this time feeling incapable of speech, had gone with her meekly. Indeed she had to fight the inclination to lay her head on that big motherly bosom and sob out her grief and worry.

Mistress Bunkerton, apparently quite unawed by the presence of the Queen, kept darting fierce glances at her husband, as if daring him to open his mouth and question her authority. But she had been as good as her word. Sweeping aside the feeble protest of the ladies, she herself had undressed the Queen. Tucking her in the narrow bed, the best she had to offer, she had placed a heated brick, wrapped in a woolen shawl, at her frozen feet. With the Queen safely in bed, Mistress Bunkerton had then returned to hectoring her husband. Under her strident supervision, he lugged cots, chairs, and even an old couch up the steep and narrow stairs, for the Queen's ladies, who, defying Mistress Bunkerton, had refused to be parted from their mistress.

The Queen looked about her. In the light of the one candle Mistress Bunkerton had left burning, she studied her ladies. Mary Rowhampton, the youngest of them, appeared to be sleeping peacefully. She lay curled up in a chair, her golden hair falling over the armrest and touching the floor. But most of them moved restlessly, limbs twitching, mumbling now and again, as though even now their dreams were haunted by that nightmare journey from Holland to England.

Henrietta Maria gave a rueful grimace. They were lucky to be sleeping. Would that she might follow their example. Oh, Charles, my darling, I have prayed for you! Night and day I have prayed for you! Are you safe, are you well? I shall lose my mind if I do not soon reach your side! Sighing, she pressed her hand to her aching head.

Lady Morton heard the sigh. She was lying on the frayed couch with the sagging middle, now she sat up and looked at the Queen. "Are you all right, Madam?"

"Margaret! You startled me. I had thought you to be sleeping. Aye, I'm all right, but I feel very restless."

Lady Morton's gray eyes studied her. In some ways the Queen had changed. She seemed to have shed much of her petulance and her arrogance. She was warmer, far more considerate of those who served her. There were even times when she was gentle. She had always been deeply religious, but now she seemed to have blossomed into a fanatic, and that was a side of the Queen that she could not like. All the ladies who served her, whether they be Catholic or not, must attend Mass. No excuses were taken. Dorothy Grove, suffering from what appeared to be lung fever, had been forced to attend. Her hacking cough did not soften the Queen to compassion, she merely raised her voice above the disturbance. The shivering Dorothy, kneeling on the hard floor, had finally fainted. When the other ladies had moved to help the unfortunate girl, the Queen had forbidden them to stir. And so Dorothy had lain there on the cold floor, the draught from the window playing upon her, until the service had ended. Only then had the Queen shown concern, and then, it seemed, she could not do enough for the girl. She had commanded her own physician to attend her, but it was too late for poor Dorothy. She had died, and was buried in the alien Dutch soil. She might have died anyway, Lady Morton told herself, yet she could not rid herself of the uncomfortable notion that the fanatical Queen had aided in that demise. So mayhap, despite her new and gentle guise, this Henrietta Maria was far more to be feared. Would God, who was loving and gentle, have turned His back on a suffering girl in order that He might continue to preach to the populace? Nay, He would not. He would have lifted the sufferer and taken her to where she might receive warmth and comfort and healing.

"Margaret," the Queen said sharply, "why are you staring at me in that odd way? Have you said your prayers? Have you given thanks to God for bringing us through to safe harbor?"

"Yes, indeed, Madam."

The Queen hesitated, as though about to challenge this statement, then she said slowly, "In many ways you grieve me, Margaret, for I have noticed your reluctance to give thanks to Him to whom it is due. However, I will take your word for it this time. Soon, before I sleep, I too must kneel and repeat my thanks to Him."

"But, Madam, you will take a chill."

"The sufferings of the body are secondary. Lie down now and try to rest."

"Yes, Madam." Fearing that the Queen might conceive the idea that they should both kneel, or even that the others should be awakened to join them, Lady Morton settled down hastily. Through half-closed lids, she continued to study the Queen. Whatever else Henrietta Maria might be, one could not deny that she had courage. On that long and terrible and danger-fraught sea journey from Holland, she had been unflinching. They had finally landed here, Bridlington Quay, on the wild and rugged coast of Yorkshire, but they had thought never to see England again.

Lady Morton shuddered as she remembered how the ship had heaved and plunged beneath them. Tossed like a cork on those waters, lashed by gray and mountainous waves, the deck awash with spray, it had been a terrifying experience. But the real terror had been yet to come, for suddenly, appearing like a phantom from out of the curtain of rain, there hove an enemy ship. *Strong Arm of God*, the ship was called, and its Puritan admiral knew that the Queen was on *The Dreadnaught*. He had been determined to capture her. She would never forget that dogged and relentless pursuit. Wind had howled through the riggings, sounding like a million demented souls. Lightning forked the sky, and the rumble of thunder combined with the crash of cannon balls, which, barely falling short of their objective, sent up great walls of water. The pursuit ship, looking like a giant and sinister white-winged bird, drew nearer and nearer, until it seemed that she would surely take them. They could hear their own captain shouting orders, and then they felt the ship make a sweeping turn. Somehow, they found, they had managed to outrun their enemy.

In the cabin below, the Queen had conducted her prayers as though nothing was happening. Her voice rose above the terrifying din and confusion, exhorting God to defend them from their enemies. Perhaps God had answered her, Lady Morton thought, for it was surely a miracle that they had managed to elude the pursuit ship.

When the battered ship had put into Bridlington Quay, the Queen had barely waited until they were all ashore before bidding them to kneel and give thanks. Captain Peterson, who had declared himself to be a staunch Episcopalian, hadn't liked it at all. At first he had refused to kneel. But so fierce was the Queen, so commanding her aspect, that he had finally sank grudgingly to his knees. Lady Morton, kneeling beside him, had heard him mutter, "Cursed Catholics! I want none of their mummery. I'll say my own prayers, thank you. A Catholic Queen! Damned if I shouldn't have let Batten take her!"

Lady Morton's lids were heavy. Her last thought, before surrendering to sleep, was the name she had heard Captain Peterson utter. Batten. Was that the name of the enemy admiral? It must be. Batten. She would remember that name.

Soon she must leave the warmth of the bed, the Queen thought regretfully. She must not lie here in gross comfort muttering her prayers. Such sloth would not be pleasing to God. But for the moment, if He would forgive her, she would lie here and brace herself for the effort. Hastily, Henrietta Maria crossed herself. It was not fitting to even think that way. Nothing was too much to do for Him, no discomfort too great. She stared with feverish eyes at the sloping ceiling, almost as if she expected to see God's stern face there. The candle flickered in the wind that came from the slightly opened window and sent racing shadows across the ceiling. She blinked her eyes. It might be that she was slightly delirious from all she had had to endure, but now those shadows were turning into the marching armies of the Roundheads. Even in Holland she had heard of the progress of those wicked men. Those men, under Cromwell, who, in destroying the churches and the cathedrals, spat upon God!

Henrietta Maria pressed a hand against her shaking lips. God would surely punish them for such desecration. She turned her head from side to side on the pillow. And now, as she thought of her husband, her dark eyes became wide and bright with fear. What was to become of him, that good and well-intentioned man? What was to become of them all? The battle of Edgehill, fought in 1642, had seemed like a wonderful triumph for the royal cause. The Roundheads had fled before the two wings of cavalry. The right wing led by Prince Rupert, the left wing by my lord Foxe. It had been a victory for the royalists, but there had been a great many wounded. The Roundheads had fought back savagely. Oliver Cromwell had been there with his trained men. It was Cromwell who had pursued her son Charles and his friend, Marcus Milford. The two boys, seeing the Royal Standard fall into enemy hands, had rode forth to retake it.

Henrietta Maria shivered. She had never loved Charles as she loved James, but he was after all her son. It was very frightening to think of him on the battlefield. He and his brother James, who had also been present, might well have been captured. Had it not been for the timely charge of the royalists, Cromwell might have taken them.

Henrietta Maria's always vivid imagination showed her the scene. She heard the thunder of cannon, the sharp barking blast of the musketry. She saw the choking black smoke spreading in an acrid haze over the field. The stench of blood raw in the nostrils, the pitiful screams of the wounded. Screams mingling with trumpet blast, the pounding of hooves, the flash of sunlight on drawn sabers. Cavalry charging with the resounding yell, "For King and country!" Long hair of cavalier blowing across the dead face of enemy soldier. The gay and the somber united in death!

Henrietta Maria struggled to subdue her imagination, but it would not be subdued. She heard the spiraling shout as the Royal Standard was captured. There was her son Charles, young and fearless, his long, black hair streaming out behind him as he galloped forward, dark eyes glittering, his mouth tightened to a thin line of determination. He would be heedless of shouted warnings, for Charles, she knew, could be conveniently deaf when he chose. He would send his horse leaping over those sprawled bodies. His one aim to pluck the Standard from the hand of the enemy soldier who bore it aloft in insolent triumph. He and Marcus Milford, who was never far from Charles's side, had, between them, retaken the Standard. Young Milford had done more, he had, before the cavalry had borne the Prince to safety, killed a man who was creeping up on Charles. For the first time, in the cause of his friend, his sword had been bloodied.

In his letter to her, the King had made much of this incident. "If you could have seen the boy, dear heart," he wrote with enthusiasm. "He whirled his horse about so abruptly that the animal reared. Recovering himself, he leaned from his saddle and thrust his sword right through the throat of the would-be-assassin. Never have I seen such determined and swift action. He killed for Charles, his friend, and he exulted at the time, but afterwards he was sickened. The memory of the deed haunts young Marcus yet. It was brave doing in one so young. We owe him our son's life. I will always be grateful to him."

Henrietta moved restlessly in the bed. But, yes, she thought, she too was grateful. She must remember to reward him. What could she give him to show her gratitude? She thought of Marcus

Milford's face, his bearing, the expression in his dark eyes, and she frowned to herself. There was nothing she could give him. He would scorn reward. He was in all respects, save for his age, a man. Aye, one could not reward Marcus Milford as one would a child. Her thoughts returned to her son. Again she shivered. What a terrible risk he had taken! He, the heir to the throne! He must be taught, forcibly if it prove necessary, that he must not expose his person to danger. Had he died, why then, of course, James would have been the heir to the throne. James! The next King of England. Henrietta smiled with pleasure at the thought. James, her darling biddable James. He was not stubborn like his brother, and what a wonderful king he would make. A Catholic King. James, she knew, could be brought to see reason. But what was she thinking about? Henrietta Maria was appalled and sickened at the pleasure the thought gave her. What manner of mother was she if she could think that way? She must be a very evil woman indeed. Nay, from now on she would think of Charles, not James. The tears were cold on Henrietta Maria's cheeks, and she put up her hand to wipe them away. She would try to love him, she would indeed, and she would remind him that he must preserve himself at all costs. For England's sake, for their sake!

James's face, so handsome and appealing, rose up before her mental vision. He was so much handsomer than Charles, yet, strangely, not nearly so beloved. Hastily she forced herself to go over the events that had happened since her departure for Holland. She herself had raised sufficient money to send her husband supplies of arms and ammunition, but it had not been enough. Oh, just at first the supplies she had sent might have been of some small help, for with the beginning of the civil war the King had made triumphant progress. He had won many battles, including Edgehill, but now, with the rise of Oliver Cromwell in the military field, things appeared to be going badly for him. Cromwell, she could no longer doubt, was not merely a narrow-minded bigot, he was a successful, strong, and ruthless military commander, a man greatly to be feared. But nevertheless, it had seemed, in those early days, that nothing could stop the King. He had all but succeeded in reaching London, where he had hoped to force the surrender of Parliament and bring an end to the war. Perhaps he might have accomplished his aim, but Charles was not ruthless. He had thought of his army, so much smaller than the army of the rebels, and he had decided that he could not expose his men to such grave risks. And so, regretfully, he had desisted. He had taken Banbury, after a fierce fight. At Brentford, he had had another victory. Finally, he had marched into Oxford, where the still loyal people had greeted him with much acclamation. To the best of her knowledge, the King was at Oxford now. It was there that he had set up his civil government and his military headquarters. God grant that she be with him soon!

Henrietta Maria thought of the many negotiations for peace, both from the King and from Parliament. But Parliament's terms, designed to humble the King and to retain their own power, would have made of Charles merely a puppet to dance to their tune, and they were not and would never be acceptable. It was a black time for England and for the King, and steadily becoming blacker. Parliament went from strength to strength, while the King, in many cases, was forced to fall back. The power of the hated Oliver Cromwell increased with each passing day. There were other powerful names in Parliament's forces, Fairfax, Hampden, Essex, to name a few, but somehow it was of Cromwell that one always thought first. His menacing shadow, his iron determination, seemed to hover over the country like a clenched mailed fist. Cromwell, who had trained his famed Ironsides himself, turning them into an invincible, unbreaking fighting force, seemed determined to bring down the monarchy. He seemed to have a personal and deadly hatred for the King. Even in Holland, word of his grim threat had been brought to her—

"We will cut off his head while it yet wears the crown!"

"O God, save my husband! Save England!" Shivering with

fear, Henrietta Maria thrust the covers aside. Heedless of the cold, she knelt beside the bed and entreated God to watch over her beloved husband.

Admiral Batten was furious. His ship, *Strong Arm of God*, and four of the other ships in his fleet were anchored now in Bridlington Quay, facing the narrow fishermen's cottages that lined the quay its full length.

Dirty hovels, the admiral thought contemptuously. But one of them, he felt certain, sheltered that Frenchwoman who called herself the Queen of England.

"Queen!" he muttered to himself. "That bitch is responsible for all our troubles. Had it not been for her ill advice, and for a King weak enough to allow himself to be dominated by a woman, England would now be at peace. It was her, her constant goading, her damned determination to bind us once more to Catholicism that has brought us to this pass!" His hands clenched at his sides. "To think that I almost had her, would have had her for sure had it not been for my cursed, slovenly crew!" He glared in the direction of the cottages. "I know you're there. You'll not escape Batten twice, you Catholic strumpet!"

Batten, in common with most people, was convinced that the Queen had been the prime mover in the war that now ravaged the country. Forgotten were the King's friendly overtures to Parliament, forgotten the obstinancy with which they had met even his most reasonable request. A culprit was needed to appease their consciences, and Henrietta Maria, the foreigner, stood accused. The King was weak with love for her, the people cried. She wheedled him, bewitched him, and it would not have been long before they were once more fleeing the terror of Catholicism, with its witch huntings, its inquisition, its burning of heretics. Aye, if Henrietta Maria had her way, she would rekindle the fires at Smithfield!

The crew looked at each other uneasily, and in each heart fear stirred. The admiral's red brows were drawn together in a fierce frown, and he had not once moved his eyes from the row of cottages. They knew that look from past experience, and it boded no good. What was he thinking about? What was he planning? Was the Queen resting in one of those cottages? He'd set his heart on capturing her. When he failed, largely because their hearts were not in the effort they had been asked to put forth, there was not a crewman aboard that had not heaved a sigh of relief. Take the Queen prisoner! They trembled at the thought. Holy Christ, should the King win through to victory, they'd all have their necks stretched! Batten's lips were moving again. He was planning some deviltry, the mad red-headed bastard!

Batten's light-green eyes narrowed as a thought came to him. The Queen was in one of those cottages, he did not know which one, but did it really matter? If one had taken her in, then they were obviously all in it together, all traitors. It was therefore his duty to destroy that nest of traitors. If by so doing the Queen fell into his hands, and he cared not if she be alive or dead, his glory would be the greater. In years to come they would talk of him as the man who destroyed the evil eating at England's heart. Also, the government were not ungrateful for services rendered. They would see that he was well rewarded. His throat was tight and dry with excitement as a plan began to form. Murder? Slaughter? Nay, they could not call it that. They would say only that it had been a necessary and courageous action.

"Stonerton," Batten swung round and faced his second-in-command. "The Queen is in one of those cottages. I want her!"

Stonerton gaped at him. "Sir? Which cottage, sir?"

"I don't know which one, dolt! Pass the word along to the other ships. All cannon are to be trained on those cottages. When I give the word they are to fire simultaneously, and keep on firing until I give the order to cease."

The hairs on the back of Stonerton's neck prickled. "Fire on the cottages, sir? But that would be wholesale murder!"

"Are you presuming to question my orders?" Batten shouted.

"If you are, Stonerton, you'll find yourself clapped in irons!"

"But, sir, would it not be better to send a party to search the cottages?"

Batten stared at him for a long moment, then he turned his head and shouted, "Bramwell, Spencer, forward. Take this man below and clap him in irons!"

He waited until the two men had led an unprotesting Stonerton away, then he raised his voice again. "Eyerton, come forward."

When the man stood before him, he repeated his order. Eyerton was shocked into speechlessness, but, less courageous than Stonerton, he hurried to carry out his mission. Batten smiled grimly as he saw the shaking of the running man's head. Cowards, all of them! But he was not afraid to act.

Batten paced up and down impatiently, barely able to wait until the cannon were trained upon the cottages. By God, he'd rake them with shot from end to end! He'd smoke out that French bitch! He cared not how many died, so long as she fell into his hands.

"Cannon trained on target," came the shout.

"God save the Queen!" Batten muttered mockingly. The captain of each ship stood stiffly at attention, their faces turned toward him as they awaited his signal. He stepped forward, making sure they had a clear view of him. Satisfied, he raised his arm, then dropped it abruptly. "Fire! he shouted. "Fire!"

Henrietta Maria toppled over on her side as the cottage shook beneath a giant blast. Tracers of fire streaked the dark sky, lighting the room with a weird glow. The floor trembled beneath her, and she could hear screaming all about her.

"God preserve us!" Lady Morton was standing over her, trying to drag her to her feet. "Madam, are you hurt?"

"No!" Henrietta Maria rose quickly. "What is it? What is happening?"

"Madam, the ships!" A scream from the window. "The ships are firing on the cottages!"

Henrietta Maria stumbled to the window. People were pouring

out of the cottages, children were crying, women were screaming frantically, and all the time the terrible bombardment went on. The cannon spat forth death and destruction. One man fell, yelling hoarsely and clutching at his stomach. A running, shrieking woman, blind with terror, fell over his prone figure. Others, following, fell on top of her, making a writhing, screaming mass.

"My God! My God!" Henrietta Maria pressed her hand to her mouth. She must not scream. If she showed terror, her ladies would become more demoralized than ever.

"Madam!" In her agitation, Lady Morton took the Queen by the shoulders and shook her. "Do you realize what has happened? 'Tis the pursuit ship. That man is here, he is outside, he is determined to capture you!"

Henrietta Maria's brain swum in terror and confusion. She felt a chill that was not caused by the raw night air. The pursuit ship, *Strong Arm of God*, it had followed them here. It was unbelievable, like something out of a nightmare. Because of her, they were firing on the cottages, killing innocent people! She drew a deep shuddering breath. It must not be. She could not allow it! With one of the few unselfish impulses of her life, she said as firmly as she was able, "I will go out to them, Margaret. They want me, no one else. When I appear, they will stop this murder!"

Lady Morton lurched as another salvo hit the cottage. "No, Madam, you must not!"

"I must. I will!"

"You ain't going nowhere, dearie," a voice said from the doorway. "Nowhere near them ships, that is."

Henrietta Maria swung round. Across a floor that sloped oddly, Mistress Bunkerton stood in the doorway. Beneath a white cap, her hair was dishevelled, there were smears of dirt and blood on her face, and her night gown was torn down the front, exposing part of her ample breasts. Behind her stood her husband, looking meager beside her. Mistress Bunkerton advanced into the room. "One o' you blow out that candle," she snapped.

Henrietta Maria felt the woman's hands fumbling at her shoulders. "Here's your cloak, dearie. Nice and dry it is now. Me an' my man's going to take you out the back way. You an' your ladies can run down the slope. We'll point out the way. You won't be seen by no one on them ships."

"You would do all this for me, and you don't even know why those ships are firing?"

"Nay, I don't know. But I can bloody well guess. 'Sides, you're the Queen. I sees my duty, an' I does it. Ain't no more to be said."

"But the people? They're killing them! How can I go?"

"They'll stop that firing soon," Mistress Bunkerton soothed her. "An' when the folks get over their screaming an' carrying on, they'll likely remember that they got cellars same like us. Now you come along o' me."

"You are very kind."

Mistress Bunkerton ignored this. "There's a hill at the bottom of the slope. You shelter behind that an' you'll be perfectly safe. When them bastards have gone, I'll come an' fetch you. Then we'll see about getting a message through to somebody. Tommy Billington, he's got himself a good horse, an' I know he'd go for you."

She began to lead the Queen to the door. "Come on, ladies, follow close." Still talking, she led the way down the flight of steep stairs. Turning left, she opened another door which led to the outdoors. "Can't give you nothing to light your way, 'twouldn't be safe, but the slope's smooth, an' you can't miss the hill. I'd take you down the cellar with us, but that wouldn't be no good. When them swine stop firing, they'll be bound to search each place." She turned to her hovering husband. "You got them blankets what I asked for, Will?"

"Yes, dear."

"Aye, I see you have. Well, don't stand there gaping at me with your mouth open like a fish. Hand 'em out. Can't have the ladies taking a chill, can we?"

"No, dear."

398

Mistress Bunkerton said lightly, "Man o' few words is my Will. But he's a good man all the same. You wouldn't think it to look at him, but he's devoted to Your Majesties."

Henrietta Maria swallowed a lump in her throat. "I shall never forget your kindness," she said emotionally. "God will reward you. And you may be sure that the King will hear of this."

"Sakes!" Mistress Bunkerton said roughly, trying to hide her own emotion. "Don't you start crying now, dearie, or you'll have me doing it. Like I said, I'm only doing my duty. You don't want to go bothering the King with all o' that stuff. Got enough on his mind, he has."

"All the same, I shall tell him."

Mistress Bunkerton gave an uncertain laugh. "What'll he do, I wonder, make me Lady Bunkerton. Like that, I would." She laughed again, to show that she was joking, then she gave the Queen a gentle push. "Be off with you, and God bless Your Majesty."

Echoing her dutifully but none the less sincerely, came Will Bunkerton's quiet voice. "God bless Your Majesty." In a sudden spurt of independence, he added, "And may God bless the King, and make him victorious!"

They found their way down the slope. Lady Sarah Middleton, missing her footing, rolled helplessly the rest of the way. Brought up short by the hill, she was found to be frightened but unhurt.

The Queen was never to forget those hours. The booming of the cannon, seeming to their inflamed imaginations to become louder, the fluttering wings of disturbed birds, the scuttling sounds of small night creatures, the furious barking of dogs, the belching smoke that, drifting down the slope, caused them to cough chokingly; the damp raw cold seeping through blankets and the shuddering chill of icy ground beneath bare feet, but overriding it all, the overwhelming fear. Some of the ladies were crying, others complaining bitterly of the cold.

Henrietta Maria wished to show them an example. She was the Queen, she reminded herself, she must not show fear. She must be strong and, by her fortitude, shame them out of their weakness. She knew of only one way to do this. "You will all kneel with me," she commanded. "We will ask God for protection, and for the strength to bear the long hours ahead of us."

The young Countess of Baselstone gave a moan of protest. "But, Madam, the ground is wet, and I am already chilled to the bone."

"Your devotions to God will warm you," Henrietta Maria answered sternly. "Come, is there one here who would think of their comfort before their duty to God?"

Nobody answered. Knowing that it was useless to argue, they knelt on the wet ground. Heads bowed, automatically making their responses, they thought of warm beds, of hot food, and great leaping fires.

Even Henrietta Maria, though she struggled against it, succumbed to the same weakness. Why could she not be a true and unflinching daughter of God? But she would make up for it. If God led her back to the King's side, she would devote many hours a day to her prayers.

Dawn found most of them sleeping. But the Queen, her back resting against the hill, was wide awake. With her eyes on the orange and pink-streaked sky, her lips continued to move.

Mistress Bunkerton, coming to find them, saw the Queen's moving lips. Praying, the poor dear soul, she thought. Aloud, she said, "Come on back to the house now, dearie. You shall all have a nice hot breakfast in front of a big fire. All's well now."

Henrietta Maria started. The cannon had stopped their booming, but she had not been aware of it. "They have gone?" she said faintly.

"Some time ago. I waited to make sure they wasn't coming back."

"Are many hurt?"

"A few. Not as many as you'd think though. Except for one man, it ain't too serious. Like I said, most o' 'em had the sense to hide in the cellars. You come along o' me now. That Tommy Billington, he's all ready to ride. Take any message, an' go anywhere Your Majesty bids him, he will."

"You are so good! God is so good!" Henrietta Maria took a step forward. Sighing, she crumpled at the woman's feet.

Mistress Bunkerton knelt beside her. " 'Tain't nothing," she assured the awakened ladies. " 'Tis only an ordinary swoon. The strain has been too much for her."

Chapter
Twenty-Two

My lord Foxe, his dark brows drawn together in a frown, stood in the doorway surveying the scene of conjugal peace on the lawn. The Queen, clad in a pale-pink satin gown, sat on a chair. Her skirts, embroidered with blue and green birds, were spread about her like the petals of some vast exotic flower. Sunlight glinted on her piled black hair threaded with pink ribands with the whole surmounted by a small lifelike bird with widespread wings. She looked young and gay and carefree. Seated nearby in another chair, his legs carelessly thrust forward, was the King. His long hair was rumpled, for he had been romping with three-year-old Henry. There were grass stains on his white satin breeches, and the marks of Henry's fingers on the white gold-embroidered satin of his jacket. Henry, at this moment, was playing happily with the scarlet ribands that decorated the knees of the King's breeches. Seated at the Queen's feet, his head resting against her knees, was the Queen's favorite son, James. The rings on Henrietta Maria's fingers flashed in the sun as she gently caressed the boy's hair. The King, looking almost as carefree as the Queen, bent to address a laughing remark to Henry. The boy, laughing back, reached up a fat dimpled hand to clutch at a lock of his father's hair.

"A beautiful picture, is it not?" a voice said from behind Brett.

Brett turned swiftly. Marcus Milford, with the Prince and Meredith, had come up behind him and were standing close. Brett frowned at Marcus. "I vow you are too harsh, my young friend." He glanced swiftly at the Prince, wondering what his reaction might be to the sarcasm implicit in Marcus's remark. The Prince's dark eyes were brooding. He seemed to be concentrating on a problem of his own.

"The King has much on his mind," Meredith reproved Marcus. "It is only natural that he would wish to enjoy himself now and again." She craned her head forward. "Look, Brett, there is Tony and George."

Brett nodded as he watched his son and the young Duke of Buckingham join the party on the lawn. He was aware of the feelings that had prompted Marcus's remark. Like himself, the boy's mature mind had seen the folly of the King idling in peaceful bliss with the Queen. It seemed wrong, it was wrong, while men schemed to remove him from the throne. The Queen, who had been reunited with the King for some time now, seemed to have completely forgotten her terrifying experience at the hands of Admiral Batten. Her logic seemed to be that, having escaped, she could forget indefinitely the troubles that wrenched England apart. Indeed, the only reminder of that grim time and of the civil war itself, was in her inexhaustible prayers. No matter what she might be doing, the Queen would suddenly rise to her feet and call her ladies to her. Then, having despatched a messenger to bring the rest of the Court from their duties, she would sink to her knees and conduct one of her long and wearying prayer sessions. These sessions were resented by the many who were not Catholic. But because the King was indulgent to her, the ladies and gentlemen, with secret rebellion in their hearts, knelt with her. When she was not praying or making her confession to the priest, Henrietta Maria was laughing and gay. She light-heartedly presided over them all, and at this small Court in Oxford, she seemed to have created Utopia for herself and the King. The King was more adoring in his attitude than ever he had been before. Because he admitted her into his confidence, discussing many secret matters with her and asking her advice, which she freely gave, Henrietta Maria was content. Never before had she been consulted on matters of state, and this new sense of power went to her head like a draught of strong wine. The men of Charles's war council were alarmed. They were afraid that the King might listen and act upon Henrietta Maria's advice, which, being guided largely by her emotions and the passions that swayed her from moment to moment, was invariably foolish, not to say foolhardy. Brett, however, was convinced that the King offered her this tender attention solely because he loved her, but he would never dream of taking her advice seriously.

A finger poked Brett in the ribs. "If you please, my lord," said Meredith's indignant voice, "I have asked you three times if I might be allowed to pass. If you will use your eyes, you will see that the Queen is beckoning me to join her."

"So she is." Brett stood aside, giving her a slap on the rump as she passed. "Though what Her Majesty wants with your company is a mystery to me, shrew."

Her eyes met his, something slumberous and inviting in their depths. "I can be very good company, my lord, as I will show you later."

His dark brows rose mockingly. "I vow, m'lady, that I can scarcely wait for the proof."

"You will be sorry for that remark." Laughing, she went to join the little group on the lawn.

Brett smiled after her. She was as beautiful as ever, perhaps more so with the added dignity of maturity, even though that dignity was of appearance, if not attitude. Her figure was still slender and gracefully curved, her hair very bright against the white lace of her gown. She was a curious mixture, his Meredith.

At one moment she would be loving and tender, and, though he knew it to be only an act staged for his benefit, the prelude to some special favor she desired, even humble and submissive, the perfect wife. The next moment she would be seething with rebellion. She would be quarrelsome and headstrong, opinionated, and so cursed stubborn that he was ofttimes tempted to knock her head hard against the nearest wall. Life with Meredith was a series of squalls, but in between the squalls there would be sunny interludes of sublime happiness and contentment. And then there were the other times, when she would be chasing after some crack-brained scheme, which was sternly suppressed, usually, by himself. Not unnaturally, this would lead to further squalls. But if Meredith made life uncertain, it was certainly never dull, and in that uncertainty one thing remained constant, her love for him. Of Meredith's love he could always be sure, as she could be sure of his.

Brett became aware that Marcus was watching him. For once the boy appeared to be off-guard, and there was a hungry, almost a wistful look in his eyes. "What is it, Marcus?" Brett asked.

"I was thinking of how happy you and my lady Foxe seem to be," Marcus said quietly. "It is a rare thing, is it not, my lord?"

"Nay, lad," Brett answered gently, "it is not so very rare. Many married couples are extremely happy."

Marcus shook his head, and there was a look in his eyes that pained Brett. "I believe it to be rare," he said slowly.

"But you are not necessarily right, are you?"

Marcus looked at him uncertainly. "You have achieved that rare thing, therefore it is easy for you to say. But for myself, I think I would find it very hard to give my love and my—my—"

"Your trust, Marcus? Is that what you would say?"

"Aye, my lord. I do not think I could ever bring myself to trust a woman."

"When you fall in love, you will find it surprisingly easy."

"But—but love can be evil sometimes. It can weaken and make one less than a man."

Brett knew that he was thinking of his father and of his mother, the woman whom he so hated. "Do not let one bad example blind you to the good in others, lad," he answered him.

"I spoke of no example, my lord."

" 'Twas but an observation," Brett said, surrendering to that stiff pride.

The Prince of Wales, who had been leaning against the wall, his hands thrust into his deep lace-trimmed pockets, quite aloof from the conversation, spoke abruptly, "Didst know that my mother is with child, my lord Foxe?"

Brett, who had not known, felt both surprise and consternation. "I did not, Charles," he answered. "I know not whether to be pleased or sorrowful. These are perilous times, and one cannot help but feel concern for the Queen. A small child may add to her burden."

Charles looked at him with his somber eyes. "I think as you do, my lord. My father has been very happy in this reunion with my mother, but now I sense a difference in him. It is as though he knows that they must soon part again." The Prince leaned forward and looked through the door at the King. "The tide of this war turns against us, my lord, bringing our previous victories to naught. Gloucester is lost to us, and once again the Scottish rebels are showing their hand."

Brett looked at him with pity. It was a heavy burden for such a young lad to bear, and yet he knew that that young and astute brain was fully capable of grasping the situation. When he spoke again, it was with respect for that intelligence. "The King still holds all the north of England, though, I admit, 'tis with a tenuous grasp at best. As for this business with the Scots, I must confess that it has me worried."

"You have heard the rumor that Sir Harry Vane is about to negotiate an alliance with the Scots against the King?"

"I have heard. Unfortunately I believe it to be more than a rumor. I believe that it will inevitably come to pass."

All the youth seemed to drain from the Prince's face. He looked haunted. "If such an alliance should be, my lord, then we are lost."

Seeing the expression on the Prince's face, Marcus threw Brett an indignant look. "Nay, Charles," Marcus said in that gentle tone he used to no one else. "Nothing can be said to be lost until the last battle has been fought."

"Well said, Marcus," Brett spoke with a heartiness he was far from feeling. "Shall we join the King?"

There were tears in the Prince's eyes, and Marcus moved quickly to shield him from my lord Foxe's penetrating eyes. "Nay, my lord," Charles said in a muffled voice, "there are things I must do. I will join my father later." He turned and walked away. Reaching the end of the corridor, he said without looking back, "Plague take you, Marcus, must you dawdle. Hast forgotten that you planned to show me something?"

Marcus looked blank for a moment, then he said quickly, "Aye, Charles, I remember."

"Then get a move on. I'll not wait all day."

"You'll wait until I am ready," Marcus said, moving after him.

"Od's fish, but you are a plaguy, insolent rogue. I know not why I put up with you."

"Nor I with you," Brett heard Marcus answer.

Brett smiled to himself. He had heard the tears in the Prince's voice. The little by-play had not deceived him. Instinctively, in times of trouble, the Prince relied on Marcus's rather stringent company to bring him needed comfort. Marcus did not speak softly to his Prince, unless softness was needed, for it was not his way. He rallied, commanded, hectored, and jeered until he provoked such a spark of anger in Charles that the dangerously emotional moment would pass. But Charles, even angry, knew of the deep sympathy that Marcus kept so well hidden. He knew the real impulse behind his abrasive words. All through his life, Brett knew, Charles would turn to Marcus. Others might fail him, but Marcus never! Those two, so unalike in many ways, understood each other very well. The friendship between them, begun in hostility on Marcus's part, would last a lifetime.

Dismissing thoughts of the two boys, Brett's brows drew

together in a frown as he considered the dismal place that England had become. The tide was slowly and inexorably turning against the King. And now, where once the people had admired his resistance against the tyranny of Parliament, where they had once cheered on his victories, they now did so no longer. The people wanted peace. It was clever propaganda that had convinced them that it was the King's arrogance, his selfish obstinancy that gave no thought to the needs of his people, that caused him to decline all the reasonable terms that Parliament offered. It was the King who kept the war raging. Parliament, and that clever and so mercilessly vindictive man, Oliver Cromwell, had become the heroes, the King the villain and the enemy of England! All theaters, all games, or other places of amusement were either banned or closed throughout the length and breadth of the kingdom. The maypoles, that harmless amusement of the people, were pulled down. The ceremony and the festivities of Christmas were rigidly suppressed. Instead, Christmas was proclaimed as a day of fast. For these things, too, the people blamed the King. It was his fault, they said, the fault of him and his Catholic wife that their England had become such a dark and dreary place. Whoever heard of an England without maypoles to celebrate the spring festival, without games, without fun and laughter and feasting? Hooray for Cromwell! Hooray for his soldiers, the brave and invincible Ironsides! that was the people's parrot cry these days. God be with the good man, Oliver Cromwell, the brave, the bold, the fearless! Cromwell, who sought to rid them of a tyrant King whose aim was to suppress them, to drag them down to the depths of degradation, that they might, like mindless puppets, obey his terrible will. Give them Cromwell, who would turn England back to a place of happiness and contentment, a place of green and drowsing peace.

There were many, of course, who did not believe this. But those who dared to declare for the King, who were bold enough to state that he was not to blame for the present misery, were dealt with harshly. Parliament, and the people's popular representative, the ubiquitous Oliver Cromwell, rode the crest of the wave now. And in that same wave the King and his cause were slowly drowning.

"The tyrant King who would force them to obey his terrible will," Brett muttered. Gentle Charles Stuart! Were it not so tragic, it would be laughable. God curse Parliament! And may He consign Oliver Cromwell to the fires of hell!

Brett looked across at the King. He was leaning back in his chair. He was not laughing now. Sunlight, filtering through the trees, dappled his face, and where it was shadowed, it seemed to hold deep hollows. He looked gaunt and terribly exhausted. Brett cursed himself. The King tasted despair, it was written there in his face, and he had begrudged him this small and peaceful interlude. Henrietta Maria was a vain and infuriating woman, but she did love the King, and that love which she showed more and more these days, must be of great comfort to him. Brett saw the Princess Elizabeth approaching the King. She stopped beside him, giving her quick, rather anxious smile, and placed a caressing hand on his shoulder. Charles's face lit up, and he drew the child onto his lap. Grave eight-year-old Elizabeth, with her pale, pointed, and pretty face, her mop of dark-brown curls, and her big, thickly lashed hazel eyes, was another comfort to the King. Next to Charles, the gentle girl was his greatest solace.

Henry gave a jealous cry. Angrily, he tugged at Elizabeth's green skirts, trying to drag her from the King's lap.

The King laughed. "You must not be jealous, Henry, 'tis a sin." Henry's face lengthened, and the King reached out an indulgent hand and helped the boy to clamber up. "You may sit on Elizabeth's lap, if she gives you permission to do so." Elizabeth nodded. "Then that's all right," the King went on. "Now we may all be comfortable together."

"Papa!" Elizabeth suddenly exclaimed in her clear sweet voice. "You must never go away and leave us! Promise me that you will not!"

Henry glanced from his father's to his sister's face, and his eyes filled with tears. Charles did not notice, he was looking intently at Elizabeth. "Why, my darling," he said tenderly, "you are trembling. What is it? Tell Papa."

"It is a dream I have," Elizabeth said in a shaking voice. "In my dream you go away from us, and we never see you more. Oh, Papa, it must not be. I could not bear it!"

"Hush, hush! 'Tis only a dream. There may be times when I must leave you, but I will always return, I promise."

"But it is not only the dream. I have heard people talking. I have heard them say that you will become a prisoner of Parliament. That they—that they w—will cut off your head." With a strangled cry, Elizabeth hid her face against his shoulder. "Oh, Papa, I love you so very much!"

Brett saw the drawn look about the King's mouth, the fear in the Queen's eyes. "Elizabeth!" Henrietta Maria's voice rose shrilly. "How dare you repeat such wicked nonsense!" Her distracted gaze flickered to Henry, who, thoroughly frightened now, was crying in earnest, and clinging with both hands to his father. "Stop it!" she shouted. "The sound of your crying pierces my head like a knife! Get down at once, both of you. You will tire your father."

"You must not let such gossip upset you, dear heart," Charles said, managing a smile. "As for the children, they are not tiring me."

But Henrietta Maria was thoroughly frightened by Elizabeth's words, and she could not hide that fear. She got to her feet so abruptly that her knee bumped sharply against the still reclining James's head. "That little sniveling fool!" She glared at Elizabeth with an expression in her eyes that was almost hatred. "We must all go inside now, we must pray for the safety of your beloved father!" she babbled feverishly. "Come, come, children, all of you. And you, my lady Foxe, attend me. We must pray, 'tis the only way!"

Charles looked at the Queen's twitching hands, at her white face, the muscle leaping beside her mouth. She will be on her knees for the rest of the day, he thought with resignation. "Henrietta Maria, you must not allow yourself to become so upset. All is well, my love, all is well. Pray if you wish, but do not force the children to remain too long on their knees."

She did not seem to hear him. "They must pray," she muttered. "All must pray with me!" With a whirl of her pink skirts, the Queen turned and hurried away. The King, staring after her, saw that her lips were already moving, her hand clutching the rosary dangling from her belt.

Reluctantly the King released the children. "Go then, my darlings." His warm smile embracing them each in turn drove some of the fear from their faces. "Pray with your mother, as she wishes. But you must remember this, you are not of her faith. When you make your devotions to God, I would have you utter your own prayers." He stroked Elizabeth's hair. "Your mother is very upset. Mayhap you can console her."

The children, headed by James, the rear brought up by Tony Foxefield and an unusually sober-faced Duke of Buckingham, went slowly after the Queen, but not without many backward glances at the King.

"You are stupid, Lizzie," came James's loudly belligerent voice. "Do you think I would let anything happen to our father?" His walk took on a slight swagger. "I would kill anyone who dared lay hands upon him!"

Elizabeth bent her head meekly. "I was silly, James. I'm sorry. Charles will keep him safe. And then there is Marcus, too. They would not allow harm to come to our father. I should have remembered that."

"Charles! Marcus!" James shouted, his male pride insulted. "What of me?"

"And me!" Tony and George cried in unison. "After all," Tony added, "we are older."

Not to be left out, Henry shrieked, "An' me! Me!"

Elizabeth stopped walking and turned her anxious smile upon them all. "You too, dear James. All of you."

The King was moved by their determination to aid him, but he raised his voice commandingly. "That will be quite enough. Your mother is waiting for you. Hurry, please!"

The King waited until the children had disappeared around the corner of the tree-shaded walk, then he turned his eyes to the open door of the building opposite him. "My lord Foxe," he called. "I saw you a short while ago. I know you are still there."

Smiling, Brett stepped out into the open. "As usual, Charles, you are perfectly right."

"Naturally," the King answered. "I am fortunate in knowing, my friend, that wherever I am, you will not be far behind."

Brett thought to himself that the friendship between Charles and himself was similar in many ways to that between the Prince and Marcus. Seating himself in a chair beside the King, he crossed his legs casually. But there was nothing casual in the expression in his eyes as he said, "So here I am, Charles. Do you wish to talk?"

The King nodded. "I do, Brett. Talking can sometimes help to clarify things in one's mind."

Brett looked at him closely. The lines beside Charles's mouth seemed deeper than before, he thought with a surge of compassion. He looked infinitely weary and much older than his years. "The war, Charles?" Brett questioned gently.

"What else." Charles's shoulders lifted in a faint shrug. "But first I would ask you how fares my lord Butler?"

"He will be up and about in a day or two, I am told. He is very anxious that I should assure you of his devotion and of his desire to serve Your Majesty in all things."

Charles smiled. "He does not need to tell me that. Say to him, if you should see him first, that I will visit him as soon as may be."

"He will like that. It will cheer him immensely. In succumbing to this illness, he feels that he has let you down."

"Nonsense!" Charles leaned forward in his chair. "Brett, what is it that ails our friend? I had thought it was his heart, but now it does not seem to me to be any specific thing."

Brett smiled wryly. "His heart is weak, of course, but I believe he is quite simply wearing out. He is slowly dying from the pain of loving a worthless and conscienceless woman. You must have realized, Charles, that where his lady is concerned, my lord Butler is deplorably weak. Had I been he, I would have thrown the slut out long ago."

"Even if you loved her?"

Brett's jaw set firmly. "Even so, Charles."

Charles flushed as he thought of his own weakness where his wife was concerned. He was as much in bondage to a woman as was my lord Butler. Brett was different. No matter how much he might love, he would never allow himself to be helplessly bound by that love.

Brett said, still watching him closely, "But it was not of my lord Butler you wished to speak, was it?"

Charles clasped his hands loosely over his knees. "You are right. The war goes badly, Brett."

Brett nodded. "But we will never give up. We have had some victories, a few setbacks. But what of that when we know our cause is right?"

"Cromwell believes as fully in his cause," Charles said, looking at him with shadowed eyes.

"Cromwell!" Brett said impatiently. "I am constantly hearing the man's name. Is he then our only enemy?"

"Sometimes it seems that way. If I be King of this country, then Cromwell is king and prime mover in this war."

"Nay. He is nothing!"

"But you are wrong, Brett," Charles said seriously. "I could never like the man, but in his own field he is great. Forget not the times we have faced him at Stamford, at Grantham, Gainsborough, Chalgrove Field, and many other places. They were but small skirmishes, but sufficient to show us that he is the Ironside that Rupert named him. Sufficient to prove that he is unbendable, unbreakable. He is a fanatic, a narrow-minded and joyless bigot, and my sworn enemy, but I cannot deny his great courage."

Brett, who secretly agreed with him, could not however bring himself to say so. His eyes on Charles, he waited for him to go on.

"A treaty has not yet been sighed, Brett," Charles said with an obvious effort. "But it will be. There is to be an alliance between Parliament and the Scots against myself. Sir Harry Vane is already on his way to Edinburgh to negotiate with the Scots."

"What!" Brett looked at him in utter dismay. "I have heard rumors, and I feared the outcome, but I did not believe it had gone this far. When did you hear of the departure of Vane?"

"This morning."

"And is the information reliable."

"Utterly. Sedgemoore, who works closely with Vane, but who spies for me, is fully conversant with the terms of the treaty. The treaty is to be known as the Solemn League and Covenant. It calls for the destruction of the Church of England, and for Presbyterianism to reign in its stead throughout my three kingdoms. Money will be granted by Parliament to the Scots if they, in turn, will send an army into England to crush the Royalists before the opening of the next campaign."

Dumbfounded, Brett stared at him. "How can you be so calm, so unmoved? Know you not that this alliance could spell failure to your royal cause?"

"I will never give up, if that is what you mean," Charles said with a flash of his old spirit. "But in a day at most that treaty will be signed."

"You trust Sedgemoore? You believe him?"

"With all my heart. He despises the Parliamentarians, but he works with them for my sake. Each day he risks his life in my cause, and he has given me much valuable information."

Brett saw once again the fair, taut-skinned face, the steady blue eyes of Brian Sedgemoore, the Earl of Berkleyholt, and he recalled his disappointment and disgust when the young earl had declared for Parliament, and had spoken out against the King in heated terms. He had liked the man, admired his clear, fair

414

judgment, and he had been unable to reconcile that attitude, so unlike him, with the man he had thought he knew. Despite his concern, a grin spread across Brett's face. "So that is my lord Berkleyholt's game, is it? By God, I should have known!" He looked indignantly at Charles. "I had thought you trusted me," he exclaimed. "Why did you not tell me of this before?"

"You became so very stiff and correct whenever his name was mentioned, that is why."

"You should have made me listen. By God's precious breath, what a fool that young rogue must think me!"

"Nay, he believes you act a part, even as he does."

"Well, that is something to be thankful for." Brett sobered. "Charles, this means that we must map out a new plan of campaign. If we are to gain any advantages, we must proceed with great secrecy and caution. What are your commands for me?"

The King spread out his hands. He appeared to be examining each nail with great care. "You would do anything for me, would you not, Brett?" He looked up quickly. "When you told me that, you spoke truth?"

Brett looked at him sharply. "You know it well, you have always known it. What need have you to question me?"

"No need, my lord Foxe. 'Twas but my way of easing into what I must now request of you."

"Request of me?" Brett's uneasiness deepened. "You know very well that you may request anything of me, Sire. Anything within reason, that is."

"Brett, the Queen is with child. She is very precious to me, it would not be too much to say that she is more precious than my crown. But I realize she is in danger here. I have been putting off the moment when I must send her from me to a place of greater safety, but I can put it off no longer." He paused, looking at Brett as though expecting him to understand his meaning.

A monstrous suspicion had entered Brett's mind, but he forced himself to speak quietly. "Go on, Charles."

"My lord, to whom but my most trusted friend, and his equally trusted wife, would I commend the care of the most precious object in my life?"

Brett drew in his breath sharply. Surely he must have misunderstood him? "Charles!" It was an exclamation of outrage. "You cannot mean me?"

"I do mean you, Brett. You and my lady Foxe must accompany the Queen on her journey to Exeter. You must see that she is settled comfortably at Bedford House, and prepare thereafter to await with her the term of confinement." He looked at Brett pleadingly. "I trust you, only you. I know you will do this for me. The Queen's whereabouts will inevitably become known. She will need your strength to support her, your daring and resourcefulness."

There was anger in Brett's eyes. "I? I stay at Bedford House coddling a woman, while you and others risk their lives! Nay, not even you may ask it of me. I'll not do it, Charles. Meredith may go, but not I! Curse it! A man would be useless to the Queen at such a time."

"Nay, Brett. Would I ask for such sacrifice if I did not believe the Queen to be in grave danger? The Parliamentarians would give much to lay hands on her. Have they not already tried to impeach her on a charge of high treason? I have said that I trust only you to protect her, and that is true. Go with her, Brett. Give me that much peace of mind, I beg of you!"

A flush mounted Brett's face. The King could command him, but he chose instead to plead. Brett's brows drew together in an angry line. How could he remain impervious to this tortured man, his King and friend? How could he deny him the peace of mind so essential to him in the fighting of the war? "Very well, Charles," he said stiffly, "if you so command."

"I have not commanded. I have requested."

Brett tried to hold onto his anger, but could not. The prospect of being with the Queen for so long appalled him, but for Charles's sake he must bear it. Remembering the King's words,

416

he said, "I know. 'Twas but my way of easing into an assent to your cursed request."

At Abingdon, on a day that was bright with sunshine, the King took his leave of the Queen. He kissed her again and again. "God watch over you, dear heart," he said tenderly. "Go with my lord and lady Foxe now. They will protect you in my absence."

Henrietta Maria was hysterical. She could not control the fear in her heart, or her sense of dark forboding. "Charles! I will not go. Oh, my lord King, allow me to return with you to Oxford!"

Charles shook his head. He looked at her for a long moment, as though seeking to impress her forever on his memory. In his heart, too, there was fear. When would he see her again? When next they met, would he come to her as a victor, or as a dethroned king? He looked into dark eyes, swimming with tears. He saw her pale, trembling mouth, the bleached whiteness of her face, the fluttering of the green veil that bound her dark hair, and he turned quickly away to hide his emotion. "Your ladies will get too far ahead," he said in a choked voice. "You must go now, my love."

"No!" She flung herself at him, her fingers clawing at his back, forcing him to turn. "As you love me, do not send me away! If you allow me to go, then I shall know that you never loved me!"

"Oh, Christ!" Charles's voice was anguished as he caught her to him and crushed her in his arms. "I love you, do you hear me? I love you more than my life, myself! But you must go. I will not expose you to danger!" He thrust her from him so roughly that she staggered. "Never again say that I do not love you!"

"Then I will not say it!" her voice rose to a scream. "I promise that I will never do anything to displease you, if you will but let me stay. Please, Charles, please!"

Brett, looking on with grim eyes, slid down from his horse, and assisted Meredith to dismount.

Meredith approached the sobbing Queen. "Madam," she said, putting an arm about her shoulders, "do not make it harder, I beg of you."

Henrietta Maria turned a tragic face to her. "He does not love me! If he loved me, he could not send me away!"

"He loves you," Meredith soothed, conquering an inclination to slap the hysterical woman. "It is because he loves you that he can send you away. Can you understand that?"

Brett saw the tears on the King's cheeks, and he wanted to look away, fearing that the King might be embarrassed to remember that he had been witness to his anguish. Charles made no attempt to hide his grief. "Look after her, Brett," he begged in a breaking voice. "Promise me!"

"I give you my word, Sire." Brett put his hand on the King's velvet-clad shoulder and squeezed it in a rough attempt at comfort. "For the love of God, Charles," he exclaimed in a goaded voice, "don't do this! Come, pull yourself together. There is a limit," he went on, forcing a light note into his voice, "even to my endurance. And I like not to see you so completely destroyed."

Charles nodded and managed a shaky laugh. "Aye, 'tis unseemly behavior on the part of a king, I know." He turned his head and looked steadily at Brett. "With you she will be safe. That is my comfort. I must go now, for I can endure no more!"

With a final nod to Brett, he moved toward his horse. The gentlemen accompanying him stared straight ahead, apparently blind and deaf to the small drama. Without looking at the Queen, the King mounted his horse. "Ride!" he shouted.

Henrietta Maria stared with wild eyes after the galloping figures. Sun touched Charles's long, dark hair, the red velvet of his jacket, the foam of lace at his cuff as he raised a hand in farewell. "Good-bye, my love!" his voice came to Henrietta Maria faintly. "Good-bye!"

"Charles!" she screamed. "Don't go! Don't leave me!"

The riders turned a corner and were lost to sight, but it seemed to Henrietta Maria that she could still hear the echo of Charles's voice. "Good-bye, my love! Good-bye!"

Frantically, she whirled to face Meredith. "Oh, my dear God!" she shrieked. "I have lost him. I shall never see him more!"

Without quite knowing why, Meredith found herself shivering. Cold fingers seemed to touch her spine. Almost she could believe the Queen's wild statement. At a loss to account for her own sensations, she stared at the distraught woman. "Madam, you must not say such things. Of course you will see him again."

Henrietta Maria shook her head violently. "No, I know that I shall not! I—I feel it!" Covering her face with her hands, she sank down at Meredith's feet.

Brett came toward them. "Madam!" his voice was a command, forcing the Queen to look up at him. He stared into her tear-streaked face and, despite himself, he felt pity stir. But it would not do, he thought. Queen she might be, but he could not allow such scenes to go on. He would not. "I feel deeply for you, Madam," he said in a purposely hard voice. "However, the King has placed me in charge of your welfare, and that being so, I tell you now that there must be an end to this nonsense." He reached down and lifted her in his arms. "Do we understand each other?"

Henrietta Maria stared into his face with her tear-glazed eyes. "You are cruel!" she whimpered. "I am the Queen of sorrows, yet you have no pity. You are against me, everybody is against me!"

Brett carried her to her horse. None too gently, he settled her in the saddle. "I am sorry if you find me unsympathetic, Madam. I will not stand for hysteria, it is best you know that. It is bad for yourself, for the child you carry, and for those of us who are forced to listen to your wailing and screaming."

Now his words penetrated in all their enormity. Anger lit her eyes and her cheeks flamed with furious color. "How dare you, my lord! I remind you that you speak to the Queen!"

"When you behave like a Queen, Madam, I will need no reminder."

Henrietta Maria's hands clenched on the embroidered reins. "Oh!" She almost choked on her anger. "Leave me, you insolent lout!"

"As you command." With a mocking bow, Brett turned away.

Henrietta Maria sat stiffly upright in the saddle. When the order came to ride, her eyes were still smouldering, but the tears were dry on her cheeks. Refusing to be hurried, she moved forward at a dignified pace. Her mouth was sullen with anger as she thought of the obnoxious and brutal my lord Foxe.

Matching her horse's slow pace to Brett's, Meredith said in an awed voice, "How could you bring yourself to speak to the Queen so? She will probably never forgive you."

Brett shrugged. "She will, in time. If she does not, I will survive. In any case, anger against myself will consume all other emotion. It is better so."

"Ah, the wily fox speaks!" Meredith gazed at him in exaggerated admiration. "I think I love you."

His taut face relaxed into a grin. "If you know what is good for you, wench, you had best be sure."

"I shall make up my mind in my own good time, my lord."

"I have promised myself to administer a thrashing to the Queen, should she merit it. Remind me that you stand in need of the same treatment."

"The Queen?" Meredith stared at him, half believing him. "Not even you would dare!"

"Would I not?" the tone of his voice banished her doubt. "She has been placed in my charge. And you know well that I am not a patient man. If I am to be faced with endless hysteria, I would dare anything. If only for the sake of preserving my own sanity."

Meredith giggled. "I believe you really would, Brett."

Brett's jaw tightened. "My lady," he answered, "you may be certain of it."

The Queen stared straight before her. My lord Foxe had humiliated her. He was quite indifferent to her suffering, and he had treated her with disrespect. He was a churl, and she would like to see his arrogance humbled. Aye, she would even like to see his head lopped from his shoulders, if she might be allowed to handle the sword. The Queen shivered as thoughts of Charles, her beloved, tried to pierce through the angry mist that bound her. Hastily, she nursed her anger against my lord Foxe. In concentrating on that, she felt safer. Fear and anguish awaited, but she would not think of it yet. Not yet!

Chapter

Twenty-Three

My lord Foxe paled as another frantic scream sounded in his ears.
It had a sound of doom, he thought, as, exhausted by his incessant pacing, he dropped heavily into a chair and fixed his eyes on
the door of the chamber in which the Queen lay. How much
longer? When would she give birth to the child!

The struggle had gone on for hours, or so it seemed to his
inflamed imagination. It was a marvel to him how one small and
fragile woman could endure such torment. He had not been
present at the birth of his own son, but he shuddered to think of
what Meredith must have undergone. But surely the Queen's
child must be of giant size, if she had not yet managed to eject it
from her womb.

He took his kerchief from his sleeve and mopped his forehead.
What was the matter with him? he asked himself. He had faced
many dangers in his time. Sword thrust forward at the ready, he
had ridden into the very teeth of the enemy. Several times he had
been wounded in combat, but the wound, however severe, had

not prevented him from despatching a Roundhead soldier or two. He had known only a normal fear at those times, the fear any man might know when Cromwell's Ironsides made one of their historical advances. But nothing he had known could be compared with this. The Queen's agonized screams had the effect of turning him into a quivering coward. He wanted to leave this room where the sounds of her travail could be so clearly heard, but he conceived it to be his duty to stay, and he could not bring himself to do it. He thought enviously of her ladies, who, in a moment of weakness, he had dismissed. They had retired gladly, as he would like to do now. Their fearful twittering, the apprehensive glances they had kept casting at the door of the chamber had annoyed him. Now he found himself wishing they were here. They had been company of a sort. He would at least have had somebody on whom to vent his irritation when the waiting grew unendurable. Aye, and why should they escape? Why should they not suffer as well as he? He put the kerchief away. If only she would not scream. He could bear anything but that!

"Coward!" Meredith had called him, when she had come to him for a brief moment to report the progress of the birth. She had laughed at him. " 'Tis amusing the way you men will tremble before such a natural thing."

Well, he was trembling. He felt quite ill, but he could not help it. Now Meredith was back in the room, and God knows what she might be doing. He found it surprising that the Queen, relaxing the marked hostility she had shown her, had insisted that she be present, as well as the skilled midwife, who had helped with the birth of the other royal children, and Sir Theodore Mayherne, the King's own physician, the only one the King trusted to attend his wife.

The Queen's voice that had sunk to a whimpering moan, rose again to a full-throated scream. Her English quite forgotten at this time, she cried out in French, "Help me, Lord! I can fight no more!"

Brett shuddered. His lace stock seemed to be choking him. With quivering fingers, he loosened it. The June day was confoundedly hot, he thought, hotter than any he recalled. The windows were wide open, but it was still stifling. It was more than cowardice that he felt, but Meredith did not know that. Combined with his cowardice was a distress of mind. He could not rid himself of the uncomfortable feeling that it was his brutality that had forced on this tortured birth. The Queen should not be in labor yet. She had not been due to deliver for at least another week. Perspiration broke out on his forehead as he recalled yesterday's scene.

All day the Queen, in the most unreasonable frame of mind she had yet shown, had been issuing her commands in a high-pitched querulous voice. A score of times she had lost her temper, stamping her small foot imperiously, shrieking at her ladies, breaking into stormy, hysterical tears. Her delicate face, slightly puffed with pregnancy, scarlet with rage, she had slapped the face of Lady Joan Sunderland for some trifling fault. When the girl broke into tears, she herself had joined her, declaring that no queen, no ordinary woman, had ever suffered as she suffered. Sobbing out her husband's name, entreating God to send him to her in her hour of need, she had hurled ornaments against the wall, her hysteria rising to fresh heights as they broke and littered the floor with sharp fragments.

Brett had turned from these tantrums in disgust. He had walked out of Bedford House, leaving Meredith and the other ladies to deal with her. It was when he returned that the climax came. Bowing before the Queen, he had seated himself in a chair.

"I do not recall giving you permission to sit in my presence, my Lord Foxe," Henrietta Maria had cried in a rising voice.

"Your pardon, Madam." Brett rose. Bowing again, he asked, "May I have Your Majesty's permission to be seated?"

"No, you may not. And do not use that tone of voice to me."

Brett felt anger rising, but he suppressed it. "If my tone was offensive, I beg your pardon."

"You are using the same tone, my lord Foxe. I cannot bear your sarcasm, your arrogance!"

Brett said wearily, "Then it would seem that I must again ask your pardon. Shall I retire, Madam? 'Twill relieve you of the necessity of looking upon me.''

Henrietta Maria stared at him, her eyes narrowed and spiteful. ''Nay, my lord Foxe, you will not retire. You will kneel before me instead, and you will reavow your loyalty to our royal cause.''

''I?'' He looked at her in complete astonishment. ''Not even the King would ask this of me.''

''But I do ask it. It would seem to me, my lord, since first we came here, that you have consorted with many odd and suspicious characters.''

Brett had made certain friends. All of them were loyal to the King. Through these men, he had kept abreast with the tide of the war. From them he had learned that the King, failing to strengthen his position, had often been in dire peril of being captured by the enemy. Prince Rupert, at his best in war, still blazed a glorious path. But all the Royalists might do seemed doomed in the face of Cromwell's growing influence, his ruthless stamping out of all resistance, his open threats against the King.

''Well, my lord, what have you to say for yourself?''

''Nonsense, Madam,'' he answered the Queen abruptly. ''That is what I have to say. My loyalty is not and has never been in question. You know it well.''

Bright color stained Henrietta Maria's face. She began to shake. ''Kneel!'' she screamed. ''I have commanded you to kneel, my lord!''

He came to stand in front of her. Looking into her rage-distorted face, he thought of all he had had to endure through this woman. He had put up with her screaming passions, her unreasonableness, her rudeness, her incessant demands, and he had stamped down the impulse to treat her as he would have any other woman of like nature. But this was too much! ''Save your energy and your breath, Madam,'' he said coldly. ''I refuse to encourage you in your stupidity.''

''Stupidity?'' Her jaw dropped slightly. ''You say that to me! To me!''

"I do indeed." His voice softened slightly. "Unreasonable I have always found you to be, Madam, but this time I do not hold you entirely to blame. Doubtless your condition is affecting you. Come now, will you not compose yourself? You will do harm to yourself and the child."

"You insolent knave!" She rose slowly from her chair.

"If I seem insolent, Madam, I pray you to forgive me. The truth is that I do but seek a sane and calm approach to your many bewildering moods."

Her breast rose and fell rapidly with her agitated breathing. "This is how I forgive you, my lord!" Her hand flashed upward and she hit him savagely across the face.

Brett's teeth cut into his lip with the force of the blow, and he tasted the salt of his blood. He grasped both her wrists in his hands, pulling her close against him. "You may thank the saints," he hissed, "that I still remember that you are the Queen!"

"And why should that fact deter you, my lord. Since first we met I have been the Queen, but that did not prevent you from threatening me. Go on, strike me! But remember this. You will pay for it with your head."

"Even so, were you in healthy condition, you would feel the sting of my hand. You need your backside reddened, by Christ you do! But you are a woman who is with child, and I am forced to remember that."

"You—" Agony lanced through her body, silencing the angry words she had been about to hurl at him. "Oh!" she moaned.

Instantly he released her. Half suspiciously, he said, "What is it?"

She moaned again, swaying toward him. "The child comes!" she gasped. "You have done this to me. 'Twas not due yet!"

"What!" Without further ado, he had picked her up and strode over to the door.

Her ladies, who were in the inner room, flocked about him as he emerged. The Queen lay in my lord Foxe's arms, apparently senseless, her face bloodless, and the yellow satin of her gown creased. They cried out, they wrung their hands. It was not until Brett ordered them curtly to send for the physician and the midwife, and to prepare Her Majesty for labor, that they came to their senses.

The capable midwife, arriving, had taken charge. She ordered Brett from the room, bidding him at the same time to take the ladies with him. "For I'll not have those fluttering useless creatures getting in my way, to say nothing of disturbing Her Majesty," she had said briskly.

He had left thankfully, but not before he had been given a glimpse of the Queen's body arching upward with a strong spasm of agony.

"Be born at any time, I'd say," Mary Kestler, the midwife, had remarked with some satisfaction. "Don't you worry, Your Majesty, this child is impatient to be born."

Impatient to be born, was it! Brett thought grimly. Well, then, it must have changed its plaguy mind. Doubtless, like its mother, it was stubborn, and was refusing to move.

A scream, louder than the rest, brought Brett to his feet. He stood there, the blood pounding in his ears, his hands clenched at his sides. In the silence that followed that scream, he heard the thin wailing cry of a child. It was born then! Thank God! But what of the Queen? Had his brutality killed her?

It seemed to him an interminable time before the door opened and Meredith came into the room. She exclaimed at the sight of him. "Brett! What is it? You look about to swoon!" Anxiously she went toward him. "Come, my love, sit down, else will you be falling."

He was annoyed by her solicitude, for it seemed to him that he could detect a hint of laughter beneath it. He sat down gladly, however. "One would think you were the anxious husband," Meredith went on, her hand stroking his hair, "instead of the Queen's stern and implacable guardian."

He brushed her hand away impatiently. "How fares the Queen?" he demanded.

"She is very weak," Meredith answered, "for 'tis her worst birth to date, so Mistress Kestler informs me."

In his anxiety, he glared at her. "But she will live?"

"Of course she will live, my love. She is stronger than she appears."

He relaxed in the chair. "Thank God for that! I thought I had killed her."

"What mean you?"

"I will tell you later." He breathed deeply. "It is over, and all is well. 'Tis all that matters."

She was still looking at him curiously. "You do not inquire for the child."

"From the time he has taken to be born," he said bitterly, "no doubt reserving all his strength for the thrust, I am assuming that he is strong and healthy."

"To the contrary, a somewhat frail child, I would say. But it is not a he, 'tis a she."

"Mistress Kestler said the child was impatient to be born. When it delayed its appearance, I should have known its sex. Who else but a female would be so cursed contrary?"

Meredith laughed. "But she is the prettiest little thing. I vow you will be quite enchanted."

"I doubt it," he remarked gloomily. "All babies look alike to me. I only pray that she does not have her mother's disposition."

"If the King loves her, she cannot be so very bad."

"Ah! Now that is something I have never been able to understand. Charles must be crazed."

"You speak treason, my lord."

"So I do. Then you must report me, must you not, my lady Foxe?"

"When next you annoy me, my lord, I will give some thought to it."

When my lord Foxe entered her room for the first time, ten days after the birth of the Princess, Henrietta Maria knew from the look on his face that he had grave news to impart. Her eyes flew to Lady Morton, who was seated beside the bed holding the Princess in her arms.

Lady Morton rose instantly. "If Your Majesty will excuse me, I will return the child to her nurse."

Scarcely waiting for the door to close behind her, the Queen looked at him with dread. "The K—King?" she faltered. "He is not—Nothing has happened to him?"

"Nay, Madam." Brett seated himself in Lady Morton's vacated chair. "The King and the royal children are well."

She studied him. He looked very weary. He had forgotten to remove his plumed hat, and the dark-blue velvet of his jacket and breeches was spotted with the light summer rain that was still falling. For the first time she softened toward him. "What is it, my lord?" she said almost gently. "What news do you bring?"

"Madam," he spoke each word carefully so that she might understand. "I have received word that my lord Essex advances upon this city."

Her color faded, but she said haughtily, "Essex, that traitor! I fear him not."

"Forgive my blunt speech, Madam, but only fools or the unimaginative are devoid of fear." He leaned forward, fixing her with his eyes. "I do not believe you are a fool. Essex is the King's most bitter enemy, and yours. He has sworn to return you to London, and there, he swears, you will answer to Parliament's charge against you."

"I?" Her dark eyes widened, and now he could see the fear in them. "To what charge must I, Henrietta Maria, answer?"

He was sorry for her. Sorry that his words must break down that haughty barrier she had erected against fear. "Madam, they do accuse you of having levied war in England. 'Tis you, they say, who by injudicious counsel to a man who loves you beyond his country and his crown, have brought England to civil war."

Henrietta Maria gripped the sheet in both hands, her knuckles whitening. "But that is ridiculous! 'Tis a lie, my lord!"

"I know it, Madam. You have had some influence upon the King, that much is true. But he is his own man. However, that is the belief of Essex, and of many people. His avowed intention is to take you. He will do it if he can."

"I see." Henrietta Maria's smile was bitter. "Doubtless he will achieve his object. We have no army here to defend us. We cannot stand against him."

"Nay, Madam, you underestimate me. When Essex arrives you will, with God's help, be far from here. You cannot walk so far, and I have ordered a litter to be constructed. We will, of course, have horses, but I fear the jolting would not be good for you. I intend to make our way to Pendennis Castle. 'Tis near the Lizard, in Cornwall."

"I know where Pendennis Castle is, my lord." Henrietta Maria answered with a flash of spirit. She looked at him angrily. "Do not treat me like a child."

"I was not aware that I was doing so," Brett answered her calmly. "Once we reach our destination, I will put you aboard a vessel, and you will be conveyed to France." Anticipating her next question, he added. "Worry not, there are many friendly vessels whose captains we may approach."

"But—but I cannot go. What of the Princess?"

"I understand your feelings," Brett said pityingly, "but you cannot take her with you. The journey will be hazardous enough. 'Tis certain that we will be forced into hiding many times before we reach the castle. 'Twould be quite impossible were we burdened with a new-born child. For the sake of the Princess's health, and for your own peace of mind, you must leave her behind."

"But—"

"There can be no buts. Forgive me, Madam, 'tis the only way. Leave her in the care of the lady whom you trust the most."

Henrietta Maria seemed unaware of the tears trickling down her cheeks. "Th—that would be L—Lady Morton. I do not trust many women, but I do trust M—Margaret." She leaned back against the lace-trimmed pillows, her tears flowing faster. "Oh,

430

my lord, is there to be no end to my sorrows? I have lost my husband and my children, and now I must also lose my little Princess!''

'' 'Tis but a temporary parting,'' Brett assured her hastily. "Very soon you will all be reunited.''

"Can you tell me that in all truth?''

Brett hesitated. He wanted to comfort her, but it would be folly to give her false hope. "Nay, I should not have said that, Madam. Would to God that I could assure you that it be truth. I do, however, sincerely believe that it will be so.''

Henrietta Maria heard the sympathy in his voice, but she also noted the wary expression in his eyes. "If you fear my hysteria,'' she said surprisingly, "you need not, my lord.'' Pleased with the effect of her words, she went on, "In the past, I have behaved very badly. But there is another side to my nature. I can see that 'tis time to show it to you.''

He stared at her. "Indeed. I must confess that I had not thought to hear such words from you, Madam.''

"I know it. But there is a lot you do not know about me.'' Adding to his surprise, she smiled warmly at him. "It may be that I am not as bad as you think me. Mayhap I can be brave if need arise. Aye, resourceful and enduring too. What think you of that?''

"I know not what to think, Madam. But please go on.''

"I will. I believe that a litter will seriously impede us. Therefore, my lord, no litter.''

Brett's eyes narrowed. What new game was this? For the first time since he had known her, she spoke as a woman, not a spoiled child. But he answered her with his customary brusqueness. "Nonsense!''

Henrietta Maria was content. She had sensed the change in his attitude. She both loved and hated this man; it had always been so in their relationship. But now her affection for him was uppermost. She longed for his respect. She longed to shine in his eyes. "No litter,'' she repeated quietly. "I will walk when you walk. Ride when you ride.''

431

"It is a long way," Brett protested uncertainly. "I fear it will be too much for Your Majesty."

Henrietta Maria shook her head. "I have made up my mind. It will not be too much for me. Have you forgotten that I am my father's daughter?"

"And so, Madam?"

"So, although you may not think it, he has endowed me with some small speck of his courage and endurance."

Brett hid his smile at the picture this statement brought forth. Courage the man had had in plenty, and he had been France's most loved and revered King. But for Charles's sake, he hoped that that stallion of a man, Henri of Navarre, had not also endowed his daughter with his lecherous nature. Even a small speck of that would be too much. His smile broadened as he thought of the Prince of Wales, who, from his observation of the Prince's general behavior with the wenches, might well have fallen heir to Henri of Navarre's lechery. Aye, he doubted not that the lovable and charming young Charles would be his maternal grandfather all over again.

"I see no occasion for smiling, my lord," Henrietta Maria rebuked him. With that new and charming seriousness, she went on, "You must remember, my lord, that not only will a litter impede us, it will also make us conspicuous. Which is surely something we must avoid."

"I have worried over that problem," Brett answered. "Very well, Madam, if you are sure, it shall be as you say. My lady goes with us. There may be another, of Your Majesty's own choice, but no more. We will all do our best to save you any unnecessary fatigue and strain."

"I am sure of that." There was bright color in Henrietta Maria's cheeks. Her tears had dried and her eyes were sparkling. "But you must all look to yourselves, my lord. I believe I will be able to take care of myself. When do we depart?"

"Tomorrow. It can be no later."

"Then tomorrow it shall be. I will be ready."

Brett rose to his feet. He did not know her in this mood, but he

432

found himself liking her. He took her hand in his and raised it to his lips. "With your spirit and courage to aid us, Madam, I know that all will be well."

Delighted, she smiled up at him. "And have I pleased you at last, my lord?"

"You have indeed, Madam. Now I am fully aware that I speak to the Queen." He released her hand. "I ask you to excuse me now. There are arrangements to be made." Bowing, he turned away.

"My lord," her voice stopped him at the door, "where will this all end? Think you we will be victorious?"

He hesitated. He wanted to tell her the truth as he saw it, to speak to her as a mature woman, yet still he could not entirely trust her moods. "Things do not go well," he ventured.

There was fear in her eyes, but she spoke quietly enough. "What of the King? No matter the outcome of this war, he will be safe, will he not?"

Safe? Brett thought. If only he could be sure of that. There was a chill possibility he sometimes entertained, but how could he speak to her of that? Would Parliament, if they emerged victorious from this tragic war, dare to lay violent hands on His Majesty's sacred person? Surely they would not dare! Not even Cromwell, for all his oft-repeated threats, would have the courage to commit regicide. Avoiding her eyes, he answered quickly, "Worry not, Madam. He will be quite safe. None would dare harm the King."

After he had gone, Henrietta Maria did not call her ladies to her side. She lay still, her eyes brooding. She had caught the expression on my lord Foxe's face, and his hastily uttered words had not comforted her. "None would dare harm the King," my lord Foxe had said. But what if he should be wrong? Oliver Cromwell was a man greatly to be feared, and, remembering his threats against the King's life, she shivered violently. It would seem that only the death of the King would please that man!

Her heart twisted in the first real anguish she had ever known. Her fingers touched the cross suspended on a fine gold chain about her neck. "Oh no, Charles, it must not be! I love you so very much. I would not want to live without you!"

She clutched the cross, as though seeking to draw comfort from the contact. "Dear God, I will endeavor to be different, more worthy. Spare my husband, I pray You. Help me to be all that a wife should be, so that when he has need of strength, I may support him with mine. I will comfort him, warm him with my love. I know that I am vain, selfish, spoiled and arrogant, for thus I have been brought up to be, but with Your loving and gracious help, I will overcome these faults that I may be more pleasing in Your sight, and in his. I will be a good daughter to You, a good wife to my husband. I will strive to turn the hearts of heretics to the True Faith. My children are not a lost cause, for I will never give up. I will struggle with them endlessly, and in the end they will embrace the True Faith. The light of Thy countenance will shine upon them, this do I vow! Dear Lord, punish not my husband because he be heretic. With him too will I work, striving my utmost to bring him to Thy Grace!"

When Meredith entered the room some time later, the Queen slept. She had been crying, Meredith noted, for the tears still shone on her cheeks, and her fingers clutched the small gold cross.

Meredith stood thoughtfully beside the bed, looking down at her. Brett had told her of his conversation with the Queen. Would she ever understand her, Meredith wondered, this woman who seemed to be so many women in one? She had so many guises. There was the haughtily arrogant Henrietta Maria, there was the quiet and courageous woman, this one rarely seen. There was the vindictive, the affectionate, the bad-tempered, the generous, the religious fanatic. Which was the true woman?

Meredith looked at the slim fingers clutching the cross. Whatever woman Henrietta Maria might be, she would always be the fanatic. That was a part of herself that she could not, and perhaps did not want to change. She derived great comfort from her religion, which was how it should be, but that did not excuse her hectoring of others not of her faith. For instance, there could be no doubt that Henrietta Maria loved the King, but him too would she see subjected to torture, if, by so doing, it would bring him to her faith.

Meredith shivered. She neither liked nor disliked the Queen, yet, because she was the Queen, she would do all in her power to serve her. But, in her fanaticism, there was something terrible about her at times. Not only terrible but merciless, self-destructive, that could eventually destroy both herself and those she loved.

Meredith turned away from the bed and went softly over to the door. It had been agreed that the Queen should be disguised for her journey into Cornwall. That journey would be fraught with so many dangers that she trembled to think of it. Would the Queen endure? Would this courage she had displayed break at the first test?

With her hand on the latch, Meredith turned once more to look at the sleeping woman. Maybe she would endure because there was no other alternative. And Henrietta Maria, if she knew aught about her, would have commanded God to see her through to safe harbor. The Queen's fervent belief in the Almighty in no wise prevented her from issuing to Him her commands. Smiling at the last thought, Meredith left the room, closing the door quietly behind her.

When the King entered Bedford House, he was triumphant, but staggering with weariness. He had fought his way to Exeter in order to reach the Queen's side. He had set out when he had first heard the news that the Earl of Essex marched upon Exeter. The Earl's avowed intention was to take the Queen prisoner, and transport her to London, where, he had said, she would answer for her crime against England. At first the King had not believed that the man would carry out his plan. But when the incredible news was brought to him that Essex had actually had the audacity to place a price upon the head of the Queen of England, he doubted no longer.

With only a small force to aid him, the King left Oxford for

Exeter. There were many small skirmishes on the way, for the Parliamentary soldiers seemed to be everywhere. But the King was determined to reach his destination, and the men fighting with him caught his fire. On each occasion they put the enemy soldiers to ignominious flight. With only one man wounded, and he only slightly, the King came to Bedford House.

Entering the great Hall, followed by his weary men, whose long locks were powdered with dust, their high leather boots splashed with mud, and the signs of strain evident in all their faces, the King felt almost happy. He was here, where he had so longed to be. For a few days, in the company of Henrietta Maria and his new born child, he would endeavor to forget the war. He had beaten Essex to his goal. When the Earl finally arrived, he would find himself facing not one helpless woman, weak from childbirth, but a small and formidable force. It was typical of Charles that he gave no thought to the danger in which he might find himself. His mind was filled with only one thing, his wife and his child.

"Sire!" Her red silk gown rustling as she advanced toward him, Lady Morton sank down before the King. "I—I had not thought to see Your Majesty here. 'Tis a pleasure and an honor."

Charles was not altogether sure of the pleasure she was expressing. She looked, he thought, pale and frightened. "Pray rise, my lady." He waited until she had done so. "And now," he said, smiling at her, "where is the Queen?"

Lady Morton was too agitated to respond to the smile. She wrung her long, white hands together. "The—the Queen has gone, Sire. I fear you are too late."

"Too late?" Charles's heart quickened with sudden terror. What did the woman mean? He had received reports that Her Majesty and the Princess were in excellent health. The Queen had suffered a little more at this birth, but she had come successfully through her ordeal. And now here was this woman telling him that he had come too late. He swallowed, trying to ease the dryness of his throat. "I understand you not," he forced out the words with some difficulty. "What mean you?"

Lady Morton saw the fear in his eyes, and she realized that he had misconstrued her words. Dismayed, blaming herself for her clumsy way of expressing herself, she said quickly, "Nay, Sire, you have misunderstood my meaning. The Queen and the Princess are quite well. 'Tis merely that the Queen is not at Bedford House."

Charles felt weak with relief. "I see," he said, wiping the perspiration from his forehead with the back of his hand. "I confess that you did alarm me. Be so good as to inform me of the Queen's whereabouts."

"I cannot, Sire. None here knew her destination. My lord Foxe felt that it would be safer so. But all is well, for my lord Foxe returned this morning. He will explain all."

"I trust so." Charles glanced at his men. "My men are weary and in need of refreshment," he said to Lady Morton. "Pray see that their needs are filled. After that, go immediately to my lord Foxe. Tell him that I wish to see him at once."

"Yes, Sire. My lord is sleeping. But I will awaken him." Lady Morton hesitated, wondering if the King might change his instructions. When he did not, she hurried away.

When Brett entered the room just off the hall, his expression was scarcely welcoming. Bowing before the King, he exclaimed with the privilege of an old friend, "What do you here, Charles? It may be that Essex will arrive at any time. Have I escorted the Queen to safety, only to have you fall a prisoner into his hands?"

Charles looked at my lord Foxe's weary face, at the blue velvet jacket, which, he guessed, had been hastily donned, for it was badly creased and splashed with mud. "You need have no fear for me, my lord," he said quietly. "I can take care of myself. Where is the Queen?"

Brett's grim expression relaxed. "On her way to France, Sire. My lord Essex had made his intentions too plain for my peace of mind. With the Queen as hostage, your surrender would quickly have followed." He saw Charles's face tighten, and he added, "The Queen would have been an excellent bargaining point, you know it well, Sire. 'Twas a risk we could not take. The Queen is safe. 'Tis a weight gone from your mind, surely?''

''I should have been consulted.''

''You placed the Queen under my protection. There was no time to consult with you. And you did say, at the slightest risk, I was to act independently.''

Charles was silent for a moment, then he nodded. Disappointment, though keen, gave way to gratitude. ''You are right, my friend, I did say so. You have done well.'' He grimaced. ''But 'twould seem that I have come all this way for nothing.''

Brett smiled. ''Not quite, Charles. I would hope you would wish to greet your daughter.''

''My daughter!'' Charles's face lit up. ''Of course. I had forgotten the child. Take me to her.''

''I will. The Princess has been placed in Lady Morton's care. The Queen desired it so.''

''A wise choice. My lady Morton is an excellent and trustworthy woman. Well, why do you just stand there? I am impatient to see my daughter.''

''One more thing, Charles, and then we will go. What of the Prince of Wales?''

The glow of eagerness faded from Charles's face, leaving it drawn and tired. ''I know what you would say. For his own sake, the Prince must leave me, even as the Queen has done. One by one I am severed from my family. Sometimes I think I will never see them more.''

''Come,'' Brett said bracingly, ''I'll have none of this dismal talk. Have you thought where you might send the Prince?''

''To the western part of England. Charles will be among the loyalists there. If their sympathy and loyalty be waning, it might be that he will help to rekindle it. I will send him in the charge of Edward Hyde and my lord Colepepper.''

''Excellent. Now come, Charles, the Princess awaits her father.''

''Plague take you, Brett!'' Charles exclaimed with momentary irritation. ''I like not your soothing voice. Am I a child that my daughter must be held out to me like some cursed sweetmeat to comfort me?"

Brett grinned. "I regret that I was so obvious. But we all need comfort at times, Charles. Perhaps you most of all."

"I miss the Queen," Charles answered, following him through the door, "and I know I will miss that young rogue, Charles. He has been an inspiration to me, he and Marcus Milford. Both of them so young, so eager, so sure that right must triumph. Yet often do I ask myself if right can triumph. I find myself wondering if my cause is already lost."

Brett glanced quickly at his brooding face. "Doubt not, Charles. We will emerge victorious."

"Will we? The Parliamentary triumphs are overwhelming. As for Cromwell, it seems that he cannot lose a battle. He and his Ironsides stand shoulder to shoulder, sweeping all before them. Cromwell and Fairfax, backed by other of the Parliamentary generals, rule England this day."

"Not for long, Charles. Not for long!"

"I wonder. The Royalists will fight to the finish, but their strength has been badly depleted. On all sides they are finding themselves cut off."

"Have done!" Brett said roughly. "I like not this defeatist talk!"

Charles shrugged. "I had thought it understood between us that I might confide in you. You do not imagine that I talk to my men in this way?"

"Nay, I know you do not. And of course it is understood between us, Charles. It is only that it grieves me to see you in such low spirits."

Charles's gloom lifted as they entered the nursery. He smiled at Lady Morton. "Where is my daughter?" he asked.

"Here, Sire." Bending over a satin-draped cradle, Lady Morton picked up the child and handed her to the King. "She is not yet named, but I am sure you would know Her Majesty's desire."

Charles held the child gingerly and looked tenderly into the crumpled, rose-tinted face. "She is beautiful." He glanced at the fluff of red-gold hair. "Her hair is a pretty color, but there is not much of it, is there?"

Lady Morton hid a smile. "It will grow, Sire."

"I hope so. Mary and Elizabeth had a thick growth when they were born." He rocked the child gently. "And what shall we name you, my little one?"

The Princess yawned widely. "So you are not interested, Madam," Charles said, laughing. "But you must have a name. I will call you Henrietta Anne. Henrietta after your mother, and Anne after your grandmother. There, there, my daughter, how will that be?"

Henrietta Anne sucked at her tiny fist, then broke into a loud and angry wail.

"I can tell that she likes it not," Charles said, hastily returning the Princess to Lady Morton. "But Henrietta Anne it shall be."

A commotion outside arrested their attention. They could hear muffled shouts, and the louder sound of tramping boots.

Lady Morton clutched the child to her and shrank back. "My lord Essex!" she breathed.

"Nay, my lady," Brett reassured her, "he would not have been allowed to pass so easily."

With the King at his side, Brett started toward the door. Before he could reach it, it was flung open and the Prince of Wales and Marcus Milford stepped into the room.

The King stared at them, his frown ominous. "Charles! Marcus! What do you here?"

Disregarding the frown, the Prince grinned at him. "Marcus and I thought that what you could do we could do, Sire. And here we are."

"How dare you!" the King thundered. "How dare you expose yourselves to such dangers, you young fools!"

The Prince's grin faded. "There was no danger, Sire. We did not encounter one patrol. If I have angered you, I beg your pardon."

The King's anger began to fade. "Oh, well, you are here, and

440

safe. God looks after fools and children, I suppose. I suppose you came to see your mother and your sister?"

The Prince nodded eagerly. "Yes, indeed, Sire." He looked at Lady Morton. "That is my sister, I take it, who is making that infernal caterwauling?"

The King could not refrain from smiling. "No doubt because she realizes that she has a fool for a brother." He stood aside. "Your mother is not here. I will explain later. But you may see Henrietta Anne."

"Henrietta Anne? What a big name for such a small bundle."

"Sire," Brett said solemnly to the King, "you must not linger long. I will ask that a meal be prepared for you, but then you must be on your way."

"We will not stay for a meal, Brett. We will take the food with us and eat it on the way."

"Then I will instruct the cook." Brett smiled at Marcus as he passed. "And how fares Master Marcus Milford?"

"Very well, my lord," Marcus answered with his usual gravity.

The Prince took the child from Lady Morton. "Listen!" he exclaimed, with a delighted smile. "She has stopped crying. Come and look at her, Marcus. Is she not a little beauty?"

Marcus obediently bent over Henrietta Anne, who now seemed perfectly contented. "A pretty child," he commented.

"Pretty?" the Prince cried. "She is beautiful! She knows she is safe in her brother's arms, don't you, my little sweetheart?"

"She could scarcely know where she is," said Marcus, the logical.

"She knows," Charles insisted. "And look there, she is smiling at me."

Marcus was struck by this. "Why, so she is."

Lady Morton looked at the King, who grinned at her with understanding. The Prince seemed so delighted, that she refrained from telling him that it could scarcely be called a smile.

"You seem very taken with the baby, Charles," the King said. "It was not so with your other sisters."

"They were not like this one," the Prince replied, still gazing with enraptured eyes at the tiny face. "Henrietta Anne is very special. Ah, but we do not like that name, do we, my little one? It is too stiff and heavy. I shall call you Minette. My Minette!" He turned to Marcus. "Would you care to hold her?"

"I?" Marcus drew back. "No, Charles, I thank you."

"She will not break. Later, when she is older, it may be that you will regret this lost opportunity."

"Thank you, Charles. If I do regret it, I will not mention it to you."

Charles returned to crooning over the baby. "We will ignore him, will we not, my Minette. If he does not see that you are a very rose of beauty, then his case is hopeless."

"The hair," Marcus said unexpectedly, pointing to the fluff of red-gold adorning the baby's head. " 'Tis my favorite color. In my opinion, all females should be born with such a color."

"Ah, Minette, Marcus has paid you a compliment. You must treasure it, for you will never hear the like from him again."

The King shook his head in bewilderment. Charles loved his sisters and brothers, for his was a warm and loving nature. But this child, Minette, as he called her, seemed to have cast a spell over him. He could not seem to have done with gazing at her. Mayhap, he thought, Henrietta Anne was special to him because she had been born in the midst of their trouble. Perhaps he looked upon her as a symbol of better times to come. "Charles," the King said gently, "return Henrietta Anne to my lady Morton. We must be on our way. 'Twould be dangerous to linger."

"I suppose so." Regretfully, Charles handed the child over. "I pray you, my lady, take very good care of my Minette."

"I will, Your Highness. I will guard Minette with my life."

"I am sure of it, my lady. Forgive me if I seem rude, but Minette is my special name for her. To others she will be Henrietta Anne, but to me, always Minette."

"I understand, Your Highness. I will rephrase my words. I will guard Henrietta Anne with my life."

The Prince winked at her. Moving closer, he rested his hand on her slim waist. "And guard yourself, my lady, for you are most fair."

"Wh—why thank you, Your Highness," Lady Morton answered, flushing.

"Charles!" the King said sharply. "We must not be so familiar with our elders."

After they had gone, Lady Morton replaced the child in the cradle. The Prince was only a boy, but she found herself remembering that look in his dark eyes with distinct pleasure. Only a boy, and yet there was something about him that compelled admiring feminine attention. She herself was no exception.

She smoothed the covers over the baby. Remembering the King's words, she murmured, "I am not so very old, after all, am I, Henrietta Anne?" She made a wry grimace. "But perhaps too old to be flattered by a boy's dark flirtatious eyes."

Chapter Twenty-Four

There was an unusual flush in the Prince of Wales's cheeks, and
the eyes with which he regarded his father were openly defiant.
"I will not go, Sire. Dost truly think that I would journey into
safety, leaving you behind to face danger?"

Marcus Milford, who was, as usual, in the Prince's company,
moved uncomfortably. Meeting the King's eyes, he said quickly,
"I beg you to excuse me, Sire. I know you wish to speak to the
Prince alone."

The King regarded the tall, straight figure in the dark-red
velvet suit indulgently. The boy's darkly handsome face looked
stiffer and more remote than ever, owing to the embarrassment he
was suffering. It was the Prince who had insisted that Marcus be
present at this interview, and he, reluctantly, had followed him.
Now he was anxious to be gone.

"Nay, Marcus," the King said, "I wish you to stay. 'Twould
seem to me that your influence over my son is greater than mine.
That being so, I may need your help to persuade him."

"Persuade him, Sire?" Marcus's rare smile appeared. "But surely Your Majesty has but to command."

"Well!" Charles turned such an outraged face upon Marcus, that the King had difficulty in suppressing a laugh. "I thought you would be with me, but 'twould seem that I am betrayed on all sides."

Marcus's brows rose. "I swear, Charles, that you are far too dramatic. If you would but listen to wise counsel, you would not believe yourself betrayed."

"It is what I might have expected of you, Marcus," the Prince flared. "You do not suffer and feel as I do. I swear you are as cold as a mackerel on a slab. You have no emotions, no deeper feelings."

"You know that is not true," Marcus answered in an austere voice. "But I forgive you, you are such an addlepate that you know not from one moment to the next what you are saying."

"How dare you!" The Prince retired behind a dignity he was far from feeling. "You forget that you speak to your Prince."

"Since you remind me that you are my Prince, then may I say that your childishness offends me."

"You may say nothing. I do not give you leave to speak."

Marcus's lips curled into that faint sardonic smile that always had the effect of infuriating the Prince. "Very well, Your Highness. I will wait until it pleasures you to give me leave."

"Curse you, Marcus, I've a good mind to punch your head."

"Your Highness may try. But, as usual, you will lose the battle."

"Od's fish, I will show you differently."

"Gentlemen," the King hastily intervened. "Entertaining though this battle of words is, I must beg you to return to the point at issue."

"Sire, I have said I will not go," the Prince repeated stubbornly. "I refuse."

The King's face altered. "As you reminded Marcus, I now remind you. You forget to whom you speak."

"No I do not, Sire. I speak to my father."

"And also to your King. As your King," Charles went on, his voice softening, "I can and will command you to go. But as your father, I beg you."

"Sire. You expect me to travel to the west of England, with only old Hyde and Colepepper to bear me company?"

"There are also the gentlemen of your retinue," the King pointed out.

"Aye, but they are worse than Hyde and Colepepper. Surely you would not wish me to face Hyde's constant lecturing, and my lord Colepepper's heavy and humorless jokes, to say nothing of the gloomy faces of the others?"

"Lectures you may endure, also jokes. It is the danger I do not wish you to face."

"You will be facing it, Sire."

"That is a different matter. I am the King, my place is with my troops."

"I am the Prince. A son's place is by his father's side."

"A son's place is to obey his father," the King retorted, losing patience.

Abruptly, the Prince changed his tactics. Opening his dark eyes very wide, he said solemnly. "I would go, Sire, indeed I am eager to go. 'Tis a question of my conscience, however. It will not allow me to desert Your Majesty."

"You may tell your conscience, Charles, that you will be far more valuable to me in the west of England. It may be that you will glean valuable information. Certainly, seeing their Prince, I believe that the people will become more fervent in our cause."

The Prince knew that he had lost. No matter how many protestations he might make, he would be forced to go, there was no way out. "Very well, Sire," he said, breaking the heavy silence that had fallen. "It would seem that I have no alternative. There is one request I would make, though."

"What is it?"

"I ask that Marcus accompany me."

Before the King could reply, Marcus said sharply. "You know that is impossible, Charles. I have explained why."

446

"You refer to your father's condition, Marcus?" the King said gently.

Marcus's mouth quivered, but his answering voice was steady. "I do Sire. I believe that he is dying. He would wish me to be at his side." Now his voice roughened, and there was a distracted air about him. "There is no one but myself and Mrs. Thomas to care what happens to—to him. My sister J—Jessica loves him, but she is only a babe. There is no one else, Sire. No one."

"There is myself, Marcus. I love your father."

Marcus's eyes were brilliant with tears. " 'Tis very good of Your Majesty to say so."

"Nay, 'tis not good of me. I speak truth." The King held out his hand. "Come here, lad."

Marcus went to him slowly. Stiffly, hesitantly, he placed his hand in the King's. "Pray forgive me, Your Majesty, but—but do not attempt to console me." He laughed shakily. "It might well prove disastrous."

The King squeezed his hand and then released it. "Then I will not, Marcus. But you must not be ashamed of a natural emotion."

"Marcus," the Prince said softly, "there is also another who cares. Myself."

Marcus made a choked sound. The King rose hastily to his feet. "Come, Charles," he said beckoning. "I believe Marcus would prefer to be alone."

"He may prefer it, Sire," said Charles, "but he isn't going to be alone."

The King hesitated, minded to command him to leave the room. Then, remembering the strong bond between them, he changed his mind. "Very well, Charles," he said. "But I will wish to see you later. There are arrangements to be made, things to be discussed."

The door closed behind him. Several minutes elapsed before Marcus spoke. "You should have gone with the King, Charles. Unless, of course, it pleasures you to see me make a fool of myself."

"You are the fool if you think that," Charles said in a determinedly cheerful voice. "It does pleasure me, however, to find that you have human emotions."

Marcus turned to him, and Charles saw that he was in control of himself again. Only the smudges beneath his eyes betrayed him. "Were you ever in doubt, Your Highness?"

"Nay, 'twas just my poor attempt at a joke. And don't call me 'Your Highness,' you stiff-necked donkey."

Marcus turned away again and strolled over to the window. "The day is fine," he commented. He leaned nearer to the window. "There is quite a collection of birds upon the lawn. Do you hear the din they are making?"

"Curse the day," Charles exclaimed. "And curse the birds." He walked over to stand beside Marcus. "Do you realize that we are soon to be parted? It may be years before we see each other again. Don't you care?"

Marcus continued to stare through the window. "I care, Charles," he said at last. "But there is nothing we can do about it."

"And how am I to go on without you?"

"I don't know. When it comes to looking after yourself, you're such a fool."

"A fool, am I. We'll see about that. And why i' plague don't you look at me?"

Marcus turned his head. "It will not be years, Charles. As soon as I am able, I will join you." He hesitated. "In the meantime, know that you have all my loyalty."

Charles stared at him. "By God, Marcus," he cried, "It must have pained you to force out those words."

"Not at all." Marcus gave him a cool look. "They came surprisingly easy."

"You are a strange one, Marcus. Damned if I know what I see in you."

A faint smile touched Marcus's lips. " 'Tis undoubtedly my overpowering charm."

"Bah! You will be returning to Milford Manor in the morning, will you not, Marcus?"

"Aye, I must go."

Charles held out his hand. "Friends, Marcus?"

"Friends, Charles." Marcus took his hand and wrung it.

"Forever," Charles insisted. "Come hell or high water."

"The old oath again? Aye, Charles, come hell or high water."

"And you promise to join me as soon as it be possible?"

"I have said so, have I not?"

"Aye. But where is the harm in having you repeat it?"

"No harm. 'Tis simply a waste of words."

"And Milford never wastes words," Charles jibed. He sobered instantly. "Marcus," he added, "I trust you find my lord Butler well."

The dark eyes were instantly shuttered against him, and Charles, to his great exasperation, felt that even he, close as they were, had intruded in a place where Marcus did not wish him to go. Then realizing that Marcus merely sought to keep a tight hold on his emotions, he said, "All right, curse you, I'll say no more."

"It would be as well." Marcus turned to the door. "I have things I must do, if you have not, Charles." He looked into the Prince's downcast face. "It will not be long, Charles, before we meet again. Think you that you can keep out of mischief without my steadying influence to restrain you?"

"Steadying influence! In your own way you are as mad as I. How can you be sure that it will not be for long?"

"I believe you know as well as I that my father is dying. When he is gone, I will no longer stay at Milford Manor."

"It may be that you will be forced to stay. You are not yet of age, you know."

Marcus's head lifted arrogantly. "My years will not count in this instance. I will be the head of the household, and, as such, I will do as I please."

"And what of Jessica?"

"Jessica will be placed in Mrs. Thomas's care. As for my mother, she will instantly leave my house."

Charles looked at that cold and implacable face. Even now, he realized, he did not know Marcus entirely. The ruthless side of Marcus's nature had never been turned against himself. "But, Marcus, you would not turn her out?"

Marcus frowned impatiently. "If you think that, Charles, then you do not know me. She will not be exactly penniless, you know. She has an adequate income, which will continue after my—my father's death. If she cares to, I will allow her to live in the house in Banbury Square." His lips curled. " 'Tis big enough to entertain a platoon of her lovers."

If she were starving, Charles thought, I wonder if you would care? Do you really hate her that much, my friend? He said slowly, "It would seem to me that you are very unforgiving."

"Where she is concerned, yes."

"You know, Marcus, I would not like you to be my enemy."

" 'Tis true, if sufficiently injured, that I would make a bad enemy," Marcus said shortly. He looked at Charles intently, and there was a smile in his dark eyes. "But since I believe you quite incapable of injuring me, it need not concern you."

"But I might one day, Marcus. Perhaps unintentionally, without realizing that I was doing so."

"This is a ridiculous conversation, Charles. Rest assured that I could never hate you. So, if you unintentionally injure me, I must put up with it, must I not?"

"Well, I'm glad to hear that." Charles stared at him. He was as gay and light-hearted as Marcus was cold and remote, but somehow they fitted together in the perfect friendship. Marcus was of the same age as himself, yet always, when they held a serious conversation, he had the feeling that he was years older than himself. Marcus awed him at these times, but somehow also inspired his pity. There was such a strangeness about him, such an air of unhappiness. He had been wounded deeply, Charles was sure of that, but even to him Marcus would not speak of that other and secret side of himself.

"Well, Charles?" Marcus's voice cut across his thoughts. "You have seen me before, I believe. So why the devil are you staring at me?"

Charles grinned. "Was I staring? I'm sorry." He turned away. "Well, go, if you're going. I shall miss you, curse you. So leave me alone to wallow in my self-pity."

Marcus laughed. "You will wallow until a pretty wench catches your eye, then all will be forgotten but the conquest." He clicked his tongue in mock censure. "You are far too young for these amorous adventures."

"Too young? Nay, Marcus, where the wenches are concerned, I was born ready, willing, and able. But it does not behoove you to pass disparaging remarks on my youth or my conquests. You have professed to a great dislike of females, but thus far it has not stopped you from tumbling them between the sheets whenever opportunity arises. And, whilst servicing the lady in question, didst ever think of yourself as too young?"

"I was born old, I think. Each wench I have serviced has always assured me that I am the equal of someone twice my age. There, I have given you my testimonial. What pray is yours?"

"Oh, my youth, too, is entirely disregarded. The wenches do not ever make mention of it. I am known as the perfect lover."

"Certainly," Marcus said dryly, "you are making sure that you have enough practice. On that note, Charles, I will leave you. Good-bye, until we meet again."

"Good-bye, Marcus. And you make sure, plague take you, that this parting is not of long duration!"

It was only after Marcus had left that Charles became aware that his parting words had been tactless. A short parting could only mean an early death for my lord Butler. If the parting be long, it meant that he still lingered, and was perhaps recovering. Charles shrugged. Marcus would understand that he had not meant it so. No one else understood him half so well as Marcus.

Chapter
Twenty-Five

The King sat in a hard-backed chair in the coffee room of the King's Arms Inn. The small-paned window facing him was curtained in bright orange, the curtains looped back with green silk cords. On the dark oak-paneled walls hung copper ornaments, giving a note of cheer to the otherwise somber room. Behind him, a fire crackled in a huge brick grate, for the May morning had turned chilly, and he could feel the heat on his back. Seated about the fire were his companions, who had accompanied him on his flight from Oxford.

The King turned his head to study them. There was my lord Foxe, his legs, encased in high black leather boots, thrust out toward the blaze. He looked strangely unlike himself with his short-cropped hair beneath a steeple hat of sober gray. He was clad entirely in gray, except for his boots. On his plainly cut jacket, his only adornment was a wide white collar edged with a thin frill of lace.

The King's smile was bitter. What of himself? He certainly did not look like a king. His hair, too, had been cropped to just below his ears, and his beard hacked until it was naught but an untidy stubble about his chin. To think it had come to this! The King of England a fugitive from his own people!

To distract himself, the King glanced at my lady Foxe. She too was dressed soberly, but her apparel, unlike that of the King and my lord Foxe, was that of a woman of means. Her brown dress was of a rich, heavy silk, the ruffles at the hemline and the cuffs of fine French lace. Her bright hair was drawn back from her face into a modest twist in the back of her neck, the twist held in place by a brown riband. Her high-crowned brown bonnet, the inner brim lined with white lace, was tied beneath her dimpled chin with wide brown ribands. She looked to be a prosperous merchant's wife. The King and my lord Foxe traveled with her as her servants. Seated on either side of her, garbed in black, with plain white linen collars and cuffs, were John Ashburnham, a gentleman of the King's bedchamber, and the Reverend Michael Hudson, the King's chaplain.

Looking down at his own rusty black clothing, the King made a slight grimace. There was not even a feather to brighten his black steeple hat. Upbraiding himself for caring for such vanities at a time like this, the King turned his head away and looked down at the paper in his hand. On the paper he had written, in his fine flowing script, "Tuesday morning, May 5th, 1646." He had meant to write to the Queen, but somehow the words just would not come. He crumpled the parchment in his hand and threw it on the table beside him. Settling back in his chair, his eyes on the light rain falling outside, he thought of the train of events that had brought him to this moment. His own Parliament, refusing his overtures, had refused to receive him at Westminster. Now he waited in this inn, in Southwell, to receive the Scottish commissioners, who, reversing their position, had offered him protection from his enemies, should he agree to surrender his person into their hands.

Sometimes, the King thought, it all seemed to him like a long nightmare, from which, he prayed, he would shortly awaken.

The rebellion of his people, the rise of Cromwell. The many battles, some won for the Royalists, but far, far more lost to Cromwell and his forces of the Eastern Association, the Ironsides, as they were popularly known. The battle of Newbury, in which neither Royalists nor Roundheads could justly lay claim to victory. Chalgrove Field, Prince Rupert triumphant, and John Hampden, the Parliamentary General, lying dead, the tall, standing corn waving about him. The battle of Marston Moor, the King's army scattered, and Cromwell in possession of the battlefield. The long summer months, with Cromwell constantly on the move, attacking Royalist positions, striking like lightning, his well-trained forces advancing. The Roundhead soldiers were afraid of Cromwell, the iron man who ruled them, and, because they feared him far more than the Royalist forces, it made their victory inevitable. Cromwell, maintaining his policy of the strictest secrecy, so that not a whisper of his movements reached Royalist ears. And then, finally, that bright summer day, June 14th, 1645, in which he, the King, had witnessed the collapse of all his hopes. That bloody battle of Naseby, which had given final victory to the Parliamentarians.

Shuddering, Charles saw that battlefield again. The infantry, commanded by General Fairfax. Cromwell's son-in-law, Henry Ireton, with his cavalry. The infantry, muskets primed and ready. Cromwell himself, commanding another wing of horse. Charles closed his eyes, seeing his own cavalry go plunging into the battle, their shouts in his ears, "For King and country!" The Roundheads advancing, always advancing like a solid wall of death and destruction, their voices raised in song, "God is with us. Eternal God defend us ever!" Prince Rupert and Prince Maurice, their charge brilliant, but wasting time in fruitless pursuit of the enemy. Cromwell's horse charging the Royalists from the rear and the sides.

Charles sighed deeply, remembering the Roundheads' surprise attack on all sides, their horses plunging forward as if to trample their enemies into the blood-soaked mud of the battlefield. My lord Foxe crying "Halt!" as the Royal army broke and ran before the charge. Himself crying out in desperation, "Stop! In the name of God, stop!" He had drawn his sword, crying out again, "One charge more, good gentlemen, and we will win this day!"

Charles opened his eyes. The rain was heavier now. With his infantry scattered, fleeing in all directions, some of them, even as they ran, captured and taken prisoner, going to who knew what fate, he had had no choice but to retreat. So he, with the ever faithful my lord Foxe, had left that terrible scene of carnage. As long as he lived, he would remember those broken bodies, the anguish on dead faces, the gaping wounds, the flies settling on shattered flesh and bone, the steam still rising from the dulled coats of dead horses. The bright tunics of his men dyed with their own blood, their hair coated in mud, some of them unrecognizable, their faces smashed by the flying hooves of Cromwell's cavalry. Aye, as long as he lived he would remember, and he would grieve for those young lives lost in his cause.

Charles's hands clenched on the arms of the chair. He and my lord Foxe, accompanied by Prince Rupert, who had somehow escaped the onslaught of the Roundhead horse, and a small troop of infantry, had made their way to Leicester, from Leicester to Ashby-de-la-Zouch, to Lichfield, to Bewdly, and to Hereford. As he rode beside my lord Foxe, he had told himself that he must not give up hope. Did he not still have Montrose in Scotland, and had not Glamorgan promised that he would send Irish troops to his aid? Just before they reached Abergavenny, they had parted with Prince Rupert, who returned to Bristol, where, he had explained, a siege might be expected at any hour. The King, knowing he must call himself fugitive now, entered Wales in the company of my lord Foxe. But his days there had seemed endless, and his nights haunted. And so he had left once more to pursue his hazardous adventures. Knowing that at any moment he might be betrayed and captured, he had not really cared, the heart had gone out of him. It was my lord Foxe who had kept his spirit alive, who had refused to allow him to lapse into that moroseness which more and more sought to possess him.

"Of a certainty we are temporarily broken," my lord Foxe had said, "but we will recover. You cannot lose, Sire, not in the end. So for God's sake light up that gloomy face of yours!"

"The end!" The King rounded on him fiercely. "I know not when or what the end will be, and neither do you. You say I cannot lose, but I have lost! So seek not to cheer me with your false words of hope!"

Riding beside my lord Foxe, the King thought of the defeat of Montrose in the north, and, bitterest blow of all, of his nephew Prince Rupert, who had betrayed him. For had not Rupert, when Fairfax began the siege of Bristol, surrendered immediately to the enemy. He who had held such a strong position. "We cannot win," Rupert had been quoted as saying, "therefore I esteem it to be best to surrender gracefully and preserve our dignity!"

"Dignity!" the King thought. Rupert the brave, the dashing, to do such a thing. It was beyond belief! And so, disillusioned, heartsick, he had written to Rupert, telling him that he was discharged from his service, and requesting him to leave England. It was typical of Rupert that he would not allow such a stain to remain on his character. Accompanied by Prince Maurice, he had sought audience with the King. At that audience he had entreated his uncle to see his action not as the disloyal act of treason it appeared to be, but merely an act of indiscretion. The King, because Rupert was the son of his sister, had allowed Rupert to believe he accepted this as an explanation of his conduct, but in his heart he still called it treason. Rupert, studying the King's face, and finding it devoid of passion, had been satisfied. Feeling himself absolved from any hint of treachery, he had bowed his way from the King's presence. Shortly after that incident, he and Maurice had left England.

Glancing at the King's brooding face, my lord Foxe had gone on to say, "While the Prince of Wales lives, the royal cause will never be lost. When the Prince departed for the Scilly Isles, he removed himself still further from danger. A wise move on the part of Hyde and Colepepper to take him there. I understand that the Prince raised serious objections to the move. I am glad that reason finally prevailed.''

The King smiled for the first time, ''Ah, but the Prince is no longer in the Scilly Isles.''

''What!'' Brett exclaimed in dismay. ''You are not telling me that he is coming back here to face this turmoil?''

''Nay.'' The King shook his head. ''And I thank God for that mercy. He has joined the Queen in France. It might be that he would have resisted, had not Marcus Milford arrived on the scene to persuade him. They are both in France now. I understand that the young Duke of Buckingham will shortly join them.''

''Charles, Marcus, and George,'' Brett said thoughtfully. ''In that case I imagine that Tony will likewise be clamoring to go. He will, of course, have some difficulty with his mother. Had Meredith her way, she would keep him in leading strings. But he is of an age now where we cannot really command him. Were we to try, he'd probably run off without our consent. Aye, you may be sure that Tony will take ship for France.''

The King's face saddened. ''You know, Brett, I still find it difficult to believe that John is dead and that Marcus is now my lord Butler. I suppose I should remember to call him thus.''

Brett smiled. ''You will remember, Charles. Marcus has a natural dignity, and such a presence for his age that he could be no other than my lord Butler.'' He laughed. ''They are a couple of rogues, Charles and Marcus. Tony and Buckingham are quite inexperienced beside them when it comes to tumbling the wenches.''

The King returned his smile. ''Aye, and Tony and Buckingham are older. Charles takes after his grandfather, I fear. His maternal grandfather.''

''And Marcus?''

''Let us say that the lad has a natural bent for that kind of thing,'' the King returned dryly.

''I had thought he despised females.''

"So he does. I deplore to see his nature so twisted out of shape through the fault of his mother, but that does not prevent him pleasuring himself with the wenches. But I fear that Marcus will never form a lasting attachment with any female. He is far too contemptuous of them."

"The day may come."

"I take leave to doubt it. She would have to be a most unusual female to hold Marcus's interest for more than a week. His chronic suspicion and distrust would, I imagine, be hard to fight."

"I suppose he sees something of Lady Mary in all of them."

"Aye," the King agreed. "Or thinks that he does."

"If a lady does succeed in conquering him, we must take off our hats to her."

"I would do so with the greatest of pleasure. I have grown very fond of Marcus, and I think that I have, in part, penetrated the barriers he erects. I would like to see him happy."

The King's thoughts drifted away from that conversation rather reluctantly. He would have preferred to dwell on that rather than his present troubles. But they were too persistent, niggling at his mind until he was forced to face reality. After the defeat of Naseby, the war was too all intents and purposes at an end. But negotiations, fruitless for the most part, still went on between him and Parliament. He himself, determined that Parliament should recognize the authority of the church and the crown, would not listen to any suggestion for an alteration in the rights and privileges pertaining to both. On their side, the Parliamentarians were determined to reduce the church and crown to nothing. And so it was that the King's council urged him to enter into negotiations with his erstwhile enemies. That they were still his most implacable enemies was proved when they refused to listen to anything, however reasonable, that he might have to say. He listened to Montreuil, the ambassador extraordinary sent by the King of France, whose object was to act as mediator between the King and the Scottish commissioners, who were showing a disposition to befriend the King. The terms of the Scots were hard, however. The King of England must, if he valued their friendship, take the covenant.

Charles frowned, remembering his rage at that time. "I will do anything within reason," he replied. "But I tell you now, good gentlemen, I would rather lose my crown than my soul. If the trend of the times is such that Presbyterianism must rule the souls and the hearts of my people, then I will tolerate it. No more! You ask too much of me!"

To their argument that, through their influence, he could regain his crown, he had returned the same answer.

After that, there was, for a time, only an ominous silence from the Scots, then, to his surprise, they returned a soft answer. He need not take the covenant. They begged His Gracious Majesty to remember that, while his own Parliament refused to allow him to come to Westminster, they, his loyal Scottish servants, were prepared to receive him into their army.

"But this I cannot do," Charles exclaimed to Montreuil. "What purpose would it serve?"

"Your Majesty," Montreuil answered smoothly, "I greatly fear that your only safety lies with the Scottish army. They are gentlemen of their word. They have said that they will receive you with the honor due to their sovereign, and that they will at all times respect your royal person." Montreuil toyed with the enameled snuff box in his hand. Snapping it open, he took a pinch of snuff. He did not ask permission, and this act, small though it was, served to indicate to the King his lowered position. Montreuil returned the box to his pocket. "I repeat, Your Majesty, there is no question that your safety lies with the Scots."

"Even were I to consider it," he had answered Montreuil, "you know well that I am watched on all sides."

Montreuil smiled. In the tone of one who admonishes a child to listen and to take heed, he said, "General Fairfax is advancing upon Oxford. Should Your Majesty fall into his hands, your position will be perilous indeed. The civil war is over, but they will capture you if they can. A deposed King would be a magnificent trophy."

459

"I am not yet deposed, sir."

"It is only a matter of time before you are formally declared so. You need the Scots."

"You are strangely insistent, sir. In any case, I have always heard that General Fairfax is an honorable man. If he conveyed me to Westminster, I believe that I could successfully plead my case."

Montreuil looked at him pityingly. "I do not doubt General Fairfax's honor, but he has his orders. You are not wanted, Sire, 'tis best to face that fact. Whatever offers and accommodations you may make to him, Fairfax, whether or no it be against his inclination, will be forced to reject them. He will return you to London, but not in honor, as you desire, and have the right to expect, but as a prisoner. But, if Your Majesty is prepared to assume a disguise, it may be possible to escape from Oxford before the general's coming. For instance, you might travel as the manservant of my lady Foxe, save that she will not be known by that title."

"So that I may then proceed to the welcoming Scots," Charles answered bitterly.

"Exactly so, Sire. And a great welcome you will find," Montreuil assured him, quite unruffled by the King's attitude.

What else could he have done? the King thought. On April 27th, armed with forged passes, he had ridden over Magdalene Bridge, accompanied by Mistress Fawcett, as Meredith was to be known, John Ashburnham, Michael Hudson, and my lord Foxe, known on his pass as Master Tobley. Now they were here, at the King's Arms Inn, awaiting the arrival of Montreuil and the Scottish commissioners.

Aware that a silence had fallen, the King turned his head again. He met Brett's eyes, and the expression in them filled him with apprehension. Brett had been against this move. "I do not trust the Scots," he had said. "Montreuil assures you that you will be taken to London and held as prisoner if you do not take advantage of the Scottish offer. But have you thought, Charles, how easy it will be for the Scots to make you prisoner, if such be their inclination?"

"And do you feel it will be their inclination?"

"I do, Charles. I find myself filled with uneasiness."

Always before, Charles thought, I have listened to my lord Foxe, and, in general, I have taken his advice. But this time, I have not. Will I regret it, as that look in his eyes is telling me that I shall?

The other two men were gazing into the fire, but Meredith was watching him wide-eyed. She too seemed to have taken on some of my lord Foxe's uneasiness.

"It is not too late for you to depart," Charles said suddenly. "I am arrived safely at my destination, thanks to all of you." He leaned forward, his manner urgent. "Go! Go with my blessing."

Brett got up and walked over to the King. "What is it, Charles? Are you regretting that you allowed Montreuil to persuade you?"

Charles shook his head. "My lord, how can I know what to think? I am beset on all sides. But if your suspicion be correct, I would not have you taken prisoner with myself."

"If we go, will you come with us?"

"Nay. I am weary of running, weary of hiding. The time has come, my lord, when I must put my trust in someone, else am I entirely lost."

"Then we stay, Charles."

"I beseech you to go, my dear friend." Charles looked at the others. "All of you, all my dear friends."

"Where you go, we go. It can be no other way."

Meredith made a soft sound of pity as she saw the moved look on the King's face, the tears that filled his eyes. Rising to her feet, she ran to him. "Sire! Dear Sire!" She fell to her knees before him. Taking his hand, she pressed her lips to it. "Know you not that we will ever be yours to command?"

"If I did not, my lady," Charles said, smiling at her, "then I

461

would be a very stupid man.'' He looked across at the other two men. "John, Michael? You are free to go, you know.''

John Ashburnham and Michael Hudson rose. "We are not free, Your Majesty,'' Ashburnham replied, "because we have not that wish. I stay!''

"And I, Majesty,'' Hudson echoed. He looked round, his bright eyes including them all in his glance. "I fear Your Majesty is burdened with us, for I can see that we all have a like determination.''

" 'Tis a very loyal picture, I perceive,'' Montreuil's voice said from the doorway. He looked at the kneeling Meredith. "But it will not do, Your Majesty. Suppose it had been the innkeeper who entered, instead of myself?''

"But it was not,'' Charles answered coldly, realizing that he had little liking for the tall blond man with the piercing brown eyes. He looked beyond him at the group of men standing behind him. "Come in, gentlemen, I pray you.''

The four Scottish commissioners, headed by Montreuil, advanced into the room. One by one they bowed before the King. Retiring to a few paces, they looked uneasily at each other. At last, when the silence grew strained, one of them spoke. "My name is Ian MacGregor, Your Majesty. I am empowered to ask if you, Sire, surrender to us your person willingly?''

The King hesitated, but only briefly. "I do, sir.''

MacGregor bowed. " 'Tis well, Sire.'' His blue eyes swept over the King's four companions. "We have no orders to take these people.''

Brett stepped closer. "Yet you will take us,'' he said in a harsh voice. "We will not leave the King.''

The man's face darkened. He seemed disposed to argue this point, but a murmur from his companions caused him to change his mind. "Very well,'' he said stiffly. "Doubtless accommodation can be arranged.'' He turned to the King. "Your Majesty will not object to signing a paper? 'Tis merely a formality, proving that you come to us of your own free will.''

Charles's eyes met Brett's. He thought that he read a warning in them, but he was not sure. He said quietly, "Of a certainty, gentleman." He held out his hand. "Give me your paper."

Silence descended once more, the only sound in the room the scratching of the King's quill.

Oh, Charles, Brett thought, looking at the King's downbent head, his moving hand. God send that you will not regret this move! God send that my suspicions prove incorrect! He looked at Ian MacGregor. The man was smiling, but somehow he did not trust that smile.

Following them from the room, some thirty minutes later, his heart was heavy. It was wrong, he thought. I know it, I feel it!

Meredith's hand was on his arm. Her face looked so white and strained that Brett forced a smile. "My lady," he whispered. "I do not care for you in that bonnet. I fear it does nothing to aid your looks."

"And they need aiding, I suppose?" she answered in a low, indignant voice. "Be silent, my lord, lest your extravagant compliments overwhelm me."

"Merry," he bent his head nearer to hers. "Go home, my love. These gentlemen will not seek to detain you."

"And leave you? Certainly not!"

"I can take care of myself."

"Aye, but a fine mess you'd make of it. I stay."

He made one more effort. "Tony will need you."

"Tony is in France. And there he is likely to stay for a long time. Seek not to get rid of me, my lord, for you cannot do it."

Seated in the carriage, opposite the King and Brett, Meredith listened to the lumbering wheels of the vehicle following them, and she found herself praying, "Dear Lord, let the Scots prove friends. Let them not show to the King the faces of enemies! Aid him, comfort him! And if we do find that we have walked into a trap, restrain my lord Foxe from exercising his fiery temper against our enemies. For I do not want him harmed!"

Chapter
Twenty-Six

The men bearing the sedan chair proceeded slowly along Whitehall. They were on their way to Sir Robert Cotton's house, which was the destination of their royal passenger. The men tried to make their minds a blank, for neither of them wanted to remember that Sir Robert's house was conveniently situated near Westminster Hall, where the King was to be tried for his life on a charge of high treason against the English nation. Walking bare-headed beside the chair was my lord Foxefield. Struggling to control his emotions, he stared fixedly ahead. Slightly behind him was Herbert, the King's personal attendant. The nobleman and the loyal servant. The only two permitted to attend the King in his hour of need.

Behind the stiffly drawn up guards lining the streets, their uniforms a note of color in the gray drabness of the day, were crowds of people who had gathered to watch the King pass by. News of the trial of the King of England had leaked out. Though, it was quickly realized by the more knowledgeable, it was not so much a case of leakage as a subtle spreading of the news. It was

464

hoped that the King's enemies would be there to shout and boo. However, those who felt so inclined were intimidated by the suggestion of violence about them. The tide had turned once more in favor of the King, and the majority of the people, men and women alike, were silently weeping. Small children, looking up at the grieving adults in wonder, began to weep in sympathy. Those of them who had at one time thought they had genuine grievances against the King, forgot them now. Bitterness against the rebel government had taken its place. They were crippled with heavy taxes, oppressed by the soldiers, and their minds went back with increasing longing to the days when King Charles had ruled. All eyes were on the sedan chair, the focal point. It was their own King, the prisoner of a government they were rapidly learning to detest, who passed by. Their King, who must shortly begin the fight for his life. There was not one of them there, not even those who openly proclaimed themselves to be his enemy, who doubted that the King would emerge triumphant from his ordeal. In most faces there was a sullen resentment of this indignity to his royal person. How dare this upstart government lay hands upon their King! How dare they confine him, force him to answer to charges like some common felon!

A wave of emotion passed through the assembled poeple. Some of them remembered him walking through the park, the streets, attended by his gentlemen. He had a ready smile for all who passed by. They remembered his gay and colorful clothes, his plume-laden hats, his long locks that were always so exquisitely curlcd. What a contrast to the drab clothes of Oliver Cromwell and the members of the Houses. Now, instead of smiles, there were sober faces. The people could no longer enjoy themselves, for all places of entertainment had been closed. They must be restrained in their clothing. Any riband, even the smallest piece of lace, was frowned upon. To laugh aloud was a positive sin. The emotion gripping them was so palpable that the soldiers holding the crowd back felt their hearts begin a heavier beating. They tightened their grip upon their muskets and braced themselves in anticipation of a possible rush.

A man cried out in a shaken, almost hysterical voice, "It was only yesterday that I saw the King. He was seated in his carriage. I saw his eyes on me, and out of respect for him, I took off my hat. The King did likewise to me. But the soldiers guarding him were displeased with my act of reverence. They dismounted, then they seized me and threw me into a ditch. Think of it, my friends, we are not allowed to show reverence to our own King. For shame! For shame!"

Alarmed by the ominous muttering behind them, the soldiers stole quick, furtive glances at each other. Would they be able to hold this crowd back? Would sympathy for King Charles overcome the rigidly imposed law and order?

My lord Foxefield heard nothing, saw nothing, was conscious of nothing but the nightmare. He had warned Charles not once but several times that the Scots were not to be trusted. How tragically right had he proved to be. The Scots had held the King a prisoner for nearly a year. In that time they had constantly harried him to take the covenant and to establish Presbyterianism in all three kingdoms. They had said to him, "If Your Majesty will do this, we will proclaim you King of Scotland. And from that point, Sire, we will work zealously to restore you to the throne of England."

The King found himself deeply offended by these machinations, and he firmly refused their offer. After that, he was uneasily aware that the baffled Scots could and possibly would use him to make bargains with the English Parliament, who were equally anxious to have his person in their possession. Time had dragged by. There had been many discussions between the Scots leaders and the English Parliament. Then the Scots made their infamous bargain. If the English would pay them the sum of four hundred thousand pounds, they would surrender the person of the King and withdraw their armies. The English government accepted their terms.

Brett winced at the memory. As long as he lived he would never forget the King's shocked and haggard face when he heard of this bargain. Wild-eyed, he paced the room. "Oh, God!" he cried out in his agony. "I am sold and bought!"

Meredith, who was present, had forgotten everything but the need to comfort the King. When, exhausted, he sank into a chair and covered his face with his hands, Meredith ran to him and took him in her arms. "There," she said, soothing him as if he had been Tony. "There, there, we will not let this happen. We will find a way out!"

Gently Charles released himself from her cradling arms. "If there were a way out, my lady," he said, attempting a smile, "I am sure you would find it." He touched her cheek with his finger. "Do not be too sympathetic, else will you unman me. I must accustom myself to face these trials."

There had been no way out. Nothing that they could do. The King was taken to the Palace of Holdenby. On the way, he had said to Brett, "I am thankful, my lord Foxe, that Hudson and Ashburnham managed to escape from Newcastle. It may be, as they hoped, that they can do something to aid me." He put his thin hand on Brett's arm and squeezed gently. "It is selfish of me, I fear, but I am glad that you and your lady are with me. Without you, I would feel completely deserted."

It was then that, for the first time in a great many years, Brett felt an inclination to weep. Instead, he had forced a light note into his voice, "Bah! You know well that you will never be rid of us." The light note failed as he added, "As long as you live, as long as you have need of us, we will always be there, Charles."

A shudder shook Brett. As long as he lived! Dear Christ, to what had the King of England been reduced? He thought of their weary journeying from one prison to another. For the most part the King had been treated with respect, but they were still prisons. From Holdenby, whence he had been removed by Cornet Joyce and a troop of five hundred horse, acting, Joyce said, on the authority of the army, the King had gone to Childerly Hall. There he had met with Oliver Cromwell and General Fairfax.

Cromwell, his normally pale face red, had spoken defiantly to

467

the King. "I am aware, Sire, that Cornet Joyce informed you that he acted upon the authority of the army. I hope, however, that you will believe me when I tell you that I had no part in it."

Charles noticed that General Fairfax was regarding Cromwell with open contempt. "I find it hard to believe that you had no part in Cornet Joyce's action," Charles said quietly. "One might say that you are the army. Such instructions would have surely had your full and complete knowledge."

Cromwell did not answer at first, for he had become aware of Fairfax's contemptuous expression. Flushing a deeper red, he glared angrily at the General. "I am sure Your Majesty is aware that Fairfax too has no small part in the army?"

Charles answered him in a cool voice. "Aye. General Fairfax is a good soldier and a man of honor." His eyes appraised Cromwell. "You too are a good soldier, a genius in fact, but you are not a man of honor."

Cromwell lost his precarious hold on his temper. "It is not for you to insult me!" he shouted. "You are no longer of account. You are nothing!"

The King smiled. "But I know who I am, and in what account I hold myself." His light, faintly amused tone was not lost on the fuming Cromwell. "Deny it though you may, my good sir, I am Charles Stuart, King of England, and will be until the day I die."

"That day may not be long in coming," Cromwell growled.

Charles, noticing the dangerous glitter in Brett's eyes, threw him a warning look. He spoke to Cromwell in an even voice. "Your remark cannot but rejoice me, sir. I would sooner die than live under these conditions."

"You would sooner die?" Cromwell's lip curled. "We will see how we may accommodate you."

"You are a brave soldier and a brilliant organizer," Charles answered him. "These admirable qualities, however, do little to mitigate a personality that I find offensive in the extreme. You will leave my presence at once."

" 'Twill pleasure me to do so. I do not care to look too long upon a ruined man, and one who has ever been but a poor excuse for a King!'' Jamming his hat on his head, Cromwell strode away.

General Fairfax looked uncertainly at Charles. "Sire," he said hesitantly, "permit me to apologize for myself and for Mr. Cromwell."

Charles smiled. "For yourself, General, there is no need. You do your duty as you conceive it must be done. But I know well that you bear me no personal animosity."

"Indeed I do not, Sire. There are many things in which you and I could never be in agreement, but as a man, I like you well. I fought in this war because I believed in the principles for which it stood." A look of distress clouded his face. "But now all these good and righteous things seem to have become strangely twisted. Sire, I no longer know what to believe."

"Never lose faith in yourself, General," Charles said gently. "I am the last one who should tell you this, yet that is my advice to you."

Fairfax stared at him. Then, as though unable to help himself, he went down on his knees and bowed his head. "Whatever may come of it, Sire," he said huskily, "I find that I am unable to forget that you are the King. If ever I should discover that I have fought on the wrong side, my life will become unbearable. But right or wrong, I earnestly crave your forgiveness."

"You have it, General. But pray rise to your feet. If your superior should view this act of homage, he might conceive it to be his duty to punish you."

Fairfax rose without haste. "You are the King, Sire," he said, bowing low. "Others may forget it, but I cannot."

Charles's eyes followed him as he strode away. "He is my enemy," he said softly to Brett, "but an honorable enemy. I wish that things might have been otherwise, for Fairfax is a good man, and would have made a staunch friend."

It was true, Brett thought. As long as Fairfax continued to believe in the things for which he had fought, he would be the King's relentless enemy. But he was honorable, and he would have no desire to take the King's life. But Cromwell would.

469

Others like him would. How weary the King must be, how little rest he was allowed. After his short visit to Childerly Hall, he had been forced to follow after the army. For more than four months he had been continually on the move. The only bright spots in that harrowing time were, as he passed, the cheers of his people. Cheers which the soldiers had been quite unable to suppress. Then there was the short visit from the King's children, the Princess Elizabeth and young Henry, the Duke of Gloucester. The meeting took place at the Greyhound Inn at Maidenhead. The children were accompanied by the Earl of Northumberland, whom Parliament had made their guardian.

Seven-year-old Henry, forgetting dignity, gave a squeal of joy when he saw the King. Flinging himself into his father's arms, he hugged him tightly. "Papa! Papa!"

Elizabeth, twelve years old, grown tall and slender, had a gravity of expression that did not, however, detract from her quite astonishing prettiness. She smiled shyly at her father before rebuking Henry in her gentle voice. "Henry, you know quite well that you must bow to our father. You must not throw yourself into his arms as though you have been taught no manners at all."

The King hugged the boy closer. "Nay, my daughter," he said, holding out his hand to Elizabeth, "let us forget decorum for the moment. Let us be as other fathers and children, and greet each other with all the joy that is in our hearts."

Elizabeth placed her hand in his. Then suddenly, impulsively, for her, she drew her hand away and wound both arms about his neck. "How I have missed you, my dear, dear Father!"

Later, when the King was seated at a table with Brett and Meredith either side and the children facing him, he said in a low, troubled voice, "Elizabeth, how do you and Henry go on at Syon House?"

For a moment Elizabeth hesitated. Brett had the impression that she was sorting words in her mind, choosing them with care that she might not add to her father's worries. "It is pleasant there," she said finally. "We are kindly treated."

Henry frowned. "They do not beat us, if that is what you mean, 'Lizabeth," he chimed in, "but I for one do not like it there. I want to see my Mama and my new baby sister. I want to see Charles and James. Oh, Papa, when will we all be together again?"

There were tears in Charles's eyes. "I wish I knew, my son. I can only tell you that your mother and little Henrietta Anne are both thriving, for which God be thanked. As for Charles and James, I feel sure that you will see them soon."

Henry looked resentful for a moment. "When James escaped from St. James's Palace, why did he not take 'Lizabeth and I with him?"

"It was not possible, Henry. James had much ado to take care of himself. I was relieved beyond measure when word was brought to me that he had landed safely in France."

"I am angry that we could not escape with James," Henry said, his eyes beginning to shine, "but when I think how he escaped, I am not so angry." He giggled. "Was it not a great joke, Papa? Imagine James dressed up as a woman, and passing under the very noses of our enemies. I wonder if any of those men tried to flirt with him?"

Elizabeth glanced nervously over her shoulder. "Hush!" she admonished the boy. "Be careful of what you say."

"I will not! I am glad James escaped. I am glad he managed to fool those bad men."

"So am I. But you must not call them bad men."

"Why not?" Henry demanded belligerently. "They are our enemies, and that makes them bad men." He glared at the Earl of Northumberland, who was seated a little distance from them. "They are all bad men. I hope one of them tried to flirt with James and kiss him. James would have given him such a punch!" His eyes began to sparkle again. "Aye, James would probably have killed the rogue!"

"Do be quiet!"

" 'Lizabeth is too nervous, is she not, Papa?"

Brett laughed, saving the King the necessity of answering.

"Your words conjure up an amusing picture, Henry. The thought of James held in the brawny arms of a soldier, struggling to preserve his virginity, is highly diverting."

" 'Tis only in Henry's imagination, my lord," Elizabeth said, looking at Brett with her grave eyes. "I am sure that such a thing could not have happened." She glanced at Meredith. "Do you not agrcc, my lady?"

Meredith gave her a warm smile. "I do. We must pay them no attention, for they are being foolish."

Henry looked inclined to argue this, but after a moment he went on wistfully. "Do you know, I think that I miss Charles and Marcus most of all? I would that I could be with them."

"I miss Charles," Elizabeth said, her smooth forehead wrinkling, "but I am not sure if I miss my lord Butler. Marcus was always very polite and respectful to me, but I had the impression that he did not like me very much."

"It is because you are a girl," Henry said importantly. "Marcus thinks girls are silly, as I do. And do not call him my lord Butler again, 'Lizabeth. He will always be Marcus to us."

Elizabeth did not answer him. From the corner of her eye she had seen the Earl of Northumberland rising to his feet. It was the signal that the visit was over. Tears sprang into her eyes. "Oh, Papa!" she cried in a breaking voice, "soon the Earl will be taking us away, and I had so much I wanted to say to you!"

Charles reached out and took her trembling hand in his. "Do not distress yourself, my Elizabeth. There will be many other times when we will meet and talk."

She looked at him, her eyes too tragic, too knowledgeable for a girl of her years. "I hope so, Papa. But sometimes I cannot help but wonder what is to become of us."

Frightened by something he saw in his sister's face, Henry sprang to his feet. Glaring at the Earl, he shouted, "I will not go! I wish to stay with my Papa. You cannot make me go!"

The Earl of Northumberland came closer and looked apologetically at the King. "I am sorry, Your Grace," he muttered, "but I have my orders. I trust that you understand, Sire?"

"I do." Charles rose to his feet. "Come, Henry, all is well. "Do not cause a scene and make me ashamed of you."

"But, Papa, I—"

"No, my son," Charles interrupted, "say good-bye like a man. Comfort yourself in the knowledge that we will soon meet again."

For a moment it seemed that Henry would rebel. Then, unconsciously responding to the appeal in his father's eyes, he bowed low. "I take my farewell of you, Your Majesty," he said in a clear and steady voice. "As you have said, we will soon meet again." He looked at Brett and Meredith, his eyes overbright in his white face. "My lord, my lady," he said, inclining his head.

"Bravo, my little Duke!" Brett said softly.

Henry's pale face flushed with pleasure at this compliment from a man whom he admired intensely. His eyes smiled his appreciation. But when he turned once more to the Earl of Northumberland, his bearing was haughty. "I am ready, my lord," he said in a cold voice. "You need not fear that I will try to escape you."

"I am sure you will not, Your Grace," the Earl replied gravely.

Elizabeth was shaken out of her reserve. She was trembling as she curtsied before the King. "I bid you farewell, Your Majesty."

Charles raised her from her curtsey and took her into his arms. "God be with you, Elizabeth, my darling," he whispered. He held out his hand to Henry. "And with you, my dear son!"

It seemed to Brett that something inside Charles Stuart broke as he watched his children depart, for he was never quite the same again. The melancholy to which he was naturally prone deepened. He scarcely seemed to notice when his little retinue of gentlemen, who had joined him at Childerly Hall, were ordered to depart. But, showing that the leave-taking had indeed affected him, he said to Brett, "I believe, if you and your lady were ordered to depart me, I would do something desperate!"

Brett believed him. He was, he thought, perilously near the

breaking point. It was fortunate that the King's enemies, who seemed so anxious to strip him of comfort and companionship, had apparently taken the presence of himself and Meredith for granted. But if the time ever came, Brett resolved, when they were ordered to leave the King, it would be he, not Charles, who would do something desperate.

They were still with the King when he was taken, under the guard of Colonel Hammond, to Carisbrooke Castle, of which Colonel Hammond was the governor. When the King proceeded through the town of Newport toward the castle, he was immensely encouraged by the loyalty of the inhabitants, who cheered him to the echo, and by a simple act of homage from a young girl. The girl, pointedly ignoring Colonel Hammond and the small party of soldiers guarding the King, handed him a half-opened rose, and said in a loud, defiant voice, "God bless Your Majesty! We are all with you, every one of us!" She glared about her, as though defying anyone to contradict her. Nobody did.

Smiling, the King pressed the rose to his lips. "In my dark hours, mistress, which I fear will be many, your kindness and loyalty will comfort me."

So began the King's imprisonment in the fortresslike Carisbrooke Castle. For a short time he was not uncomfortable there, for Hammond had given over his own rooms. But Colonel Hammond who, because he was the nephew of one of the King's trusted chaplains, Henry Hammond, had been thought a friend, soon proved that he was nothing of the sort. He was a stiff military man who thought only of his duty. To Hammond, the King, by force of circumstances, was virtually dethroned. The King had refused to meet the impossible terms of the Parliamentary members who came to visit him at the castle, and to the governor, this made the sovereign responsible for the overthrow of the English Constitution. Angrily he refused all requests made by the King, no matter how simple.

Hammond's ire grew when it became known that a large proportion of the people were once more rallying to Charles. In

474

Wales, the people proclaimed him King. The uprising in the King's favor was so violently loyal that Cromwell, with several regiments riding behind him, journeyed forth to put down the rebellion. He succeeded. But for a time there had been serious alarm within the ranks of the King's enemies. The guard about Carisbrooke Castle was doubled. It was reinforced yet more when Captain Burley, a one-time naval officer, caused a drum to be beaten through the streets of Newport. "To the aid of the King!" the captain shouted in a stentorian voice. "Come men, come lads, come one and all! We'll have our King released from his prison, or we will die in the attempt!"

Before the small rebellion was crushed, several did die. The fiercely loyal, elderly Captain Burley was hanged.

The King made two attempts to escape, but neither succeeded. His spirits rose again when, despite the spies all about him, he managed to smuggle out letters to the Queen. It was Meredith who made this possible. She took fantastic risks that the King might have this small comfort.

In September of 1648, fifteen Parliamentary commissioners arrived in Newport, their object being to treat with the King. So Charles, having given his word that he would not attempt to escape, left Carisbrooke Castle and took lodgings in the home of Sir William Hopkins. That meeting between the King and the Parliamentary commissioners lasted six weeks. It was a hopeless situation from the first, for everything remained as it had been before. The King found that he was not expected to have a mind of his own, but rather, like a puppet on a string, to submit meekly to the demands of his enemies. One of the articles submitted by Parliament was that the King should give up those friends who had loyally aided him in the civil war. He refused, and the Treaty of Newport, as it was called, came to a dismal end.

Brett was alarmed by the lowering faces of the commissioners. He felt that the King's refusal to meet their demands placed his life in serious danger.

"Sire," Brett said, "I am greatly concerned for you. I beg you to reconsider Parliament's proposals."

Charles smiled that new and weary smile, but there was a ghost of a twinkle in his eyes as he answered. "This from you, my lord Foxe? Did I not know better, I would believe you to be turning coward."

"Aye, Charles, I am turning coward. But for you! For you! Listen to me. If you do not reconsider, I fear that your life may be in danger!"

Charles shook his head. "Their proposals are absurd and insulting. And one of them, impossible. I will never betray my friends. Hast forgotten, my lord, that you are one of those friends?"

"I have not forgotten, but I can take care of myself. So can the others. In the name of Christ, Charles, I beg you to look to yourself! There is not a one of us that will think of it as a betrayal. We will know that you spoke only to save your life."

"And are you so sure that my life is in danger?"

"Aye, Charles, I am very sure. Word has been smuggled to me that some officers have met to draw up a remonstrance against you. For the blood that has been shed during this cursed war, they are demanding that you be punished. But this threat might yet be averted if you meet the demands of Parliament."

Charles was silent for a moment, then he said in a tired voice, "In the long run it will make no difference, Brett. If, as you say, they wish my life, they will find a means of taking it."

"Charles, you must submit for the time being. It will give us time to arrange your escape."

"I regret, Brett, my friend, but I cannot submit. My conscience is already heavily burdened. I will do no more. Nay, not even to save my life."

Once more the King's words to the Parliamentary commissioners rang through Brett's head. It was almost as though the King were repeating the words in his ear. To the departing men, he had said in a voice weighted with sadness, "My lords, I doubt if we shall meet again. I would wish you to know that I have made my peace with God. I thank Him most humbly for past blessings bestowed upon me. I think I can say that I will, without fear, suffer all that my enemies may contrive to do to me.'' His dark eyes flashed angry fire as he pointed an accusing finger at them. "But think not that I am ignorant of the plot against me and mine. My true pain comes with the sight of the suffering of my people, and with my great fear that men are preparing many evils for them. And these men are those who, while constantly prating of the public good, work in secret to further their own ambitions!''

After the King had finished speaking, the men went silently away. Brett, observing them, knew that they were greatly shaken by the King's words.

At nights, in the darkness of his bedchamber, Brett could find no rest. Tossing and turning, his brain burning, he tried to think of ways to save the King from his certain fate. They will take his life! The words were beating hammers in his brain. They will seek to impress upon the generations to come that, in murdering the King, they did but work for England's good. They will say that the King worked for his country's destruction!

It was not until the soldiers came for the King, this time removing him from the house of Sir William Hopkins and transferring him to grim Hurst Castle, that Brett truly understood that his worst fears were to be realized. Before, he could tell himself that he was worrying for nothing, that he was surely wrong. Now he could no longer do so.

Hurst Castle! He would never forget it! Wrapped in the nightmare of memory, Brett walked on beside the sedan chair quite oblivious of the gaping crowd. In his mind the castle rose up before him once again. A gray place, a forbidding place, with its great thick walls standing upon barren earth. A place to shudder at, and yet it was here that they had lodged their sovereign. The King's room was small and dark and comfortless. If he was to find his way about, candles must burn at all hours. The whole castle was impregnated by the foul odors that rose from the swamp ground about the castle, and it seemed, too, always to be bound about by dense fogs. Small wonder that in that place not fit to house a dog let alone a man the King's health should suffer. There he had lived for some time, uncomplaining, except occasionally to his closest friends.

The soldiers came for him again, and once more the King was on the move. But this time he went with joy in his heart, for Major Harrison and a troop of a thousand men had come to escort him to his favorite residence, Windsor Castle.

Brett's mouth tightened. The King had been happy at Windsor, he had almost begun to hope again. But Brett still had his spies. These men, staunchly loyal to the King, reported to Brett that the Commons had voted that the King be summoned for public trial.

Brett thought of the quiet dignity with which Charles had accepted this further blow from fate. When he had been told that he must now be transferred to London to stand trial, he had simply said, "If it please God to forge me in the fire of adversity, then I am ready."

Brett put his hand on the side of the sedan chair. Almost immediately he felt the warm pressure of the King's fingers on his. " 'Tis a tragic thing that a King must stand trial for his life," Charles said in a clear voice, "and it will be my life they will demand, I know it, Brett. But the fight is not yet over. When I am dead, my son Charles will be King of England. Help him, my dear friend, help him to bring this long and bitter struggle to an end, so that he may have a new and glorious beginning." Again the King's thin fingers pressed Brett's. "God save King Charles the Second!"

His eyes stinging with tears, Brett responded, "God save King Charles the Second!" The words were no sooner out of his mouth than his heart gave a horrified leap. What was he saying? His words implied that the King of England had already been tried and condemned!

His thoughts must have reached the King, for Charles said calmly, "Nay, Brett, do not torture yourself. We both know how this sorry business must end."

Brett looked down at him. Despite the King's calm manner,

there was pleading in his eyes. "I will help your son, Charles," Brett said quickly. "I promise you!"

With a last pressure, the King's hand fell away. Brett could think of nothing more to say, indeed, he had no words to express his raging inner grief. There were many, he knew, who would seek to restore a Stuart to the throne of England, and he hoped sincerely that he would have a part in it. The young Lord Butler certainly would. Cromwell and his cohorts would most certainly seek the death of the King's son, even as they now sought the King's. But it must not be. Young Charles must live! He must live to fulfill his destiny!

Chapter
Twenty-Seven

It was all over. The savage mockery of a trial, everything. The King of England had been condemned to death!

On the morning before his death, Brett watched with pain-filled eyes as the King put on an extra shirt to shield him from the cold. He wanted to say something to Charles, anything, but his throat was too constricted. He envied Herbert, the King's personal attendant, who was frankly crying. It would be a relief, he thought, to break down, to be able to sob out his misery and despair. But in the face of the King's calm acceptance of his fate, he could do no less than endeavor to uphold him in his hour of need.

The King, looking up, caught Brett's eyes upon him, "You are no doubt wondering why I trouble myself with an extra shirt, my lord Foxe?" he said, smiling. "I have a reason, believe me."

Brett swallowed and managed words. "Knowing you, Sire," he said hoarsely, "I am sure of it."

The King nodded. "The Thames is frozen over. Indeed the

weather is so severe that without this extra shirt I might begin to shiver.'' His eyes met Brett's. ''I would not wish to shiver. My people might remark it and believe that I shivered out of cowardice.''

''Charles!''

The King smiled at Brett's involuntary cry of protest. ''Come, Brett, you have ever been one to look facts in the face. You must do so now. I am to die, there is no gainsaying it, is there?''

''Nay, Charles,'' Brett answered with all the bitterness of his grief and his rage. ''No gainsaying it at all.''

''Brett.'' Charles went to him and laid his hand on his rigid arm. ''Listen to me, my dear loyal friend. You must believe me when I tell you that I do not fear death, that it is not terrible to me.''

''Oh, Christ, Charles, do not!'' Brett turned from him abruptly.

Charles sighed. ''For this at least, be glad for me. Oh, I did fear death, but no longer. I thank my dear God that He has laid His consoling hand upon me. He has prepared me to face what must be.''

''Charles,'' Brett said in a tight voice, ''no doubt it relieves you to talk, but I do not think I can stand much more.''

''And my good friend fears he will show the shameful weakness of tears?'' Charles moved away from him. ''But you must not be ashamed, Brett. My good Herbert is not.''

Brett glared at Herbert's tear-streaked face, then he looked directly at the King. ''Nay, Charles,'' he said in a loud voice, ''I'll not cry for you. I'll waste no tears. Instead, I shall get on with the business of living, and its purpose, which shall be to vindicate you.''

''Amen to that, friend.'' The King sat down on a bench beneath the narrow window. ''Come, Brett, Herbert, pray to sit down. Colonel Hacker will be here soon to escort me to Whitehall, and there are things that I must say.'' He waited until both men had seated themselves before resuming. ''I wish to make disposal of my few remaining possessions.''

"Sire!" Herbert exclaimed in a choked voice.

Charles put his hand on Herbert's shoulder and pressed gently. "Come, you have upheld me thus far, Herbert. Only a little farther to go."

"Yes, Sire." Herbert bowed his head, his tears dropping on his black breeches.

"Good." Charles patted the heaving shoulder, then released it. "For you, Herbert, my striking clock. For you, Brett, my gold ring with the crest, and for my lady Foxe, my emerald thumb ring."

"Charles," Brett said desperately, "I want nothing. Think you that I need a momento to remember you by?"

"Or I, Sire," Herbert put in.

"Nay," Charles answered gently. "I know you need nothing to remember me by. 'Tis simply that I wish you to have them. Now pay me close attention. To my son Charles, I leave my bible, which, in this time of trial, I have found my greatest consolation. To my son James, my silver ring. To Henry, my catechism, and to Elizabeth, my daughter, my book of sermons." He paused. When he went on his voice was slightly unsteady. " 'Tis little enough to leave, I know, but 'tis all I have." He turned to Brett suddenly and gripped his arm fiercely. "To my daughter Mary, her father's dear love. And to my wife Henrietta Maria, my love and adoration as ever. To little Henrietta Anne, Charles's Minette, a loving memory." His fingers tightened, then fell away. "Tell them, my lord Foxe, let them know that I ever loved them, and that my last thoughts I shared with God and with them."

"I will tell them, Charles, have no fear." Brett's eyes met the King's. "And I will give to Henrietta Anne more than a loving memory. I will make her see you, hear you. She shall know your strength and goodness, and she shall walk in pride because you were her father."

Because Charles was moved, he tried to pass it off lightly, "Such words from my blunt-tongued, mocking friend! I had not thought to live to see the day."

"Yet you have, Charles. I would to God that—"

"Nay, Brett, do not say it. What is done is done. Nothing can save me now."

In the heavy silence that fell between them, the knock on the door was startlingly loud.

Charles stood up as Colonel Hacker, accompanied by the Bishop of London entered the room. The colonel, a short, burly, red-faced man, stood in an attitude of stiff attention. Without looking directly at the King, he said, "Your Majesty, it is time to depart for Whitehall."

"I am ready." Charles stooped slightly so that the shorter Herbert could place his cloak about his shoulders. "After you, Colonel."

Colonel Hacker looked at him then. "Your Majesty," he faltered, his pale-blue eyes brilliant with suppressed tears, "I must tell you that I deeply regret—that I—I—" he stopped, unable to say more.

"I know what you would say to me, Colonel," Charles said gently, "and I thank you for it. It is one more comfort that I take with me."

Colonel Hacker inclined his head. "If Your Majesty will follow me."

Charles, with the bishop beside him, and followed by my lord Foxefield and Herbert, stepped out into the biting cold of the January day. For a moment he paused, taking a deep draught of the crisp air, then he went forward. The guards fell into place behind him.

Charles was amazing, Brett thought. He walked through the park as jauntily as though he were out for an ordinary stroll. He even made small jokes to the captain of the guard, telling him that if he and his men could not manage to march faster, they would lose him altogether.

They were not far from Whitehall when an ugly incident occurred. A big man, dressed in a long coat of drab brown, a wide-brimmed hat pulled well down over his eyes, darted from the shelter of some trees and fell in beside the King. For a moment the man said nothing, then he made the gesture of drawing a finger across his throat. "Your bloody Majesty's going to feel the bite o' the axe soon, ain't you," he said loudly. "Blunt is that axe, I knows. You ain't going to die quick."

Sickened, Charles turned his face away. His expression murderous, Brett took a quick step forward, only to be restrained by the bishop's hand upon his arm.

"Captain!" the bishop addressed the captain of the guard in a cold, commanding voice. "Do your duty, if you please. You will either arrest that fellow, or have him driven away."

Before the captain could give a command, the man sprang away. Laughing, he ran back to the shelter of the trees. "You'll feel the bite," he called. "I promises you!"

For Brett, the rest of that day passed like a slow and neverending nightmare. If he felt this way, what must Charles be feeling? It was ten o'clock when they had arrived at Whitehall. The rooms in which the King was lodged to wait out the time before his death were comfortable. But in their very comfort, they emphasized the horror of what was to come. It was here that Bishop Juxon came to administer the sacrament to the King. In the middle of this, a knock sounded on the door. Five ministers, ignoring the King's refusal to see them, stood without. Nye, the leader of the group, looked defiantly at the Bishop. "We come to pray with the King," Nye said.

"The King does not wish to receive you," the bishop said, his face cold and set. "Go away, if you please."

"We bring God's word and his consolation," Nye insisted.

The King came forward then. Looking only at the bishop, he said, "Pray thank the good gentlemen. But tell them that as they have so often prayed against me, they shall never pray with me in my agony. They may, however, if they wish it, pray for me."

Defeated, the ministers turned away. Listening to the drone of the Bishop's voice as he prayed over the King, Brett wanted to smash his hands through the window panes. He wanted to shout to whoever might be listening, "Murderers! Murderers!"

When Meredith arrived some two hours later, she went straight to the King. "Sire, I am here."

Charles looked surprised. "I had not expected you, my lady Foxe." He looked at Brett. "Mayhap it would be better if your lady does not stay."

Before Brett could answer, Meredith said in a steady voice, "I hope that is not a command, Your Majesty, for I intend to stay. Forgive the disobedience, but I must stay."

"I understand." Charles put his arm about her and held her close for a moment. "We have been together this long time, and you would be with me to the end. But, my lady, it is not a pretty thing to see a man die."

Meredith looked at him for a long moment, then she pressed her wet cheek against his. "I know, dear Majesty, but do not send me from you!"

"If I did, would you go?"

She drew away from him. "Nay, Sire."

Charles laughed. "Then there is nothing more to be said. I am happy you are here, my lady. Your presence comforts me."

When dinner was served, the King, who had decided to touch nothing after receiving the sacrament, refused to eat. "But," he added, "it will please me greatly if the rest of you will eat."

"Sire," the bishop protested, "you must eat something."

"Must I? Nay, I think not."

Meredith, to whom Brett had related the story of the King's extra shirt, said cunningly, "The weather is very sharp, Sire. Without some food to sustain you, it might be that you would faint, perhaps falter."

The King looked sharply from Brett to Meredith. But, obviously struck by her words, he consented, though unwillingly, to eat a small piece of bread and to drink a glass of wine. "It would never do, my lady," he said, turning his dark eyes to Meredith's flushed face, "if I were to faint. I would never live it down."

"Nay, Sire, indeed you would not." Meredith turned away to hide her tears.

It was almost two o'clock on the following day, January 30th, when the King stepped onto the scaffold. The scaffold, draped all in black, had been built to accommodate at least sixteen people, most of whom were already assembled there. Just beyond, troops of soldiers ringed the place of execution about. Drawn up at stiff attention, they stared straight ahead. There was no lack of spectators, for the roofs of the nearby houses were crowded with those who had come to view the death of a king.

Brett felt sick as he followed Charles's slight figure onto the scaffold. He could feel Meredith's hand trembling violently in his, and he wanted to order her curtly to go away. Only the knowledge that she would refuse restrained him.

With burning eyes, Meredith stared at the block in the center of the scaffold, the axe beside it, and the tackle which was to be used to drag the King down to the block, should he refuse to kneel. Unconsciously Meredith's head rose proudly. They had no need of tackle with which to drag down the King. Charles would die with dignity, with pride. As he had lived so would he die. Her eyes fell on a long object covered with a black velvet cloth. It took her a moment to realize that it was the coffin that would house the King's body. A clumsy movement from a passer-by pulled the black velvet cloth away. She saw that the coffin was made of deal. It was cheap, roughly made, unvarnished. The King was to lie in that! Despite the chill of the day, perspiration broke out on Meredith's forehead. She clamped her lips tightly shut to suppress her cry of outrage. Outrage was lost in a wild terror as she saw the King's executioners mounting to the scaffold. The two men, apparently determined to conceal their identities, were like hideous figures from a nightmare. Their faces were covered by full masks, and through narrow slits their eyes glittered. Both wore obviously false wigs, one a brilliant red, the other night-black. From beneath the masks curling beards reached almost to their knees. They were wearing frieze breeches and tight fitting upper garments of a dull brown.

Brett, seeing them, drew in his breath sharply. Dear God! he prayed, his fingers tightening bruisingly about Meredith's hand. Let this hideous charade of death be over soon. Those macabre figures are to execute the King? Which one will swing the axe? Will it be red wig or black wig? God, how much more can he stand? How much more do You expect him to stand? His silent prayer broke and scattered when he saw that the King looked his way. He forced his dry lips to smile and, as he had done so often before, he gave a reassuring wink. Agony rose in a fresh hot wave as he saw the King respond. Oh, Charles, my King, my friend! He became aware that the King was about to begin his speech. Through the roaring in his ears, Brett tried hard to concentrate.

The King's voice came clear and steady. "I shall be very little heard of anybody here. I need not speak. Indeed I could hold my peace very well, if I did not think that holding my peace would make some men think I did submit to the guilt as well as the punishment. But I think it is my duty to God first and to my country to clear myself as an honest man, a good King, and a good Christian. I shall begin first with my innocency. In truth I think it not very needful for me to insist long upon this, for all the world knows that I never did begin a war with the two Houses of Parliament. And I call God to witness, to whom I must shortly make an account, that I never did intend for to encroach upon their privileges—"

The King's voice went on, but Brett was no longer listening. What would it do to England, this terrible act of regicide? Could a country that had put to death its crowned and annointed King, ever rise from the ashes of self-destruction? What of young Charles, the Prince of Wales, who had been willing to surrender his person to his enemies, if, in exchange, they would release his father? His offer had been ignored. The King was to die. They were determined upon it. Anger boiled in Brett's veins. First the King, then the Prince. His enemies would hunt him down, if they could. They would put him to death. His eyes slid to the most baleful enemy of them all, Oliver Cromwell. Cromwell was watching the King with an air of barely restrained impatience. He could not wait for the King's speech to end, he could not wait for the moment when the King would lay his head upon the block!

Meredith felt the tensing of Brett's figure, and she looked up in alarm. His eyes were fixed on Cromwell's face. "Brett!" she whispered. "Brett, please! You can do nothing."

Brett tore his eyes away with some difficulty. Bending his head so that his lips were on a level with Meredith's ear, he whispered, "By Christ and all His angels, I swear they'll not get their hands on the Prince!"

Meredith said nothing, but her fingers squeezed his in answer. Her heart began an agitated beating as she realized that the King was nearing the end of his speech. Well, what had she expected, a miracle? That the King would be reprieved at the last moment?

Charles's voice was lower now, but no less clear. "I shall not hold you much longer. I will say only thus to you. That in truth I could have desired some little time longer, because I would have put that which I have said in a little more order. Therefore, I hope you will excuse me. I have delivered my conscience. I pray God that you do take those courses that are best for the good of the kingdom and your own salvation."

There was a tense silence when the King's voice faded. Then the bishop stepped forward. "Your Majesty's affection toward religion is well known," he said in his deep grave voice, "yet it might be that you should say something further now." He looked at the King inquiringly.

Charles smiled into the gentle, anxious face. "I declare before you all that I die a Christian, according to the profession of the Church of England, as I found it left me by my father."

Charles turned to Colonel Hacker. "Sir, I will not be much longer. I hope that you will permit me to exchange a few last words with two people who are very dear to me?"

Colonel Hacker bowed his head in assent. He stepped to one side as my lord and lady Foxefield approached the King.

"My lady, Meredith," Charles said, "I beg you not to cry."

He tilted her face with his hand. "Give me a kiss of farewell."

"Sire! Sire!"

"Hush! My kiss, if you please."

Meredith's soft lips pressed against his. "God bless you, my beloved and gracious Majesty!"

As Meredith made to draw away, the King pressed his lips once more to hers. "That for my Queen, my wife. Tell her that I die loving her!" Releasing her, he turned to Brett and held out his hand. "Farewell, my old friend, my wily lord Foxe. We will meet again."

Brett's hand crushed his. "Will we, Charles? If only I could believe that!"

"Believe it, Brett," Charles said simply. "It is true."

Brett's eyes searched his. "Aye, Charles, it is true." With a swift movement, Brett bent his head and kissed the King on both cheeks. "God keep you, Sire!" Stepping back, he bowed low. Beside him, Meredith sank down in a curtsey.

The King handed his cloak to the bishop, smiled once more, then turned to the executioners. "When I kneel before the block," he said in his quiet voice, "I will say a very short prayer. When I thrust out my hand, you will please strike swiftly."

"Your hair," the red-wigged executioner mumbled. He handed the King a cap, and gestured to him to put it on.

"Certainly." With steady hands the King put on the cap, making sure that all his hair was tucked beneath it. "There. Is that better?"

The executioner nodded. Bishop Juxon stepped forward again. "Fear nothing, Your Majesty, there is but one stage more. It is a short one, and it will carry you from earth to heaven. And there you shall find great joy and comfort."

"I thank you for your words, good Bishop. And to all my friends a last farewell."

Charles knelt before the block. I am afraid, he thought. Dear Lord, I am afraid! Give me courage, let me show no fear. Unto You do I commend my soul!

Those who watched saw the faint smile on the King's lips as he

489

laid his head on the block. His hand made a jerky movement. The red-wigged executioner lifted his arm. The blade of the axe flashed in the fitful sunlight as he brought it down against the King's exposed neck.

A groan went up from the onlookers as the head dropped into the straw. Grunting, the black-wigged executioner bent forward. Pulling off the cap, he grasped the head by its long hair and held it aloft. "So die all traitors!" he roared.

Brett took Meredith's hand again and led her away. January 30th, 1649, he thought. A day to remember forever. The day when Englishmen murdered their King. A day when the country entered into the darkest period of her history. "God save King Charles the Second!" he murmured beneath his breath.

Soft as his voice was, Meredith heard him. She smiled at him through her tears. "God save King Charles the Second!" she repeated.